KEEPER OF THE LIGHT

Contact: lesleymavery.author@gmail.com

Cover, interior design, and formatting by Aubrey Labitigan

Jai Design

Contact: facebook.com/designjai

Published by Autumn Hearth Publishing

ISBN: 978-1-965906-01-9 E-book

ISBN: 978-1-965906-00-2 Paperback

ISBN: 978-1-965906-02-6 Hardcover

ISBN: 978-1-965906-99-6 Dustjacket

AUTUMN HEARTH
PUBLISHING

For my parents.

To my loving mother, who gave the greatest gifts of all. She taught me to love, and taught me to read, and taught me to love to read.

And to my dad, who built our cottage, and a world of possibilities.

Thanks for everything.

KEEPER OF THE LIGHT

LESLEY M. AVERY

Prologue

A monster loosed from Pandora's Box, The War Between the States leapt to life—A living thing with a voracious appetite for destruction. There were those who had welcomed it. Those with misplaced dreams of gallantry and glory. Thought by many to be a minor inconvenience that would last a few months, it had grown more vicious with each passing hour as it crept across the land. Now, the very ones who had nurtured it, and called it forth, both North and South, had become its sorry victims praying for their deliverance. Fear thickened the air, and the monster crept closer.

Chapter 1

South of Boston, Massachusetts, March 1863
Two years into the American Civil War

Far to the south it could be cannon, but not here. Not yet. Here it was only thunder proclaiming its threat of rain, and the damp night air and piercing winds bore it witness. The ominous sounds seemed Heaven's mimicry of the endless guns of war, and a reminder of Man's atrocities.

Here in the North, the wind reached icy fingers down the collar of a lone rider, and urged her onward. Katherine needed no prodding. In spite of her heavy coat and manly attire, she was cold to her very core, and tired from her long fruitless ride. She would like nothing better than to be home by the fire, but the way was dangerous, and the going slow.

Far below the narrow cliff trail, ocean waves crashed with quickening tempo along the rugged New England coast, and the horse quivered with anticipation as they reached familiar ground. Katherine pulled the brim of her hat lower against the stinging wind and squinted into the darkness, letting the tired animal pick its way along the rocky path, toward their goal.

They were getting close now, and she was filled with both relief and dread. It was much too dark to be out on the cliffs, but this was practically her backyard, and both horse and rider knew the crooked way by heart. She had scampered through these rocks and caves with her brother and sister, and though she tried to ignore it, her mind stitched a patchwork from pieces of an idyllic childhood. Sultry summer days with the ocean as their playground, the clear crisp beauty of autumn, and howling winter winds that swept off of the Atlantic and shook the eaves of their snug cape style home, prompting scary tales of the sea from her brother, and squeals of relished fright from her sister and herself—*How she missed them.*

The family owned a larger house in Boston, and the cottage was originally intended to be a summer retreat, but every year they had come sooner and stayed longer and somehow the roles of the two houses were reversed, with the smaller one more often referred to as home. Katherine's father, Phillip Lawrence, was a sea captain, like many in the area, but unlike most, he owned several of his own ships, and held shares in a number of others. She thought of him now. Intelligent, capable, and stubborn, he had built the sturdy cottage himself, and provided well for its defense against a lifelong siege from the sea. Standing on a bluff, in defiance of the elements, it stood strong, with heavy timbers and a thick slate roof. "Better yet," as he liked to say, it was built of fieldstone hauled from further inland. More than a house, it was a home, filled with the warm personalities of the Lawrences themselves. Like a beautiful crystal Katherine had owned since she was a child, the cottage was a solid thing, but full of life. A wonderful treasure that sparkled with a magical light, and touched all who came near. It held the light of love, and if her father was its builder, her mother was its keeper, for it was her gentle loving way that centered all of their lives. Here was Katherine's sanctuary. Shelter not only for her body, but her soul. Here were her memories, her freedom, and her strength. She had to reach the cottage. It was all she had left.

It was this house that rose before her now, barely discernible in the enveloping darkness, but unlike other days, no welcoming lamp burned at the window to proclaim the promise of warmth within, and no bit of laughter escaped its threshold to ride the night air.

The first drops of rain had fallen, fat and plopping, when she reached the yard, and she was thankful she had made it home before the skies opened up in all their glory. With a sigh, the young woman removed her hat, and released a tumble of blonde hair that reached to her waist. "We're in for it this time, Matty," she spoke aloud to the horse, while she stripped her of the saddle and blanket. "Poor Matilda." She gave the beautiful black a hug, paying almost no attention to the empty sound her voice made in the darkness.

Taking up the lantern, she entered a tack room that separated the stable from the rest of the house, and passed through to the large kitchen. Thunder rumbled closer and the rain poured down in earnest, as she crossed the slate floor and lit another lamp on the table. Mentally she gave thanks that the stable and house were attached, making it much easier to tend the animals in bad weather… Especially blizzards. *And thunderstorms!* She added, when a deafening crash sounded overhead, and a vivid flash of lightening turned the night sky to day.

She soon had a fire dancing in the grate, its warmth chasing the dampness to the far corners of the room. She removed her oversized topcoat, a hand-me-down claimed from her brother, and while she waited for the kettle to boil, she took up a lantern and began to wander through the rest of the house. In the library, at the front, three large leather wing chairs waited like old friends with open arms, and a beautifully carved writing desk stood in one corner. It was Katherine's favorite place in the world, but she found little comfort there this night.

In the living room that had often overflowed with family and friends, her mother's piano waited to be brought to life, and the great fireplace, which stood back-to-back with the one in the kitchen, waited dark and empty. The stilled hands of time seemed to mock her from the mantelpiece, where her father's collection of clocks once ticked in chaotic symphony. Finding them an annoyance, she had let them run down, save one. What was time but a tormentor that moved too quickly, or too slowly, and always contrary to what one wished?

She passed the bedrooms and the room used for bathing, the only light the small halo around her lamp. There were two smaller rooms upstairs. One had belonged to her brother, William, and the other, she had shared with her sister, Dorothea, or 'Thea,' as they often called her.

She circled back to the kitchen, setting the tea to brew and laid out a simple supper for herself, the china, and the silver, so familiar a part of their everyday life together, *all reminders.* Her eyes lit on each of the other chairs, *all empty.*

She lived with ghosts, and they tormented her. Deserted rooms echoed with warm conversation, and shadows of smiles hung like cobwebs in dark empty corners… *the corners of hell. Hell was not as some thought it then. Not fire and brimstone, but an eternal cycle of dark quiet rooms, traveled alone with one's own thoughts.* Thunder cracked and popped again and Katherine jumped. The rain drumming on the roof only magnified her loneliness. "Stop it!" She scolded herself, feeding the fire, but the thought was barely formed before she was lost again in reflection, making her way to the guest room.

The pleasant room held a comfortable bed, and fewer memories than any other room in the house. She pulled off her riding boots, *a gift from her father.* He traveled the world and spoiled his family with the most wonderful surprises. Exchanging the old clothes that had once belonged to her brother, she chose a long flannel gown from amongst the silks and satins, and settled into bed. With equal hope and doubt, she closed her eyes.

Sometime later, her mother called from the next room. Poor Mother, she had been sick, for so long now, but Katherine was sure she would be well soon. As she had done so many times in the past months, she helped her to bathe and wash her hair, and helped her back into her freshly made bed. She brushed the reddish-gold curls, and turned to place the brush on the dresser. When she turned back, her mother was gone.

Cold fear gripping her heart, she began to search. She heard the piano, and ran into the living room, only to find it cold and empty. There were voices in the library, but when she reached it, there was no one there. Sweat dampened her forehead, and her heart beat wildly. *Her mother needed her!* She hurried through the deserted kitchen, crossed the back porch, and ran out into the yard. Her pulse pounded in her ears, and she gasped for breath taking the winding path that led to her mother's garden and the small pond. but when she reached the gate, she stumbled and fell. Blinded by tears, she rolled to her feet and tried to run on, but again and again, she fell...

Katherine sat up. The tears were real, and her heart was still pounding. "Oh, Mama," she cried out to the darkness, and turning her face into the pillow, she sobbed.

Eventually, the tears subsided, and casting about in her mind for some diversion, she fingered the gold cross that hung around her neck. *Enough!* she protested. Was there nothing she could do, or say, or look upon, that wouldn't lead her to yet another painful memory? It seemed a never-ending chain that held her a desperate captive, and there was no escape. Her tired mind flitted this way and that, and settled on the journal entries she had written such a short time before. The last few pages dragged themselves across her exhausted brain and she hadn't the strength to stop them:

Nov. 11, 1862—*Dr. Gardner came again—Mama is very bad—she has told me not to cry but of course, I do.*

Nov. 12, 1862—*Much worse, Dear God, this must turn out right— Thea is coming—I wish Papa were here.*

The next day there was no entry. The words did not exist that could express her feelings on that day. The final entry read:

Nov. 16, 1862—*Thea came. I have written to Father. I love you, Mama. Help me, I don't know what to do.*

That day they had laid Mary Katherine to rest out by the lilacs, near the garden that she loved, and Katherine had never written in her journal after that. She had placed it at the bottom of a seldom used drawer, and those times when she happened across it, she pretended not to see it.

She had gotten quite good at pretending. Pretending she was brave when she was scared to death, pretending she might be happy again, when her very heart was broken, and pretending there was hope for the future when… Thoughts of the future returned her to the reason she had ridden out alone, but mercifully, in the wee hours of the morning, sleep found her once again.

Chapter 2

"Forget it, Evelyn. You know I don't like dances."

"You really should get out, you know. It will help to take your mind off things."

Short of stature, with a sturdy build, Evelyn Wiley, put Katherine in mind of a loveable bulldog with a rapacious appetite for life. Her soft gray curls were in puzzling contrast to her pink childlike complexion, and twinkling blue eyes. Eyes that now followed Katherine's every move, making her extremely self-conscious.

Evelyn emptied the large basket of provisions she had brought, and began breaking eggs into a bowl. She eyed the young woman while she worked. The puffy eyes, the dark circles, the too thin figure… "You haven't slept well." It was a statement, not a question.

Katherine, setting the table, shrugged and looked away. "I'm fine."

"Of course you are. You're heartsick, you're still half in shock, and you look like you've been run over by a team of wild horses, and," she added, "I'd give my eyeteeth to know what you've eaten for the past week."

"It's good to see you too, Evelyn," quipped Katherine. She smiled affectionately at the older woman. "I wasn't expecting you until later."

"There's little enough work, only mourning dresses." Evelyn

referred to the sewing and repair shop she ran from her rented house in the village. "I'm so sick of looking at black dresses, I had to get away." What she didn't say, was that as the war dragged on, the local people didn't have much money, and it was getting harder to make ends meet, but all that aside, she was not so easily distracted from her topic. "It won't hurt you to go to one dance."

Katherine winced and shook her head, "I don't think so. Besides, there's not an eligible man within miles," she exaggerated.

"*He's* around…"

Silence flooded the room. Katherine felt as if she were swimming underwater, too far from the surface, and in desperate need of air. Ignoring the heavy thudding of her heart, she struggled for control and took a deep breath.

"*You've seen him?*" She asked, in a small voice, not sure she wanted to know, and at the same time not sure she believed Evelyn, although she could not have said why. This was her friend, she loved her like a mother, *but still,* there was something about the look on her face… Feeling guilty, she cut off her mutinous thoughts, and studied the older woman.

If anyone had any news it would be Evelyn. Living where she did, in the nearby village, and part of, if not the heart of, its formidable grapevine, she always seemed to know everything. *Yes,* Evelyn would know, and Katherine would trust her.

The older woman hesitated. The girl was at such a low point in her life. She wanted to give her something to hope for without hurting her, but having decided on this course, she was now slightly dissuaded, seeing the poor thing turn white at the mere mention of the one man she had ever shown any real interest in. There was more involved here than Katherine had let on. *How had she missed it?* She probably knew Katherine better than anyone now, but the girl had always been a tangle of contradictions. Evelyn weighed her options. *Should she lead her on, or was it too cruel?*

She wouldn't hurt her for the world, but right now this girl needed something to live for. *Well, sink or swim…* Taking a deep breath, she set sail for shallow waters. "His ship's been sighted." *It wasn't entirely a lie… his ship had to be somewhere, and someone must have seen it.* She glanced at Katherine and grew uncomfortable under the young woman's searching gaze. The look she saw there before the girl turned away, both encouraged and surprised her. She took a chance and struck blindly at the awkward silence, "Do you love him, Katie?"

Katherine looked at Evelyn and away again, a slow blush warming her cheek, and in her distress, she spoke too quickly, "You can't be serious. He probably doesn't even remember me by now. I only met him once—formally, anyway, and you know how that ended."

"Sometimes it only takes once, Kate, and we don't know the whole story."

Katherine didn't answer. She was remembering that night, something she rarely allowed herself to do. When she did, it was never fully and openly, but as she did now, one moment at a time. Because she was afraid.

As a child, she had played on the cliffs with William. He, a typical older brother, would stand at the very edge and taunt her to come closer. Always, she accepted the dare, too proud to admit her secret fear of heights, but each time she had looked down at the rocks far below, she met the dizzying effect that made her feel as though she would be pulled forward to topple over the edge. She preferred to stay back, with only an occasional peek over the edge to test the fear. And so it was within her memory, she stayed far back, always careful not to get too close, lest she fall over the edge and be lost.

In this moment, she was dancing—floating. She could hear the music, and feel the strong arms that held her close. She could see the brilliant white of his shirt against the dark navy of his coat, and the room a blur of color in the background as they swept across the floor. If she wanted to, she could look up into his face, but that was getting too close to the edge.

"Katie?" Evelyn waited patiently, all the while trying to read Katherine's heart through her eyes.

Katherine gave a short bitter laugh. "How could I?" *I don't want to love him. I don't want to love anyone. It hurts too much.*

Her wayward mind conjured a pair of deep blue eyes and sent them forth, but determined not to waiver, she pushed them to the furthest corner of her memory. The dark prison where she kept under heavy guard all the things she could not bear to look upon, constantly struggling to keep the door closed. Here were her monsters, and her pain, and all the things that would hurt her if she let them out. She would like to keep love there, locked away, but love was strong. *You can't fool yourself,* counseled the distant voice of her mother, but Katherine cut it off, and poured another cup of tea, hoping Evelyn wouldn't notice.

"Have you been living on tea again?" The other woman never paused, just nodded toward Katherine's cup, muttering something about certain people with tea in their veins.

Katherine was grateful for company, after her long lonely night. They ate for a few moments in silence, before Evelyn broached the other subject, they had both avoided. "Did you find out anything?" She caught the slight frown before the younger woman answered.

"No, I was hoping you might have heard something."

"No, I'm sorry. *Nothing yet,*" Evelyn amended, "It hasn't been so long Kate, don't cross your bridges... *You know.*"

Katherine nodded and pushed away from the table. Taking her cup, she began to pace the length of the kitchen, "I'm trying to have hope, it's just that... I can't shake this feeling." She wrestled with determined tears, and turned to the window to collect herself.

Evelyn wisely let her be. She knew that grief, like any great wound, needed time to heal, and once healed would leave a deep and lasting scar. Even that would fade with time. *But it still ached,* she mused, *like old bones on a cold winter's night.* Her heart went out to the young woman. So much had changed. Her brother, William, who had practically been raised to run the family business, had been busy since the beginning of the war, commissioning and supplying many of the smaller ships that would make Lincoln's naval blockade a reality. The last time they had seen him was when he had left for England, and it had been months with no word, leaving Katherine to take over the work at the family's shipping business.

Dorothea, Katherine's younger sister, had married Keith Sawyer, before the beginning of the war, and moved with him to New Hampshire. Keith had been wounded early on, but at least he was home. And Mary, mother, best friend, and co-conspirator, had died in November, ripping the center and the light from their lives. And now Phillip, Katherine's father... That was why Evelyn was here now. She studied the distraught woman who had begun to pace again. Her green eyes were so like her mother's, and there was found, in better times, a hint of laughter, and a promise of wisdom beyond her twenty-seven years. Yes, she was pretty like her mother, and stubborn like her father.

Katherine continued her pacing, and looking at her lithe body, Evelyn was reminded of the time when Katherine was about twelve and Mary had given a luncheon. An old and dignified friend, Hetty Parker, had honored them with her presence—a rare occurrence. Young Kate, always a tomboy, had rushed in from her play, and Hetty had informed all present, in no uncertain terms, that Katie was fortunate to be built like a boy, with wide shoulders, a slim waist, and long legs.

Katherine had flushed scarlet, while Mary, feeling her pain, had tried in vain to divert everyone's attention. Meanwhile, Hetty had continued with adamant nodding of her wise old head, assuring the embarrassed young girl that this was indeed a blessing, and once she had filled out, she would be the envy of all the girls that ostracized her now, and left her with the boys for playmates.

Mrs. Parker had been right. Their little tomboy had grown up in fine form, and although it was the last thing Katherine cared about, Evelyn found great satisfaction in the envious looks cast at the young woman by her old childhood enemies, especially Cecilia Johnston. She smiled to herself remembering how she had sat with Mary, at the many parties they attended, and watched the young women test the waters. Katherine had always set her own course. She did not flirt, and she would not act the helpless female. But at every dance, she was the one the young men returned to again and again, drawn by her honest beauty and natural grace. *Well, every dance she would go to…* If not for her mother's gentle coaxing, she would have stayed home, as she did now. *Yes, the problem was how to get her out more.* "Still waters run deep," she mumbled to herself.

Katherine had watched her friend for the last few minutes, and witnessed the satisfied smile that had spread across her face. "*What?*" She queried, more than a little suspicious.

"Hmm?" Returned Evelyn, plucked from the midst of her time travels.

"What were you thinking just now? You were grinning like the cat that got the cream… Oh, now you've got me doing it!" Katherine broke off and scoffed at Evelyn's look of delight.

"I was remembering Hetty Parker, and her gift for prophecy."

"Oh, *that.*" Katherine was sorry she had asked, and blushed at the memory, even after all the time that had passed. At the scheming look in her friend's eyes, she wasted no time in defending herself. "I said forget it, Evelyn!"

Throughout the rest of the day, each busy with self-appointed chores, they didn't mention the morning's conversation again, but each in turn returned to the part that most concerned her.

Evelyn had her answer. Katherine was hopelessly in love with a man she barely knew, and God only knew where in the world he was… *But what to do about it?*

And, somewhere in the deep secret chamber of Katherine's heart, there flickered a tiny flame of hope, and as much as she wanted to, she couldn't bring herself to smother it. Soon she would ride out again, and she must have something, however small, to cling to.

Chapter 3

On the appointed morning, Katherine awoke to the comforting sounds of someone busy in the kitchen and the beckoning aromas of bacon and freshly baked bread.

She had slept better last night. Probably because she and Evelyn had walked down to the beach in the cold fresh air and talked until after eleven. She had been so tired she had gone right to sleep. With her first clear thought of the morning, she decided her friend had probably planned it that way, and gave an appreciative smile. Still, she was tired, as she dressed in her men's clothes and her riding boots, and made her way to the kitchen.

"Good morning! Tea's ready." Evelyn, as usual, stood toe-to-toe with life, and ready to spit in its eye if need be.

This morning, her energy left Katherine feeling all the more tired. "Morning," she mumbled, as she slid into her chair and reached for the teapot.

"Didn't you sleep well? I could have sworn the way you were yawning…."

"I did, thanks to you." She could tell by the elder's look of satisfaction, that the night air had indeed been administered as medicine for what ailed her.

Little by little, Evelyn had drawn from her like a poison, all the thoughts that churned in her head and chased her through her dreams, or at least enough of them so Katherine had been able to sleep. Maybe that was the way to deal with these things, one at a time, because together they were quite overwhelming. "I feel like I could sleep for three more days, that's all," she said, while Evelyn placed such a heaping plate in front of her, that she winced at the sight of it.

"That's grief, Kate. There're two kinds of tired. There's body tired, and there's mind tired. Your body's rested pretty good maybe, but your mind is exhausted. It's like there are two parts of your brain. See, there's a fact side, that takes things in, and there's the emotional part that has to figure out how you feel about those things, and what to do about them. Now, when something real awful happens, the fact side takes it in, but if the emotion side can't accept it, you have this argument within yourself. It's like a mental battle, and it makes you tired because it never settles. No matter what else you're doing, even talking to someone else about other things, somewhere inside you, that fight is going on, and until you can deal with it, look right at it, and find a place for it, you'll be fighting yourself. You can't lock things away."

"You know what it's like!" Katherine said in awe, looking at her friend in a new light.

"Yes. I'm glad I didn't lose you altogether with my ramblings. I don't want you to think I'm crazy."

"No, what you said is exactly right. I thought it was just me. I thought I was losing my mind." For the first time, Katherine wondered at the loss Evelyn was facing. She knew she had lost a husband years ago, but Mary had been her best friend. To her shame, she was so wrapped up in her own grief, she hadn't given it much thought.

They sat together for a time, and having reached such a comfortable plateau, Evelyn hated to change the mood, "Well dear, you'd better get going, it's a long ride."

"I know. I just hate to go while you're here. I could wait a day or two, it wouldn't matter I suppose..." Not liking the sound of her words, Katherine broke off her sentence. "I didn't mean..."

"I know dear. Anyway, I planned on your going now, so I can be here when you return. You go on and get the horse ready, and I'll clean up here and pack your lunch."

"You're sure?"

"Really. Now go! The sooner you go, the sooner you'll be back, with good news, God willing."

Katherine headed for the stable, to ready Matilda, her mind on the journey ahead. *Her father was missing.* There, she allowed the thought to form fully in her mind, because Evelyn was right, she had to deal with it. Not only her father, but his whole ship and crew. *They were overdue.* That sounded better. They were *overdue* well over a month now, according to his plans in his last letter. Plenty of time to worry, what with blockades, enemy ships, and privateers added to the usual risks of being at sea, and the sea itself.

Phillip Lawrence, had left the running of the business and mundane ship acquisitions to his son, and son-in-law, and had gone off chasing adventure, and disappeared. For the past weeks she had made the two-day ride to Boston at regular intervals, in search of any information the incoming ships might have, each time torn between her hope for news, and her fear of what it might be.

Halfway there, at the end of the first day, she would stop at the home of Captain Caldwell and his wife Judith, old friends of her parents. If Ezra Caldwell had been recently to the Boston docks, he would have a report for her. If not, he would escort her the rest of the way the next day, and they would stay overnight in the city. They would check the docks together, and reverse their path in a few days' time. In the meantime, Katherine would check in on the house and the office to see if anything was needed.

This, though, would be her last trip. After this, if there were no word, she would close up the cottage, and move into the larger family home. Evelyn had convinced her it was foolish and dangerous to ride back and forth like this, and harder on everyone concerned. Katherine had reluctantly agreed. She was loath to give up what was left of her happiness for the confines of the city, but she did have a lot to take care of. Of course, there *could* be good news, and this was the thought she tried to hold on to, while leading the horse out into the yard, and saying her goodbyes to Evelyn.

A few passing hours found her well on her way, loaded down with good wishes, her leather satchel, and enough food to feed six grown men. She had chosen the cliff trail once again, always her preference, because it would bring her to the Caldwell's by nightfall, it was less, if *ever* traveled, and because she enjoyed the view. The day held no hint of the spring that was only weeks away, and she snuggled deeper into her coat, as her breath frosted the air.

She rode easily, guiding Matilda on the rocky path through the scrub pine and strangled oaks that seemed to grow here on determination alone, as if Nature in her cruelty, had cast them out on this barren ground to find what root they could, and challenged them to live. Scrawny and stunted, painfully twisted, sculpted by the Northeast winds, their beauty lay in their strength and perseverance, their courage to try, and to thrive where others would wither and fail. Like true New Englanders, they were survivors.

A side trail wound downward to a stretch of sandy beach, and here Katherine stopped to eat her lunch. The sun was high now, and warmer, in a clear azure sky, and the ocean spread infinitely before her. She sat with her back to the cliffs, and watched the teasing wind play tag with the ocean, coaxing the somersaulting waves into whitecaps.

The lacy white against the deep blue, aided her persistent mind as it pressed for an answer to her longing. She wished…

She didn't want to admit what she wished, but the forlorn cries of the gulls overhead seemed to be echoed in her heart. She tried to ignore it, but out here where there was no one to witness, no one to read her eyes, or interpret her actions, here she could be honest with herself, and she knew the answer was not in her mind, but in her heart. She took a deep breath, and released a sigh. It wasn't fair. She didn't want to think about him, but he was always there, ready to step forth as soon as she let her guard down. *She wished he were here.*

It was strange… She had only been with him twice, and yet, from the first moment, she felt she had known him always. She recalled Evelyn's words, "*It only takes once.*" Her mind drifted back almost two years… a lifetime ago. It was April, right before the war began. South Carolina had seceded from the Union the previous December, followed by six other states within weeks. She remembered well, the feeling everyone was trying so hard to ignore. There was a constant tension in the air, as war brewed on the horizon.

Katherine and her parents had stolen a quick trip to the cottage, even though April was early in the season, and they also planned a visit to Dorothea's new home in New Hampshire. With the trouble that was sure to come, Phillip expected to be away, and they wanted some quiet time together before the impending turmoil struck home.

While Katherine was apprehensive, she had felt too, the coming loss of her unconventional lifestyle. She couldn't go on forever, running around like a hoyden, dressed in her brother's clothes, riding like a Cossack, and swimming like a mermaid whenever she felt like it. She had counted on that last summer to enjoy herself, before the gossipmongers and matchmakers tried again to rope her in, and smother her in their layers of social proprieties. She was already long passed the usual age for marriage, but her mother had married late, and she had thought little of it.

It had been these thoughts that rode with Katherine on that long ago morning, while she and Matilda thundered down the beach below the cottage. Determined to make the most of her freedom while it lasted, and to forget her problems, she had thrown herself into the ride, abandoning herself to the exhilarating salt air, and the graceful power of the animal beneath her.

This was all she wanted, to be free to do the things she loved. *Why couldn't people leave her alone?* As she rode, the sleeves of her white shirt rolled past her elbows, her deft hands on the reins easily guided the excited beast in their charge down the shore.

The day had grown warmer, and she decided to leave the beach for the shaded road that led to the village. They had taken the sandy path that went by the side of the cottage, and she held Matilda to a walk, lest her parents chance to view her from the window, and tease her at supper for racing about. Like conspirators, they passed through the side yard, and entered the lane, welcoming the shade of the pines and the occasional oak or maple with their fat buds and tiny newborn leaves.

Out in the lane, the powerful horse soon had enough of the slow pace, and was eager to be off again, and the rider more so. Now out of sight of the house, she let out the reins and bent low in the saddle, letting the horse stretch out fully, racing down the narrow road. She was considering whether to take the south road, toward Gleason's house. Gleason, their only neighbor within a few miles, a friend of her father, who would sometimes act as caretaker, and feed the animals, when the family was away. She hadn't seen him for a while… *Gleason, who, with his heart of gold and lack of personal hygiene, was a prime example of taking the good with the bad…* she smiled to herself. *Or,* she thought, *she could take the right toward the village,* when from that very turn there appeared a horse and carriage directly in her path.

Before she could think, she had already reacted, using all her strength and skill to control the horse. Matilda reared high in the air and Katherine clung to the saddle. When the flailing hooves again hit the ground, the horse would have bolted, but the bit was held hard to the right, and she turned in circles, prancing and snorting in protest before she came to a stop beside the open vehicle.

Katherine had concentrated on calming her treasured horse, and there had been no time to be afraid, but now she had to face the driver, and she was embarrassed by her carelessness. Her hands rested meekly on the saddle horn and she studied them, thinking what she should say before she looked up tentatively, and met a look of surprise in mesmerizing dark blue eyes. She caught the flash of a beautiful smile and registered a riot of dark curly hair, and a surge of warmth passed through her chest. "I'm sorry," she said, and glanced away. She was breathless from her efforts, and talking was difficult. "I was going much too fast, please forgive me," and she added, "Are you all right?"

He certainly looked all right. She chanced another glance in his direction before she looked away and back again, taking in the nervous horse and obviously rented buggy, wishing its occupant would say something.

"I'm fine, thank you," he answered in a deep warm voice, causing a strange prickling at the back of her neck. "I…" he hesitated, and Katherine forgot her shyness and looked at him again. *Was he having trouble speaking?* He wasn't out of breath; there hadn't been anything for him to do, really, except to watch her either stop, or come crashing into him.

"It was as much my fault," he offered, with that smile that showed a perfect dimple in each well-tanned cheek, and again, that strange feeling invaded her chest, as he continued, "I was going too fast as well, and I… don't know… the road. Are you? All right, I mean," he added, at her look of confusion.

"Better than I deserve, thank you," she smiled again, glad they had both escaped with nothing worse than jangled nerves.

"I…" He didn't finish.

To her embarrassment, he stared, and she felt herself blush, not realizing she already had so much color it didn't show. *Of course! He must think her some wild thing come out of the woods, flying at him like that.* She raised a hand to her hair, and was, for once, embarrassed about her choice of attire, for her clothes were much like his. She noted the high polished boots, tan britches and soft white shirt open at the neck, with the sleeves rolled up; the difference being, where her clothes were old and oversized, his appeared to be new, and fit snugly across his wide shoulders and hugged his thighs. "You were saying?" She prompted, wanting to get away from this man who made her wish she were different somehow.

"Yes, I wonder if you could tell me where Captain Lawrence lives. Phillip Lawrence? It's somewhere near here. At least I *think* it is," he added, with a little laugh and shake of his head. "I don't seem to be thinking very clearly," and he offered her that melting smile.

She didn't answer at first, the breath seemed to have left her body. She liked hearing him speak and wished he would say more. He had a slight touch of an accent, and for the moment she couldn't place it. It was more the rhythm of his speech that was different, and something with the R's. *Maybe Irish… or Scottish?*

Their eyes locked, and she was lost for a long moment before she became aware that he was still waiting.

He spoke again, "Miss…"

For some reason, she chose not to supply her name. "Have you business with Captain Lawrence?" She asked, and immediately apologized. "I'm sorry, that was rude of me. He lives down there." She pointed back the way she had come, and at her movement Matilda stepped sideways shifting her weight, and growing impatient. "It's a short way down this lane, straight on, you can't miss it. It's a dead end to our… Toward the house."

"Thank you." He made no move to leave. "*Your* horse?" He asked, with that odd inflection that tickled her heart.

She nodded.

"Beautiful," he said, but his gaze had never left her face, and she blushed again, averting her eyes.

"I have to be going," she lied. She didn't have to be going. She wasn't sure she even wanted to now. The danger had long passed, but she was still breathless and uncomfortable, and her heart was pounding. "Goodbye," she spoke softly, "and again, I apologize for my recklessness." She turned Matilda and walked her away, but changing her mind, she turned the horse around, thinking to catch him.

He hadn't moved. With an embarrassed smile, she rode closer, avoiding his eyes until she reached his side again. "Mister..." She was aware she had turned the tables on herself, when instead of his name, he gave her a delighted smirk and a quick flick of his brows.

With a smile and a nod, she conceded him the small victory. "*Sir,*" she started, and paused to take a deep breath, "I wonder if I might ask a favor of you?"

"Try me," he grinned.

"I wonder if you would be kind enough not to mention our accident, I mean *near* accident, to the Lawrences." Katherine was more leery of being teased than chastised by her parents, but aside from that, there was something about this meeting, that she wanted to keep to herself.

"Do you know them, then?" He asked seriously.

"Yes."

"I'll say nothing," he decided, after a pause, seeing she wasn't going to elaborate. "But, does not one favor deserve another?"

Katherine's chin went up.

"For my sworn silence, I ask something in return."

She waited, knowing by his smiling eyes that he baited her.

"It will cost you..." He turned his head and searched the treetops as if for inspiration, "your name." He laughed at his own verbal strategy.

This time it was Katherine who paused, giving thought to her next move. She tried to ignore the strange feeling in the pit of her stomach. "Agreed, my name, for your silence."

"Agreed." He put out his hand, challenging her to take it, and seal their bargain.

She hesitated. They were strangers, and she had the familiar thought that her behavior would be shocking to the stalwarts of her mother's sewing circle. She knew she should not have lingered here, should not have talked with him so long, if at all, and certainly should not touch him! *Oh, for Heaven's sake!* She met his hand with a firm grasp and his eyes with a defiant stare. She was not prepared for the warmth that traveled up her arm at the contact, and would have pulled away, except for the dare in his gaze.

Their eyes held, and he asked again, "Your name?"

Matilda shifted, and he let go of her hand so she could take better control of the reins. Once again, she turned the horse to go before she answered him with a grin, "My name is Katherine."

"Katherine… a strong name." He studied her for a minute as if making a decision. "It suits you, Katherine." He pronounced her name, rolling the "r," and making her appreciate it as she never had before.

"You're Scottish!" She blurted, pouncing on the elusive evidence like a cornered prey, and instantly regretting her lapse of manners. "I'm sorry."

"You're sorry I'm Scottish?" He was clearly enjoying her struggle.

"Oh, no, I was trying to guess, and I… You *are*, aren't you?"

"Aye, I am that." He spoke this with an unmistakable burr, and a playful grin. "Partly at least, unless you have cause to regret it?" He gave her a beseeching look that passed through to her heart, and caused the breath to catch in her throat.

"No," she whispered, in the only voice she could find, noticing the day had grown unbearably warm. "You have an intriguing way of speaking. I rather like it." If she were too forward, she didn't care.

At least she was honest, and under the spell of his eyes she could be nothing else.

"In that case, Miss Katherine, I am more Scottish than I have ever been before." He laughed, breaking the spell, and leaving her wondering of what nonsense he spoke.

She sifted through her wealth of feelings, and searched for a reason to leave, but found none, save she had already said goodbye, and she didn't know what else to talk about. "Well, goodbye again," and moving as if in a dream, she nudged the horse forward.

"Wait, your name… Katherine, what?"

"You didn't say it had to be my full name."

"Not fair!" He protested, laughing at having been bested, as she went on her way.

"Miss Katherine…" he called, and she stopped, and turned in the saddle, not meeting his eyes.

"I consider a little recklessness a very admirable quality."

She glanced once more into his eyes before she turned away, and felt again the rapid pounding of her heart. Taking an unsteady breath, she rode on until she was sure he was gone, and then turned to stare after him down the empty road. She *had* been reckless. Not only her riding, but also her behavior, and she wondered to which he referred. She sat for a while, pondering who he was, why he had affected her so, and why he sought her father.

The better part of an hour passed, and thinking he would be gone, she had cut back to the cliff trail above the beach that would bring her to the back of the house. He was just leaving, and she watched from the woods as he stood on the porch talking to her father.

He was taller than Phillip, something she couldn't have known from their meeting on the road. She waited while the men shook hands, and she remembered her reaction to his touch. He climbed into the buggy and she watched him drive off, the sea breeze ruffling his dark hair, and she found herself wondering what it would be like to smooth those wayward curls. Surprised by her thoughts, she had called herself a fool, and ridden toward the house where her father stood on the porch.

The memory she held of Phillip that day, was the way she always pictured him. In her prolific mind, the porch broadened and became the deck of a ship, putting him even more at home. Feet braced apart, hands on the rail, his sky-blue eyes ever seeking life's next challenge. A gust of wind whipped his thick blond hair back from his face, and his full reddish beard framed his smile. As a child, she had thought of him as a Viking king, who sailed in and out of their lives like a visitor from a storybook, always laughing and telling wonderful tales.

Drifting back to the present, Katherine sighed, and wondered where the two men were now. Wherever they were, she prayed they were safe.

Chapter 4

"Have you any idea of the worry you caused us? Any number of things could have happened! A young woman, riding around alone at night, and who knows *what,* lurking out there!"

Katherine stood, and tried to look properly contrite, squeezing in a "Yes Ma'am," whenever Judith Caldwell gave long enough pause, although in truth, she was not more than an hour later than her last visit.

"If it wasn't for the war, I should have sent the boys out to search for you."

Judith had aged. Katherine noted the gray streaks in her dark hair and the worry lines around her eyes. "If it wasn't for the war," she reminded her gently, "I wouldn't be here now, Mrs. Caldwell."

The older woman regarded her keenly, trying to discern any hint of sarcasm. Out in the hallway, Judith's only daughter, Louise, waited, and periodically grimaced over her mother's shoulder, causing her friend great effort in holding back an ill-timed smile.

Katherine's mind wandered while the woman ranted on. Judith wasn't difficult to understand. She didn't try to be hard and shrewish; it came quite naturally. She had a tongue like a sword, quick and cutting, and like any sharp object, it needed to be handled with caution. Many times, her victims had fled, extremely wounded, leaving poor confused Judith wondering what was wrong, and never considering it might have been something she said. Perhaps now though, Judith had reason to lash out at the world. She had sent four sons off to war, and she lived every day on the edge of her nerves.

"You must be tired dear, and hungry. Louise will show you to your room, and I'll have a tray sent up. Captain Caldwell, has retired for the evening, and I shall do the same."

Upstairs the girls waited until they were behind the closed door of the guest room, before they burst into giggles. "*Really, Katherine*, who knows *what,* could be lurking out there!" The younger girl tried a stern impression of her mother, and raised her hands like claws.

Louise, the complete opposite of Judith's harsh countenance, had not an angular feature on her soft round face. Gentle, petite, and very pretty, only her coloring was like her mothers in her dark chestnut hair and brown eyes. But where Judith's eyes were hard and penetrating, Louise's were a warm golden brown that glowed with genuine concern for others. What nature had withheld from Judith in softness, it had given to her daughter tenfold. Even her voice was quiet and soft, making her efforts at imitating her mother, all the more ludicrous.

Their laughter subsided and Louise glanced shyly at her friend, and looked down at the sculpted carpet. Katherine guessed what she wanted to ask and sought to save her the embarrassment. She had known for a long time that Louise had a mad crush on her brother, but, sworn to secrecy, she had never told him, waiting to see if he would come around on his own, and eventually, he had. *Now, if he would only propose…*

"No, Lou, I'm sorry, I've still no word from William, and I can see you haven't either, but you know how the mails are," she added, trying to sound encouraging.

"Oh Katherine, it's terrible, I can't seem to think about anything else." She blushed, having been so open about her feelings. "Besides…"

she went on to cover up, "Knowing you, if there *were* any news, you would have come flying over here at midnight, no matter what was *lurking out there!*"

They laughed a little, while Louise wiped at a stray tear, and Katherine hugged her, each acknowledging the terror that was most assuredly out there, and had torn the peaceful tapestry of their lives to shreds.

"Why *were* you late?" Louise asked, breaking away.

"I stopped for lunch, and I just got carried away by my thoughts," said Katherine, sitting on the bed to remove her boots.

"Anyone I know?"

She received a warning look.

There was a knock on the door and Nora, the Caldwell's housekeeper, entered, carrying a tray of food, and of course, a large pot of tea.

"Hello, Miss Katherine," she greeted her, "I'd a welcome speech all planned," she whispered, "but I hear you already got one!" Placing the tray on the bed, she winked at the girls, and headed for the door before she spoke again, "There's plenty of tea," she grinned, and with a knowing look to Katherine, she disappeared down the hall.

Katherine poured out the tea and, motioned to Louise to join her on the bed. She could tell by the thoughtful look, that Lou hadn't forgotten their conversation and tried to draw her away from it. "Did you honestly think I was that late?" She questioned.

"*I didn't*, but you know how mother is… Any excuse," she shrugged. "*So*, you were telling me about the man of your dreams," she tried abruptly.

"Why is it, you're so shy all the time, except when I want you to be?"

Louise gave her a broad mischievous grin, helping herself to some brown bread. "I thought you might like to talk about him that's all."

"Who?"

"The man you were daydreaming about."

"I never said I was." Katherine was laughing now.

"Yes, but *I know*."

"Maybe…" she started, and changed her mind, "…maybe it was my father."

"Oh, I'm sorry, Kate," Louise colored pink and nearly choked on her tea. "I was only teasing."

Looking into apologetic eyes, so like a scolded puppy, Katherine fought a nagging guilt. Lou was her best friend. In fact, she was her only girlfriend, aside from her sister, and she knew their friendship had placed the girl on the outer edges of the inner circles.

Katherine suspected her friend knew more than she wanted her to. After all, they knew each other well, and though she had never talked too much about her feelings, Louise *had* been at the dance that night. *Maybe everyone at the dance knew how she felt*, but she didn't want to think about that.

"I was," she relented.

"What?" Louise said in a small voice, sipping her tea.

"Thinking about him," she grimaced, hating her admission.

"Oh."

Her good humor easily restored, Katherine burst out laughing, "*Oh?* Is that all you have to say?" She asked, leaning into the pillows.

Her small bit of boldness gone, Louise retreated into her shell, "I don't want to pry."

It was that lack of prying that eased the way for Katherine to speak, "It scares me to think about him," she said, in such a low whisper that she could barely be heard.

Louise was taken by surprise. "I didn't think you were afraid of anything." She paused, "None of us knows if our men are coming home, Kate." She looked down at her hands.

"I know, but even if he comes out of the war, I already know it won't be…" She stared at the far wall as tears spilled from her eyes and slid unheeded down her cheeks.

Panic rose in her chest, and Louise found it hard to breathe. Katherine couldn't be despondent. She was the protector, the one who never gave up. Judith was a burden, to be endured, but Katherine and Mary Lawrence, were her role models. It was there she had found kindness and humor, encouragement and strength. If Katherine lost her way, Louise was doomed. "Kate, *please*, don't," she pleaded, tears filling her eyes as well.

Katherine, sat upright, and drew her sleeve across her eyes. "What's wrong?"

But Louise only cried harder. How could she explain?

Katherine got up and held her by the shoulders, waiting for her to calm herself. "What is it?"

"It's… *I don't know*, you're always in control, and if you give up, I'll have no hope."

Katherine was not sure she understood, but she did grasp that her tears had extremely affected Louise.

"Don't worry about me," she forced a small laugh, "I'm fine. I wonder if you could help me though," she said, getting the other girls attention. "You're in love with William… could you tell me what it's like?"

Louise brightened, and stopped crying at the mention of her favorite subject. "Oh, it's…" She stopped. "You know very well what it's like." She smiled through her tears, "It's awful!"

In the small hours of the morning Katherine stretched in the soft feather bed. She searched her foggy mind for the cause of the expectation within, and the nagging regret of… *What?*

Boston, she placed the first, and… she closed her eyes in concentration. …*Louise*. A slight frown crossed her brow. She had said too much. But what *had* she told her? That she loved him? No, of course not, because she didn't. Her heart twisted in protest, but

Katherine ignored it. Oh yes, 'That she had thought about him.' *Well, that wasn't so bad,* she supposed, but something taunted at the edge of her memory. Something Louise had said… Her mind cleared like the receding tide, yielding the words she searched for. In their clarity, a small frustrated moan escaped her, and she turned her face into the pillows. The soft fortress offered no haven from the attacking syllables as they drilled into her head and through her heart, *"You know very well what it's like…"* For the moment, at least, she could muster no defense.

From the downstairs hallway, the muffled hail of the grandfather clock interrupted her torment, and Katherine counted off the hours. Three… four… five. Five o'clock. She pondered getting up, when the decision was taken from her by a soft tap on the door.

At her call, Nora's happy face appeared, leading a small parade. In she came, with a cheery, "Good morning," and two maids who swirled about the room in quiet efficiency. When they had left, Katherine was supplied with hot water, her dress, which she had carried in her travel bag, newly pressed, and an assortment of under garments. Nora also conveyed a message from Judith Caldwell stating that Katherine should "Feel free to make use of the suitable attire which she had provided." This was followed by a wink from the amiable housekeeper, and a grimace from Katherine.

It had been this way since her first visit. Katherine had decided, at the ripe old age of twelve, that it would be a cold day in hell when she ever wore a corset. Wisely, she had kept this declaration of independence to herself, and not told her mother, but so far had been true to her vow.

Judith, of late, had placed her nose where it did not belong, and was of course, appalled at Katherine's refusal to conform, and considered it her duty to set the wayward girl on the right track. She was probably waiting downstairs for Katherine to descend, 'Transformed,' as she called it, 'into a proper lady.'

As in the weeks before, Katherine pushed aside the offending implication that she did not have the proper clothing, and washed and dressed. This time, in a black dress suitable for travel, with the straight lines and simple style she preferred, its single adornment, a jet brooch that had been her mother's. She left the extra chemises and petticoats, which she knew were borrowed from Louise on the bed. She had brought what she needed and would, once again, tell Judith so. Avoiding the corset conflict however, had been a bit more of a problem. The first time, she had left it lying with the other things, and after she had departed for the day, Judith had found it, and voiced her disapproval upon Katherine's return.

The solution was simple enough. She did now, the same that she had done on her more recent visits, and slipped it under the mattress for Nora to find later. Having braided her hair and pinned it up, she was as ready as she could be, and went downstairs for inspection.

Judith missed her cue, and Katherine was relieved to find Louise alone in the dining room. Upon her entrance, Louise did a slight double take, and gave her a grin.

"Please, not you too," Katherine whispered, not certain who was within hearing distance. "Well, you *do* look different, you know. I'll bet I'm not the only one who will look twice at you today." In truth, Louise thought her friend was always splendid no matter what she wore, but this time there was something else about her. The somber color of her dress, and her sedate hairstyle, gave her an aura of cool elegance. She looked serious and serene and *very…* She searched for the right word. *Capable?* Yes, like she could handle the world and all of its problems. Personally, Louise thought she probably could, but to tell her any of this would embarrass them both, so she settled for something they could be comfortable with, "You look like your mother."

"Thank you," said Katherine, who thought this was the only compliment she would ever need. She would have said more, but Judith made her belated entrance, followed by Nora.

"My dear, how lovely you look! Your complexion is too tanned of course, and your dress rather plain, of necessity, I know, but what a difference! And your waist is so slender." She lowered her voice while discussing such personal things. "You see what the proper garments can do for a lady?" She was too busy nodding approval to herself, to see the look of amusement that passed between Katherine and Louise, and paid no mind to Nora's sudden exit.

The ride into the city with Ezra Caldwell was quiet and uneventful. As they drove along in the buggy, Katherine watched the scenery and offered an occasional comment to the old family friend. To her he was the perfect image of a sea captain, with his old faded cap, full gray whiskers, and brawny weathered face. She considered him a good friend, and a competent advisor, and although they spoke little, the silence was a comfortable one.

It was late afternoon when they rounded the last turn, and overlooked the forest of masts that was Boston harbor. Ezra looked fondly at the young woman who dozed against his shoulder, and gently woke her. "Katie, we're here."

"Oh, I'm sorry," she sat up and smoothed her hair, surprised to find she had slept.

"I'm sure you are, the ride being as exciting as it is," he teased, and gave her a wink. He considered offering to stop for refreshment, but he knew her well enough to know she would rather get on with her business.

Ezra slowed the buggy when they drew closer, and they searched in the distance for her father's ship. She caught the pungent odor of the docks, so different from the open sea. As they drew closer, the bustle of the busy wharf filled her with excitement. Ships of every description covered the harbor, some at anchor, and some at dock, so many that it seemed she could leap from one to the other, much like stepping stones in a garden. Passengers and cargos loading and unloading, coming and going, created a kaleidoscope of color and action. She had grown up here around the docks, and had learned some things she probably shouldn't know. *Now, though, out there on Georges Island, there were Confederate prisoners…* She was pulled from her musing when Ezra caught her attention, and nodded toward the far end of the wharf. Katherine's heart leapt. For there at long last, was her father's ship the 'Mary Katherine'.

As they pulled up by the ship, there was no shortage of admiring glances, or willing hands to help the young woman from the buggy, and Katherine waited impatiently for her slow and deliberate escort to join her onboard. Radiant at the anticipated reunion, she turned to find Mister Brown, second in command and her father's right-hand man. He approached reluctantly, eyes studying the deck, hat in hand.

"Brownie!" She greeted him, impulsively kissing his cheek. "I've been so worried. What's happened? Why are you so late? And where is my father? I…" Intuitively she knew something was missing from his easy-going demeanor, and stiffened warily. "What's the matter?" She whispered, searching his face for some clue.

He looked into her eyes, and then over her head to the distant horizon, twisting his hat in his hands. He swallowed hard, and when Katherine could have screamed, he spoke. "I'm sorry Miss, the captain is not with us."

Her eyes sought help from Ezra and moved to Brownie again, *"Has he gone ashore?"* Her voice was a broken whisper, because she knew that was not what he meant.

Chapter 5

Katherine sat in a quiet corner of the great square house that was the Lawrence's home in Boston. Nathan and Gladys, the caretaker and his wife, had retired hours ago, and the atmosphere was thick with silence. Seated at her father's massive desk in the study, she read again his last letter, with the usual report of the voyage and the war, and how he expected to be home soon.

She thought of her vibrant father, now dead, and the concept was beyond her grasp. She could picture him, her Viking King of other days, laughing, joking, counseling, teaching, loving—*but not dead. Not gone, never to return.* She felt much like she had when Mary died, but she could find no tears. Instead of the heart wrenching sobs she had known then, there was nothing but a deep void. She was drained of emotion, and her feelings were far away, while her able mind clicked with the answers to what now had to be done. She had to tell her sister. She would notify Evelyn that she would be staying longer than expected, to settle business matters, and make the arrangements for refurbishing the ship. She would need Ezra's help.

Brownie had told her, her father had received her letter, and she found some comfort in the fact that he knew at the end he was not leaving his Mary behind. He had been buried at sea, which was what he had always wanted. She struggled with the sadness that he would not be beside her mother in the little cemetery near the cottage, but there was no doubt in her mind her parents were together now, once again sharing that special bond between them.

Among his personal things from the ship was his journal, strapped and locked. She had the key, but what if he had written of her mother, or worse, her mother's death, as she had? No, she could not read it now, *if ever*, and locked it away in a drawer of the desk. There were several letters to be posted, mostly to military people she didn't know, and one for Cecil Johnston, a family friend, and father of her childhood nemesis, Cecilia.

Carrying the letters to the front hall, so they could be delivered in the morning, she studied the familiar handwriting, so painstakingly neat, and so at odds with her father's impulsive and daring personality. *How could this have happened? Why?* Brownie said they were chasing down a ship attempting to run the blockade, while Phillip had stood in full view, in the light of a new dawn, calling for more sail. So that's what he had been up to… He had never told her, but she knew he had taken on something dangerous, throwing himself into it with that devil-may-care attitude. Ascending the winding staircase on the way to her bedroom, she gazed down at the hall below and recalled the night at the start of it all…

In April, 1861, when President Lincoln had declared a coastal blockade of the Southern states, it had been hailed as impossible, even laughable. To guard almost four thousand miles of coastline, including two hundred ports, the U.S. Navy had ninety ships, half of which needed repair. Many were scattered to the four corners of the world, leaving a handful available for immediate action. However, several months later, as the war gathered steam, the Navy was growing rapidly.

Lincoln's 'paper blockade' was becoming a reality, and by August, young men were leaving the area in droves to fill the call for recruits.

It was not a happy occasion, but a festive one just the same, and, true to her nature, Cecilia Johnston, had to be at the center of all things. Cecilia, true to form, had wrapped her doting father around her little finger, and arranged for a lavish farewell ball to be held at the Johnston home on the Saturday evening before the men were to sail.

Katherine, also true to form, had not wanted to attend. She remembered the subtle logic of her mother, and the broadside of Evelyn, who had been brought in for reinforcement.

"Why give her the satisfaction?" Katherine had argued, "You know she doesn't invite people to be nice. She invites them so she can feel superior, and to show off her father's money. *Please*, you know how she feels about me, and I'd have to *thank* her for inviting me!"

Her dear mother, who knew too well how to reach her, had simply pointed out that the ball was to honor the men who were leaving, including Phillip and William, and that the invitation was extended by Cecilia's parents, and therefore, the only ones to be thanked were Mr. and Mrs. Johnston.

Evelyn had professed disappointment in Katherine's lack of courage, but all Katherine had to do was stare, until the corners of Evelyn's mouth twitched and she looked away. She had known it was a lost cause, when the two women had begun to go through her closet, and she had thrown up her hands in exasperation, and informed them she would wear her newest dress. If it wasn't up to her whether she went or not, she should at least be allowed to decide what she would wear.

It was her father, though, who had made certain she would attend the ball, when he had called her into his study and told her how much he would miss her. He had given her his charismatic smile, and told her he looked forward to dancing with her himself, and besieged her with compliments until Katherine began to grow suspicious.

"And?" She prompted, her laughter bubbling forth, at his

sheepish look.

"And I have another new partner, and I sort of promised him a dance with my beautiful daughter." He looked at her hopefully, and when she rolled her eyes heavenward, he hurried on, "Trust me Kate, he's a good-looking man and more importantly, a good man. I'm sure you'll like him."

Katherine had given him a doubtful look. This wasn't the first time she had been elected to play hostess to associates of Phillip, to make an even party or round out a table, and she usually didn't mind, but her father's idea of '*good looking*,' included anyone who walked upright, as long as they were decent and honest. At least they were all well-mannered. She had never known her father to do business with anyone who wasn't.

"All right," she agreed reluctantly, giving him a long hug. "Who is it this time?"

"Captain Galloway. He's going to meet us there. Thanks Katie, you won't be sorry. He's first rate, like you."

"*First rate,*" was high praise indeed, from her father, a compliment he reserved for few things, and fewer people.

In Katherine's imagination, there grew a vision of someone who could win her father's respect. Older than he, probably, with silver hair, and lots of white whiskers. Someone like Ezra, the typical sea captain, *unlike Phillip*, who in her opinion was not the least bit typical.

High spirits prevailed that night, in spite of the war, or perhaps because of it. Her sister Thea, was away visiting Keith's parents, and William had left early to pick up Louise, leaving Katherine, to ride in the coach with Evelyn and her parents. They were a striking couple, the slender woman with beautiful red-gold hair, and the dashing captain, in his dark evening clothes. She was very proud of them.

As her father ushered them into the Johnston's foyer, Katherine paused to look around and caught her breath, for there, waiting at the doorway to the main room, was the very man she had envisioned. She noted the square build, the neatly trimmed white whiskers and the kind smiling eyes. Her only surprise was that she had been so accurate in her foresight, and with a smile she turned to her father awaiting the introductions.

"Ah, Mr. Galloway, good evening." The formalities taken care of, the party proceeded into the large room, to be greeted by the Johnston's. Cecil and his wife Amelia were fine people, but the sole product of their union, once their pride and joy, had become their everlasting cause of distress. Now, too late, they were beginning to question how a daughter that had been given everything she had ever wanted, had become the selfish, spoiled woman, who lived her life with rampant disregard for the feelings of anyone around her.

Katherine went first, the better to get it done with, the happy music and gay atmosphere, doing little to assuage her uneasiness. She greeted Mr. and Mrs. Johnston, and moved on.

"Good evening, Cecilia," she offered to the young woman before her, dressed in violent yellow taffeta, whose white-blonde hair and pink cheeks seemed too delicate for the onerous personality beneath. She was a pretty girl, a half foot shorter than Katherine, with a voluptuous figure which she flaunted to the utmost, screaming for attention with the bold colors that had become her garish trademark.

Cecilia Johnston seethed with ill-disguised malice as she eyed her rival, her calculating gray eyes busy taking in the gown of dark green silk, from its sweeping hem to its low neckline, and half sleeves that revealed Katherine's exquisite shoulders.

How she hated this girl, with her golden skin and hair, worn up now like a crown, her willowy body, and her confident manner. She had always hated her. How many times she had endured the dreaded admonishment from her parents to—*be like Katherine—act like Katherine.* She loathed them all—the whole family, who seemed so content with themselves, and were so liked by everyone, it seemed they could do no wrong. Cecilia had tried. How she had tried to get back at Katherine. She had spread countless rumors about her, *playing games with the boys, riding that beast of a horse all the time,* but people had laughed it off, and her own mother had hinted she could do with more exercise. As they grew older, she had tried spreading stories about exactly how *'friendly'* Katherine was with all the boys. She was always with them, everyone knew that; But the Caldwell brothers had called her aside, and threatened her with stories involving her reputation— *stories not altogether untrue*—and she had ceased her insinuations. No one had believed her anyway.

They *liked* Katherine, they *trusted* Katherine. *What was the matter with people?* Couldn't they see her father was richer than Phillip Lawrence? *At least she thought he was*—and the Johnston's had a larger house, and they gave more parties—Cecilia was at a loss to understand it.

Beneath the disapproval of her father's scowl, she struggled for a greeting. "Katherine," she mumbled, and indicating the gold cross that the other girl wore, she spoke with a smirk, "Lovely cross."

Katherine forced a tight smile to meet the narrowed eyes, for it was a familiar game. The cross was a heavy piece, formed by several strands of gold twisted together. It was quite unique, and had been her grandmother's and before that her great-grandfather's. She seldom wore any other necklace, and it was the one thing Cecilia complimented her on each time they met, doubtless calling it into comparison with her more elaborate jewels.

Katherine also spoke for Cecil's benefit, "Thank you, Cecilia. As you know, I treasure it."

Her rival frowned, *what did she mean, treasure?* The simple piece of jewelry did not look valuable to her. Eyeing the older gentleman behind Katherine, she decided on a new tactic.

"Why, Katherine, is this your new beau?!"

Roderick Galloway had been watching the exchange in quiet amusement, and drawn his own conclusions. Katherine turned to make the introductions, and he stepped forward, taking Cecilia's hand.

"We've met," he said aside to Katherine, and turned to Cecilia again. "How do you do, Miss Johnston? I am pleased to see you again, but I'm afraid you are mistaken. I am but a business associate of Captain Lawrence, and as I am quite free for the evening, you would do me great honor if you would promise me a dance."

Again, under the watchful eye of her father, Cecilia dared not be rude, and uttered her consent. She glared at her rival's back as the elderly man escorted Katherine away across the room.

Katherine, noting the satisfied mien of her new found friend, knew he was privy to her ongoing feud with Cecilia. "Thank you, Captain Galloway, I know that was strictly in my defense, and I consider it too great a sacrifice. I'm afraid now you'll have to dance with her."

"My, my, such hostility there," he said, glancing across the room, and giving a forced shudder. "Are you so deserving?"

In answer, she shrugged her shoulders and gave him a helpless look.

"I think not," he chuckled. "I must correct you, my dear girl, on two counts. The first, is *she* must dance with *me*, and I may not be able to avoid stepping on her wee toes."

"Oh, it's been sometime then, since you've danced?"

"I didnae say that lassie. It's only that I may not be able to resist," he whispered, with a twinkle in his eye that earned a laugh from Katherine in sudden understanding.

"And the second, Captain?"

"Aye, that's it, I'm not a captain, it's *Mr.* Roderick Galloway," at your service, just the same," he said, clicking his heels together, and making a half-bow.

"Oh, I'm sorry, I was sure my father said, '*Captain*' Galloway'."

"That would be my nephew…" he surveyed the crowded room expectantly, while Katherine recovered from her confusion.

"Ah, there he is now. Late as usual." He gestured toward the crowded hallway, near the entrance.

Katherine turned in the direction of his outstretched arm and searched the busy throng, trying to decide which could be a relative of the pleasant man beside her. Her eyes swept face after face, discarding those she knew, and considering those she didn't as possibilities. She had no idea, of course, and was about to turn to her friend for help, when a shock ran through her chest, and the breath caught in her throat. There, framed in the huge double doorway, was the stranger from the cottage road.

She looked away. At the wall, at the band, anywhere but there. There, where he stood searching over the crowd, as she had. Her traitorous eyes moved of their own accord to once again touch his face in light caress. She turned away, hoping he had seen her, and praying he hadn't. She didn't have to look at him. She knew that face so well. It had haunted her night and day for the past months. Her heart began to beat heavily, and she wanted to hide.

"My Dear, is something amiss?" Roderick asked, now waving his arm in a beckoning motion above the crowd, and looking at her, in concern.

"Thank you. I'm fine. It's quite warm in here." Katherine, gaining some measure of control, used the first excuse she could think of. "Have you found your nephew?"

"Yes, here he comes."

She turned again toward the doorway, anxious to welcome some diversion to her tumultuous feelings, and knew she was lost, when it was the stranger who started toward them. She saw him through a tunnel, the crowd dwindling to a blur, the music barely discernible over the beating of her heart, and his uncle's accent registering belatedly in her brain.

He came across the room with long confident strides, resplendent in his Navy uniform. A slight grin teased the corners of his mouth, at his uncle's frantic attempts to gain his attention. As he got closer, his gaze fell upon Katherine. Their eyes locked, and he paused but a moment, before proceeding to her side, a slow smile growing on his handsome face.

"Uncle Roderick," he greeted the older man, shaking hands, while his eyes remained with Katherine. He tore his gaze away and spoke to his uncle. "Up to your tricks again, I see, charming the ladies." His eyes moved again to Katherine, and back to his uncle expectantly.

"I was covering for you, my boy, as usual," Roderick, who had not missed the looks exchanged between the two, went on with relish, studying his nephew. "I believe this young lady is your partner for the evening." Turning to Katherine, he said, "Miss Lawrence, my nephew, Captain Devin Galloway. Devin, Miss Lawrence."

Devin Galloway took her hand, and grinned into her eyes, "Miss Katherine Lawrence," he bowed low, "I have found you at last."

Roderick's suspicion was confirmed. "You've met before," he stated, his eyes full of mischief. "Dinnae tell me this is the girl you..."

"Perhaps you'd like to dance, Miss Lawrence?" Devin spoke in an overloud voice, cutting his uncle off, and giving him a dark scowl.

The older man chuckled, "Perhaps I'll see about finding a partner for myself," and with a nod to Devin and a bow to Katherine, he left them.

Devin, hiding a smile, had offered her his arm, and Katherine had walked beside him on a private cloud, past Cecilia, to the dance floor…

Cecilia. She alone was as disturbing as any nightmare. Katherine punched her pillow, and tossed and turned in her bed trying to get comfortable. She should stop now. It wasn't often she let herself relive that evening. That one night when she had known more joy than she could ever have imagined.

With a sigh of resignation, she again eased open the door to the past, to let the truth step forth, and there he was—as tall, dark, and mesmerizing as the last time she had seen him. She stayed very still, while the emotions she had corralled for too long, stampeded through her heart, trampling her resolve.

She was dancing in his arms, one hand held warmly in his, the other resting on his shoulder. His dark hair brushed his collar, beckoning her fingertips, and it was with great effort she had not reached to touch his curls. She dared look into his eyes—*Eyes like the ocean,* deep, dark, and powerful, pulling her as surely as the tides—*And that smile,* so unfairly framed by dimples that must have been placed by the Devil himself.

The smile widened, and realizing she had been staring, she lowered her gaze to his chest, taking a trembling breath. It wasn't his looks alone that captivated her. They certainly affected her, but it was something much more. Something she couldn't explain, that took control of her at his mere presence and shook her to her core.

Brave now, in her recollections, she sought out every detail. The shiny gold buttons of his coat, his shirt, so white against the deep tan of his wrist. The clean fresh scent of him, and the wealth of longing she had felt, when in that moment on the overcrowded dance floor, another couple had collided with them, and she had, for a moment, been pushed up against him. Flushed with embarrassment, she had refused to look at him, until the music ended. Shyly she raised her eyes expecting that teasing grin, but instead met a gentle smile of understanding.

"So, it's Miss Lawrence."

Katherine only nodded. She had not said a word since he had first taken her hand. Her heart was still pounding, her throat was dry, and if she were to speak, she feared her voice would fail her. She felt the awkwardness of the silence, but he seemed content to stare into her eyes.

"I suppose it was nearly a draw," he said.

She struggled to grasp his meaning.

"You have my name in return," he explained. Seeming at a loss for words, he took a deep breath and glanced about the room. "Would you like something to drink?"

"Please," she managed, and he led her to a quiet corner where she could sit, before he went on his mission.

Katherine tried to calm herself. Now he knew her name. He knew Phillip was her father, and where she lived. How many times in the past weeks had she cursed herself for not telling him the first time he had asked her? Perhaps he would have sought her out, and asked to call on her. She would at least have known who he was, and had a name to go with the face in her dreams. *Devin. Devin Galloway.* Now he was here and she couldn't even speak to him. She summoned her courage, took some deep breaths, and smiled her thanks when he returned with two glasses of punch, and sat beside her. She let the cool liquid soothe her throat, and tested her voice. "Thank you, Captain."

"Please call me Devin," he said, staring intently into her eyes once again.

Katherine hesitated, looking around. "But we've just met."

"I know, but I'd like to hear you say my name, and besides," he paused, leaning close to her ear, "I feel I have known you always."

Katherine blushed, beset by a surge of emotion, as his breath came warm against her neck. *Was it possible that he felt as she did?* "I know, I..." She glanced about, making sure they were not overheard.

"You feel it too," he said, "I can see it in your eyes." He smiled, "Do you believe in love at first sight?"

She would rather have died than answer that, because she wasn't sure if he were serious, but secretly she couldn't deny it, the feelings were so strong within her. But this was crazy, they barely knew one another! Did it always happen this way? *Did it ever?*

Always listen to your heart, her mother had taught her, but her heart was telling her to throw herself into his arms, and to kiss him as she longed to do. In her more rational brain, Katherine knew such an action would not please her mother, who was dancing just across the room. The absurdity of it, mixed with her nerves, made her laugh, raising an inquisitive brow on that beguiling face that was much too close.

Her smile faded and she leaned toward him, drawn by some unseen power. "Devin," she whispered.

"Hello, Katherine, may I have this dance?" She jumped and nearly spilled her punch, but Devin took the half empty cup from her hand, as he stood.

"Oh, Russell! Of course," she recovered, hoping she had not been as close to Devin Galloway as she had felt. She could have sworn there were scarcely inches between them.

"Devin Galloway… Russell Caldwell," she spoke quickly, covering her nervousness, "We've known each other since we were children."

"How are you, Captain?"

Devin shook the proffered hand. "Fine, thank you, and yourself?"

"Well enough, all things considered," Russell answered, his dark eyes giving a dubious look downward at his new uniform. "I'll feel better when I've stolen the lovely Katherine from such a fine man as yourself, sir." Russell laughed heartily, and giving an enthusiastic salute, led Katherine away to the dance floor. He didn't notice, as she did, that the captain had not laughed at his jest.

Once on the dance floor, Katherine was claimed again and again, as the dancing continued into the night. She danced with her father and brother, with Roderick, and all the Caldwell boys. Wherever she was, she could feel the warmth of Devin's eyes on her, even while he danced with other women. She caught sight of him dancing with her mother, and she could tell by the way they both smiled in her direction, that they were discussing her, and her face grew warm, as she wondered what they were saying. He danced with Cecilia, and she was surprised to feel her stomach churn with jealousy. She had never been jealous of Cecilia, but the way the woman pressed close to him, and the familiar way she smoothed his collar… Katherine was ill at ease, and wondered how well they knew each other.

"Oh, Devin," Cecilia gushed as they danced past, and Katherine fought another strange twinge. She excused herself from the dancing, and left to get another glass of punch.

When she turned from the table, Devin was at her elbow. "Katherine…"

There were a few other people near the table and she gave him a warning look over the rim of her cup.

He paused, while a vision of liquid green eyes burrowed deep into his soul to make a home there, and belatedly, he remembered to breathe. He gave her an exaggerated bow that made her smile. "*Miss Lawrence*, I believe this next dance is mine," he rasped, taking the cup from her hand, and drinking from the same place her lips had touched, deliberately staring at her over its rim.

Katherine turned scarlet at his impetuous behavior, "Devin!" Her voice was barely a whisper, but she was yelling at him just the same. She glanced nervously to the corner occupied by the stern old matrons of this particular society, with their gray faces and black dresses. They were always there somewhere, stiff and proper in their manner and their dress. Always on the lookout for some fresh scandalous morsel to devour, and woe to the one who provided it.

"Relax, no one was looking," he laughed, and swept her into a waltz. "I knew I could get you to say my name again. Let them all turn inside-out with indignation." He looked so pleased with himself she had to smile. He held her firmly, the warmth of his hand burning into her back, seemingly pushing her heart more into her throat so she could barely breathe, and when her eyes met his, the heat of his stare said much. Her hand tightened on his shoulder involuntarily, and her heart beat wildly, when he waltzed her across the room and through the doors into the August night.

Cecilia, watching Devin as always, saw them go, and seethed again with hatred. *How dare he!* She had done everything she could to keep him with her, and now, of all people, he had gone off with Katherine. Her father was close by, and she chose not to make a scene… *yet.* She couldn't have him always watching her too closely. She had new friends, and she had plans. There was money to be made from this pathetic squabble they called war, and she was smart enough to see it. All she needed were some funds to get started, and she was well on her way. She would deal with Devin later. She smiled to herself, and wandered over to entice the handsome John Ambrose to dance with her. She would watch. Katherine would return, and she would be waiting.

"Will you walk with me, Katherine?" He asked, and she could not refuse. She took his arm, reveling in his nearness. They walked through the quiet gardens to a secluded spot at the back of the property, and stood listening to the gentle sounds of the evening.

"Katherine, I think you know how I feel about you. I wish I had found you sooner, I would have arranged things differently. I'm sorry. I would rather be with you, but I've committed myself. I feel so trapped. I wish I had known…"

He didn't finish, and she wondered what he was trying to say. *Arranged what things?* She knew many of the girls were marrying before the men left, or had promised to wait for their sweetheart's return. She didn't know what he had in mind, but she knew in her heart, if he asked her, she would wait for him, and if he didn't, she would wait anyway.

He went on, and she felt a stab of disappointment as he continued, "I shouldn't ask, but would you meet me tomorrow morning, before I sail… please?" He pulled her into his arms, searching her face, and lowered his mouth to hers.

Katherine stood motionless, captured by his intent gaze, and watched him move closer, as if in a dream. There was the sudden realization that she had wanted him to kiss her from the first moment she had seen him, and had, even then, somehow known this would happen. The first warm brush of his lips was gentle, *asking,* and brought a shock of wonder. She had been kissed before, but it had not felt like this…

He paused to look at her, a note of surprise in his expression, but she wanted more, and told him so with the tilt of her head. Trembling with restraint, his lips pressed hers more insistently, warm and soft.

Her heart turned over in her breast, and her blood began to hum. *…Never like this.* She slid her arms up around his neck, burying her fingers in his hair at last, and pulling him closer.

Encouraged by her response, Devin deepened the kiss, gentleness yielding to passion. How he had waited for this moment, wished for it, dreamt of it. He kissed her again, insistent and searing. He sought to be closer, and she opened to him, shared with him. His tongue slid in to touch her soul, and he knew nothing else.

The sun rose in Katherine's center, a burning mass of heat and light that filled her with liquid fire. She clung to him, giving in to the love she could neither deny nor understand.

Devin covered her face and neck with kisses. His heated breath by her ear shooting sparks through her soul. She closed her eyes and held to him, and when his warm mouth brushed across her shoulder and moved to the top of her gown, she was sure he must feel her heart pounding.

Her breasts strained against the soft fabric, seeking escape from their silken prison, and were momentarily freed, only to be recaptured by his fevered caress. She gasped, lost in this new sensation, welcoming the warmth of his touch that both worshipped and enslaved her, as he whispered her name. She hadn't known it would be like this—*Could be like this!*

She held her breath while his kisses formed a molten path across her skin to claim first one welcoming peak and then the other. Katherine was caught in an all-consuming fire. Eagerly she yielded to him, welcoming, willing him to want her, to have her, and to give of himself in return.

He pulled her to him again, seeking her mouth, his tongue caressing the dark velvet depths, and pressed her against the length of his body, boldly displaying his desire. With searching fingers, she found the buttons of his coat, and his shirt, spreading them wide to instinctively press her softness into the crisp dark hair covering the solid muscles of his chest. The contact made her gasp again in pleasure, and she felt a wild urgency deep within, spiraling out of control toward something only he could give. Only, "Devin."

He stopped and looked at her, his eyes wide. "Saints, Katherine, I'm sorry!" He took her by the arms and turned to seat her on the stone bench, frantically arranging her clothes. *"Oh, God, I never meant for this to happen."* He knelt before her, his head bowed, trying to catch his breath while buttoning his shirt.

Katherine sat, stunned by his sudden desertion, ill with rejection and unspent desire. Her hands shook while she adjusted her gown, her mind reeling. *He was sorry?* But listening to his apologies, the world settled around her, and cold logic began to cool her ardor. He was right, she wasn't thinking, *but she wasn't sorry. She would never be sorry… Unless of course, he thought less of her, but that did not seem to be the case.* "We should go in," she said reluctantly, thankful for the darkness that hid her burning flesh. She didn't tell him she hadn't spoken to stop him, but had been lost in ecstasy, and was barely aware she had uttered his name. She *wouldn't* have stopped him, and the thought frightened her. She had been listening to her heart.

They walked in silence, her hand on his arm. When they reached the courtyard, Evelyn appeared out of nowhere, falling in behind them as if she had been there all the while. They had been gone for some time; Katherine realized. *Leave it to Evelyn*, the last Katherine had seen of her, she had been dancing with Roderick.

Inside, Devin bowed and left the two women to avoid as much gossip as possible, and Evelyn drifted away. Katherine started across to the hallway where her parents were getting ready to say their good-byes.

Halfway across the room, Cecilia grabbed her arm and spun her around. "You bitch!" She hissed, into the startled girls face, keeping her voice low so the few remaining guests didn't hear.

Katherine was much too elated to be bothered by yet another of Cecilia's tirades. She was meeting Devin in the morning, and she knew he would ask her to wait for him. "What is it, Cecilia?"

"You've got your nerve!"

Katherine had never seen her so angry. "For Heaven's sake, Cecilia! Tell me what's bothering you!"

The girl's eyes had narrowed to slits of cold gray ice. "Stay away from Devin. If I ever catch you near him again, I'll make his life a living hell!"

Katherine did not understand. "What do you mean? What right have you…?"

"I have *every* right. He is my fiancé!"

Katherine's eyes fell to the diamond Cecilia flashed on her left hand, and her heart fell to the floor.

Chapter 6

The strong grip of yesterday clasped her heart when she stepped into the Johnston's foyer. She could almost hear the haunting melodies of that long ago evening, and feel the arms that held her. She kept her eyes straight ahead when she was led past the ball room to the rear of the house and Cecil Johnston's study.

"Katherine, dear girl! Come in, come in!" He hurried from behind his desk to give her a fatherly hug, and show her to a chair. "How are you? I'm so sorry about your father. He was a great man, and my closest friend. You know, if there's anything I can do..." *Poor child*, she looked lost. *Indeed, she was.* Her whole world had been taken from her in one way or another. She bore it well though, he decided, admiring how she sat straight and tall, her head held high—*If only his own daughter—Oh, well.*

"I'm fine, and thank you." She couldn't talk about Phillip right now. "You look well, Mr. Johnston, how have you been?" She thought, studying the tall rotund man before her, that he always appeared the same, solid and pleasant, with sparse pale hair and watery gray eyes behind his wire rimmed spectacles. Cecilia took after her father in coloring, but her temperament was purely her own.

"Can't complain. Wouldn't help anyway." He gave a sad smile, and folded his hands on his desk. The silence weighed heavily, and Katherine began to wish she hadn't come.

"How is Mrs. Johnston? …And Cecilia?" She forced herself to add, to be polite, and because she liked Cecil—*Loved him*—she thought, to her surprise. He had been there all her life, and she loved him like an uncle.

He sighed, and gave her a very speaking look over the top of his spectacles, and she knew he was not pleased. "Amelia's fine. Cecilia's been away, but she's coming back soon—She married, you know. She eloped."

She hadn't known, and the crushing weight settled on her chest. She opened her mouth but no sound came forth. She hadn't thought of that. She had never thought beyond that night, when Cecilia had hissed those words— *"My fiancé."* The words had echoed through her brain, as a black cloud had gathered at the edges of her vision threatening to overcome her. She had never fainted in her life, and she had prayed to God, that there at Cecilia's feet not be the first time. With pure determination, she had stared her enemy in the eye, and wished her well. Walking straight and tall, she had made her way to the door, said her good-byes, and left, with Cecilia's voice echoing in her ears. She somehow managed to face her parents, and Evelyn, in the coach. When they inquired about her evening, and the handsome captain, she had shrugged, and told them only that she would not be seeing him again, crushing the look of anticipation in their eyes, and they had ridden home in silence.

All that night, the sharpness of the words had cut to her heart, and the next day, when she didn't meet him, and instead had wandered through narrow alleys and backyards in the gray morning mists, in case he should look for her at her house, it was those words that had tormented her. The added burden of saying good-bye to her father in the pre-dawn hours, proved too much for her defenses, and being alone, she had let the tears fall.

It had been well after noon when she returned home, and she knew he had long since sailed. The weeks that followed, were much the same, as though she still wandered in a fog, hearing Cecilia's voice. And then it became Devin's voice she heard, *"I am committed. I wish I had found you sooner." So that was what he meant.* She had thought it was the war, with all its uncertainties…

"Katherine?" Cecil Johnston regarded the pale figure with concern.

"Oh," her voice barely a whisper, "I'm sorry, I guess I'm not feeling as well as I thought. I came to deliver this." She rose, and held out the letter from her father. "I think I'd better go now."

When she reached the door, she paused, and summoned the best smile she could manage. "Please tell Cecilia and her husband that I wish them happiness."

Cecil, did not comment, but instead, rose to wish her well, and turned his attention to the papers on his desk, never seeing the single defiant tear that had crept passed her iron will, and never knowing it was he, who had ground her last grain of hope to ashes.

Katherine, once again, left the Johnston home with her head held high above her shattered heart. The depressing gray of early morning had turned to a cold drizzle, and Casey, the twelve-year-old groom, and son of her caretaker, was waiting on the porch. With his older brothers in the war, and a diminished staff at the house, he had begged to be her driver and coachman. She had her doubts, but had not been able to resist the charming towhead with the pleading brown eyes. Now she was sorry, entering the dry interior of the coach while he stood in the rain. With the fervor of the very young, he assured her he didn't mind, and scrambled like a monkey to his high perch, setting the horses in motion. Settling into the seat, she flipped the hood of her cape off her head. The cape was black, like her dress. Almost everyone was wearing black these days. She had worn it because it was expected, and too, because it suited her mood. Now in the darkness of the closed coach, it seemed she could disappear into the blackness that surrounded her.

Hot tears started from the corners of her eyes and she brushed at them with determination. *Dammit!* She wasn't going to cry. If she started, she might not stop. She lifted the leather shade on the window and peered out at the deserted street. Outside everything was gray. The sky, the buildings, the cobblestones, even the hollow clopping sound of the horses' hooves, if it had a color, she decided, would be gray. She dropped the curtain, and everything was black again. Cold and black and empty.

I wish them happiness. Did she? She leaned her head back and closed her eyes, searching within herself for an honest answer.

She wasn't angry with Cecilia, *at least about this.* How could she blame her for wanting him? *What woman wouldn't?*

Was she angry with him? She saw again those haunting eyes, and tasted the warm urgency of his mouth on hers. The memory of her own desire burned upward to scorch her pride. *Why? Had he already been engaged to Cecilia when he had met her? He must have been. But how could he love a cold hateful person like that?*

She knew better than anyone, that you couldn't control love. Love happened where it would. She also knew there were other reasons for marrying besides love, and she knew not all men were faithful. *Had he used her? Could she have been fooled so completely? No, that was not possible… Was it?* Her mind skimmed over the thought, afraid to look too closely. *She had been so sure it was love.*

Strangely, she did want him to be happy. *Because she loved him.* A hot trembling confusion stirred in her heart. She turned in the seat, pulled up her knees, and curled herself into a ball. *Yes,* she wished him happiness—and she wished she could die.

By mid-afternoon, the annoying drizzle had been nurtured into a steady rain, which seemed like it would go on forever. This was fine with Katherine, who, still stuck deep in the mire of her dark depression, didn't think she could stand to see a bright sunny day.

Ezra had been over to have lunch with her, and had now left to see to some more business matters involving her father's partners. He was helping her take care of everything, and Katherine was grateful, as she stood at the front window of the drawing room, and watched his huddled figure receding into the rain. When he passed from her view, the street was once again empty, and she was once more alone.

For a while she watched the wind at play, twirling down the street like a happy child, skipping through the gathering puddles in gleeful abandon. For some reason, it reminded her of her sister, and she wished Thea were here now. She had written to her, of course, but it would be weeks before she could get everything in order, and she could visit. At least Thea had Keith. He had been wounded early in the war, and he was home with her and their daughter, Amy. *Amy a wonderful little girl.* A tiny insight scurried across her rambling thoughts, but it was too quick, and she could not grasp it. She stood very still trying to recall it, but it was gone, and somehow, she felt its loss. She sighed, and stared down the deserted street. No one was coming.

Her mind formed the painful query, '*Who is there to come?*' and at this, she hurried from the room and slammed the door, leaving the question behind. She crossed the foyer to the study, and drawing the drapes, and lighting a lamp to change her mood, busied herself with paperwork and matters of the household. From time to time, she came to, and found herself staring into space, but would plunge in again, admonishing herself to snap out of it. Once, while searching for a folder of receipts, she opened the drawer where she had placed Phillip's journal, and she paused, running her fingers over the cover, reconsidering whether she should read it. As before, she decided she was not ready, and emptying everything else from the drawer, locked it again.

The mantle clock chimed four, and she looked up in surprise. She had managed to deplete a good part of the afternoon without realizing it, feeling the evidence only now, in the ache in her back. She rose, stretching, and covered a small yawn.

Gladys knocked and bobbed her head in the doorway, "Would you like tea, Miss Kate?"

"Yes, thank you Gladys, that would be wonderful."

The housekeeper took a sideways glance at the young woman, who had the look of shock about her eyes… and the way she stared off into space all the time, it simply wasn't healthy. "Are ya all right, Miss?"

"Yes, really, only I'm a little chilled, I think I'll start a fire."

"I'll get Nathan."

"Oh, that won't be necessary, you know me; as long as you promise not to tell?" Gladys, much relieved by the teasing look and small smile, left happily, seeing a little of the old Katherine among the ruins.

There was no kindling in the study, and Katherine left its dark comfort, for the more cheerful drawing room. Laughing at herself over its closed door, which she had slammed in her fugitive exit, she opened it wide, trying to force the heavy mood away from her.

This room was more cheerful she admitted, surveying the pale walls. She drew the drapes and decided a fire in here would do just as well.

She knelt before the hearth, and struck a light to the tinder, but it would not catch in the damp down draft. She could hear Gladys in the hallway, and shifting her weight, she reached for another sheet of old newspaper, and scrunched it beneath the grate to set it afire.

"There's a visitor, Miss Kate," Gladys said, setting the tea service on the table

"Who is it?"

"I don't know, Miss, he's coming up the walk now."

"One?" She asked, her eyes on the newborn flames.

"Yes, shall I show him in?"

"Please."

"I'll get another cup." Gladys spoke more to herself as she quit the room.

Another condolence call, just when she was feeling a little better. She hated these uncomfortable visits, but she understood people felt they had to do *something*, and what else was there?

Satisfied the kindling would catch, she sat on her heels, and brushed a stray lock of hair from her face. She pushed herself to her feet, and a strong hand grasped her elbow in assistance.

"Oh!" She said, startled, glancing over her shoulder, "I didn't know…" The sentence died on her lips and she ripped her arm from his grasp. She stepped backward, her overwrought heart colliding with her ribs. *Oh*, she mouthed, but this time there was no sound.

He watched her take another step back, and his warm smile of greeting faded. She reminded him of a trapped animal, her incredible eyes overlarge in her white face, as she frantically searched the room… *For escape?*

"Katherine, It's me, Devin. I didn't mean to scare you. It's only me."

Katherine stared. *Yes, He was here… after so long.* She hadn't been prepared. Hadn't expected him to appear out of nowhere. A few times before, she had heard he was in the city, and she had stayed away purposely, passing up the cottage for Evelyn's house in the village. She hadn't wanted to see him. She was afraid. Afraid of what it would do to her. *And she had been right.* All the months she had spent trying to heal her broken heart, all her denial, all her resolve, crumbled at his presence, and she could do naught but stare at the face she remembered so well. The curling hair, longer now, the startling hue of his eyes, and his dimples, ready to blossom at his slightest smile… *He needed a shave.* She frowned, common sense returning with that tiny bit of logic. "I wasn't expecting you."

He was much relieved to see her eyes focus again, and he had to smile at her obvious understatement. He took a tentative step toward her, and then another, relieved that she did not move away.

There was a weary sadness about his eyes, and she could only wonder what sights he must have witnessed. She reached to press her hand against his bristled cheek. "You're all right?" She asked, her voice a breathless whisper. In answer, he turned his head and pressed a light kiss to her palm, and she snatched her hand away as if she had been burned. "What are you doing here?"

Before he could speak, Gladys returned with another setting, and wondering at the strangely silent couple, she shut the door on her way out.

Devin stooped and added a few pieces of wood to the growing fire, and stood to find Katherine still staring as though lost in thought. "I wanted to see you, of course. I'm very sorry about your father, and your mother. Maybe you should sit down."

She nodded her head, but did not move. Why did he have to come now, when she was trying so hard to be strong?

They stood studying one another, noting the price the long months had extracted from each. He had not seen her when he had first entered the room, crouched where she was, by the fireplace. Then she had moved, brushing at her hair, leaving a smudge of soot on her cheek. He had thought she resembled a child, stooped to play a game; a little girl, small and fragile that he wanted to hold and comfort, until the haunted look left her eyes.

How different she seemed from the first time he had seen her, thundering toward him on her huge black horse, her complexion heightened, her eyes sparkling like champagne, and her hair flying around her shoulders like a golden cape. Her breasts heaving beneath the open collar of her shirt and her skill working the reins, had brought to mind, Athena, the goddess of war and wisdom. There was that too, in the depths of her eyes, that drew him to her. He had never met a woman with such spirit, and she had ridden straight into his heart.

He had sat a long time, that day, trying to sort out his feelings, before going on to see Phillip Lawrence. True to their bargain, he hadn't mentioned her, but later, he had searched the village and the city, looking for her every chance he got, and nearly driving his Uncle Rod crazy. He hadn't known she was Phillip's daughter at first. She hadn't said so, when he had asked her for directions, and when he had returned to ask Phillip about her, the cottage was empty. He had called here, in Boston, looking for Phillip, and it was the caretaker that had told him they had gone to New Hampshire, and that Katherine was indeed a Lawrence. Soon after that, he had left the area to visit his own family, returning just in time for the ball. He had only hoped she would be there as Phillip had promised. He should have known she was a Lawrence, she was very like her parents, and the fact that they were both gone, would account for much of the change in her.

She shivered in spite of the fire and he stepped closer and took her hand.

"Your hand is like ice."

She pulled away, but gave a tiny smile that caught at his heart for its sadness, and he smiled in return, although he felt more like crying. Of all the atrocities he had seen, the sorrow in her eyes brought him the most regret.

She noticed the rain drops that sparkled like diamonds on the brim of the hat in his hand, and on his navy great coat. Seeing the direction of her gaze, he tossed the hat, and it sailed the short distance to the hearth. She watched it land squarely on target, and was speared by his piercing look that seemed to pass right to her heart.

Holding her eyes with his own, he unbuttoned his coat and held it open in invitation.

She hesitated, weighing the consequences, but the prize was too great. *Just this once…* she stepped into the warm haven close to his heart and felt herself come alive again. Only this, she would take and keep always, making the most of what little was left to her.

Devin wrapped the coat about her, and held her close with trembling hands. He closed his eyes, and swallowed the lump of fear that caused him to think she would turn away from him. She was all he thought about—the reason he had struggled to survive the hell of the damn war. He had to know why she had run away without a word that night, and not met him before he left the next morning. He had waited two hours at their chosen meeting place, and, cursing himself for waiting so long, he had begun to search for her. He had run all the way to her house from the docks, sweating, and stumbling up the stairs to find Nathan, who told him they had left to see Phillip off. Feeling sick to his stomach he had run all the way back, grabbing at strangers to ask if they had seen her, panic pressing tighter with each negative answer.

Racing against time, blinded by frustration, he had headed for his ship, and slipped and fallen on the stone quay, opening a gash in his knee. He had rested his face on the cold stone, and cursed the war, the world, and everything else he could think of. Several of his crew had carried him aboard, calling him their first casualty, and while the surgeon stitched his knee, he had in desperation, written a letter, addressed it to Katherine, and paid a boy on the docks to deliver it.

The few times since then he had returned and been able to look for her, it was as though she had vanished. Today, when she regarded him, there was no evidence that she recalled the words of the message that he had hung all his hopes on, but he had come to find out what had happened. That he would die without knowing, and without winning her love, had been his greatest fear.

Katherine stirred against his chest. Well warmed, and content for the moment, she could have stood there for the rest of her days. He was here, safe and whole in her arms. She was realizing only now, how much she had feared for his safety.

His strong hands caressed her shoulders, and she moved to kiss his shirt over his thudding heart. She had willed her mind to forget, but her body remembered all too well its role in her surrender to this man. Deep within, the forsaken coals of her passion stirred to life. Her breasts brushed his chest and she felt their traitorous response as his hands came up to massage her neck. This was heaven, just being near him, but she knew it was wrong.

She rolled her head back relishing the touch of his warm fingers, and he could not resist her parted lips. He was so careful, kissing her tentatively, not wanting to scare her away. Still, he felt the power of her kiss that he remembered from so long ago, surging through his blood, a current that pulled him helplessly under her spell.

She rose on her toes to fully surrender to his mouth, in a reply that took his breath away, and left him staring at her for a long moment, until she lowered her eyes in confusion and guilt. She hadn't meant to kiss him, and she stepped away.

Mercifully, Gladys knocked, and Katherine went to stir the fire, hiding her burning face, when the woman entered.

"Did you need anything else, Miss?"

"Yes, please, Gladys, more tea." Katherine mumbled, without looking up, smoothing her hair into place.

"Take your coat, sir?" Gladys offered, and not so much as raising an eyebrow at the untouched table, took the damp garment Devin handed her, and left to get more tea.

Now what? Katherine stayed at the fireplace trying to gather her scattered nerves. She returned the poker to its stand, and chanced a look at Devin, who still stood in the center of the room with a puzzled look on his face. She directed the anger she felt at herself. She was a fool. She had only meant to be near him for a moment. She should know better. A little of him would never be enough, and she could never have all of him. It was a fact she had to face.

He was safe, for the time being, and she could be grateful. But nothing had changed, *except for the worse. Instead of Cecilia's fiancé, he was her husband!* The thought brought a stab of agony to her heart, and tears stung her eyes.

"Katherine, what is it?" Devin asked.

"Cecilia," she whispered.

Devin scowled. "She's home."

She couldn't speak past the tightness in her throat, and shook her head, fighting to keep the tears from spilling over. She didn't want to think about Cecilia now, she had her whole life to think about that, but only these few minutes with him.

"Katherine, why did you not come to meet me? I need to know."

"How could you think I would? I couldn't. It wasn't right, what happened between us."

"But of course it was right. I love you. Did you not get my letter?"

She shook her head and began to cry.

He saw the tears again in her eyes, and the desires she had started raging through him, paused in the face of uncertainty, and a growing pity. Whatever it was, it was something too large for her to work around right now. He was certain she had been on the verge of hysteria when she had first seen him. Perhaps with Phillip's death, on top of everything else, now was not the time to press her. God willing, he would have time. "It's all right Katherine, we can work this out," he comforted.

She gave him a look of disbelief and sadly shook her head.

Gladys returned, exchanging the teapots without a word, and Katherine moved to the sofa to pour. Devin sat beside her, and taking out his handkerchief, leaned close. She would have shied from him, but at his scowl she thought better of it, and surrendered to his ministering.

She sat very still, while he dabbed the tears from her eyes and wiped the smudge from her cheek, folding the gray and white cloth and tucking it into her clasped hands, before he sat back to drink his tea, studying her.

The child vanished with the smudge, and before him sat an elegant woman, in a high collared black dress, with her hair neatly coiled at the base of her neck. Cool and distant. *No, not cool,* he thought, that was the wrong word for her, for he knew too well the fury of passion that she hid just beneath the surface, and the thought of it warmed him.

"I'm sorry about your father," he said, to change the direction of his arduous mind.

She nodded, regarding him, over the rim of her teacup, reminding him of the night of the ball, and afterward in the garden, when he had held her at last, and had been so completely overcome by his feelings for her. He had meant only to kiss her, and he remembered the dizzying emotions that had erupted within, when he had first touched her lips. Her response, and the soft scent of her, the taste, the feel of her, had overwhelmed him. He had gone much too far… *He must have insulted her.*

"How did you know?" She asked, interrupting his thoughts.

He took a deep breath, and set down his cup with a clatter, looking at her in surprise.

"What?"

"About my parents, how did you know?" She repeated, tilting her head.

"Cecil."

Katherine shifted her view to the fire, a slight frown creasing her brow, "Of course."

Devin took the opportunity to study her profile, and finding it difficult to be so close and not touch her, he reached out and ran one knuckle along the line of her jaw. Her frown increased, and he moved his hand to cup her chin and turn her face toward him. Pain flashed in her eyes, before she closed them, shutting out his pleading look.

"I'm sorry, Katherine. I'm sorry for what happened, but I can't change it now." When she didn't respond, he stood. "I'd better go," he said quietly, and went to retrieve his hat before moving to the door. "If you want me, if you need anything at all, I'll be at Cecil's."

"Devin..." She didn't want him to go, but she didn't dare ask him to stay.

He paused with his hand on the doorknob not looking at her, "Yes?"

She had to say something now. "Are you happy living with Cecilia?" She needed to punish herself, to rip open the wound and feel the pain anew, so she wouldn't ask him to stay.

He didn't see the tears that fell, and she didn't see the frown that he gave the solid wood of the door.

His situation was *almost* ideal at the moment. He had been afraid she would be bothered by Cecilia, and he was determined to win her over, but he knew he had to tread lightly. He could hardly tell her the woman wouldn't keep her hands off him… "No. She hasn't changed."

Long after he had gone, Katherine sat staring into the flames, clutching the grey and white plaid handkerchief, absently tracing the embroidered initials 'D. T. G.' with her fingers. *He loved her*. He had said so. She wondered what the 'T' stood for, and where he had been for so long. There were so many things about him she didn't know— Would never know.

Devin strolled down the rain-soaked street, not entirely displeased. He hadn't settled things with her, but he would, and now that his work would keep him close by, it would be soon. He hadn't told her that, but she would find out soon enough.

Chapter 7

As daylight faded, evening stepped silently forth in her moment of glory, to create an enchanting world of pink shadows and black silhouettes, softening the harsh beauty of the rugged terrain. Forlorn and furious, Katherine traveled the rocky trail that led her to the cottage, for once immune to the grandeur of her surroundings.

She shoved aside the graceful pine boughs, riding with an uncharacteristic peevishness of mind and manner. It was earlier than her last return and the way was lighter, but her heart was not. The near-argument she'd had with Judith Caldwell had left her fuming and she fought to control Matilda who skittered nervously, sensing the mood of her mistress.

Who was Judith, to tell her what she could and couldn't do? She couldn't live in that house alone, in the middle of nowhere, unmarried, unchaperoned. *What would people think?* It wasn't proper, she said. And, *SHE* had decided, it was best for Katherine to live with *HER*!

"Pigs may fly," Katherine muttered aloud, trying to think of something she liked little enough to compare to the meddling Mrs. Caldwell. In Judith's parlor, she had been polite, and as calm as she could, while they *discussed* the situation, or while Judith demanded, and she had listened, and she had left as soon as possible.

Katherine hoped her mother was proud of her, because as taxed as she was, it had taken a great deal of her self-control not to knock Judith on her... *chair*, she mentally supplied, in case her mother was somehow privy to her thoughts.

Wasn't Proper? What *was* anymore? Was it proper that at this moment the whole country was torn in half, and thousands upon thousands were dead or dying, with no end in sight? Brothers against brothers, fathers against sons, uncles, cousins. It was beyond comprehension. The world was upside down. But here in their tiny corner, it wasn't proper, according to Judith, for Katherine to live alone. If she wasn't so upset, she could have laughed at the absurdity of the whole situation.

It was a long ride and her mind had turned to more important issues by the time the cottage came into view. Instead of the stark shell that she dreaded, soft orange light spilled from its windows in greeting, offering a small bit of comfort, and by the time she had finished with Matilda, she was wondering why she had let Judith Caldwell upset her so. Granted the woman was intrusive, but she was concerned, and in either case, she had no real say in the matter.

Retracing the path of their conversation, she stumbled over the one word whose sharpness had stabbed at her pride and tugged at her weary heart, '*Unmarried.*' Before the war, women who weren't married before her age were the rarity. But now with so many men gone away, and so many that would never come home, it had become just another fact of life—*or of war*. So, she was unmarried. It wasn't as though she were sixteen and on her own. She would never marry. There was only one man she would ever care that much about, and he was married to someone else. She paused, resting her forehead against the door to the kitchen, before she entered to find Evelyn.

With an outward bravado, that would have made her father

proud, she marched into the room, tossing what she hoped was a normal "Hello," in the other woman's direction, crossing to stand before the fire.

Evelyn stood by the table wiping her hands on her apron, and awaiting a clue to Katherine's disposition. When the young woman faced her, shoulders squared, booted feet spread apart, arms folded across her chest, she felt between them an immense void, she could find no way around.

It was Katherine who broke the silence. "Well, you know."

"Yes, I know. I'm *so* sorry Katie."

Growing uneasy under the others gaze, Katherine exhaled heavily and shrugged, dropping her arms by her sides. When Evelyn crossed the room offering her comforting embrace, she was stopped at arm's length when Katherine placed her hands at her shoulders. "Please don't."

The half-whispered plea, and desperate look, gave Evelyn the bearing she needed. "Well, supper's ready, and I've got water heating. I thought you would enjoy a nice hot bath." She spoke briskly, urging Katherine to the table, and serving up her favorite chicken pie and pouring her tea, "How was your ride, dear?"

Katherine took to the small talk with unusual zeal. She talked of the travel, the weather, the war news, and related her run-in with Judith Caldwell, all the while chattering brightly.

Too brightly. Evelyn contemplated the rapid speech, the jittery movements, the high-strung voice, and wondered how long it would be before Katherine reached her breaking point.

"Have you considered what you're going to do?"

"What do you mean?" Katherine asked, afraid Evelyn was siding with Judith.

"Will you stay here?"

Katherine studied the food on her plate, "There are a lot of things to go over yet, and I'll have to keep up at the office, and there's

William… But for now, things will stay pretty much the same, and I want to stay here as much as possible."

Evelyn searched for another topic, and seized on the one that had brought a light of hope to the young woman's eyes a few weeks ago. "Any word of Captain Galloway?"

Katherine leapt up from the table. All the loss, anger, and resentment, which festered within her young mind, seemed to burst forth at the thought of acknowledging this latest insult, this added injury, to her already battered soul. "Don't!" she shouted, "Don't ever mention him! Do you hear me!?"

Surprised at her own reaction, she stopped and stared, as tears filled Evelyn's eyes and coursed down her cheeks. Never had there been harsh words between them, and she was ashamed of herself for speaking so. She knelt before her friend's chair, and took her hands, "I'm sorry, Evelyn, I didn't mean it. I'm not angry with *you*. Please understand," she begged, "I can't think of them all at once, and I can't *not* think about them. I don't even know who to cry *for*." Her voice broke, and she gave in to the great racking sobs that would prove a tiny beginning to the healing of her tortured heart.

Katherine, who had meant to offer solace, now became the consoled, as she knelt with her head on the same lap where she had so often found comfort as a child. Evelyn unwound her braided hair and freed the burnished tresses, brushing them into place with cool sympathetic fingers.

"It's all right Katie, cry all you want, it's the best thing." *It was the only thing. That and time.* The poor girl had been just beginning to have a better outlook when she had last seen her, and now with her father gone, and whatever else had happened…

Even those with great cause can only cry so long, and Katherine's tears eventually subsided.

"Feeling better?"

"I feel foolish," she replied, reaching into the deep pocket of her trousers for a handkerchief, and wiping her eyes.

"You needn't you know," Evelyn informed her. "You're like my own daughter, Katie."

"I know, but I shouldn't have said what I did. I didn't mean to make you cry."

"Oh, forget it. It takes more than a few words to wound an old war horse like me. I was crying for you, dear, I hate to see you suffer so."

A few minutes passed in silence, before Katherine moved to her seat, and Evelyn poured her another cup of tea. "So," she hedged, "About the captain... *Is he...?*"

Katherine made a tragic sound that was part laugh, part sob, "Oh, it's worse than that, Evelyn. *He's married!*"

"*Oh, my.*"

"Yes, and not only married, but to Cecilia." She had meant to finish the statement in a light flippant tone, but barely managed a disconsolate trickle.

"*Oh.* I had heard she eloped, *but...*" Evelyn didn't know what to say. She had seen Devin Galloway with Katherine the night of the Johnston's party, and she had thought for sure time would heal whatever stood between them.

Their eyes met across the table and they winced in unison, and Katherine smiled, albeit sadly. She took a deep breath. "Well," she offered, "That's that, and I'm not going to think about him ever again."

The wise older woman nodded her acceptance of the brave announcement, but she knew better. She had been in love once, and she had at last deciphered the initials on the handkerchief Katherine was twisting in nervous hands.

Katherine leaned her head against the rim of the tub and luxuriated in the steamy warmth. She was sore and tired, but not defeated. *You're only defeated, if you don't try again,* she told herself, *and you can always try again.* She had been dealt some lousy cards lately, but she'd had so much before. Perhaps life had a way of evening things out, she reasoned, taking the soap and lathering one long leg and then the other.

She had lost both her parents, but she would rather have had Phillip and Mary and lost them, than to trade places with say, Louise Caldwell or Cecilia... *Whoever,* she cut off another reminder of *that woman,* and of *him.*

She paused in the midst of soaping a shoulder, as a handsome visage floated before her presenting a familiar plea—The heart wrenching look he had given her as they sat on the sofa.

What had he to look sad about? He's the one that went and got married. Katherine felt the same anger and confusion she had that day in the drawing room, and sat still, letting the thought form fully in her mind.

Even if he had been engaged when they met, did he have to go ahead and marry Cecilia? Broken engagements were difficult, sometimes scandalous, but if he had cared about her—He couldn't have—At least not the way she cared about him. The thought drove her despair to new depths. *No,* if he felt the way she did, he would have done anything to get out of marrying someone else. It was too late now. *What's done is done,* as Evelyn would say. She would have to stop thinking about him, and it wouldn't be easy. Thank God she had Evelyn. *Poor Evelyn, she was perhaps more alone in the world…* Katherine paused. In her fertile mind was conceived a plan that would give birth to a solution for both of them.

The last days of March were hardly discernible from the gray April that followed, but May worked her magic, prodding the sleepy earth into bloom. Even Katherine felt a resurrection of her spirits as the world sprang to life around her.

Evelyn had accepted her offer, and moved out to the cottage to stay, taking over the guest room, while Katherine moved into her parent's room, and the easy companionship of the two women proved an excellent balm to the trials of life. They had spent a pleasant morning cleaning the flower beds around the house, and now, in the heat of the exceptionally warm midday, had gone their separate ways to seek relief.

Evelyn, who had chosen the kitchen with its cool stone floor, was relaxing at the table with a cold drink, when she heard the jingle of harness through the open door. Moments later, she hid her consternation, as Devin Galloway appeared at the threshold. It had been so long since she had seen him, she had barely recalled what he looked like, but now as his commanding presence filled the doorway, she found herself feeling sorry for Katherine. If the poor girl was trying to forget this man, she had her work cut out for her,

"Come in Captain," Evelyn said rising, and moving more into his line of vision. "I'm glad to see you're still whole after all this time."

White teeth flashed in amusement at the blunt greeting, as Devin stepped into the cool interior. "It's much better in here," he acknowledged in appreciation. "Mrs. Wiley, isn't it?"

"I'm surprised you remember; it's been so long." She indicated a chair, and poured another glass of cider.

"You're Katherine's friend," he said, as if that were reason enough for him to remember her, and she fought the urge to ask about that which was none of her business.

"Is she here?" He asked, taking Evelyn by surprise.

She hadn't even thought of lying to him, but now she weighed whether it would be in Katherine's best interest. *No*, it wasn't her place, and there was something about the hopeful look in his eyes… "Yes, she's here. She's down on the beach. But Captain," she cautioned him, as he rose to tower over her, "she's been through so much, and, well, with everything that's happened…"

"Don't worry, Mrs. Wiley, I've come to ask her to forgive me." He could hardly explain that he had come to apologize for attacking her in the garden and tearing her clothes off, so he left it at that, and hurried toward the beach.

In deference to the heat, Katherine had donned a skirt of crinkled cotton, and a matching cream blouse whose sleeves were trimmed at the cuff by narrow bands of pale green satin. The same ribbon wove down both sides of the placket, framing a row of tiny pearl buttons, and trimmed the waist band of the skirt. She had abandoned her shoes, as she often did, here in her private world, pushed up her sleeves, and undone a few buttons to catch the cool ocean breezes.

Devin stood at the top of the sandy bluff, and watched the lone figure as she walked along the water's edge, her skirt caught up and over one arm and her long hair hovering on the wind. She made a lovely picture against the background of the ocean, and he promised himself as he looked down upon the lonely path of her footprints, that no matter what he had to do, he would one day walk by her side.

She waded deeper into the still cold water, and stood with one hand shading her eyes, looking out at a passing ship. It was in much closer than most that passed, and she watched for some sign of trouble, but they were traveling at a good speed, and were under full sail. She was still watching, when she sensed a movement behind her, and twisted around, to discover the enigma of her dreams staring back at her.

Still shading her eyes, she looked into his, steadying herself against the wave of sensation that was sure to come. She felt it as always, lifting her heart as though to carry it on foaming crest, and deliver it to that one, who stood at once, too far away, and much too near.

Neither spoke, and after a long moment, she turned again toward the vast expanse of the ocean, silently petitioning the heavens to send her strength, before she went to meet him at the water's edge.

"Dare I hope the war is over, Captain?" She asked, referring with a graceful sweep of her palm, to the absence of uniform, replaced by well-tailored trousers tucked into high riding boots and a casual white shirt, the sleeves of which, were rolled up to reveal heavily muscled forearms with a fine covering of dark hair. She was reminded of the first time she had seen him.

Katherine did not see the small light of hope that fled his eyes, at her use of the more formal title. "I'm afraid not. Even we pawns of fortune are allowed a break, Miss Lawrence." He considered it a step backward from his goal, but if she wanted formal, she would have formal. Her face had lost its pale gaunt look, since he had seen her last, and her complexion was already tanned a light gold by the spring sunshine.

"You're looking well," he observed, as she stepped from the waves and dropped her hem, hiding shapely calves and pretty ankles from his warm regard. "All of you."

She scolded him with her eyes, and looked away, fighting the magnetism that would draw her to his tall form. "I suppose you'll be spreading it about the countryside that I have actual legs," she said in mock contrition, seeking safety in light banter.

"What?! And send the saintly covey to early graves?" He placed his hand over his heart. "Miss Lawrence, you wound me, for I am not so careless for the sensibilities of elderly ladies."

Katherine's smile faded. "I see," she said, meeting his eyes briefly, before she turned to continue her walk along the shoreline, knowing he would join her. "Is it only the younger ones, then, of which you are so careless?"

There it was, Devin thought, she was letting him know he had treated her shabbily— and he had. Now he would have his chance to make amends.

He came around to face her and took her by the shoulders, "Katherine, I apologize. I should never have done what I did, and I didn't mean to hurt you, but I..." He thought she had wanted him as much as he had wanted her, as much as he wanted her right now, but those didn't seem to be the right words. "I thought you were agreeable. I thought you understood."

Understood?! Her outraged mind screamed in protest. *Understood that while he had made love to her in the garden, he had been engaged to someone else? Someone he had every intention of marrying?* She jerked away from him and continued walking. "Oh, I understand all right. I understand the kind of man you are, and I want no part of you!"

Her heart cried out in denial, as she spoke the heated words, but she walked on, not looking at him. She had no choice. He had a wife, and considering the way she felt about him, the less she saw of him, the better.

For a moment, he stood stunned, but with three long strides, he caught up with her, and took her elbow, turning her to face a disbelieving half-smile. "You can't be serious…"

"You've left me little enough choice," she said, pulling her arm from his grasp, and stomping off with him right behind.

"Look, I can see where you might think a show of feminine pique is called for, but you enjoyed that night as much as I did, you can't deny it! Surely, you're not going to let your pride keep us apart?"

She was outraged. There was a lot more than her pride between them, but it was that pride that loomed large now. They reached the end of the crescent shaped beach. Here the sandy bluff behind them graduated into the rocky cliffs, and a tumble of huge jagged rocks had fallen across the beach to form a natural boundary, extending like an arm reaching into the sea. She turned to confront him; her head held high. "How can you think you can still be with me? I'm not one of your backwater whores!"

His eyes widened in surprise, and he wrestled a grin. "Why, *Miss Lawrence!* Where did you learn such language?"

But Katherine was too insulted, and too furious to be charmed by his grin, or to care what he thought. "Damn you, Devin Galloway. Would you please go!"

He searched her blazing eyes but found no quarter. "*You can't mean that.* Katherine, I remember..." He remembered everything. How she had caught fire in his arms and branded him with a heat he could feel even now. "I thought you cared for me," he pleaded.

"Well, you thought wrong." She spun away from the anguish that bolted to his face and folded her arms to keep from throwing them around his neck.

This was far more than the obligatory protests of the other females of his acquaintance, not that there had been so many. He genuinely liked women, but disdained the ones with false coquettish ways, thinking they could play men for fools. This one was different. He had known that the first time he had seen her, and he had wanted her ever since. Something didn't ring true here… But he had been gone a long time.

Devin stepped close behind her, but did not touch her, for which she thanked God. "I don't believe you," he whispered.

"Then you're a bloody, blind fool."

"Is there someone else?"

Oh God, yes! "Yes! Yes, there's someone else!" She wanted to scream at him, to shake him, but she didn't trust herself to touch him.

Devin's heart twisted at her words, but he remembered the last time he had seen her, in the city. She had given him such a rousing passionate kiss, that the memory of it still warmed him, and it was not the kiss of a woman who loved another man. "Tell me you don't love me," he challenged.

"I don't love you," she whispered, squeezing her eyes shut, hating herself, and the lie that came from her lips. "I *can't* love you!" She cried louder, the words closer to the truth, her voice breaking, and the tears coming at last.

He reached for her, but she sensed the movement so close behind, and she whirled around, bitter tears clinging to her lashes, her arms crossed. He had to strain to hear her voice, low and beseeching in desperation. "It's hopeless Devin, don't you understand? It's hopeless, and it pains me to so much as think about it. Please go and leave me alone."

Devin stared at the mixture of fury and agony as they fought for control in her beautiful face, and felt a helpless sorrow spread within his heart. "No, I don't understand, but if it's what you want, I'll go for now. Have your damnable pride, if you must. Let it keep you company and warm your lonely bed. But I don't believe you—And I won't give up."

With that, he turned and left with angry strides down the beach.

Katherine watched him go with an aching heart, and bit her lip to keep from calling out to him. It was a short time later that she retraced her footsteps to the house, finding that the serene solitude of the beach had turned to insufferable isolation.

Chapter 8

Captain Galloway tip-toed down the main stairway of the Johnston home. Although he had a considerable distance to travel, he was earlier than he had to be, and with good reason. He reached the bottom of the stairs, and nearly cursed aloud, when that reason pounced upon him in the hallway.

"Good morning, Devin, I've been waiting for you."

"Good morning, Cecilia. Like a cat waits for a mouse," he muttered under his breath.

"What did you say?"

"I said, be quiet, you'll wake the house. What are you doing up at this hour?" As if he didn't know. It was the very reason he had wanted to leave the house early, but he pretended to listen while she went through the explanation.

"Now, you know very well I want to do some shopping today, you were there when I asked Daddy for the carriage."

"So?" He stood, feeling trapped as she whined on, her impudent eyes touching him everywhere. He started down the hall, and she seized the opportunity to take his arm, and pull it snugly against her ample bosom as she walked along beside him, finishing her story.

"So, you see, since Daddy's gone already, and you've hardly spent any time with me, and you've got that great big coach to yourself, you can drop me off, and after lunch Daddy will pick me up."

Devin cursed himself, and poured his second cup of coffee. If he hadn't gotten up so early, he wouldn't have time to drop her off. As it was, he had no other excuse, and now he waited at the dining room table, while she got dressed.

At least it was a short distance before he dropped her off, he considered with relief, and a good thing *too*, or he might find himself ravaged along the way. He hadn't slept well, and rested his elbow on the table, supporting his head with his hand. Wearily he closed his eyes, and she was there… *A robe as sheer as moonlight clung to the form that rose from the waves like a spirit. A partisan wind billowed at her feet, and awarded him a fleeting glimpse of long slender legs, while hypnotic eyes drew him closer to open arms and warm parted lips. He went into those arms and she bent her head, capturing him with a curtain of gold silk and a kiss that scorched his soul…* He awoke with a start, blinking his way from a dream to a nightmare, as Cecilia stood in the doorway in a glaring pink gown, besieged by ruffles and bows.

"Poor Devin, you look unwell," she simpered, plopping a sweaty palm on his forehead. "Perhaps you should go back to bed and let me take care of you."

"No, thank you," he said, pulling away from her unwelcome touch.

Once inside the Johnston's roomy coach, Devin settled himself on the seat opposite Cecilia, and stretching out his legs, tried to recapture the dream that in the past nights had granted him little rest. Truthfully, he had told Cecilia he had a headache, and for once she was mercifully quiet.

Ezra Caldwell had the pleasure of escorting Miss Katherine Lawrence to an early breakfast. She had been in the city a week, and had already made fair progress delving into the legal maze, that was the considerable estate of her late father.

This morning, she was meeting with Ezra and an attorney, who were going to guide her through the many assets, including the ships, and the various shares in others, that were owned by Phillip. She also needed to pick out some material for the summer weight mourning dresses that Evelyn would help her with, but that was later, and first, she had decided, she would enjoy her breakfast.

The bright summer's day was already warm, but Katherine felt cool and businesslike in her dress of midnight muslin with the crisp white collar, and elbow length sleeves, her hair wound into a neat braided coil. In spite of the grueling work ahead of her, she was in a fair mood, as she walked with Ezra in the busy section of the city, with its blocks of businesses, and shops of every description.

They stopped at a smoke shop, and Katherine waited outside while Ezra went in to see if there was any tobacco to be had. Already, the streets were alive with the bustle of everyday life. The aroma of hot bread wafted from a nearby bakery to tempt her appetite, and street venders hawked their wares. Horses and carriages jostled for space avoiding early shoppers, and she watched it all with lively interest.

Like a black cloud appearing on the horizon to smother her sunny outlook, the ornate coach that was unmistakably the Johnston's, pulled close to the sidewalk a short distance down the block. Katherine had no wish to be confronted by Cecilia, and, on the chance it might be she, stepped into the shadowed alley.

The coach door opened toward her, blocking her view, and beneath it a length of leg appeared, clearly masculine, in tall black boots and gray trousers. She watched as it stepped to the ground and was joined by its twin, moving much too lively, and being much too lean, to belong to Cecil.

A strange weight spread upon her heart when the man moved

beyond the door into her vision, and her sorry eyes beheld that one they most longed to see. He looked wonderful, and elegant. in a dark morning coat over a gray vest that matched his trousers, and a flawless white shirt.

Gallantly, he reached a hand to the coach, and for a moment it was she who felt its steady guidance, so dearly did she wish it. A full pink skirt descended to the walkway, and Katherine knew by its shocking hue, it could only be Cecilia.

The dark head gave a slight nod, and the polished boots disappeared upward before the door closed, revealing a sight that hit Katherine like a blow. There stood Cecilia, her large abdomen proclaiming to the world that she was with child. Katherine's breath caught. Not just any child, but the child of the man that held her heart in his hands. She braced herself against the rough wall and stared as the coach rolled past. For one brief moment her eyes were seized by a steel gaze, and then he was gone.

Devin bolted from his seat and pounded on the roof to stop the driver, but they had gone half a block before the horses were stopped, and hanging from the open door, he jumped to the cobblestones. He ran down the street, weaving his way between children and old women, to the spot where he had seen her, but she was nowhere in sight. He looked around him at the mass of people. She could have gone in a hundred different directions, and if he thought that she wanted to see him he would have searched every single one. He knew otherwise though, and returned to the coach, cursing the morning while trying to convince himself it hadn't really been her.

Katherine paced the length of the study, her stomach churning with agitation. He was coming. She did not feel up to facing him again, but it was one of the few business details she had left to settle, and she comforted herself with the thought that after this, it would be done with. It had been three days since she had seen Devin and Cecilia, and she was trying to come to grips with Cecilia's pregnancy, though the memory still burned like the touch of a hot poker. Of course, Cecilia would have children. It was after all, only natural for man and wife to want offspring of their love. *She would.*

A picture rooted in her mind and grew—A tiny babe with striking blue eyes and dark locks, grasping a familiar masculine hand—The scene broadened to include the whole of the father, tall and proud, and beside him a woman, radiant with joy. He took her into his arms, and kissed her, stirring the fires that waited, smoldering, for his touch to bring them to life… Katherine closed her eyes, feeling the power of that touch, so well-remembered. The woman stirred in his arms and turned, and the face was not her own.

"Dammit!" With pure will, she turned her attention to the business at hand. Phillip Lawrence, in death, as in life, had provided well for his family. In addition to various bank accounts, and vast properties, he had also equally divided his more personal assets. The city residence, where she was now, had been bequeathed to William, as was Phillip's prized ship, the 'Mary Katherine,' and half of the Boston business he had worked so hard to build. Dorothea, who, on her wedding day, had received a sizable sum of money, was left the steam powered 'Sea Rose', and the smaller shipping office and warehouse properties in Portsmouth.

To Katherine, he had left the cottage that she loved, partial ownership in the Boston office, along with William, and his half ownership of the new steam frigate he had bought into at the beginning of the war. As fate would have it, the owner of the other half, and her new partner, was none other than the esteemed Captain Galloway. At present, Katherine held a rather dark opinion of fate. She wanted out.

Under the terms of the contract, either share could be bequeathed or sold, with the other partner having the option of first offer, so neither of the original partners was forced to accept a new partner they did not want. In other words, if Katherine understood correctly, Devin could sign a new contract, with her as his partner, or he could buy her share, and own the ship by himself, or she could sell her half to someone he approved of.

She ardently hoped he would choose one of the latter. She didn't need the money, and the last thing she needed, was Devin as her business partner, when she was trying so hard to stay away from him. She wanted to let the attorney handle the transaction, but had received word that Devin insisted on seeing her first.

Reaching the far end of the room, she turned to pace back again, and walked into his wide chest. "Dammit!"

"And Good afternoon, to you, Miss Lawrence."

"How did you get in here?"

"Gladys. I told her you were expecting me. I thought you were."

"Do you always creep up on people?" She said irritably, shaken by his sudden appearance, and his nearness.

"Only the ones I wish to be near." He smiled, showing his dimples and she turned away, seeking refuge behind the desk, where she sat straightening a perfectly neat stack of papers.

"You wanted to see me?" She wanted to get this over with.

"Always." His voice, rich and deep, caused shivers along her spine and she glanced away from the deep pools of his eyes.

"Devin, be serious."

"I've never been more so," he said easily, seating himself on the corner of the desk. Devin could not believe his good fortune. For weeks he had racked his brain for an excuse to be near her, and here, thanks to Phillip, he had his chance. Silently he blessed the Fates, and wondered if Phillip Lawrence had known something.

Her voice brought him back to earth. "What about the ship?"

He rose and stood before her. "I would be delighted to have you," he paused, his eyes saying much more than his words, "as my partner."

"No!" Katherine protested, her eyes wide in alarm, "I thought... Don't you want to buy me out?"

At last, he gave her the kind of attention she wanted. Flirtations aside, he studied her keenly. "Do you need money, Katherine?"

"No," she answered honestly, feeling no resentment at his blunt question. "I sincerely thought you would want the ship. And it would be for the best," she finished, not meeting his level gaze.

He frowned, opening his mouth to speak, and instead nodded thoughtfully, "I see. Well, I am sorry, but I am not in a position to buy you out in my present situation, so I guess you're stuck with me." He took a comfortable chair in front of the desk, crossing his legs out in front of him.

"I'll buy your half. Name the price."

"Thank you, but no. I need the ship, it is important to my work for the Navy."

"I'll *give* you the ship. You can have it."

"No, no, Katherine, I'll not have your charity."

"I'll sign the papers!"

Devin was cut to the heart, and rose to stroll the length of the room, lest she see it in his eyes. It was a dear price she was willing to pay to be rid of him. *Did she hate him so much?*

To Katherine, it seemed, as he stood admiring the large portrait of Mary Lawrence, that he was considering her offer, and she grew hopeful.

"You look like your mother." He smiled, and caught her with his warm gaze from across the room, "The most beautiful woman I have ever seen."

Her heart beat loudly as her mind groped for a reply. *Did he mean her mother—*in which case, she would agree with him—*or herself?* If she said '*Thank you,*' would she sound assuming? *Oh, why did he always tie* *her in knots!* The moment was passed, and she had only blushed. "You confuse me, Captain," she said, lowering her eyes, her voice soft in the quiet of the room. In the awkward silence, it dawned on her, that either way, he had complimented her. She glanced up to find him still watching her. "What about my offer?" She stammered.

"Out of the question. What would people say? A lady does not go around giving ships away to gentlemen, Miss Lawrence," he scolded, cocking an eyebrow at her, "And a *gentleman* would not accept such a gift. For shame!"

Katherine almost smiled. She knew very well how much he cared for other people's opinions, and for that matter, who would know? "Do you call me less than a lady, then?"

"If I did, it was not my intent, for never intentionally would I place myself so far to the wrong." He bowed, and no longer sure he was playing, she changed the subject.

"Seriously De… *Captain*, will you not accept my offer?"

"I cannot, in all seriousness. You must realize that."

For a moment she was stuck, and her brows drew together in concentration. "*I know!* I'll sell it to someone else!"

"No!" He looked desperate, and she stopped short. "I have first option to buy," he reminded her.

"Yes, but you don't want it, and…"

"I do!" Devin scrambled for excuses, "I cannot afford to do that right now at any price. Have a heart, Katherine, I need to keep the ship. My life could depend on it. Would you have me grovel, for a bit of time?"

"Of course not." She never meant to cause him hardship or embarrassment, and now she was torn. "I didn't realize it would be a problem. I'm sorry, I'll wait. I can wait as long as you need, it makes no difference."

Devin coughed to hide a smile behind his hand. She was so

genuinely remorseful, with her pleading eyes, and he wanted to hold her, and comfort her, and kiss that full pink mouth and... *No.* He closed his eyes, tamping down his rising desire. Brick by brick he would tear down the wall she was trying to build between them. She didn't want it there any more than he did. He could read it in her eyes. Her lovely mouth might lie to him, but in the depths of her eyes there was something else.

Katherine was concerned. Devin stood across the room with one hand on the mantle and his eyes were closed. She moved to his side, and tentatively touched his arm. "Are you not well?" She whispered, the tenderness touching his heart.

He opened his eyes, drinking in her nearness, her every move, as she took his arm and lead him to the nearby sofa. "I'm fine," he assured her, as she passed a cool hand over his brow, much like Cecilia had a few days before, when he had shoved her hot moist hands from his person.

"You feel warm," she said, going to the cabinet and pouring a liberal draught of brandy to offer him.

Devin took the glass from her fingers. He *was* warm. He was burning up, but his fever was not of illness. He burned for the touch of those same slender fingers, and he reached for her hand as she stood by, watching over him.

She moved away and sat facing him on the sofa, careful to keep a good distance between them and they sat in silence while he finished his brandy.

Katherine contemplated the situation, still searching for a way out, until he stirred. Her nerves stretched taut, but all he did was lean forward and again reach for her hand. His lips brushed warmly against her fingers, and then he was gone.

So they would be partners. "Dammit!"

Chapter 9

By July 1863, the hodge-podge mix-and-match armies had been replaced by experienced fighting men and proven officers, who had honed their skills, and were perfecting their practice of destruction. After a stunning victory at Chancellorsville, Robert E. Lee, commander of the Southern armies, continued the invasion of the North, which would lead both armies to a dramatic confrontation at Gettysburg, Pennsylvania. At the same time, Union General, Grant, continued his ongoing assault on Vicksburg with stubborn persistence, to gain control of the Mississippi river, and cut the South in half. Both battles were so-called Union victories, but resulted in unbelievable losses for both sides, with thousands upon thousands of dead, wounded and missing.

Katherine fought a private war. Devin had wasted no time in using the mutual ownership of their merchant vessel for an excuse to visit her for one reason or another. *"Did she approve of this cargo? What did she think of this or that? Was this route all right with her?"* Three times last week he had come with his nonsense, and twice already this week, had she looked up from her desk, or turned to find him there watching her, and it was only the middle of the week.

At first, she had been unwilling to see him, but he had been persistent, and she had let him have his say. He had not pressed her about her feelings, and he never mentioned Cecilia, or the day they had argued on the beach. He would appear, sit for a while exchanging a few pleasantries, ask his subterfuge questions and leave, whistling the same familiar tune.

Gradually she found herself looking forward to the companionable half-hour visits, and relaxed in his company. It was not good. For every afternoon that she spent time basking in his warm easy charm, there was an endless night of longing, of wanting him beside her, and dreaming it might somehow come true, and each morning was more painful than the last.

This morning, she had been shocked to find herself considering what it would be like to set aside her pride and give in to him. *Could she be his mistress? No!* It went against everything she believed in. Everything she had been taught. But still, the temptation lingered, and she turned from it in shame. She no longer feared him, as much as she feared herself, and what she might do. She would be glad when the week was over, and she and Evelyn could retreat to the safe distance of the cottage.

Desperately she dug for the resentment she harbored over his marrying Cecilia. No small thing to begin with, she fed it, and fattened it, to stand forth in defense of her weakening heart. What had he been thinking, when he stood before man and God, and promised to Cecilia all that he should have shared with her? *Had they a gun to his head?* Even so, if it had been her, she would have gladly died proclaiming her love for him, rather than marry someone else. Apparently, the same thought had not occurred to him, and for that, she could hate him… *Almost.*

This was no way to start the day, and she left her bed to seek out what small solace there could be found in a steaming bath. Refreshed, if not ready, she resolved to face yet another day and its attack on her nerves. She chose the crisp blue dress she had worn to breakfast with

Ezra, because its rich color and prim white collar gave her self-composure a much-needed boost. Tying her still damp hair up with a simple ribbon, and leaving it to dry in soft waves, she went down to breakfast.

It was after noon, and Evelyn had left to attend one of the endless gatherings, where the women pretended the war did not exist, and prattled on in meaningless chatter, while they rolled bandages and knitted socks to be sent to the front lines. Katherine had attended once. Evelyn had invited her along again, but the groups of widows and mourners, and the sympathetic looks they gave her made her uncomfortable. She would rather do her part in shipping ventures, and monetary donations for the widows and orphans. "All work and no play..." Evelyn scolded, but she had begged off, with a promise to attend the barbecue at the home of Hetty Parker on Saturday, and Evelyn had left her reluctantly.

Katherine's paperwork was finished, and she found herself with little to do to occupy her time. In search of some diversion, she wandered the downstairs rooms. She bypassed the newspaper, with its disheartening lists of the dead, and roamed into the family parlor at the rear of the house. Idly she approached the piano and running her fingers over the keyboard began to pick out the melody that nested in the corner of her mind. As she played, she recognized the tune Devin often hummed or whistled under his breath, and one by one the notes came.

Loch Lomond, the Scottish ballad of lost love; *how beautiful, how heartbreaking...and how fitting*, she thought.

"I didnae know you were so talented."

Almost as if she had conjured him with the haunting notes, he appeared, leaning indolently in the doorway with his arms crossed over his chest, enjoying the picture she made framed in the large window, the glaring sunlight polishing her hair from behind, and casting the front of her in shadow.

Katherine had given up being surprised by his appearances, although sometimes he still startled her. She had decided he must bribe Nathan or charm Gladys, to let him in unannounced. "Good afternoon, Captain," she said, giving him a small smile, for in spite of her morning misery she was glad to see him. He looked wonderful in his rough work clothes, a dark shirt open at the collar making him look more attractive than ever.

"Miss Lawrence. Dare I hope that your taste turns to Scotland for other things, or is it her music alone that touches you?"

"Well, I am quite fond of… her Bluebells." She laughed, ending the pretense of missing his meaning. "Were you born there?" She asked, genuinely interested.

"Do you want me to have been?" He grinned.

"That has little to do with it."

"As it happens, I was, but my parents were visiting."

"I see, and are they still…" She hesitated, considering this might be as painful a subject for him, as it was for her.

"They live currently in Nova Scotia," he supplied, "and they are quite well, thank you."

They exchanged a smile of mutual understanding, before he added, "Perhaps you'll meet them one day."

She didn't know how to reply, and moved away from the piano. She left the stream of sunlight, to where he could see her better and Devin recognized the dress he had seen her in at the marketplace. He had almost convinced himself he had imagined seeing her, and chased a phantom figure of his wishful mind. "It *was* you!" He said, pointing an accusing finger in triumph.

Katherine looked at him in confusion. "Pardon?"

"In town! I saw you, in *that* dress, right before you disappeared!" He gave her a suspicious look.

"*When?*" She was not about to admit that she had run like a scared rabbit, into the nearest shop to elude him, and watched until he had left.

"I don't know… A few weeks ago. You were by the smoke shop!"

"Oh, where you there?" She asked innocently.

"Yes, I was *there*!" Devin snapped, wondering at his worsening temper, somehow feeling he had been made the fool.

"Well, you needn't be angry, I only asked."

"You *knew* I was there!"

"Did I?"

"Well…" He was now unsure. "I *thought* you did. I thought you saw me and ran from me. What were you doing there alone, anyway?" He demanded.

"You make it sound like a crime to go to the marketplace. And who said I was alone?"

"You weren't alone?" He tried to ignore the increasing pounding of his heart, while he waited for her answer.

Oh, he was jealous, was he? He could bloody-well have a wife, but she couldn't go to the lawyer's office? Let him wonder. Let him feel a small portion of the pain she lived with day after day! "I don't see how it's any of your business," she said, quitting the room, to pass through the drawing room, and cross the hall into the study.

Devin followed, burdened by a heavy scowl, and shut the door behind them. "You didn't answer me," he stated flatly, facing her across the desk.

"Fine, I was with a man!" Katherine said, seating herself at the desk while her anger rose. She stared up at him with a challenge in her eyes, and folded her hands. "Now, was that what you came here to ask, or is there some pressing ship's business you wish to discuss, such as how many napkins do I think the jack tars will need to wipe their dainty fingers!?"

He didn't answer, but stood regarding her sarcasm with injured pride and saddened heart. So, she had seen through his excuses to steal a few moments with her, to see her smile, and hear her laugh, while he bided his time and contemplated how best to get her willingly into his arms. *And why wouldn't she?* She was an intelligent woman, and he hadn't tried very hard to hide his purpose, thinking she enjoyed his visits as much as he did. Perhaps he had been wrong, and she was merely tolerating him as her business partner. After all, there had been nothing in her look or manner, these past weeks to encourage him. Only the natural easy warmth that he had come to know was part of her personality. She had told him that day on the beach that there was someone else, and why wouldn't there be? She hadn't come to see him off the morning he had left, and he had been gone so long… *And she was so beautiful.*

His heart was leaden, but he would do what he could to salvage his pride, and he turned to where she sat waiting for his answer. "I'm sorry to have bothered you with responsibility Katherine, you being a woman, but I only thought to include you."

Fuming from his selfish jealousies, and burning from his sly insults, she rose in anger, her hands flat on the desktop, her back arched like an angry cat, and met his mocking gaze. When she answered, her voice was low and steady. "Captain Galloway, I am very able to meet my responsibilities, as you well know. If there is a legitimate problem with *our* ship, you may come to me and I will gladly solve it for you. Until, or unless there is, you can take your half-witted questions, and your arrogant attitude elsewhere." She straightened and came around the desk on her way to open the door, inviting him to leave. "Better yet, you can take the whole damn ship and turn it into kindling and leave me alone! Is that clear?"

Devin advanced toward the still closed door, where she waited, her hand on the knob. He barely heard her words, but caught their meaning well enough, and the thought burned in his brain. *He was not welcome.* Not only was there someone else, but what little part of her he had was being stripped from him. He stopped before her, looking down into the turbulent depths of her eyes in search of the spark he had once seen there. She was the most amazing woman he had ever met, and he was going… cast from her presence like a flower from the sun. Before he could think, his arms were around her, and he was kissing her.

Her hands moved to his shoulders with the intention of pushing him away as he backed her against the wall, holding her mouth captive with his own. She could feel the anger in his kiss, demanding, and taunting.

For Devin it was desperation. He had tried everything, and she was sending him away. Away from what he needed most, away from all that mattered. And he would go, if it was what she wanted, but first he would try again, with his kiss, daring her to deny she felt something… *anything.*

For Katherine it was an outrage. She wanted him to leave… *Didn't she?* What right had he to be angry, and to be jealous and vengeful when she refused him, the way she had to? She didn't want to refuse, *and it was so difficult.* She waivered in the struggle that raged within. Her lips parted, her hunger for him overcoming her willpower, even as she damned herself for her weakness.

Instantly his kiss changed from desperation to devotion, and he cradled her in the crook of his arm.

A tear born of her broken heart coursed down her cheek followed by another, and her response faded. He raised his head to search her face, and there in her eyes, was the longing look he had hoped to see, but the sadness that accompanied it was overwhelming. He released her, and she opened the door.

"Katherine…"

Her voice was a whisper, "I meant what I said, please go."

He touched his fingers to her chin, and too late, she shifted her tear-filled eyes away from him.

"You might think you mean it Katherine, but your eyes tell me differently. And your lips." He bent close and she tensed, half dreading, half wanting the kiss that would prove his words, but it never came. He gave a short bitter laugh. "You, see?"

Her answer was a resounding slap across his face. *"Get out!"* She ground out at him, *"I hate you!"* And in that moment, she did. She hated him because he was right.

The following days passed with all the speed and gaiety of a lengthy funeral procession. Several times, Katherine sensed a presence and turned from her work, but there was no one there, and she chided herself. She knew he wasn't coming, and she knew it was for the best, but she didn't know how to stop thinking about him.

She had no idea where he was. Suppose he had returned to active duty. She had no way to know. Suppose he lay wounded or dying this very minute? *Suppose he thought of her?* She cringed as she remembered her last words to him, *'I hate you'. What a horrible thing to say.* Of course she didn't hate him. She hated the reality of loving him, and knowing she couldn't have him. And she had slapped his face! She sighed. If she saw him again, she would tell him... *Tell him what?* That she loved him? No, she couldn't. But she would let him know, somehow, that she didn't hate him, and that she was sorry—If she could face him.

Chapter 10

Katherine would have been relieved to know Devin was far from the front lines. He was, however, every bit actively involved in the war, and had been, ever since his return to Boston after monotonous months of blockade duty. He had proven himself most able at anticipating and capturing the unfortunate runners, but he took no pride in his achievements. Of more than forty thousand men in the U.S. Navy, a very small percentage were seasoned sailors, and it took only opportunity, experience, and a handful of well-chosen men, to stand out from the crowd, all of which he had been fortunate enough to have.

It had begun to sicken him when he captured the daring blockade runners, only to find their ships loaded with meat and medicine for a starving and suffering people. He held no hatred for the gallant Southerners. He deplored slavery, yes, and he stood against secession, but he admired the people on both sides who gave their all for what they believed in, and if that made him less than a loyal Northerner he didn't care.

It was the gun runners he detested. Not the ones from the South, who were simply doing their duty, but the ones from the North—The profiteers. The filthy traders, who were not in the war for cause or honor, but for self-profit. The ones who stole Union arms, and sold them to the needy South for outrageous prices, and in doing so, were arming the enemy against their own. They were the ones he enjoyed capturing on pure principle.

When the opportunity arose to transfer to his current duty, he was more than willing to volunteer. Heavy shipments of arms were getting through to the South from the Boston vicinity, and they needed someone who knew the area. Devin didn't know it that well, but he didn't proffer that information, and so far, he was getting the job done, finding an advantage in the fact that he was also largely unknown in the area. Thus far, he had tipped off waiting forces, to shipments of pistols packed in lard barrels, and barrels of gunpowder disguised with a top covering of flour.

His latest project was acting as a buyer in hopes of recovering a large quantity of stolen Enfield rifles, and he was getting close. The problem was, it didn't leave him much time for solving his plight with Katherine, and it was most difficult to work with her so sorely on his mind.

Perhaps this sunny Saturday would be different. He was attending the Fourth of July barbecue at the Parker's, whose property bordered the Johnston's. He wasn't much in the mood for socializing, but one never knew what one might learn from casual chatter, and in his new role of 'merchant,' he should make an appearance. Besides that, with any luck Katherine would be there, and he needed to know if she had forgiven him. *Katherine, the woman who hates you*, an inner voice taunted, but he shrugged it off, tying the spotless cravat beneath his freshly shaven chin.

He had avoided escorting Cecilia, by having a previous business engagement before the barbecue, and leaving her in her father's care. But now as he stood in the Parker's yard, she hurried to his side and claimed his arm.

He was introduced to John Parker, who had been wounded, but was more than happy to have made it home, and in whose honor they were all gathered, and to John's wife, and his grandmother Hetty. All the while he talked, and laughed, and met, and greeted, his hopeful eyes trolled the crowd for the single sight he cared to see, but they did not find her. Perhaps she wasn't coming after all. She *was* in mourning, but so many people were in mourning these days, exceptions to the rules of etiquette were shifting, lest there be no guests left to attend anywhere. At that moment, he spotted Evelyn, and grew hopeful, and he began to cross the yard toward her, when his gaze chanced on Katherine at last.

She sat in a secluded corner where rows of chairs had been set out in the shade, and to the rear of the group of the vicious older matrons she so disliked. She sat stiff and proud in her dress of black, with its plain neckline and narrow sleeves, her hair once again in its neat coil. Even in her dark and plain clothes she somehow stood out, he thought, like a queen among the peasants. She wasn't looking at him, but beyond, and he turned to follow her line of vision to Cecilia, a short distance behind him in the crowd. He changed direction, thinking to first lose Cecilia before approaching her.

Katherine had seen Devin. He was easy to spot in his white suit and pale blue vest. She hadn't expected him to be there, but she had been aware of him from the first moment of his arrival. *How could she not be?* His was not a presence that was easily dismissed. She had seen him walking across the yard with Cecilia close behind, and she had known when he spotted her. When he immediately turned and walked the other way, her heart fell. *What did she expect?* Hadn't she told him to stay away from her? Hadn't she told him she hated him? Her cheeks flamed, and she bent her head to her folded hands. Sometime today she would find her chance to apologize.

It was well past noon when the meal was ready and everyone flocked to the long tables to fill their plates. Katherine flowed with the crowd, and in its ebb found herself left near Cecilia and her parents, who stood not far from Devin. Face to face, she could hardly ignore them, and she would not give Cecilia the satisfaction of thinking she was affected by her in any way. She took a deep breath and willed herself to speak, although the words did not come easily. *Think of mother, think of mother...* "Congratulations, Cecilia, on your marriage and on your child," she lowered her voice, "I wish you all the happiness you deserve." Turning to Cecil and Amelia, she said, "You must be very proud," but she did not meet their eyes. She could not, and did not, look at Devin, but turned to take her plate back to her seat, although she no longer had an appetite for its offerings.

"Why, thank you, Katherine," Cecilia purred, delighting in the moment, thinking she might have something her rival would envy. "And how about you, still no man of your own?" Katherine shook her head and kept her eyes on Cecil, while his daughter rambled on... "You poor thing. Well, don't despair, you're not too old—*yet.*"

Katherine gave a tight smile and went on her way. Only Devin, who had observed the exchange while keeping his distance, read the pain in her eyes, and the set of her jaw that told him of her self-control. He had seen that look before. But Katherine was upset before Cecilia spewed her cutting remarks. *Why?*

Devin knew Cecilia well enough to pick her simple mind, and as he admired the receding black skirt, he cast the bait, and turned his charming dimples on the catty one, "What do you suppose is wrong with *her?*"

Cecilia, delighting in his attention and his apparent distaste of Katherine, practically swallowed the hook. "Oh, she's jealous of me, Devin. She has always been jealous of me, ever since we were children, and now that I'm married, and have a child on the way, I suppose she just can't stand it."

"I see." Devin replied, managing to keep a straight face. He hardly thought Katherine was likely to be envious of Cecilia, *and hadn't she implied she was involved with someone?* If he were to solve this riddle he would have to fish for his answers elsewhere.

Dancing had started for those so inclined, and Cecilia, who always had to be at the center of things, had drifted away from him at the first strains of the music, leaving him free at last to approach Katherine. He circled the edge of the large crowd and came up behind her, where she sat once more alone, in the shade. As he reached her, the matronly gaggle rose as one, and moved across the yard to keep a closer eye on the dancing. Taking a seat in the row behind her, he leaned forward and whispered, "How do you suppose they do that?"

She did not jump. She had watched him weave his way around and heard him approach. She was trying to collect her thoughts, readying what she would say, but his question drove the words from her mind. "What?" She asked, turning so she could see him out of the corner of her eye.

"Those women." He nodded toward the group of older ladies. "How do you suppose they get about, if they don't have any legs or ankles under those skirts?"

Katherine gave a small laugh at his nonsense, and relaxed a little, relieved he would speak to her. "You're a jester, Captain Galloway."

"Aye." He loved to hear her laugh.

"A fool." She said, watching the old women cross the yard.

"Aye, a fool for you, Katherine."

She stopped laughing as the sincerity in his voice plucked at her heart, and it grew quiet. Here he was, being kind to her, after what she had said. She turned more in her chair, and her eyes sought his before she began to speak, "I fear I am the fool. I pray you will forgive me my temper."

"I would forgive you anything. You must know that. It is I who should apologize, for giving you reason to hate me. I was not much of a gentleman. But if you forgive me for that, I'm afraid you may still hate me for this, because I'll never be sorry I kissed you. *Never.*"

Katherine's heart was full, and she lost herself in his eyes, their color heightened by the hue of his vest. His tan showed dark against the white of his collar and he looked very handsome. Her gaze was warm and misty as she told him in all honesty, "I could never hate you, Devin."

He grinned a lopsided grin and raised a skeptical brow, "'Tis a far cry from the meat I hunger for, but to a starving man even a crumb is welcome."

She did not reply, and at the sad shake of her head, he knew she was not changing her mind about him, she was only feeling remorse for her outburst earlier in the week. He had gained precious little ground, but it was to be cherished, and he would give her the space she seemed to need. "It is enough to know that you don't hate me." *For now*, he added mentally. "I will leave you as a friend." He patted her shoulder and rose to leave. "Before I go, would you answer one question for me?" She waited, and he asked doubtingly, "Are you jealous of Cecilia?" He braced for a flare of temper or a flip retort, but she sat for a long moment with her head bowed, before she nodded in the affirmative. Devin was incredulous, *"For God's sake, why?"*

In a voice so low he had to lean close to catch her words, she answered, "Why wouldn't I be? She has everything I could ever want."

His brow wrinkled in thought, he took a few steps, and turned back, "You dislike her very much, don't you?"

Katherine looked him in the eye, "That's three questions."

He couldn't help but smile. "Then it was very gracious of you to wish her happiness." He turned to leave.

"Wait." She couldn't let him think her better than she was. "In truth, I did not." She glanced away.

"But I heard you."

She looked down at her hands again, "I only wished her the happiness she *deserves*." She would have confessed more fully, but he had already caught the barb and gone chuckling on his way.

In the waning heat of the evening, Devin sat apart from the revelers, his back against the bole of a towering elm. He was deep in thought. How could Katherine possibly be jealous of Cecilia? *She was a hundred… no, a thousand times more woman than Cecilia would ever be. So, what was it?* Something Cecilia *had*… The baby? Most women wanted a baby, he supposed, and surely Katherine would, but first she would need a husband. She couldn't be wanting for male companionship. Certainly, he had made his feelings for her clear enough, *but she didn't want him,* and, to his relief, she had turned away at least a dozen eager men while he had watched her this very afternoon… Cold apprehension gripped his heart, as his mind formed an appalling conclusion. He jumped to his feet, and scanned the jovial mob for a likely candidate. Evelyn would know, but she was too shrewd.

There, that pretty girl that had arrived a short time ago. William's girlfriend. *What was her name? Louise?* Yes, Louise Caldwell, she might know, but she might remember him, too. Who was that she was with… *her mother perhaps?* Devin moved through the crowd like a stalking panther, with Judith Caldwell as his prey. Never had he been so intent in his purpose, or so leery of his prize.

Katherine left her hard chair. The sun was low in the sky, and she was no longer sheltered from its dying rays. For most of the afternoon she had been content to sit and watch Devin, as he sat across the yard, but he had disappeared over an hour ago and had not returned. She surmised he had joined the dancing, when he had headed in that direction, and he was probably enjoying himself. He was a good dancer, as she remembered, but he was probably good at everything.

Her head ached, a combination of the sun and her tightly braided hair, and it was not being helped by the loud music and the increasing clamor of the joyful throng. No doubt much of that joy had poured forth from a bottle or a keg, she deduced, walking in the fading light. She left the mob behind, as the fireworks started overhead, and took the pathway that led through the backyard and into the gardens beyond. Out of sight of the house now, she uncoiled her hair, and undid the braid, letting it fall loose and running her fingers through the heavy mass to massage her scalp.

Mrs. Parker had always kept a beautiful garden, and Katherine wandered aimlessly, enjoying its twilight wonders. At the end of a winding pathway, she came upon a bush of white roses and picked one perfect bloom, cherishing its sweet fragrance. White was for joy, but she was not feeling very joyful, this day… She found herself at the very back of the property and stopped to look around. If she went behind the hedge…

Devin had left the crowd and strolled to the Johnston's yard, to sit where he often came when he had problems to work through. Lately he seemed to be out here most of the time, but never before had he been so despondent. Judith Caldwell had been an easy mark. *So easy.* A few smiles, a mention of his friend and partner Phillip, a concerned inquiry over '*Poor Miss Lawrence*' and what she must be going through, and the woman had opened like a book.

"You don't know the half of it!" She had exclaimed. But he did. He had guessed. Her next line sadly confirmed it, when she whispered, "The man she was in love with, married someone else! Can you imagine? Poor, poor girl."

"*No!*" He had said, encouraging her to speak the words that would break his heart.

"Yes, he did!" She nodded knowingly, lowering her voice to the barest whisper, "I overheard her telling my Louise that the man she loves married Cecilia Johnston and left dear Katherine devastated."

Now Devin sat on the stone bench, his head in his hands, trying in vain to find a flaw that would change the meaning of those words. Words he wished he had never heard. Katherine was in love with Cecilia's husband. That would explain many things... Why she wanted him to leave her alone, and why Cecilia bothered her so. She had said there was someone else, but he had hoped it was a lie, and now... *Anything would be better than this.*

Cecilia's husband, Everett Price, was the very man Devin suspected of heading the gun running operation he was trying to crack—he and another man, John Ambrose. He even suspected Cecilia was involved. That was why he was boarding with Cecil. A likely enough arrangement. Cecil was his only acquaintance in town, and it was not extraordinary that Devin would stay there, and it put him right in the middle of things whenever Cecilia and Price returned to town. One major drawback was, that this time, when Cecilia had returned, Price had not, and Devin found himself fighting off her sickening overtures. She had never made any secret about her feelings for him, even though he had turned her down cold. There was a time before she got married, when she had started acting like she had some kind of claim on him, until he had let her behavior be known to Cecil. He had made it clear he had no intentions toward her whatsoever, and she had looked elsewhere. But now that her husband was out of town, she had again launched an outright attack to gain his attention.

Hell could never freeze that solid... *But what about Katherine?* How could she love Price? The man was a sadistic monster. The thought tore at his heart... and if she did, was she part of his network? And if Price were captured... and Cecilia, and... "Oh Saints, help me," he beseeched the night air.

Katherine parted the bushes and stepped through, searching over the low stone wall for the alcove where Devin had taken her after the dance so long ago. *A little farther...* She paused, peering into the deepening shadows. Yes, there was the bench, and... She sat on the wall and swiveled her legs over and she was on the other side, when she heard someone speak. *Devin?* He did not lift his head as she approached, and she touched his shoulder, "Devin?"

This time it was he who jumped, right to his feet. He stood blinking, not sure whether he had conjured her in his dreams yet again.

"Are you all right?" she asked, wondering how he came to be there.

"Yes. You startled me."

"So, you see how it is, then."

"What!?" *She had an uncanny habit of reading his mind.*

"Turnabout is fair play?" She tried. "A taste of your own medicine? You surprise *me* all the time."

"Oh. Yes, I see."

Katherine stepped closer to see his face in the moonlight. His voice sounded strained, and he seemed upset. She glanced around, searching for something to say. "I was just walking."

"Oh." He stared, and she felt the intruder.

"I guess I'll go…" She waited a moment, and when he said nothing, she turned to leave.

Devin's frown was lost in the darkness. "Katherine…" He came to stand behind her at the wall, and on impulse reached out to run his hand through the silken mass of her hair.

She closed her eyes, resisting the urge to lean against him, her insides melting at his touch.

"I've always wanted to do that," he said, his voice sounding far away. "Ever since the first day I saw you. You have marvelous hair. You should always wear it down."

She turned and sat on the wall, wagging a delicate forefinger at him. "It's not allowed, you know. Women can walk, but they mustn't have legs, and they cannot cut their hair short, but they cannot wear it long either."

"Anything else?"

"Oh yes," she smiled, "Never be alone in the dark with a gentleman. I'm afraid the list is endless."

His ghost of a smile fled, and he sat beside her. "Katherine, I learned today… I found out… What I'm trying to say, is, I think I understand something of your predicament, and I'm sorry I've pressed you so much. If you ever need me, or if you're ever in trouble, I want you to know that you can come to me." He brushed his fingers along her cheek.

Politely, she answered, "Why, thank you, Devin." *How could she go to him with her problem? He was her problem,* and the more she was near him, the worse it got.

Politely, he helped her over the wall and waved her off.

He was treating her like a friend at last, courteous and warm, and… distant. *Just like you wanted,* she told herself, while she struggled to see the path through her tears.

Chapter 11

It was exceptionally humid in early August, and Katherine lay in her lonely bed, the air heavy and close about her. Even the brevity of the shift she wore, brought no relief. The damp sheets clung to her legs as if to hold her prisoner in the sweltering room, and her long hair wrapped like cloying fingers around her neck.

In the weeks since she and Evelyn had returned to the cottage, she had worked very hard at keeping busy. The busier she was, she had reasoned, the less time she would have to think about Devin. So, in the daytime she polished, she washed, she tended the large garden, and built new flower beds, and thought of Devin. She took long walks along the cliffs, and the beaches. She swam, she sailed, she fished, and took invigorating rides on Matilda, and thought of Devin. She redecorated her parent's bedroom and reorganized the library, and read to Evelyn while she did her quilting, and all the while he left neither her mind, nor her heart.

She needed to find something else. Evelyn had suggested volunteer work, but that would mean being in the city, and closer to her troubles.

They needed to get away, and had started to discuss plans to visit Thea and Keith in New Hampshire.

The nights had been much like this one. Humid or not, she often lay awake in suffocating oppression, unable to escape the heat of scorching eyes that burned through her memory, and conjured kisses that set her aflame with desire. Still could she taste the demanding urgency of his warm mouth, and her body craved his phantom touch.

Katherine kicked off the clammy sheet and got up to pace the room, as remembered words hit her like a slap in the face. *'Have your damnable pride, let it keep you company, and warm your lonely bed.'* She could almost laugh. Her bed was warm all right, but it was not pride that kept her company, it was a hot-blooded blue-eyed ghost that would ever haunt her. Snatching up her light summer robe and a towel, she found her way in the dark and went silently out the door, taking the path to the beach. She often swam late at night in the hot weather, and if Evelyn missed her, she would know where to look.

The night air embraced her in a gentle shroud, and sure feet found the sandy trail more by habit than by sight in the velvet darkness. The only sound was the lapping of the surf, while overhead, a sliver of moon peeked through the clouds to flirt shyly with the body of the sea. Katherine stood for a few moments in appreciation of the beauty surrounding her, before she dropped her robe and towel upon the sand, and waded into the cooling waters. Waist deep, she took a breath and dove in, swimming as long and far as she could before surfacing, gasping for air. She reveled in the refreshing chill of the far depths and the strength of her body, cutting skillfully through the waves.

Tiring after a long while, she retreated to the beach to stroll its curved length, much as she had with Devin weeks ago. It seemed forever ago, and yet she felt if she turned at that moment, he would be there. She knew better, however, and walked on, ignoring the strained pressure at her throat. Reaching the natural jetty, she waded outward again and seated herself on one of the large rocks, trailing her legs in the surf. It was a beautiful night, and she couldn't help but wish she had someone to share it with. *Maybe someday…*

She tried to assemble in her mind one who might suit her. Face after face, she called up from fact and fancy, memory and imagination, those she knew, and those she had yet to meet. One by one, blond, brunet, redhead, gray eyes, green eyes, brown, they were turned by some psychic sorcery, into that very one whose form and features she was most trying to avoid. The game was a cruel one that she could not win, and Katherine brushed aside a crystal droplet that quivered at the end of her long lashes, and then blinked, coming sharply to attention.

Was there a flicker of light? There across the water… She sat very still. A few stars winked between passing clouds, and the moon briefly showed its silver smile. Perhaps it had been a reflection off of the waves, or her tears, but neither explanation rang true to her heart, and she waited, trusting in herself, scarcely breathing. It came again, and was gone, but she had seen it; a tiny flicker, too high up, and too orange to be a reflection on the water. She gathered her thoughts, her body tensing instinctively. There was nothing there where that light had been. It had to be a ship. But why here, and at this time of night? A muffled sound reached her in the stillness, and she slid into the water, crouching low against the rocks, as apprehension nibbled along her spine.

Working her way outward to the end of the jetty where the water was well over her head, she found a foothold among the jumbled stone and strained to hear above the lapping of the waves. For what seemed like hours she waited, her nerves on end, and when the sound first came, she wasn't sure she hadn't imagined it. But it was growing closer now, and more frequent, and its temperate rhythm confirmed her suspicions. The familiar creak, and quiet slap, repeated over and over had to be a rowboat, and the muffled oar locks and silent passengers could only mean they were up to no good. *But what?* She questioned, her mind supplying a hundred possibilities.

They weren't as close as they seemed to be by the sound carried over the open water, and she watched with great relief, as not one, but two boats, entered the next cove, the rocky one, on the other side of the jetty. If she were going to learn what they were doing, she would have to move closer, and without a blink to fear or consequence, Phillip Lawrence's daughter pushed off from the rocks, swimming underwater. Surfacing well in their wake, she began to follow, careful to avoid the moonlight cutting occasionally across the cove. Closer now, she could hear voices, but only snatches of what was being said.

"Are you sure…"

"Shh!"

A sudden noise, and a loud exclamation of pain was followed by an ingeniously inventive curse that she had to admire, and hoped she would remember. "Russo, you idiot, shut up!" Came a harsh whisper.

She ducked under again, swimming far past them, and hiding in the shadow of a huge boulder nearer to shore, she watched them as they landed. She counted a half dozen men in the large dories, and she waited, while they wrestled with a number of heavy crates and carried them the short distance up the beach, toward the base of the cliffs, before returning for more. From time to time, they stopped to make use of the covered lantern that had first alerted her to their presence, and then they seemed to disappear.

Katherine waited. She had been in the water a long time now and began to shiver. She wished she had stayed on the other side of them, where she would have dared to move to the beach. She knew now, they were using the large cave that she had often played in as a child, and she could investigate more closely in the daytime.

The men returned and shoved off, and when they were far enough out, she returned to the house at last, rinsing in the icy well water, before toweling off and entering the house. It was after four as she changed her shift, and taking a fresh towel for her hair, fell across the bed to speculate on the events of the evening. Almost instantly, she was claimed by an exhausted slumber, never realizing that at least for the past few hours, her mind had eluded the constrictive hold of Devin Galloway.

Standing on the shore of the far cove in the bright sun of mid-afternoon, Katherine scanned the horizon and the cliffs above. In spite of the heat, she wore her trousers and an old blouse, with her high boots over thick stockings.

She had discovered upon rising, that the soles of her feet and the palms of her hands were covered with tiny slashes from the barnacle covered rocks she had clung to the previous night, and were quite sore. Satisfied there was no one in sight, and confident they would not return in broad daylight, she crawled into the cave. The nudge of nostalgia hit squarely as she stooped in the brush covered opening. She hadn't been in here for years, and it seemed so much smaller than she remembered. The naturally hewn hollow was still good sized, but when she was a child, it had seemed enormous. The cave was deceiving, the front being a small cramped area. As children they had been warned against the danger of playing here, but of course they did, and they had called this front entrance, 'the porch'. From the rear of the porch section, the cave expanded to a large rectangular size, high enough for a grown man to stand in.

Katherine hadn't thought anyone knew about this cave, the largest of several the Lawrence children had played in, but obviously she was wrong, for here before her was clearly evidence to the contrary. Case after long wooden case was stacked against the far wall, more than had been brought last night. She moved closer, squinting in the meager light from the cave opening, wishing she had brought a lantern.

She could not open the crates, but peering closely, read a *U.S.A.* stamp on some, and from their size and shape guessed them to contain rifles. *Gun runners? Smugglers? Thieves?* Surely the army wouldn't be hiding its own weapons… not here. They had to be thieves, or runners. Her blood ran cold when she thought of those men coming and going so close to where she and Evelyn slept, blissfully ignorant of what was going on. *But where to go for help?* The military headquarters in Boston was the obvious choice, but perhaps if she waited, she could learn more before making a decision. At some point, they were sure to return.

As she crawled out into the sunlight, her head was spinning with questions… Who those men had been, how long they had been using the cave, and whether they knew about the other entrance hidden in the back, and that when conditions were just right, the cave flooded.

In the days following her discovery, the weather was clear, and the night sky cloudless. Katherine knew her 'friends' would not return without the cloak of darkness to hide them, and she had waited impatiently for a moonless night. Now, on a suitably black night, she slipped from the house fully dressed, carrying her boots and her old brimmed hat, until she reached the back steps. She stopped to pull her things on, arranging the hat over her hair, which was tightly braided and pinned to her head, and letting her eyes adjust to the dark. Rather than be caught on the open beach, she planned to watch from the cliffs above, reasoning that the view was better and the danger less. The cave was a good distance away by the trail and she set off at a brisk pace.

Several hours later, with no sign of anyone, she breathed a disappointed sigh. She had decided they would not return this night, when she froze, sitting as still as the stone beneath her. From down the narrow trail, came the unmistakable nickering of a horse and the heavy crunch of hooves moving along the gravel path, and then it stopped. A light grinding sound puzzled her, and then another, and the horse moved again, stepping lightly. Whoever it was, had dismounted, and was coming in her direction on foot. She had to decide! She could stay where she was, trying to hide in the sparse brush, she could crash into the heavier woods on the far side, knowing the noise would give her away, or she could go back up the trail the way she had come.

She chose the latter, stepping carefully, making as little noise as possible. Now and then, over the pounding of her heart, she heard the steps behind her stop, and she imagined their owner listening, and she would stop too, trying to time her movement to that of her pursuer.

Perhaps they weren't after her at all. She searched the side of the path for a spot to hide, and paused to listen. They were coming faster, nearer. She turned and ran, heedless now, of the noise her boots made striking the rocky ground. Katherine was fast of foot, but hearing the powerful strides close behind, she knew she was outdone. Sensing she was about to be caught, she ducked down, emitting a grunt of pain, when a knee of granite slammed into her shoulder, and a large form crashed to the ground ahead of her. Fearing for her life, she jumped up and ran past the prone body, but an iron grip caught at her ankle, and sent her sprawling off the side of the path to the edge of the cliff.

She landed on her back, with her head and shoulders hanging off the ledge, her world reeling upside down. She made a desperate grab at the scant undergrowth, but the frail roots came loose in her hands. Through the black void, a hand grabbed her belt and pulled her upward, until she rested on the rocky shelf. She sensed her adversary draw back his fist, and like a cornered animal she lashed out with her nails, and caught him across the face. He twisted away, losing his grip, and she pulled back her booted foot and kicked with all her might, striking solidly. The impact knocked her assailant backward, and sent her sliding helplessly over the edge.

Scrabbling and clawing, she fought for a hold, and felt herself slip. Sand filled her eyes and nose, and stones pelted her face, as she bent her body upward from the waist, and dug in her heels. There was a last-second grasp at her boot, when her heel cleared the eroded edge, but the grip of her attacker-turned-savior slid from the smooth toe, and she was falling.

Instead of the swift and deadly plunge she expected, her descent became an excruciatingly slow journey, as she bounced and skidded, skimming the punishing surface like a discarded rag doll. At each contact, she braced and dragged, gouged and grappled, fighting to the end, until at last, one hand found a hold.

The root of an old pine, thrusting out of the embankment in a blind search for sustenance, became her hope, and she seized it in fierce determination. She turned her battered body, clinging with both hands, and sought a foothold, her feet digging at the gravel strewn facing, as rock and rubble tumbled into the night. From the precarious perch, she tried to catch her breath and take stock. The sand in her eyes was agonizing, and she wiped her face on her sleeve until she dared to open them at last. They stung and watered, and there was nothing to see but darkness, so she closed them again. The surge of panic as she fell had been great, and she was feeling sick to her stomach, but since this was neither the time nor the place to be ill, she turned her mind to other things, taking slow deep breaths.

She listened, wondering if her attacker were still there. *If she called out for help, would he save her, or shoot her?* She decided if he thought she knew about the cave it would be certain death. At least, so far, she was alive, and she held her silence. Far below, a horse galloped along the beach and came to a stop, and someone began to thrash among the brush, no doubt searching for her fallen body. She stayed very still until she heard him ride off.

Her arms grew tired, and her body ached, and she dug again with her feet to gain more support. The hillside here was soft, and as her head cleared, she found she was closer to the bluffs than she had thought. Nearer to the cave, the rocky cliffs were higher and more dangerous, but as they merged with the bluffs, they gradually became more sandy and less steep, and she guessed she must be somewhere near the jetty.

Think Katherine! Think! She admonished herself, trying to concentrate. She knew this tree, whose exposed roots thrust pitifully into space, she had seen it a million times, *but what else was there?* By slow degrees the scene formed in her mind, and she heard her father's voice as she had in thousands of childhood trials, "*You can do it, Kate. You can do anything you put your mind to.*" And her mother's gentle inspiration, "*Have faith Katie, and all the rest will take care of itself.*"

Encouraged, she began to recite her mother's favorite psalms to herself, welcoming the tears of frustration that came to cleanse her tortured eyes. The image cleared in her mind, and she pictured the landscape as if she stood on the beach looking up at it. There was a gnarled mass of roots like this one, but they were high above her, and she hadn't the strength left to hoist herself upward. She remembered somewhere to her right was another pine tree, a hapless victim of the elements that had toppled lengthwise down the steep incline, but she didn't know how far away it was. Reaching blindly into the darkness and high up to her right, her fingers found another root. Testing it to hold her weight, she said a silent prayer, and let go of her original hold. Bit by bit, in this manner, she worked her way across the cliff, knowing she was heading toward the steeper drop, but to her left was the wash left by the jetty, with its loose rock and jagged edges below.

At last, her fingertips brushed the rough bark of the tree trunk just out of reach. Groping in between, she found a thin root, and when she tested it, it gave a bit, pulling like a rope through the sand. She doubted it would hold, but the strength in her arms was almost gone, and there was no alternative. She held tight throwing her weight sideways, half jumping, and half swinging.

The root pulled and held, and then snapped, and she dropped downward. She kicked her toe into the soft bank, and as she felt it give way she pushed off, and embraced the fallen tree with both arms, holding to its scaly body with a passion born of desperation. Here she rested, giving thanks for the questionable trophy, and tried to calm her pounding heart. She inched her way down the trunk, clinging to its rough surface. Dead branches scratched and clawed at her as she reached the inverted top of the tree, and faced her final test—She couldn't see the ground.

She guessed she was ten feet up. *Or twenty?* She wasn't good at judging distances, and she couldn't remember if sand or rocks awaited her at the bottom, but she couldn't stay *here*. Hanging at arm's length she let go, and dropped into the darkness.

Hitting sand and brush, she tumbled another good distance down to the beach below, getting immediately to her feet. She was afraid if she rested again, she wouldn't get up, and weak and shaking, she pushed herself onward. She kept to the brush until she reached the jetty, picked her way across the rocks until she came to the water's edge, and climbed over to the beach on the other side. With the last of her will power, she trudged across the shore toward home, trusting the constant tides to cover her tracks.

Chapter 12

Frenzied footfalls attacked the aged slate floor of the kitchen while it lay in mute innocence, its stalwart presence as eloquently consoling as an old friend. This time it was not Katherine who paced the length of the sturdy stone, but Evelyn, in the ominous silence of the pre-dawn. Katherine had not returned. Many a night she had gone down to the beach to seek escape from all that plagued her, but Evelyn had checked the beach an hour ago, and found nothing. Not knowing where else to search, she had returned to the house to wait for daylight, her imagination running rampant with disastrous possibilities. Nevertheless, when the latch lifted, she was not prepared for the appalling apparition that entered.

"Kath... My Lord, what's happened?!"

Katherine held onto the door, not trusting her shaking knees, which had barely carried her up the hill. She spoke no word, but her eyes pleaded for the older woman's aid.

Evelyn smothered the sparks of fear that had ignited with her first sight of the girl, and rushed forward to help, wondering what on earth could have brought about this state. She appeared to have been beaten, and Evelyn looked her over from head to toe not knowing where to begin. Her filthy hair was full of twigs, and hung in wisps and snarls around a face that was almost unrecognizable. Trails of tears from swollen red eyes, crisscrossed through the dirt on her face, showing scant evidence of the fair skin beneath, while dark stains of pitch mottled her jaw and blackened her hands. The dark blouse, was torn at the shoulder, revealing bloodied scratches, and the knees of her trousers hung in tatters above once bright boots, now marred and scuffed, and encrusted, like the whole of her, in wet sandy mud.

Thinking to guide her to a chair, the first thing Evelyn did was place her hand on Katherine's shoulder, jumping when she gasped in pain. "I'm sorry," she murmured, much distressed over how to proceed, until the weary specter raised its arm, and Evelyn cradled it in gentle support, as they moved to the nearby bench.

Katherine lowered herself gingerly to its hard surface. "I need your help Evelyn," she stated the obvious, wiping sand from the corner of her mouth, "I'm stiffening up. I need a hot bath, and I don't think I can manage it." She rested her head back, and closed her eyes, letting loose a long breath, thankful to have made it this far. She opened her eyes and stared at her black sticky hands as she unclenched the aching fingers.

Evelyn stoked the coals and put water on to heat with trembling hands. "Don't worry, we'll get you cleaned up." She came to stand before the battered woman and look into her eyes, "Did someone *hurt* you, sweetheart?"

Yes, Katherine thought, she was hurt. At the moment she hurt all over, but she understood the concern of her friend. "No, not that, I'll explain later." Evelyn turned her attention to getting things ready, and Katherine stared again at the fingers of her right hand, and the dried blood encrusted beneath her nails.

The soothing heat engulfed her, as she sank into the steamy depths of the tub, and savored its effect on her rigid muscles. Evelyn had cleaned the pitch from Katherine's hands and face, and now sat at the head of the tub removing the sticks and leaves interwoven through the nest of tangled hair. She watched in ghastly fascination when the heat revealed a massive purple bruise that covered the whole of her patient's right shoulder. "Land sakes, child! Whatever hit your back?"

Katherine told her the story of how she had discovered the suspected smugglers, her late-night vigil, the ordeal on the cliff trail, and her narrow escape. She included the landing of the boat, and the use of the cave as a hide-away, knowing Evelyn would push to call in the authorities.

Evelyn listened, enthralled and sick at heart, to think what might have happened. If any other woman had told her a story such as this, she would not have believed her, but there was not a doubt in her mind that it was exactly as Katherine had described. Besides, she had seen the end result, and the girl was lucky to be alive. *"You could have been killed."* She meant to scold, but the chastising bite of the words stuck in her throat, leaving an awed statement of fact.

Katherine lay with her head against the rim of the tub, a hot wet cloth covering her face, "I know," she said, quietly, "and I lost my hat, too."

A good while later, a much-improved Katherine lay clean and somewhat comfortable in her bed, having emerged slowly but surely from her grimy disguise, and drunk a good measure of brandy administered by Evelyn.

"You know Kate, you've got to have help on this one. You can't handle everything by yourself."

"Don't worry, I've had enough adventure to last me a while."

Evelyn shook her head as she closed the door on the already sleeping woman, guessing that her attitude would last about as long as her bruises.

A week later, much to her dismay, Katherine found herself once again in Boston, through the diligent prodding of her insistent mentor. Not for the first time in the past days, she questioned her judgment in having invited Evelyn to move in with her. Stiff and sore from her ordeal, she had been more or less confined to the cottage, and under the close supervision and care of the older woman. As soon as she was able, she arranged for Gleason to care for Matilda, and she had been whisked back to the city in Evelyn's buggy, the first step in reporting her findings to the nearest army headquarters.

Now, as the two women rode along in the coach, after leaving the house, Katherine was having second thoughts. But it was too late. They pulled up in front of the modest brick building, and Cody, the too young coachman, nearly stumbled in his haste to open the door for the object of his adoration.

Katherine stepped from the coach in a high-necked dress of deep burgundy that heightened the color of her eyes, her hair caught in a netting of gray silk. She gave the boy a gentle smile that brought a blush to his fair cheeks. Holding her sore arm at her side she entered the dim interior, followed closely by Evelyn. They stopped for a few seconds while their eyes adjusted to the indoor light, before they approached the desk in the center of the dim lobby, and the lone occupant seated behind it.

A rather burly sergeant, with dark hair and a ragged beard, kept his attention on the cluttered mess before him, and paid them no mind. Katherine studied the unkempt person, taking note of oily hair, and the dark stains that trailed through the matted whiskers, and continued downward to deface the front of his tunic. She decided he was no credit to the army, and disliked him instinctively. "Excuse me," she said.

Dark eyes rose beneath a furrowed brow to glare up at her, and widened in surprise at the unexpected vision they beheld. *Madonna Mia!* The sergeant came to his feet, his full height not quite meeting hers. An insolent smile showed off yellowed teeth, as he scrutinized every inch of the elegant beauty before him. "Yes Ma'am," he answered, with an exaggerated enthusiasm, that together with his leering glower, made Katherine uncomfortable, and Evelyn indignant.

"Sergeant!" Evelyn spoke pointedly.

"Sergeant Bernardo Russo, at your service," his smirk, giving lie to his guise of good manners, and his eyes never leaving Katherine. "And you are?"

Evelyn stepped forward half shielding Katherine behind her. "Mind yourself. We've come on important business…" She stopped abruptly when Katherine grabbed hold of her arm and took over the conversation. "We are looking for Devin Galloway. He is a navy captain. Would you know where we might find him?" She asked, giving Evelyn's arm an extra squeeze and shooting her a warning look.

Evelyn held her silence, as Katherine towed her toward the door, almost before the Sergeant answered.

"Why don't you try the Navy office, then? *Stupid women!*" He muttered to himself, but tried again, "If you leave your name, I will help you find him," he offered, in a second attempt for an introduction.

"That won't be necessary, Sergeant, I am sure you are right, we have come to the wrong place."

He hurried to the door and grabbed her elbow to delay her departure, and received a warning glare from flashing eyes that only made him chuckle.

Katherine met the cold black eyes and was reminded of a shark, dangerous, unfeeling and deadly. She looked past his shoulder at the notices on the bulletin board, and spoke the first name she saw there. "Macey. *Mrs.* Walter Macey." She hurried a much-befuddled Evelyn to the waiting coach.

"Do you mind telling me what that was all about, *Mrs. Macey?*" Evelyn asked, after Katherine had quietly instructed Cody to drive them in the opposite direction, and the long way around, before taking them home.

"Not at all," Katherine replied, glancing out the window, at the way they had come. "Do you remember, when I told you about the boat landing on the beach?"

"Yes."

"Well, that was the name I heard!"

"Oh, my! You think that was him?"

"I don't know, but we don't know it wasn't, and either way, I wouldn't trust that man."

"I can't argue with you there, there were plenty of things about him to dislike, but what do you think we should do now?"

"Wait, I guess," Katherine said hopefully, watching for Evelyn's reaction out of the corner of her eye, and knowing the woman's reply before it was voiced.

The following afternoon, Katherine wandered the length of the drawing room, pausing to finger an occasional knickknack and to flex her shoulder. To a casual observer, she might appear the idle daughter of a wealthy family, simply bored with the August heat, instead of a woman in serious contemplation of her limited options. Evelyn had departed to visit an ailing Hetty Parker, leaving Katherine to wrestle with the decision of returning to the army office, or contacting someone else. That '*someone else*' Evelyn had suggested, was Captain Galloway. *If Phillip had trusted him...*

The very thought of that meeting made her heart beat faster as she paced the room. Elegant in black silk, her hair once again rolled into a silken net, she fought the idea that she secretly welcomed the excuse that would call him to her side. *No!* She protested against her willing heart, there must be *someone else—Cecil Johnston perhaps, or Ezra…*

With a soft tap at the door the decision was taken from her when Gladys poked her head in, "Captain Galloway, to see you miss."

"Tell him I…" She started in panic, but it was too late, he was there, and she cut off the half-spoken excuse.

"Tell me you're not in?" Devin teased, in that voice like a caress, greeting and rebuking her at the same time.

"No, I…" Katherine turned and time ticked away, as she stood feeling the pounding of her heart that beat with something more than the usual passion he aroused in her. She hadn't seen him for weeks and he seemed pale and a bit thinner, and she stared, still struggling with her options.

Obviously, she was less than glad to see him, Devin thought, and self-consciously, he passed a hand across his forehead brushing at a wave of dark hair. "I seem to be as welcome as the plague," he smiled hesitantly, trying to hide his disappointment, when she spoke no word to deny it. "Cheer up Katherine, I didn't come just to see your pretty face," he said, moving toward her across the room.

He did look pale. Forgetting her injured shoulder, she reached to touch his face, and gasped at the pain that shot through her.

Devin looked at her in alarm. "Are you hurt?" He asked, naturally reaching to steady her.

"No. Yes, but I'm fine. I… fell." She told him the understated truth, and then asked, "Did Evelyn send you?"

"No," Devin said, confused, still studying her with concern. "I came to bring you these," and reaching inside his coat he brought forth a small stack of letters tied with a ribbon, and with an elaborate flourish held it before her eyes.

"Oh!" Katherine exclaimed, recognizing the handwriting, "They're from William!" She reached for the neat bundle with her left hand, and taking it to the sofa she began to scan the precious lines with her heart in her throat. There were four in all, short in content, except for the last, which explained how, on his way home, their ship had been damaged, so they had made port in England, and had to wait for repairs… *But he was all right! And the news was less than a month old!*

Devin watched the joy that lit her face while she read, and found his reward for the hours he had spent calling in favors, and tracking down William Lawrence. The letters were forwarded to him by a friend, by routes and reasons best left untold.

Katherine finished reading and viewed him through happy tears. "I could kiss you!" She said, forgetting herself in her enthusiasm. Blushing, she averted her eyes.

He looked on in despair, wishing with all his heart that she would, but knowing it was but a figure of speech. He released her from the uncomfortable silence, "I'm glad you're pleased. I was going to bring them out to you, when I noticed Cody had the coach out, and I thought you might be in town."

"I can't thank you enough," she said, still shy about her outburst, and not meeting his eyes. "Where… how did you get them?"

Gladys interrupted, and Devin only shrugged, smiling. "Can I get you anything, Miss Katie?"

"Please, Gladys, something cold?" Katherine turned to Devin, and at his nod, Gladys left them.

"*Katie?*" He asked, doubtfully.

Katherine smiled, "I was a little girl once, you know."

He covered her in a long slow perusal, the heat of his gaze leaving her no doubt about his thoughts, and his voice was husky when he spoke, "Aye, but no longer."

Katherine got nervously to her feet. "I'm forgetting my manners, and so are you," she added with a scolding look. "Won't you sit down, Captain? Perhaps you'd like something stronger to drink?"

"No thank you, that's fine." Devin said, seating himself and still watching her, as Gladys returned with iced tea. They sat in awkward silence, sipping their drinks, until Devin rose to leave, and relieved but saddened, Katherine walked with him to the door. "Thank you, again, for the letters. I thought you might have shipped out by now."

"I thought you were going to kiss me?" He teased, deciding at the last minute to bait her after all.

To his surprise, she stepped closer to place a tender kiss on his cheek, and rest her forehead against his chin for a blissful moment.

He pressed his lips to the golden head, and slid his hand in a light caress down her back.

Katherine winced when he brushed her shoulder, and arched away from his touch, pressing against him. She stepped quickly away.

"I'm sorry," Devin whispered, catching her left hand, reluctant as always, to leave her. "What happened to you?" He asked, studying her closely.

She stood lost in thought, remembering the impact against her shoulder with a clarity that caused her to wince again. "I just fell, that's all." She spoke with a finality that told him the subject was closed.

"Take care of yourself," he said, kissing her hand, and opening the door. Halfway out, he paused, and turned to study her again. Not with the burning look of passion as before, but with careful consideration. "Have you been in town long?"

"A few weeks. I've been very busy at the office," she said, feeling the need to lie after all. "I've had my last ride on Matilda for a while."

He frowned, "Katherine…"

She stood, refined and feminine, her hands folded at her waist, and lifted delicate brows in attention, but he seemed to change his mind.

"Nothing," he said, shaking his head as if he had made a decision, and with a wistful smile he left her.

Katherine watched him go, more confused than ever about what to do. She needed time to think. He had been so kind, bringing her William's letters, and he had the same effect on her as always, but she hadn't confided in him, or asked for his help. Something had stopped her. Something about the deep red scratches where she had kissed his cheek. Scratches she was certain had come from her own hand.

Chapter 13

With the assurance that Katherine had indeed met with Captain Galloway, and that he definitely knew of the incident along the cliff trail, Evelyn elected to stay in town and offer whatever aid she could to her friend, who was doing a bit better.

Katherine, with a sincere promise to avoid the cliffs, at least after dark, had once again scurried to the seclusion of the cottage. While her meeting with Devin had left her wondering about his connection to the smugglers, it had left her no doubt of her continued attraction to him. *He couldn't be involved, he couldn't.* Each time they met, she felt closer to the edge of her resistance, and she was losing the determined battle she fought against throwing herself into his arms. The very thought of that longed for haven made her sigh aloud. She had to stay away from him. He was like a fire that she could not control, and rather than risk being consumed, she would have to live without the light and warmth he inspired, bearing the dark emptiness of life without him. This was the task she undertook with a fierce determination, and gallant bravado, that left her in misery. For, in the way of those determined not to think of a specific topic, she could, of course, do nothing else.

Long days in the summer sun had left her skin an unfashionable golden tan, and painted pale highlights in her hair, and in the solitary week since she had returned, her shoulder, had improved considerably. She had felt well enough to deliver William's letters to Louise, but other than that, had stayed off the cliff trail as promised, confining her outings on Matilda to other paths, and her nighttime sojourns to her private beach. It was the result of one of these nocturnal visits that would shake the very foundations of her beliefs, and change her life forever.

True to habit on this sultry summer night, she had gone to swim in her shift, bringing only a towel and a robe. At first, she had been apprehensive about being on the beach at night, knowing not even Evelyn was nearby, but as night after night had passed without any activity in the next cove, she had relaxed and begun to enjoy her routine.

She had finished her swim, and was toweling dry, when across the water came a flicker of light, and the overwhelming sensation of being caught in a repetitive dream.

Fighting the impulse to flee to the cottage, she stood rooted to the spot, her senses alert and waiting. A vision of Evelyn in chastising scowl, flashed through her mind, but Katherine smothered it. She had promised to stay off the cliffs at night, and she had, and there was more here than her usual bent for adventure. Something she could not put a name to… A premonition… A wisp of warning, that stirred her consciousness, and disappeared beyond her grasp. With fierce conviction, she grabbed her robe, and turned and ran down the beach toward the jetty.

She did not enter the water this time, but climbed the familiar wall, and crept down the beach to select a hiding place at the base of the cliff. Swallowed in the shadows of the huge rocks, she settled herself to watch.

In eerie encore the scene unfolded before her, unsettling in its likeness. The rowing, the approach, the cursing and angry voices, all returned with a haunting sameness. Only upon landing did the performance alter somewhat, and she watched, as not six, but seven men jumped ashore. There seemed to be nothing to unload this time, and the men started directly toward the cave in silence. As they filed past, not far from her, she spied a shadowed form that stood taller than the rest, and caused a tingling at the back of her neck. Sense, more than sight, told her who it was, but she could not have been more certain.

Oh, God! She had hoped she was wrong in thinking he could be involved, and that his appearance on the cliffs that night had been part of his work, and perhaps he had been observing as she had. But here he was in the midst of them. Helping now, as they carried the long wooden crates and loaded them into the boats.

As they worked, Katherine sat in misery and terror, wondering what on earth had possessed her to come. She wished she had followed her first impulse and returned to the cottage, and locked the door behind her. *Why did she have to discover this?* Knowing she could never be with Devin brought her pain beyond endurance, but the possibility that the object of her love was a traitor, tore through the last shreds of her fortitude, and yet, in the deepest part of her soul, her love insisted—*It couldn't be.* She closed her eyes, and reached for her cross, seeking guidance, when a loud crash rent the silence, echoing off the stone heights like a rifle shot.

She jumped, her heart pounding, and so did everyone else. One of the men had stumbled, and a case had smashed to the rocks, breaking under its own weight and spilling its contents with a raucous clatter. With more than a few rough curses, that raised numerous possibilities of the blighted one's ancestry, the loose rifles were gathered and carried to the waiting boat. The fear of discovery now heightened; the men worked at double the pace to complete the loading. She waited barely able to breathe, as they made their way once more to the boat and prepared to shove off. One, two, three and four, and then five, left the cave, and Devin was not among them.

In terrible suddenness a second crash echoed from the cave, and Katherine knew she was mistaken. She had thought the previous sound resembled that of a gunshot, but now she could compare them, and this was by far the more terrifying. It was the unmistakable crack of a pistol. Her half-formed prayer unuttered, she sat frozen, staring at the cave opening. A lone figure emerged and strode across the narrow beach to the waiting boat, and it was not the one she had so fervently hoped to see.

"Hurry up, Russo, you lousy bastard, you'll get us all caught!" The course whisper came through the darkness, and when the heavy boat had worked its way out to sea, Katherine rose from her hiding place on shaking limbs.

Moving like a sleep walker to the mouth of the cave, she crawled through the low opening. Inside, she paused, squinting into the inky blackness and seeing nothing. She began to feel her way around the rough interior with trembling fingers, until at last she found the small candle and flint she had hidden weeks before. She crawled to the inner space, and fumbled in the darkness, to set it aglow, and taking a deep breath, she turned to face her worst fear.

Devin lay face down on the floor of the cave. Sick at heart, she knelt beside him, and set the candle down to turn him over. He was dressed well for the nights work, and on careful examination, no ugly hole gaped in the black trousers or the dark shirt that covered his broad chest. She moved the meager light closer to his head and saw the blood. *So much blood.* She reached cold fingers to test the pulse at his throat, and a faint beating answered her prayer.

Leaning closer, to search his face, she placed a hand to his forehead and found a large raised lump, she had not seen in the shadows. She ran her fingers through his hair seeking the wound, and found a long gash along the left side of his head. She was hopeful. Although the thick hair and the cave floor were soaked with blood, the shot that was surely meant to kill him, had instead, grazed his skull, but how deeply, she could not tell. She stood without hesitation and pulled off her robe, tearing it down the middle to wrap it around his head, and tying the ends to hold it securely in place.

Now what? She doubted she could move him, but she had to try. She pushed him to a half-sitting position, placed her hands under his arms and around his chest, and pulled with all her might. In rapid estimation, she placed his weight at a ton and a half. *"You damned fool,"* she whispered, not knowing if she should direct the title at him or herself. His head rested against her shoulder, as though he slept, and for the briefest instant her grip tightened to an endearing hug. "Oh Devin, my love," she whispered aloud, "please don't leave me." There was no time for weakness, and she braced herself, and pulled again, ignoring the burn in her shoulder, and fighting the tears that rose forth. By agonizing inches, and pure determination, she pulled him from the cave.

Out on the ocean, shouting and gun shots carried over the waves, but Katherine barely noticed. The noise only spurred her on to move Devin before someone returned. Her eyes fell upon the splintered gun crate and its sturdy cover, at the water's edge, and a plan began to form in her mind. With mounting haste, she unbuttoned his shirt and pulled it from him. Rolling him on his side she spread the garment out and placed the stout wooden cover on top of it. Then, moving him once again flat on his back, she tied the sleeves of his shirt around his chest, under his arms, strapping him to the makeshift raft.

She stopped to remove his heavy boots and toss them aside, and pulling her precious cargo into the surf, she towed him toward the jetty, and worked her way around its point. On the other side, she traveled the length of the beach in waist-deep water, the mocking waves echoing the name that would ever haunt her… *Russo, Russo.*

Pulling Devin to shore, and hating to leave him, she ran for Matilda to tow him the rest of the way to the house. Once there however, she could think of no way to move him up the few steps, and deciding he had been bumped about enough, she towed him into the barn and set about making him comfortable.

She passed through the kitchen and roused the fire in the grate for hot water. Sheets, blankets, towels, a scissors, a razor and the various ointments Evelyn used for her nursing, were gathered in a rapid forage through the cottage. When she rushed to his side, she was struck by how still and pale he was, and another ripple of fear crossed her heart. She set aside her supplies and dropped to her knees, bending low to feel his breath against her cheek, and place her hand over his heart. She was barely reassured, and her worried gaze caressed his face, as she untied the knotted wet shirt from his chest. She pressed a warm kiss to his cold lips, *for luck*, she told herself, and hers were the tears that rolled down his cheek.

She scolded herself, knowing if Devin were going to get the care he needed, it was up to her to give it. This was no time for virgin blushes, and spreading a sheet over his body, she reached beneath it to unfasten and remove his wet clothes.

By the time she had fashioned a soft bed of fresh straw and heavy quilts, the water she waited for was thoroughly heated. She maneuvered her patient into the comfortable nest and added several blankets. As she settled the heavy body, the phrase '*dead weight*' intruded into her thoughts and stabbed her in the heart. The discarded makeshift bandage was soaked with blood, and in spite of her determined attitude, Katherine's hands shook as she examined the wound by the light of several lanterns. To her relief, it was clean, perhaps helped by the salt water, and it appeared to be less severe than she had thought, with only the front of the gash too deep to leave to heal on its own. With intricate care she trimmed the dark hair from the edges, and washed the whole of it with hot soapy water. Unknowingly, she bit her bottom lip and held her breath, while she placed neat tiny stitches to hold the sides of the wound together before slathering on one of Evelyn's concoctions and covering all with a fresh clean bandage.

She sponged the dried salt and sand from the beloved face and hands, the long arms and broad chest, and as much of the rest of him as seemed fitting for his comfort and her modesty. As much as she tried, she could not claim immunity to the attraction of the long lean strength of him that bespoke grace and power even in repose.

Satisfied she had done what she could, Katherine blew out one lantern, turned another down low, and took the third with her to hurriedly see to her own needs.

From the roar of the pistol, Devin was lost. A blind emigrant, entering a foreign world of darkness, he neither woke nor slept, and yet he dreamed. Although aware that he hurt, he could raise no hand to help himself. He felt the warm flow of blood, and in the way of dreams, it mingled with salt tears to become a river, lifting him and carrying him from the black void of the cave, and setting him adrift in the ocean. Rocked by the gentle rise and fall of the waves, he drifted, weightless and helpless, alone at the mercy of the elements, until at last he felt the presence of another. Cool white fingers curled from the crest of the waves to touch his wounded brow, and stroke his fevered body. Soothing and arousing, the caresses continued as the sea became seducer, capturing him within her endless rhythms.

He struggled to put a face to his phantom lover, and as in a thousand dreams before, it was Katherine who rose from the waves to join him. As always, she kissed him and pulled back, but this time he did not let her go. He instead, caught her about the waist, and pulled her with him beneath the surface, where she accepted his embrace and returned his urgent kisses, as they tumbled through the surf and were left awash at the water's edge. She lay pliant beneath him, in the moonlight, her eyes as mysterious as the sea, her robe a transparent veil over her body. As if by magic the garment parted, revealing pearly breasts to his loving gaze, and eagerly she rose against him, inviting, encouraging, offering herself…

Devin moved in fevered haste to comply, but the scene grew brighter and brighter. His troubled mind stumbled in confusion, for his memory could not recall that which had not come to pass.

Katherine had hurried to bathe, and though it was but a short hour before dawn, she dressed in a nightgown and wrapper, thinking she could yet get some sleep. Returning to check on him, she knelt by his side. The wound was no longer bleeding under the bandage, but she worried over the bump on his forehead. She knew he must have struck his head on the floor of the cave, and the large lump was now a vivid purple. Carefully she applied a cold cloth to the bruise, bringing the lantern closer so she could see.

Devin fought against the light, trying to keep his vision of Katherine, but the conclusion was lost. Grappling in frustration, unable to reach the ending, his mind turned full circle and the dream began again, with cool hands stroking his brow. So real was the fantasy, he could feel her gentle touch, and the coldness of the ocean. The water trickled down his face… His eyes fluttered open, and for an instant he saw her again, there above him in her white robe, but this time he could not reach her. His eyes closed, and in his dream, he was helpless, tied to a raft that remained off the shore where Katherine stood watching. He cried out to her for help, and she lifted her arms toward him, only to push him into the currents that would carry him out to sea and leave him ever adrift.

Katherine was relieved when he opened his eyes and spoke her name, but she realized that he looked through her, and was still lost in another world. He muttered frantically and she leaned close to catch his ravings—and was sorry—for what she heard twisted her heart, and filled her with regret.

"Please Katherine, love me. Don't send me away."

Quick, hot tears filled her eyes. *What had she done? What was she supposed to do?* He sounded so hurt, and so weak.

She tried to summon the anger that had so often helped her in her resolve, but it would not come. She held his hand, and kissed his fingers, and studied the face she knew so well, almost boyish in sleep. Long dark lashes rested on pale cheeks, and the shadow of a beard showed beneath the usually dark complexion. As she watched the slow rise and fall of his chest, mesmerized by its steady rhythm, the thought she had refused to allow crept into her brain. *What if he should die? She did love him.* More than she had admitted, even to herself. Shouldn't he know that? Shouldn't they at least be honest with each other, and face up to their hopeless situation? *…And then what?* With these questions, and Devin's tormenting words echoing through her mind, somewhere in the last scrap of darkness she fell asleep.

Chapter 14

It had been six days. Six days since she had awakened to find herself with her head on his shoulder, and those devastating eyes, only inches from hers. Somehow in the night he had shared the quilt with her, and in the innocence of sleep she had snuggled close against him. She had extricated herself, and anxiously asked how he was, trying to hide her embarrassment, but he was asleep again. Since that morning, neither had mentioned the few minutes of shared slumber, and she hoped he would not remember.

Later that day, she had helped him move to her room, which had the larger of the beds, and she had taken what she needed, and moved into the room which was now Evelyn's. She had fed him, and cared for him, and watched over him, and for the most part he had slept, regaining the strength he had lost.

Now, he was feeling strong enough to bathe and shave, having borrowed her father's razor, and he was able to join her at the table for breakfast. He looked handsome as always, dressed in the dark clothes she had washed and pressed, and the boots she had retrieved from the beach. She had removed the bandage and the stitches, at his insistence.

The wound was healing well, and the bruise was just visible under the familiar wave of dark hair.

"You're sure you're well enough?" She asked for the tenth time, regarding his still questionable pallor with suspicion, as she set the table.

"I'm fine. Besides I've got to get up and around, I shouldn't be here," he admitted reluctantly. "I should go."

"Tomorrow," she said, not wanting him to leave, but knowing that he must. "I mean, I'm not sure you're well enough yet. And we haven't had much of a chance to talk."

Devin raised an eyebrow in his usual questioning expression, and closed his eyes at the twinge he had caused himself. He had expected she would be eager to be rid of him, but he would be more than happy to stay. "And what shall we talk about?" He asked, with a crooked grin.

"Oh, you know, the usual things. The war, the weather. Why someone would want to shoot you in the head."

"I see. Well, the weather is wet," he said, still grinning, glancing through the window at the gray drizzle without.

"Do go on," Katherine encouraged, studying him over her teacup, in a gesture that flooded him with memories.

"Or," he hedged, "I could ask you what *you* were doing there."

"Swimming."

"In a cave?" He smirked.

Now she laughed aloud, "I was saving your insidious hide!"

"And are you sorry?"

"Of *course* not." She said, touched by his pleading look.

Devin grew serious. He remembered his dreams, but little else, and had trouble discerning the reality of that night. Yet, he had awakened to find her beside him, as if she belonged there. "How did you? I mean, how did I get here?"

Katherine poured another cup of tea, and proceeded to tell him the whole story, from her decision to swim, to his somewhat bumpy arrival at the barn with the help of Matilda. He seemed quite interested in the commotion she had heard out on the water, but she could tell him little about it. She kept a few minor details to herself. She did not speak the hated name of Russo, but it would sit at the fore of her memory in ever-ready reference.

Devin listened intently to her matter-of-fact rendition, admiring the strength and intelligence he knew lay behind the plain words. He watched, fascinated, as her lovely features covered a range of expressions while she told her tale, her eyes wide with remembered fear, or narrowed in concentration, the soft mouth curving gently while she made him laugh with preposterous conjectures about his weight.

He had seen a bloodied garment tossed aside in the hay, before she had collected it, along with his own clothes and taken them away, and he knew he was naked beneath the quilts that first day, until she found one of William's nightshirts for him to wear, but Katherine didn't mention these things, and he didn't ask, not wanting to embarrass her. He could only wonder what he had missed.

"Does that clear things up for you?"

"Yes, except..."

Her heart fell, and she knew what he would say before he spoke.

"I remember... was I dreaming, or were you..."

She cut him off, "You called out in your sleep, and I stayed close. I guess I fell asleep." She shrugged as if it mattered little, but could not forget the burning warmth of him next to her, and the thought brought a blush to her cheek.

"What did I say?" Devin asked with concern, remembering the bent of his dreams.

Katherine studied her empty plate.

"I... couldn't make it out." She stammered.

He decided she was not a very good liar, but let the matter drop.

"You think you're so clever. You haven't answered my question," she scolded.

"Which?"

She rolled her eyes in an exasperated expression that made him chuckle. "Why were you with those men?" She changed the question slightly. "I'm beginning to understand why someone would shoot you!"

Devin smiled and looked serious again, "Forgive me, Katherine, but it would be for the best if I did not tell you. For your own safety. I can only say, it was not what you might think, and ask you to please trust me."

Their eyes met and held, "All right. *For now,*" she added, and rose to clear the table.

"Thank you, and thank you for looking after me so well."

"I suppose someone *has* to." The mood was light, but as she passed his chair with the plates, he placed his hand on her arm, "I'm glad it was you," and the caress of his voice, and the warmth of his gaze scared her more than any part of their recent adventures.

They passed the late morning hours in mutual contentment, each secretly cherishing the rare time together, and being especially careful to avoid any topic that might bring them to odd ends. Devin, delighting in her company, was at his most charming, and Katherine, though the happiest she had been in a long while, was ever on guard against any sudden advances. He had a way of slipping adulations into the tedious conversation, and turning a simple compliment into an outright proposition. By the time they had finished lunch and he went in to take a nap, it was she who was exhausted, and breathed a sigh of relief.

Devin slept for a short while, and now sat with his hands behind his head. His mind drifted, reveling in his collection of a thousand visions of Katherine—laughing, sighing, frowning, jesting, touching— He thought of her cooking and preparing their meals, and he smiled. He had never imagined her in such a domestic way, his *Athena, the adventurous,* and er accomplished this as she did everything, with a simple efficient grace. Strangely the scene brought a warm contentment, and he wished she could always be so near. Bypassing another vision of her in his arms, he settled on a safer image, one where she was intent on the care of his wound. When she had finished, she had brushed aside the hair from his forehead to check the progress of the bruise before wishing him good night. He had thought to reach for her. He wanted to touch her as he had often done, but he didn't dare. She was too close, and he wanted her so badly. It was overwhelmingly difficult to be so near and not touch.

For obvious reasons he turned his mind to other thoughts and his eyes searched the room, *her room*. It was like her, he thought, cool and elegant, yet comfortable, with an inviting underlying warmth. The dark walls were hung with several paintings of outdoor scenes in gilt frames, the woodlands and oceans, reflecting the deep blues and greens that colored the large room. Thick carpets of the same dark hues nearly covered the polished oak floor adding warmth and comfort underfoot. He took in the stone fireplace in the far corner, and the windows that faced both the side and rear of the house. Across the room two velvet chairs sat on either side of a table that held a vase of white roses. Devin sighed and his thoughts returned to the bed on which he lay. The bed where she slept. Absently his hand reached to brush the pillow beside him, wishing she were there now. Haunted by his arduous thoughts, he went in search of their source.

He found her reading in the library, seated in one of the comfortable chairs. So intent was she, she did not notice him, and he leaned in the doorway observing. She wore a summer dress of pale muslin, and he noted, with some disappointment, that she had once again braided her hair and pinned it up. The weather had worsened, the sky growing darker, and though it was but mid-afternoon, she had lit the lamp and sat bathed in the glowing light. She looked very feminine, and very lovely, and very—*studious*, he thought, finding the combination charming.

She must have sensed his presence, for though he made no sound, she glanced up to find him grinning. "Oh, hello," she said smiling.

"Hello."

She looked at him curiously, "What's so funny?"

"Nothing."

"Has the blow to your head done damage then, that you go about smiling so at nothing?" She was glad to see him looking so much better than only a few days before.

"Perhaps I'm in love." He caught her off guard, leaving her nowhere to turn, staring her down.

Silence filled the room, and she took a breath, scouring her mind for a reply—some bit of wit or wisdom that would turn the bold remark aside—but none came. "I thought you might enjoy a game of chess," she offered nervously. "Do you play?" She hoped he did. She had spent much of the time he had napped, taking a bath and washing her hair, while thinking of some way to pass the remaining hours of the afternoon. *Something safe.*

"I would, and I do," Devin smiled, undaunted by the fact that she had so abruptly changed the subject. After all, there were many hours in a day. "But I must warn you," he added, "I am very good at cornering people."

"So I've noticed." She muttered.

"Especially queens," he whispered, coming too close as she rose from her chair.

Ignoring him again, she took the lamp and led the way to the living room.

Hours later, they had played two games, and were well into the third. Katherine had won the first, and Devin the second. It seemed to her, after each move, he stared at her harder and longer, making it more difficult for her to concentrate. "Devin," she prompted again, after long minutes waiting for him to take his turn.

"Hmm?"

"It's your move."

The look he gave made her regret her choice of words, and she closed her eyes in exasperation, causing him to smile. "I was thinking..." He said, with a mischievous squint.

She *knew* he was thinking, it was *what* he was thinking that worried her.

"Perhaps we could wager on the outcome of the game."

"Perhaps," she ventured, not daring to ask what the wager might be, "but I've lived in these woods all my life, Captain."

He was puzzled, and most enchanted by her impish grin, "Why, Miss Lawrence, whatever do you mean?"

"I *mean*, that I know a skunk when I smell one."

He laughed aloud, enjoying the play. "But one small wager. Surely an adventurous girl such as yourself would..."

"*Or*," she proposed, "we could do what my grandfather taught me, in a situation such as this."

Devin knew by the sparkle in her lovely eyes that something was up, and he took the bait deliberately, "What's that?"

"Tip the board," she laughed, doing precisely that, and sending the pieces tumbling to the floor.

He couldn't help but laugh. He would have been disappointed if she hadn't come up with some defense of his obvious ploy.

"Now *you* can put away the game, while I make supper," she scolded in mock severity. "And it serves you right, you lecherous wolf!" Her words floated back to him as she quit the room.

Devin gathered the pieces and placed them in their wooden box. *Saints, she was wonderful,* he thought. This was almost worth being shot at, and he might do it again, if he could land on her doorstep. He got to his feet, placing the box on the table, and paused as he thought over her departing words. *Lecherous? Was that how she thought of him?*

He hurried toward the kitchen.

After the late supper, Devin had returned to the living room, but Katherine lingered in the kitchen seeking safety in solitude. The dishes were long done, in fact, Devin had dried them and put them away, and the kitchen was spotless, but she could not bring herself to join him. Passing the broom again and again, over the clean floor, she tried to calm herself, and it was not the approaching thunder that made her hands tremble. She should have sent him home, but this morning he hadn't seemed well enough, and now it was too late for him to travel, even to the village, especially in the storm.

He seemed healthy enough now, though. *Too* healthy, in fact, as she remembered his longing gazes and charming attentions during their meal. He had said little, but studied her in such a way that she felt it was herself he would devour—and while cleaning up afterward, he had used every opportunity to touch her arm or brush her shoulder, in seemingly casual contact. He had made her so aware of his desire… *Or was it hers?* She paused in mid-sweep, and stared off into space.

"Katherine," He called softly from the doorway, "you'll wear out the floor." He came forward to take the broom from her hands and place it in its corner.

She came to, and swallowed hard, feeling as though she had been caught at something.

"Come and sit down, I won't bite you. *Well,* I *might,*" he teased, "we lecherous wolves are like that." He took her arm and led her to the sofa, and to her relief he did not sit beside her, but wandered around the room admiring and inspecting. At the far end, he stopped at the piano and raised the cover, fingering a few odd notes.

"Would you play? Please?"

It was a simple enough request, and a welcome diversion, and Katherine consented. For over an hour she played everything she could from memory, singing shyly. "I'm afraid that's all I know by heart," she apologized, flexing her stiff shoulders. "My mother was much better at it."

"You're very good." He smiled, with that look in his eyes that so easily unnerved her.

"Thank you." She studied the keyboard, trying to think of something else to play to pass the time.

"Can you play the song you played that day in Boston? Do you remember?"

"I remember, but I don't know all the words."

"I'll help," he offered, and came to stand behind her, leaning over her shoulder, while she picked out the tune on a trial run. Nervous, and distracted by his nearness, she hit a wrong note and ducked her head wincing at the discordant sound.

Devin laughed, "Relax, Katherine, you can do it," and he dropped his hands to her shoulders, gently massaging her neck.

She was far from relaxed, but the caressing fingers felt marvelous, and she waited a minute, closing her eyes while he worked the tension from her stiff muscles. His hands moved a little lower and she started, reminding him of her injured shoulder.

"Sorry. Still sore?"

"A little." She didn't tell him it had hurt more than ever after she had dragged him from the cave. She began to play, and to her surprise, Devin accompanied, giving the words his best Scottish burr and an extra measure of sorrow.

When they finished, neither moved, until at last Katherine reached to wipe away a tear, the thought of the *'true loves who would never meet again,'* striking much too close to home. "Is that your favorite?" She asked.

"Yes, I suppose it is." He gave a short laugh, seeming a little embarrassed.

"It's very sad."

"Yes, it is." Devin was staring at the nape of her neck.

"I think there's enough sadness in the world already."

"Yes," he agreed, "more than there has to be."

She sat contemplating his meaning, his hands still resting on her shoulders, her heart racing.

"Katherine..."

"Yes?" Her voice was a whisper.

"Remember earlier when I said, perhaps I was in love?"

She nodded slightly.

"What would you think if it were true?" He asked, his voice husky. Unable to resist, he bent to kiss the back of her neck. When she did not pull away, he lingered there, and soon traced a path to her ear, as he sat beside her on the bench, his back to the keyboard.

"I would think," she whispered, her eyes closed, her defenses crumbling, "that she was a very lucky woman." She turned her head and met his eyes, and then, his lips. His arms enfolded her, cradling her across his chest, as their lips parted and met again, and again, until Katherine could no longer ignore the rising fires within, and broke away, resting her forehead on his shoulder to calm herself. His hold loosened, and when she moved to stand, he let her go.

She went to open the front window, hoping the damp air would cool her body, and clear her head, and perhaps it would have, if he had not followed. While she stood, staring into the night, he removed the pins from her hair and undid her braid, burying his face in the fragrant amber silk. He whispered her name, his voice hoarse with desire, afraid she would flee from him again.

She gave in to her heart, and leaned back against him, and his arms came around her as he whispered against her temple, "I love you." She turned in his arms and he held her close, kissing the side of her neck. "Please let me love you."

She tried to keep a hold on her reeling world. *It would be so easy to say yes, but it was so wrong*, and these were the words she spoke aloud, as she pulled away. "I can't. It's wrong, please…"

"But, it's *so* right," he coaxed, fighting the urge to reach for her again.

She placed trembling hands against his chest holding him at bay with her last ounce of resistance. "We can't do this."

Devin took a deep breath, and she wondered if he might want to strangle her, and at that moment she almost wished he would. At least it would bring an end to this hellish cycle they seemed caught in. But he only nodded and touched her cheek. He turned and went to his room, leaving her once more alone with her pride and her aching heart.

Racked by desire and indecision, she paced the length of her room, praying for guidance. *Why*, she railed, *as hard as she tried to avoid him, were they always thrown together?* Wherever she went... In the middle of Boston's marketplace, of all the times of day, and all the people who passed there, she had to see him. On the cliff trail at two o'clock in the morning, he was there. They owned the same ship for Heaven's sake! And when she had resolved to stay as far away as she could, he'd gotten himself shot in her front yard! She should never have brought him here, but there had been no alternative. She thought of the night he had been shot. Her fear when she heard the pistol, and when she saw him lying in the cave. Her mind skipped ahead, coming to rest on the image of him calling out in his half-conscious state, begging her not to leave him again.

Burying her face in her hands, Katherine tried to shut out the memory, only to have it replaced with a vision of him that day on the beach last spring, when she had told him she didn't love him, and another, in her father's study, of her throwing him out in hatred.

"*Oh God, help me,*" she cried, sinking despondently into the chair,

"I'm not strong enough for this." She searched her soul for a feeling of having done the right thing, but saw only Devin's pleading visage, and heard again those treasured words, '*I love you*'.

And what of herself? Was she not suffering every bit as much, if not more so? He would leave tomorrow, and he would go home, and soon he would have a child. What would she have? *Memories of a few stolen kisses?* She could not fool herself into thinking there would be someone else. He was everything, and when he left, she would be alone forever. She got to her feet and began to undress. She brushed out her hair, donned a dark silken robe, took a deep breath, and stepped into the hallway.

Chapter 15

The door to the other bedroom stood ajar, and the candlelight within lent a dim glow to her path. She raised her hand to knock, but hesitated, resting her forehead against the solid casing. *You're a coward*, she told herself, *too weak to stay, and too weak to go back.* In abject misery, she dropped her hand to her side and turned around to return to her room. Already on edge, she gasped in surprise and placed a hand to her heart, as Devin stepped from the shadows behind her. They stood facing each other. He, afraid to let himself believe she had come to him, and she, still undecided… and the silence grew long.

"I went to close the window," he explained, shattering the stillness. "The storm's getting worse." He waited for her to speak, but she said nothing.

It was only then she became aware of the heavy rain now drumming steadily on the roof.

Devin came forward into the faint light, barefoot and shirtless. Her gaze slid over his muscled chest and strong arms, and she ached to touch him. As she did in her dreams, she reached out a hand, and he was instantly before her, offering his arm. "Are you all right, Love?" He bent close above her to peer into her eyes in concern, and was surprised by the obvious desire he found there. Still, he waited. He had glimpsed that look before in her eyes, and always she had denied it. "Katherine?"

Katherine felt the firm muscles of his forearm hot beneath her cool hand, and her fingers tightened. Wondering vaguely how she had resisted him this long, she slid her hand from his arm to his chest in a feather-light caress. She stepped closer, her thinly clad body brushing his, as he lowered his head, and she melted into him, sharing with him a kiss that freed her of all resistance.

"Katherine?" He murmured, against her lips, asking the unspoken question.

Her voice was a whisper, "Yes, Devin, plea..."

She never finished. His mouth closed over hers, in a kiss that began with gentle assurance, sweeping her into his world where they had always belonged together, and revealing a glimpse of the glorious passion that would hold her there forever. Devin moved slowly, afraid to scare her off. His embrace was careful, his strong hands holding her gently, while his tongue tentatively entered her welcoming mouth. She met it with her own, joining and parting in a long, slow dance of courtship. Time stood still, until at last his hands slid lower, drawing her closer, while his mouth left hers to travel a slow path down her neck to cover her burning breasts, teasingly wetting the dark silk of her robe.

She pressed herself against him, feeling the rigid boldness that she needed to fill the aching void within her. Instinctively, she teased him with her touch, and her body, urging him onward.

Devin was anxious to comply. He lifted her and carried her into the room, setting her down beside the bed. He untied her sash and caught his breath when the robe slid from her shoulders and floated to the floor, revealing her full beauty to his hungry eyes.

Katherine stood quietly, unashamed, while he stared.

He ran his hands over her smooth shoulders and down her arms, raining hot kisses over her eyes, her cheek, and the corner of her mouth. He cupped each breast in turn, kissing it reverently, pausing to brush off his trousers.

Her breath caught, and she melted against his lean frame, thrilling to the feel of skin against skin, breast against breast, and the proof of his desire waiting hot and hard between them.

He lifted her again and placed her on the bed, staring down at her for a moment before he joined her, sinking into her open arms and pillaging her soft mouth of its sweet treasures.

Devin was ecstatic, she was here at last, the axis of his every dream waking and sleeping, and she had come to him freely. He had wanted her for so long, waited for her. He was starving, and here before him was a feast—*more than any man deserved.* His kisses grew tentative, and the cold touch of fear crossed his heart. He raised his head to stare into her smoldering eyes. "Katherine, you're sure... You won't change your mind? You won't leave me again?"

The flicker of doubt in his eyes tore at her heart. But she deserved it, after all, she had given in to the temptation of his kisses before, and then turned from him, and she saw how cruel it had been, for both of them, and she set out to remove all of his doubts, if only for tonight. "No, I want to be with you, I know I shouldn't, but I do." She stared up at him. "I've never..."

"Shh," he comforted, the tender love that filled his eyes touching her heart, as he took her hand and guided her to him.

She rose on her elbow, and kissed him, passing a finely boned hand across his chest and over his hard flat stomach, and Devin held his breath. She sat up, touching and exploring, satisfying her curiosity, testing, loving, and learning. She marveled at the feel of him, a miraculous combination of silk and steel, and at the power of her own touch.

Devin could stand no more of the exquisite torment, and reached an arm around her waist, pulling her down beside him. He crushed her to him in a fevered embrace, his tongue seeking and finding hers, stirring again the passion that burst forth and spread like liquid fire through her veins. His lips moved down her neck, and he kissed the velvet lobe of her ear, grazing across her shoulder, before his hand moved to cover her breast, finding the eager tip awaiting his return and he watched her eyes turn soft and liquid. His mouth followed, leaving a molten trail, as he gained the velvet crest, bathing it in the welcome warmth of his tongue. First one and then the other, he stroked and teased until she pushed upward to meet his hot mouth, burying her fingers in his hair to hold him to her breast.

Katherine was lost in a raging ecstasy. Her breath was ragged, and her heart pounded. She trembled when his heated mouth moved across her stomach in a line of urgent kisses, and a shock passed through her, as his hot palm closed over the tender flesh at the joining of her thighs, bringing a soft cry from her parted lips.

She tensed at the overwhelming sensation, and he waited, willing himself to give her time. He moved to graze her lips in soft kisses and spread soothing caresses over her breasts, her stomach and her silken thighs, until she relaxed and opened to him, inviting his touch, and his kisses grew bolder. She responded, clinging to him, and guiding his head back to her breast while he stroked with tantalizing slowness, tempting and arousing.

She burned, becoming one with the flames of desire he created, as he brought her again and again to the brink of release and retreated to leave her desperate with wanting. When she could stand it no longer, she urged him on with soft whispers, raising her hips in silent confession of her need, and reaching to guide him to her.

He came to her at last, moving with care, watching for her reaction. He paused a moment, not wanting to hurt her, but Katherine was beyond waiting and thrust upward, desperate to be one with him, and complete at last.

He moved with agonizing slowness, increasing the pace when she encouraged him, catching the rhythm and meeting him thrust for thrust. Devin was inspired, selfless in his love, knowing it was her first time, and wanting it to be right for her… A cherished memory and a loving beginning for their life together.

Katherine was desperate, knowing this was all she would ever have, and she wanted to seize every moment. She studied the beloved face above her, darkly handsome and openly sensual, as he kissed her brow and her temple, murmuring sweet words of love. She would never forget this night. She closed her eyes in concentration, frantic with need, yet unable to capture the elusive treasure that beckoned beyond her reach, as he knowingly waited, until relenting at last, sending them both over the edge into a netherworld of passion.

She drew a quick breath, feeling his ragged breathing against her ear, knowing he was swept up with her in the flood of feeling, when wave upon wave of melting desire washed over them, leaving them in warm contentment. She kept her eyes closed, holding on to the precious moments as long as possible. It was a world of wonder, of shared joy, and he had opened it for her. What they shared from the beginning was something unique, but she never dreamed it would be like this. To think, that but for an error of time or fate, it could have been like this always, tore at her heart, but she had vowed not to think of tomorrow, and at her regression tears burned her eyes, and she hugged him tightly.

Devin raised his head and touched his lips to hers ever so gently, and kissed her shining eyes where the tears had threatened. His eyes searched hers for the truth, "Did I hurt you?" He asked in tender concern.

"No," she blushed prettily, "Is it always like this?" She asked, her voice small in the large room.

"Katherine, by all the Saints, I don't think it's ever been like this before in the history of the world," he whispered against her mouth.

She returned his kiss and smiled, and he kissed her again, before he rose on his arms to withdraw from her, but she held him close. "Please don't leave me," she whispered.

"But aren't I heavy?" He questioned, remembering her teasing about his weight.

"Very," she grinned, "but there's no one I'd rather be crushed by."

His brows lifted in tandem, "I should hope not!"

Growing serious, she confessed, "you are not too heavy. It's as if I were made to hold you this way." He stayed, and they whispered, and teased, and kissed, until the mood grew serious and the kisses grew bolder. She watched his eyes turn dark with desire, and she lay very still feeling him grow inside her, marveling at the wonder of it. She smiled, and he grinned back at her, spreading her hair across the pillow, with loving fingers. "The good Lord thought of everything," she whispered, as if anyone else were near to hear.

"Amen to that."

She moved with him, and he carried her once again to the furthest heights of love, with an intensity that left them both breathless. This time he moved from her, to drop by her side, inhaling the sweet scent of her, while he caught his breath. They lay for several minutes not moving, until she felt the absence of his warmth and reached to pull the sheet over them, turning on her side to snuggle against him.

Devin rested his head on his hand to stare down at her, and she hid her face against his chest, placing a tender kiss over his heart. Touched by the sweet gesture, he recalled the April afternoon when he had warmed her under his coat, and she had done the same thing. She was totally captivating, and he was enthralled by her, caught forever in her spell, a most willing victim.

With a stab he thought of Everett Price, and wondered if she had kissed him in the same way. And held him. He crushed the sickening vision, and found joy in a dawning realization. It was her first time. She had said as much. He had wondered if they were lovers, and he rejoiced in his new found knowledge to the contrary. He tried to imagine what hold Price had over her. Knowing her, she was probably too proud to be involved with a married man, unless she loved him beyond reason, and if she did, she would not be here now. Whatever their relationship was, he rejoiced in the fact that she had chosen to be with him, and he kissed her velvet brow and nuzzled her ear. "Remember the ball at the Johnston's?" He asked.

She lay warm and exhausted, lulled by the heavy thud of his heart. "Mm-hmm."

"The next morning, I waited for you. I searched everywhere. I wanted to marry you even then. That's when I wrote you the letter."

She was drifting away from him, toward a sleep of utter contentment, but she was loath to leave him, and she tried to concentrate. She didn't remember a letter, and she shook her head, emitting a negative mumble.

"We belong together, Katherine," he whispered against her temple. "I want to take care of you."

Her tenuous grip on consciousness was slipping, but his words triggered a small alarm somewhere in her brain, and she grappled for what was wrong. *He was talking about the future.* He must feel responsible for her now, but she had made up her mind, she could never be just his mistress. "No." She murmured against his warmth, her breath stirring the covering of fine hair.

"*What?*" He asked too sharply, startling her partially awake, and she tilted her head to look into his troubled eyes.

"You owe me nothing. It was my choice."

"But we'll get married, you'll see." He was trying to convince himself as much as her, frantic to think she would turn him down after all they had between them.

She placed slender fingers to his lips. "Don't make promises you can't keep." She glanced sleepily over his bewildered features, noting again the scratches on his cheek, faded now to the slightest pink, and she caressed them with her fingertips as though she would smooth them away. "I'm sorry I scratched your face," she whispered, her eyes closing.

Devin's eyes grew wide, as her words penetrated his confusion. "Christ!" He spoke loudly, making her jump, and he held her shoulders leaning over her. "Katherine!"

She stared up at him in alarm, her heart thudding. "What is it?"

"Was that really *you?*"

"What?" *What was he talking about?*

"That night on the cliffs, was that *you* I caught?"

"You didn't catch me," she defended. She had been proud of her escape.

"But it was *you?*" He said, more calmly, the pieces falling into place. The slight body he had thought to be a boy. The light weight he had pulled to momentary safety, and the smallish boot that had slipped from his grasp. He had even considered it might have been her for a little while, but had foolishly ruled it out. "But your hair..."

"Pinned." She yawned behind her hand.

"But you fell off the bluff!"

"Yes."

"I looked for you."

"I know." She closed her eyes.

"Why did you run?"

"I didn't know it was you."

"Your shoulder... I did that."

"Mmm," she murmured, drifting.

"I'm sorry."

"It was my fault," she yawned again, "I dropped down."

"Yes," he said, "That was a great, move."

"Thank you."

He watched the corners of her mouth curl slightly, and put a hand to his chest, in recollection. "By all the Saints, woman, you've a kick like a mule!" But she was asleep.

Having been unsuccessful that night, in finding what he had been sure would be a broken body, he had returned the next morning. He had read the route of escape written in the disrupted sand and broken branches across the face of the hillside, but he had found no footprints to track at the base of the cliff, or on the beach. He remembered tipping his hat in admiration of his resourceful opponent, wondering if they might meet again, *and here she was.*

He stayed awake studying her while she slept, imagining what she had been through, and marveling at how much he wanted to keep her safe.

Chapter 16

In the small hours of the morning Devin stirred, coming slowly to consciousness. His arms were empty, and he was afraid. Afraid to open his eyes, lest this dream vanish like all those that had gone before, taking with it the beautiful night.

A feeling of peace and well-being flooded through him, replacing his usual morning despair, and he knew memories too dear, too real, to ever be imagined. Memories of Katherine in his arms, her silken limbs entwined with his own, her urgent whispers, her naked passion… His heart thudded and his eyes flew open, *Saints*, he thought, if wanting and wondering had been torment, wanting and knowing would be devastation. He needed her now more than ever, and she was there. He could feel the soft warmth that radiated from her sleeping form. The single candle had guttered to its last inch, and he leaned to his side of the bed, stretching for the drawer of the bedside table where he had seen her store replacements. In the dim glow, his fingers brushed several objects and closed decidedly on the one he sought. Bringing forth the slim taper he had lit it from the other and placed it in the stand when he was bitten by the demon, curiosity. What would she keep close at hand to aid her dreams, this fascinating beguiler who had stolen his heart? He couldn't help himself, and he reached inside the draw to explore its secrets.

A book of verse, with a touching inscription from her parents on her birthday, made him feel immediately guilty, and he replaced it. Next, he found another small volume in… *French? Did she read French?* He wouldn't doubt it, she was full of surprises. His searching digits found several other candles, and brushed over a soft cloth. *His handkerchief,* embroidered with his initials. He remembered tucking it into her hand as they sat on the sofa.

With a small spark of satisfaction warming his heart, he moved to return the linen to the drawer when something else fell to the mattress, and he picked it up frowning. There in his hand was a lock of dark hair, wound at one end with a lover's knot of thread. For a moment he was puzzled, until he remembered the mended strip of his scalp where Katherine had trimmed the interfering hair from the path of healing. No words of love could have touched him more, and he tucked the small tuft into its cloth nest, and restored it to the drawer, closing it at last. She hadn't said she loved him, and she had tried very hard to avoid him, but she *had* come to him last night, and surely this had to mean *something.* Encouraged, he slid across the bed to join her.

She lay on her side facing away from him, her hair fanned across the pillow, her arms stretched out before her as though she would flee from him even in her sleep.

Devin lifted the sheet to let his admiring gaze roam the length of her lovely back. He found the symphonic blend of fragility and strength deeply stirring, and ran his fingers down the delicate bones of her spine. Careful not to touch the shadow of her bruised shoulder, he moved against her, slipping his arm around her waist and molding himself to her supple form, not knowing how close he had come to the truth.

Katherine was running. Faced with the overwhelming prospect of the lonely life ahead of her, she had chosen to surrender to the heated desires that plagued her, giving herself up to their wanton rulings and taking away a tarnished trophy. A single night. One memory to warm and sustain her through the cold and hungry hours of all her days. Now, in sleep, the power of debate was lost to her, and she fled the turbulent shame of her troubled conscience. In her dreams, as in her mind, she ran in a futile dodging of the truth she could not face. In terror of old she raced the garden path, seeking the comforting embrace of her mother, and knowing with an icy coldness gripping her heart that she would not find it. She reached the familiar gate, and here the recurrent dream varied, drawing her deeper into its web. She did not stumble or fall, but passed the old portal with ease, and once she did, was filled with a growing warmth that spread throughout her breast and touched her heart. With sure unhurried steps she walked onward until she came to the little grove of lilacs, where to her delight she found Phillip.

He appeared as always in her mind, braced on the deck of his ship, the wind whipping around him in great gusts, and he smiled and lifted a hand in greeting. She waved, and when she looked again, Mary was by his side, smiling into his bearded face, and they sailed away into the distance. She was joyous as she waved them off on their voyage, but when they faded from her view, her happiness turned to apprehension and graduated to fear, as footsteps sounded behind her on the path.

Off and running again, she clawed her way through a black wood. Her side ached and her heart pounded in sheer terror, as she crashed through brush and briars, and found herself on the trail above the cliffs. The cottage glowed warmly in the distance, and she raced toward the beckoning comfort of home with her pursuer close behind… And she was falling, the remembered panic engulfing her senses. Through the darkness a sturdy arm snaked about her waist and pulled her against a solid chest.

She calmed at his touch, and caught in the strange world between sleeping and waking, thought that she dreamed yet. This dream, too, was familiar, for many times had the handsome captain claimed her in her most secret reveries. In absolute bliss she rolled onto her back, easily banishing guilt and shame, because in her dreams he belonged to her alone.

Devin stroked the smooth skin beneath his hand, and kissed the warm nape of her neck. Katherine had cried out in her sleep, and his touch was comforting, soothing as he cradled her. His hand moved upward, cupping each breast in greeting, coaxing the sleepy peaks to wakefulness.

A hot wetness enticed at her breast, and the stroking palm wandered down to possess her, rousing her senses. This dream too, had changed, for never before had it continued so, carrying her to such unknown heights of pleasure. Katherine stirred. She was not dreaming. Perhaps she had fallen over the cliff after all, and now she was in heaven…

She opened her eyes to find two blue flames burning into her and her lovers need questing against her hip, igniting her passions further still. She was not in heaven, would probably never go to heaven, but this was close, and if she were to be damned to eternal punishment for her sin, it was too late now, and she gave in to the consuming fires that engulfed her.

Devin teased her deliberately, entering her with tantalizing slowness, cherishing the craving that made fulfillment all the sweeter. He was making her crazy, but she held on, needing release from the sweet torment, but wanting it to last forever. She clung to him, while the ecstatic tension grew, building until she cried out in supplication and he gave what she sought, filling her body and her soul as they reached their golden goal, and came floating back to earth.

"Do you see, Katherine?" He whispered, "It's so right for us, we belong together."

And they did, she knew, and at the unbearable sadness of it, the tears came again, and this time she let them fall. For the heartache, and the joy, and the gratitude for that which she should never have known, and when he faded from her at last, she sobbed against his shoulder, knowing it was forever.

Devin rolled and pulled her onto his chest, kissing her tears away, brushing dampened strands of amber from her cheeks. "I love you, Katherine, please don't cry. I didn't hurt you, did I?" He asked, his heart twisting in concern.

"No," she whispered, "I..." She looked away. What did it matter if she loved him? It wouldn't change anything.

"What? Tell me, please," he begged, hoping against hope she would speak the words he longed to hear.

Choosing her words with care, she finished, "I'll never forget this night."

Hiding his disappointment, he kissed her, and stroked her back, soothing her to sleep. He was so sure she had been about to say she loved him. She must love him, she *had* to.

Remembering her earlier confessions about the scratches on his cheek, when she lay half asleep, he felt temptation tugging at him. *No, it wasn't fair,* and if she loved him, he wanted her to tell him in her own time. In his present position he would be happy to wait. But still...

"Katherine?" He called very quietly.

"Hmm?"

"Do you..." He changed his mind. "You kept my handkerchief."

She her brows drew together; her eyes still closed. "You gave it to me."

"Why did you?"

"*What?*"

"Why did you keep it?"

She opened her eyes, giving him a long level gaze, and Devin was glad he had changed the question. Either she wasn't as asleep as he had thought, or she had only revealed what she wanted, waking *or* sleeping.

"Do you want it back?"

"No." He smiled.

Her eyes closed. "That reminds me," she said, her breath coming soft and even, "what's it for?"

His chest fluttered with humor, beneath her cheek. *"The handkerchief?"*

She shifted, getting more comfortable. "No, the '*T*'."

"The tea?" He asked puzzled.

"Your middle initial. What does it stand for?"

"Oh, *the 'T'!*" He whispered, placing a kiss playfully on the tip of her nose.

"Mmm."

"The '*T*,' stands for..." He drew out the conclusion until the corner of her mouth lifted, in anticipation of the foolish answer he brewed. Devin found the spot irresistible and rolled her onto her back to cover the tiny grin in a lengthy kiss that spread to include the rest of her shapely mouth and the whole of her heart. "The 'T', stands for '*Tonight*,'" he whispered against her parted lips.

A laugh bubbled forth, and she smiled up at him, and then shot him a quick scowl.

"Or, *trespassing*," she scolded.

Devin had the grace to be contrite, "Forgive me?"

"Maybe."

"That reminds *me*," he mimicked, and the closeness of the moment pleased her, even while a stab of pain crossed her heart.

"What?" She asked, scrutinizing every inch of his face, while a small voice counseled through her mind—*Be happy. Be happy while you can.*

"Do you speak French?"

"Oui," her brow rose at the unexpected question, "Why?"

Devin shrugged, "I wanted to know. I want to learn everything about you." He stared and she looked away, growing uncomfortable. It was more talk of the future, a future they didn't have.

"Say something," he coached.

Again, she raised a delicate brow, which he kissed.

"Say something in French."

She searched her brain and smirked, "Voyeur!"

"Noo… not *that.*"

Katherine's eyes lit with inspiration, "Do you know French?"

"No. Well, I know what *that* is. I was only looking for a candle, honest. Cross my heart!" and he did.

She raised her head to press her lips to the spot he had crossed, and then to his mouth, in a lasting caress that flooded her with a bittersweet joy. Resting against the pillows she smiled into his eyes, knowing this was her chance, and her soft words floated to his ears. "Devin, Je t'aimerai toujours. Tu es la chanson de mon coeur. La fleur de tous mes jours… et ma raison de vivre. Sans toi, je ne suis rien."

His gaze was trapped and held, lured into shining green pools, trying to fathom the depth of love there before she broke away to hide in the hollow of his shoulder. He was desperate to know, "What did you say?"

"*Voyeur,*" she whispered, "look it up."

In the last hour of the morning, Devin stirred. His arms were empty, and he cursed the oversized bed reaching out for Katherine. She was not there.

Groggy from lack of sleep he sat up, listening, but no sound reached him beyond the singing of the birds, and the distant siren song of the ocean. Pulling on his trousers, he paused at the door of the bathing chamber, but no movement, no gentle splash, came to reassure his waiting ear, and when he touched the door, it swung open to reveal the emptiness within.

No clatter of glass or silver called cheerful greeting from the kitchen, no lamp glowed warmly in the library lending its comforting guidance to each turning page. A quick run to the bluff overlooking the beach yielded nothing but a haunting vision of a lovely woman in white. In fact, nowhere did he find the remedy that would lift his sinking heart. She was gone. Returning to the bedroom to dress hastily, he spied the bedside table and on impulse jerked open the drawer and cursed. Except for a few spare candles, it was empty. Like the cottage. Like his life, if he didn't find her.

Chapter 17

The War of Secession ground interminably onward, dragging with it the youth and heart of the young country, and leaving any hope of willing reconciliation long lost in its dust. It would be a fight to the finish, and never had American pride and ingenuity been as fierce as when she turned on her own. Torpedoes, land mines, revolving gun turrets on iron-clad ships, and repeating rifles, were only some of the horrors of destruction brought into being by both sides, in a ceaseless search for an elusive ending.

Memories of the battles at Vicksburg, Gettysburg, and Chattanooga raked with open talons across many a mother's bleeding heart, and still they fought. Month by month, hour by hour, the heavy pendulum of fate that had swung first one way, and then the other, was gradually shifting in favor of the North, aided largely by the much-strengthened blockade.

By August of 1864, the Federal Navy had more than tripled its original fleet, and its persistent patrol of southern ports was steadily squeezing shut the frail lifelines of the Confederacy. The encompassing net now captured an average of one of every three or four blockade runners, compared to one of twelve in its earlier days. This, of course, meant even larger profits for the few ships that got through, making the men who sailed them all the more determined, dangerous, and deadly.

It was this sector of the whole to which Captain Galloway had devoted his talents, dedicating himself wholeheartedly to the chase of those he considered the lowest of the low, the Northern traitors. It was over a year now since he had awakened alone in the stone cottage. At first he had been sure he would find her, but it was as though she had vanished. The days had turned to weeks, and the weeks to months, and his determination to find her, had turned into a desperate attempt to forget her. He closed his mind to all they had shared—The look in her eyes when he had held her, and the love—She had never said she loved him anyway.

Gone were the tender moments, and gentle sharing, and in their place, were the cold hard facts. She had left him, and if she *were* in love with Cecilia's husband, she had used him for a night, and he had meant nothing to her. And if he meant nothing to her, then she meant nothing to him. Indeed, he rarely thought of her. Sometimes for as long as an hour.

This was the battle that raged within, as he threw himself into the more tangible war around him, trying to forget. All the hurt, the broken heart, the injured pride, all the poison of the festering wound, was gathered and drawn together, emerging as an ugly, angry hatred directed at those most deserving. And Devin could think of no one more deserving than Everett Price.

In the past months, he had been relentless in his pursuit of the fugitive Price and his operation. Working hand in hand, with the Federal Secret Service, he had closed in on the intricate network, winnowing through the pawns and rooks, until now, when the King himself was almost cornered. That was how Devin thought of him now, *the King, and his Queen, Cecilia,* for she was clearly involved up to her neck. They were at the top of the list, along with Russo, *the bloody bastard* who had shot him, and another sadistic *son-of-a-bitch,* by the name of John Ambrose, the original partner of Everett Price, who stayed in the shadows, financing the ships and banking the profits.

He no longer thought of them as people. They were pieces on a board. Spoils to be captured, and he was obsessed with the game. Cargo after cargo had been seized or destroyed in the ruinous struggle, and Price and Ambrose were fast running out of ships and money, and with the money went the ability to hire others to do the work. Soon they must make an appearance, like rats from their hole, and Devin would be waiting.

In the cold-hearted hour of three in the morning, he stood in the rain on the rolling windswept deck of the Athena, watching. Months ago, he had volunteered his own ship—Her ship—mounting more cannon, stripping her down, and working to build her speed, and make her more battle ready. His one compromise, the imposing figurehead of the goddess Athena, he had commissioned when he had named the ship—*Before she had left him.* Although loath to admit it, he couldn't bring himself to have it removed, so she remained at the bow of the great ship, with her carved gilded hair flowing back from the bow, her proud profile ever leading him on.

He exalted in the chase, and seemed not to care whether the able vessel was turned into kindling or not. *Hadn't she granted her permission so long ago?* It didn't matter anyway. Nothing mattered now.

The grand ship of twenty-eight guns and her able captain were more than a match for most, and his tenacious attitude had netted many prizes, and earned him an outlandish reputation. More than a few men had refused to sail with him, for gossip had him labeled less than sane. Others, having witnessed him standing on the open deck, with enemy shot raining around him, swore he was already dead and returned as a ghost, or a demon, to wreak his revenge on those who had brought him down. Indeed, dressed as he was now in the dark navy issue, and caped great-coat, with his full beard and long black hair whipping about, he could be the Dark Angel himself. Still others, a heartier lot than those given to superstition, signed on eagerly, knowing here was a brave man, and an excellent captain, who knew his business and did his job well. And whether there was any credit to the rumors, or not, certainly the sailing luck of Captain Galloway had been all good.

Even now, while he searched the gray horizon, fortune was with him, hiding him in the rainy mists. True, it hid his prey as well, but he knew their scheme, and they would not be expecting any trouble this far north. He stood with his feet apart, braced against the starboard rail, and lowered the brass-bound hand scope from his eye, to pass it to the stout man by his side. "There she is, Tully. Ready the guns."

The smaller man with a sopping knitted cap protecting his bald pate, held the glass to his practiced eye. "But Captain, she's the Charlotte, from Nova Scotia, and without arms. Could be she's carryin' passengers."

"Aye, the Charlotte," Devin agreed, "but that's our man and he's crossed the boundary now. Look closer at the canvas draped along her sides, she's newly gunned and concealing it, and I'll stake my life, her passengers are a familiar sort of lead and powder." This was enough for Tully, and he went about his duty, while Devin called for full steam and a warning shot across the distant bow.

As the ominous crack split the quiet dawn, the captain of the Charlotte knew he was a doomed man. The ruse hadn't worked. In a desperate attempt to recoup their losses, Everett Price, and John Ambrose, had purchased the Charlotte, an innocent little merchant brig, manned her, and loaded her to the limit with cannon and powder, rifles and small arms, coffee and brandy, all to be sold to the Confederacy at enormous profits.

Gaudette, her newly appointed captain, and a large shareholder, had thought his leg of the voyage the easiest. He was to sail to Bermuda, where his stolen cargo would be transported to several smaller ships of light draft, best suited for the run through the blockade. From there he would take on a load of smuggled goods and go on to England to trade for more arms before making the return trip. It should have worked, but it hadn't. Someone had known, and now it was up to him to make a decision, to stand or run, and he was too heavy in the water to run very fast. He searched the mists for a glimpse of his adversary, wondering if he had a chance in battle, and his heart fell.

A steam frigate of the first rating swept in off his port bow. Bold and beautiful, full sails in play, she closed easily, firing a second warning shot. An unusual carved figurehead, a female warrior of some sort, appeared through the gray dawn like an avenging angel.

He stood in fear and admiration of the fine vessel as she approached, a quick count telling a broadside of at least ten eight-inch guns and two-twelve pounders. Two pivot guns graced the spar deck, fore and aft, and it was from one of these a third shot was fired.

As awesome as she was, Gaudette had more cause to fear his boss, Everett Price, and tried to think how best to win the battle. His orders came at last, to strike the false colors and raise the white flag. And stand by to fire.

When the colors dropped on the Charlotte, Devin barked an order, and his main sails went slack in the wind. He was in no hurry to approach the idle vessel, white flag or no. He had dealt with dozens of Price's men, and not one had surrendered willingly. Those who had been captured alive, swore it was out of fear of their employer's terrible retribution.

He avoided her starboard side and came to rest at the bow of the brig, out of reach of his opponent's broad side, his own pivot guns aimed in a giant V-shape at the runner. He noticed her captain was nowhere to be seen.

Gaudette cursed, and called for a hard turn to port, and fire on sight, as momentum still carried him forward. It was the last order he ever gave. The Charlotte drifted around to her left, and when the foremost side gun came into sight on the Athena, it was fired, as was the second, in quick succession. Both shots, hastily aimed, fell short of the great ship, and her own pivot guns cracked in unison catching the Charlotte amidships at the waterline.

The brig, still turning on hard port rudder, threatened again, when more of her cannon swung into view, but a thundering broadside from the frigate settled the matter most decisively. The Charlotte went down rapidly, with most of her side blown open and a last farewell flutter from the white flag atop her mast. Survivors from the small crew were dragged on board and held under guard, as the Athena set sail for her home port.

Devin stood on the quarter deck, watching the evening skies clear, when Tully approached him, flanked by two other men, James Hubbard, an old hand a like age to Tully, and a younger man called Lattimer who had recently signed on.

Devin eyed the newcomer, as Tully spoke, "That was a good bit that went to the bottom Cap'n," he said, referring to the smuggled goods that were usually sold at auction, and split among the crew.

"Better that being fired upon. We've made more than enough for every man aboard to live quite comfortably, if this hell ever ends. You can't spend it if you're dead."

"Aye, Cap'n. Some a' the boys was wonderin' Cap'n… How'd ya know?"

Devin turned a questioning eye on the old tar. "How did I know what?"

"How'd ya know they'd fire on us under a white flag, sir?"

"I didn't." He shrugged, turning his gaze again to the horizon.

"But, ya must'a," the old man argued, not a bit afraid of this young *specter* whom he knew to be no more than flesh and blood.

Devin smiled a shallow smile, but his eyes stayed distant. "Don't believe everything you see, Mr. Tullane. You can't trust anyone."

The older man would have replied, but he could tell the captain was somewhere far away from the racing ship, and he left him to his thoughts.

A week later the Athena, none the worse for wear, rode peacefully at anchor near Salem, Massachusetts, awaiting the return of her master.

Devin meanwhile, was deep in thought, as he strolled to a small boarding house and tavern on the outskirts of town. The demise of the Charlotte was one of the few bright spots in his dreary existence, and Maggie, the woman he was on his way to see, was another.

Once again, the gentleman merchant, in a fine dark suit, he straightened his string tie and trotted up the steps of the Golden Goose, entering the rustic keeping room.

No sooner had his eyes adjusted to the dimly lit room, but a mug of ale was placed on the bar in welcome, by the buxom red headed proprietress. "Tommy, me boy, 'tis glad I am to see ya!"

"And I you Maggie, and I'll be more so, when I've tasted some of your fine home cooking." Devin replied, looking casually over the sparse gathering of locals, and taking a long drink.

Maggie O'Leary came out from behind the wooden planking, that served as the bar, and sidled up to Devin. Vivacious and pretty, with lively green eyes, she was fond of claiming 'thirty-nine' as her age, and only the morning mirror knew differently. "Will you be stayin' this time?" She asked.

"Aye, the night."

"And shall I have the food sent up, as usual?" She placed a hand suggestively on his lapel and leaned close against him, a knowing smile playing about her mouth.

Devin looked down into her smiling eyes and slipped an arm

about her waist. For a split second, a different pair of dancing green eyes flashed before him, but with an iron will he pushed the image from his mind. "Better still," he said, not bothering to lower his voice, "why don't you show me to my room and we'll eat later."

Several crude remarks accompanied them up the stairs, as they went arm in arm to one of the rooms on the second floor. Once inside, the mood changed, when Devin locked the door, and Maggie pulled the drapes. He smiled at her as she turned from the window, and she laughed happily, crossing the room into his welcoming embrace. "Thank God, you're all right," she whispered.

"And you," he returned, as he released her. "Any news?"

"Shameful this is, Devin, shameful. If my Patrick were alive, he'd be rollin' in his grave."

Devin gave her a look of amusement at the mixed words, but she went on in a rush. "He's in Gloucester!"

"Price?"

"Yes! Mad as a wet hornet he is. Marcus came back yesterday, and the word is, Everett and John Ambrose are trying to raise the money for another ship."

"Already?" Devin cursed, "I thought we'd put them out of business this time."

"I know. You may yet have, though. They are out of funds. Even if they get a ship, they would need more money for the cargo, and they have had so many failures of late, I don't see who else would risk the investment—Or their life. Something else too, bad news, I'm afraid."

"What?" Devin asked, his senses tensing.

"J.T. has been murdered. They found him in the bay, and they're sure it was Everett."

Devin sat, thinking. In the past year, Everett had left Boston, and moved gradually up the coast to the north, trying to keep his illicit operations afloat. J.T. was another contact in Beverly, where Price was staying before the Charlotte sailed. It was J.T. who had alerted them about the Charlotte. "No proof, I suppose." He asked without hope.

"No, luv, sorry."

"Was he shot?"

"No."

Devin glanced at her, as she shuddered and drew a finger across her throat.

"Do you think he talked?"

"*No way.* I knew him." She sighed, and sat on the edge of the bed. "Unless…" She looked at Devin with a sinking heart, "I guess everyone has their breaking point." They stared at each other, both knowing what it could mean if one link in the delicate chain of secrecy were to break.

Maggie took a deep breath, "Well, we may never know. No sense dwellin' on it."

"You'll have to be extra careful," Devin warned, "and, Marcus."

"I'm keepin' 'im home, from now on. He's only thirteen, and he's all I've got. I'll not lose him to this damned foolishness."

Devin smiled at the love and pride, that leapt into her eyes, whenever she spoke of her beloved son. "Right, then." He gave her a nod of approval, "Any other trouble?"

"Not much, except…"

He waited.

"You won't believe it." She laughed self-consciously.

"Try me."

"Well, ya see, it's the locals. A few of 'em, when they've had an extra ale, and when they've got an extra coin, they've propositioned me, right out, like I was one of those regular painted hussies. Can you *imagine?*"

Devin smiled, "A credit to your acting ability dear lady, and your beauty, of course."

"Aww, go on with ya." Maggie waved him off and rose to leave. "I know one thing. When this is all over, I've got to find another place to live."

"Any place you say Maggie. I'll take care of you."

She nodded. It was what he always said, and she had high hopes he meant it. "I'll see your supper's sent up. And a bath?" She asked, knowing it was his usual want.

Devin nodded as she opened the door.

"Maggie?"

She turned.

"About the propositions..."

She waited.

"Did you accept?"

Shaking a threatening fist at him, she went good-naturedly, if red-faced, down the hall. She loved Devin. She had known him forever. It was too bad he joked so seldom these days. *He was not his old self a'tall.* She paused at the top of the stairs, her smile waning, as she thought how she'd love to get her hands on the careless flirt that had hurt him so deeply. She might do murder herself.

Chapter 18

August 1864–Katherine

Dorothea Sawyer sat comfortably in the drawing room of North Hill, her home in Portsmouth, New Hampshire. She smiled observing the antics of her small pale-haired daughter, Amy, and the child's aunt, as they played a favorite guessing game, each conjecture more preposterous than the last. For the most part, she studied Katherine, pleased at the progress she had made since the night she had shown up here, nearly a year ago, in utter despair.

Katherine and Evelyn had only come for a visit, as they had already booked passage to England, but Dorothea had known immediately something was very wrong. She had never seen her sister so distraught. The next weeks had proven her suspicions correct, as she wheedled bits and scraps of the story from her older sibling. It was a man, of course. An unavailable man, and beyond that, her sister was very closed mouthed. Even Evelyn, who had accompanied her, had little to say about the whole situation, and Dorothea had pressed no more, respecting her sister's privacy. She had, however, along with her husband Keith, and help from the birth of their son Phillip, last December, persuaded the two ladies to stay here in Portsmouth for as long as they wanted.

Evelyn, being happy wherever there was a garden to tend, and Katherine, seeming not to care where she was, had been there ever since, renewing neglected relationships. Amy, at the age of four, had immediately attached herself to her Auntie Kate, drawn to the woman so like her mother, except for her eyes, which were green instead of blue. Katherine had found in the child, an outlet for all the love she had to give, and the two had become inseparable. Gradually some of the light had returned to her eyes, and she had begun to smile again.

Still, Dorothea knew, her sister was not as she used to be. The sparkle in her eyes was missing, the smile not as broad, the zest for life forever dimmed. Or so she had thought, until last May, almost three months ago, when Katherine had given birth to a beautiful son. Since then, at least some of the joy had returned to her heart.

More girlish giggles interrupted her thoughts, reminding her to play the cruel mother. "I'm afraid it's past your bedtime, Miss Giggles."

"Oh, Momma." Large blue eyes and an impish grin looked pleadingly from mother to aunt in a familiar evening ritual.

"Come on Twinkles, I'll see you up," her mother said, scooping the small sprite in the long white nightgown, to her hip, and thinking at that moment the child looked exactly like Keith.

"I'll come along," Katherine said rising, "I want to check on Gabriel."

With Amy tucked away for the night, after the usual stall tactics, Dorothea stopped in the nursery to check on her own sleeping son, eight-month-old Phillip, before joining Katherine in her room. She smiled at the maternal vision before her, as her sister sat rocking the tiny babe. "I never thought I'd see the day," she teased.

Katherine smiled up at her, and down at the child in her arms before she spoke, "I still can't believe it. I know what I did wasn't right, but I wouldn't change the result for the world. Sometimes though, I wonder what Mother would think."

"She'd think what I think, Kate, that he's a beautiful blessing, but..."

"But, what?"

"Are you sure that his father shouldn't know? I mean, imagine if you didn't know you had a son like this."

"It's not possible." Katherine said solemnly, and Dorothea knew the subject was closed. *For now.*

Her sister left her alone with her son, and thoughts of his father. *It had been so long…* She closed her eyes and rested her head against the sturdy rocker. So long, since she had crawled from his side in the pre-dawn, and left him alone, a thought that still caused her to cringe in conscience. But she had struck a bargain with herself. To settle for a night—*One night*—and she knew if she waited until dawn, it would be more than she could stand, and she might never leave him. So she had left, without so much as a note. Little did she know at the time, she had taken away so much more than she expected.

All that time ago, and still, Devin was with her, and always had been. In everything she saw and everything she did, there was something to remind her of him, and nothing ever more so than this miniature image, with dark blue eyes and a mass of tiny black curls. God had been so kind to her, *more than she deserved*, and she couldn't help wondering if Thea was right. *Was she being unfair keeping their son a secret?* Would she survive seeing him again? *Leaving* him again? She missed him. Everyday. She missed his voice, his laugh, and his kindness, and the way he made her feel that…she mattered, when nothing seemed to matter anymore. She thought back to the months just before Gabriel was born. She had been overcome with nervousness, home sickness, and missing her mother. She wanted to get away, and planned to travel alone to the cottage to gather her soul, much to the dismay of her sister, and against the advice of Evelyn. Keith had solved the dilemma by offering to have one of the ships enroute to Boston, continue down the coast to drop her off, and return to pick her up before heading for home. It would be much quicker and easier than traveling alone and by buggy.

The ship had anchored off the beach and the men had rowed her to shore, promising to return in four days' time. Four glorious days to gather herself. Time to think, and clear the weeds from her mother's marker. But even then, she could not escape her memories, or the hold Devin had on her heart. She traveled the sandy path upward with her basket of provisions, rounding the corner of the cottage, and stopped and stared in wonder. Masses of Scottish Bluebells lined the path to the back door in welcome. They were everywhere. By the gate, mixed in with the seagrass, and out by the budding lilacs in her mother's garden. *When had he done this? And why, after what she had done?* She recalled now, as she did then, the words he had once spoken, *'I don't believe you, and I won't give up'.* She brushed at a tear, and did her best to deny that deep in her heart she hoped it were somehow true.

The following afternoon while the babies took their naps, Katherine, dressed in a cool summer dress of pale green, and began to braid her hair. In a sudden change of heart, a bleak smile touching her lips, she combed it out again and tied it back with a simple white ribbon. It was a beautiful afternoon and she sought out Amy for their daily excursion. It was a favorite time for both of them. Katherine, enjoying the company of the lively little girl, and Amy, reveling in the undivided attention of an adult. Sometimes they took a picnic lunch to the small pond nearby, or to any of the many sites of the large farm. Occasionally they took the buggy, and once in a while Katherine would hoist Amy upon the broad back of Matilda and walk the shaded pathways that crisscrossed the hills and woodlands behind the house.

"Hello, young lady, where will it be today?" Katherine asked, finding her little friend on the side veranda.

"Granny Tendwell's"

"What?" Katherine asked, not understanding.

"I want to see Granny Tendwell," Amy repeated, scrambling from the floor to take Katherine's hand. "I know she's there, Papa said."

"Well," her aunt asked thoughtfully, "where does this Granny Tendwell live?"

"Up back… *You know.*"

"That big house on the hill, you mean?"

"Yes," Amy replied, already dragging her across the backyard and into the woods. "We can go this way."

They walked awhile in silence on the sun dappled path, and soon the well-worn trail wound upward topping a small hill. The dense trees thinned and they stepped from the shade into the bright sunlight, finding themselves in the backyard of a large three-story house.

Katherine stared in admiration at the attractive rectangular dwelling of white clapboard, with dark green shutters. It had a deep, welcoming porch that ran around the whole of it, the roof supported by sturdy round columns. "Oh, what a lovely home!" She exclaimed aloud. "But, are you sure someone's here, Amy? It looks deserted."

"*I think.*" Amy replied, looking anything but sure of herself, and towing Katherine to the front.

A stone walkway led past a huge oak tree, and across the sweeping lawn to the front door. There were two large barns, and several outbuildings and caretakers' cabins in the distance, all neat and white like the house, but still no sign of inhabitants.

"*You knock.*" Amy whispered, cowed by the heavy silence, broken only by the occasional sound of the birds.

She did so casually, to please the child, sure that no one would answer. In fact, when a petite elderly woman opened the door to peek out at them, it was difficult to say who was more surprised.

Katherine recovered first. "Oh, hello, Mrs. *Tendwell?* I'm sorry to burst in on you. Amy said you were her friend, and…" by way of explanation, Katherine pulled the cowardly Amy from behind her skirts.

The woman's pleasant face cleared in recognition. "Oh! And so I am. Come in child, come in," she said, opening the door wide in welcome. She extended her hand to Katherine, as Amy scampered past them both into the hallway with a jubilant, "Hi Granny!"

"You *must* be related to Dorothea. You look so like her."

Katherine took the hand of the stately little woman dressed in black chiffon. She had the bearing of a queen, that was slightly intimidating, but beneath a crown of silver hair was a kind face with warm brown eyes, and she liked her immediately. "I'm Dorothea's sister, Katherine, which makes me the aunt of this runaway train."

The older woman smiled brightly, "I'm Helen Trendwell, although, 'Tendwell' has a nice ring to it."

Katherine smiled apologetically, while Helen stooped to coax a hug from her small neighbor. "I hope we haven't disturbed you?"

"Nonsense child, you make a dismal day a little brighter. We are about to take some refreshment, and it would please me to have you join us. My daughter Anne is in the garden, and our hired man Wes, is here somewhere. Do come along."

It was obvious that to decline was out of the question, and amused, Katherine followed as she was told. They walked down the wide center hall, and she could see it led the depth of the house to a rear entrance much like the front, the transom and sidelights of the doors flooding the space with sunlight. A grand stairway rose on the right and led to a railed balcony that ran the perimeter of the space above them on the second floor. Katherine could not contain her enthusiasm for the splendid old house. "Oh, Mrs. Trendwell, your home is beautiful!"

"Thank you dear, please, call me Helen. Yes, we've had some wonderful years here. My late husband, Robert, had it built to his specifications, and he was so particular! If you like I'll show you the rest of it later." She paused, looking around the great hall herself, and shook her head sadly. "We've come to close it up you know."

"What a shame!" Katherine sympathized, wondering if she should offer assistance of some kind.

"You see," Helen continued, "with Robert gone, and my only son, Paul... He was lost at Shiloh."

"Oh, I'm so sorry," Katherine murmured, putting a hand out to her new friend.

"Thank you dear, I know the war is hard on everyone. Well, Anne has her home—she prefers to be in town—and I'm going to stay with her, and there's no one... I had hoped to sell, but with the war and its uncertainties, no one seems much interested in an old horse farm. But I'm prattling like an old woman, which I am," she added with a smile, as she led the way through a doorway at the end of the hall, into a huge kitchen with a granite hearth. A bank of windows and another back entrance lined the rear wall, from which could be seen the neglected gardens. It was through this door that Anne appeared, a younger version of her mother with pretty light brown hair.

After a shared lunch, Helen and Anne conducted the promised tour, and Katherine fell more and more under the spell of the charming house. Amy scampered about the hallway, and Katherine scolded her, trying in vain not to smile, but Helen assured her it was all right.

There was a lovely library, cozy and warm, and a small private parlor. The overlarge drawing room was cheerful and bright, and Katherine thought it perfect. "Oh Helen, it's wonderful, how can you bear to leave it?"

Helen Trendwell shrugged. "It *was* wonderful once, full of family and friends, but it's a cold and lonely place for one little old lady. You see, it was a home then, and now it's nothing but a house." She smiled distantly, and Katherine nodded, her own eyes filling with tears, "I understand."

They crossed the hall again, and at the double doors before them, Anne and her mother exchanged glances before they threw them wide. "Oh!" was all Katherine could say, and the other women smiled, pleased with her reaction, as she walked into the center of a huge ballroom decorated in gold and white, with two crystal chandeliers, and the biggest marble fireplace Katherine had ever seen. Helen laughed aloud, "My husband, God rest him, thought he was the governor! Or at least as important… and perhaps he was. Come to think of it, the governor was here quite a few times."

Amy ran about in excited circles, stopping here and there to turn little pirouettes, on the polished floor. Katherine walked the perimeter of the room admiring the grand piano in the corner, the fireplace, and the massive dining room set on the rear wall. She returned to join the women who stood bathed in sunlight from the floor to ceiling windows, and the doors that led out to the porch and gardens beyond.

Upstairs there was a master bedroom with a separate bathing room, and off the open balconied hallway were numerous bedrooms, more bathing chambers, and a room at the front used as a private study. The back staircase continued another flight where there were several comfortable rooms for the help, and in the center of the third floor, more stairs wound upward to a widows' walk. Helen waited, while the others took in the view of the harbor in the distance.

Katherine thought the whole of it was breathtaking. When it was time to leave, and the small party descended the stairs, she paused on the landing. "You know, Mrs. Trendwell, if you're still looking for a buyer, I would be very interested myself," she said shyly.

Both of the other women looked surprised, and it was the elder who spoke. "Oh, I didn't... Are you sure, dear?"

"It's a beautiful house, and it's near my sister, and I can't go home right now… for personal reasons, and I can't live with Thea and Keith forever. I've been there too long already."

"It's a very big house, child, have you a large family?"

"No," Katherine answered looking down at the floor, "only myself, and my infant son, and my friend, Evelyn."

Helen was kind enough not to pry. In these days of sorrow, there were many things people would rather not discuss. "Well dear, perhaps someday you will. If you're serious about the house I'd be happy to sell it to someone who would care for it as much as I, and I would be most pleased if you would consider perhaps keeping my helpers. They are lovely people and I hate to put them out of work. There's my housekeeper, two maids and kitchen helpers, my cook, and a groundskeeper. They have no place to go, you see. I'm sure they would be most grateful. Aside from a few pieces—mainly the desk in the office—which was my husband's, we've taken what we want, and I think the rest can go with the house, if that's all right?"

"Yes, of course," said Katherine, growing more excited by the minute, "and you would always be welcome."

Helen eyes filled, as Anne moved close to place a hand on her mother's shoulder, "That does make it easier to let go. Bless you, child."

Helen and Katherine went to the study to discuss arrangements, while Amy played in the hall with Anne. A price was named, which Katherine found more than agreeable, and with a promise to return soon, she collected Amy and they started for home.

"Are you going to live there?" The child questioned as they worked their way down the hill.

"Yes, at least, some of the time. What's wrong, Twink?" She asked, noting the serious mien of the little girl, while they made a game of stepping from tree root to tree root.

"Can't you find people when they get lost?"

"Well of course, why do you ask?"

"Then couldn't we look for Uncle Paul?" Amy asked, a puzzled expression filling the large eyes that gazed solemnly up at her aunt.

"*Uncle Paul?*"

"Yes, Granny said he was lost, but if we look for him, maybe we could help her find him, and then she would be more happier."

"Oh, I see," Katherine said, wondering what the child knew about death.

"Well, Twink, people who are lost in the war, aren't lost like… Like your kitty was, you remember? And we searched and we found her?"

"Yes." The blonde head nodded, concentration knitting her tiny brow.

"When people say someone was lost in the war, it means they… It means they died there. Do you understand?"

The little girl considered this for a moment, and nodded. "Oh," she said, and they walked on hand in hand.

"Auntie Kate?"

"Yes?"

"Is that what happened to Gabriel's papa?"

"What?"

"Did he get lost too?"

Katherine knelt before the innocent child, and hugged her tightly to hide her sudden tears, "I hope not, Sweet. *I hope not.*"

Chapter 19

In his guise of independent merchant, Devin plied the North Shore, seeking minor cargo and major information. This time he had left Boston for Gloucester, and sailed on to Portsmouth to visit the large shipyard.

With their business completed, on this early September afternoon, most of the crew took leave for the nearest tavern, while Devin stood by the rail planning his next move.

"Excuse me, Captain?" One of three men, who were loading some merchandise onto a heavy dray across the dock, approached him. "I wonder if you could lend us a man for a delivery? We're short a hand today and this is a heavy load."

"I'm afraid everyone's gone, friend, except those who drew watch. Have you far to go?"

"No sir, we shouldn't be too long," the man said, hope filling his eyes.

"I'll give you a hand then," Devin offered. "I wouldn't mind going for a ride."

The four men loaded a heavy mahogany desk, and several rolls of sculpted carpet. Devin lifted a corner to examine the luxurious green rug with pink and white roses carved into the border. Next came a large nursery goods crate to complete the load, and he hopped on the wagon as it pulled ponderously away from the docks. Color tinged the trees against a backdrop of a brilliant sky and he enjoyed the countryside, until several miles from town, when the slow-moving dray turned off the road onto a long curving drive, and he gazed longingly over the scene ahead.

Atop a low rolling hill, in the midst of sweeping lawns and open fields beyond, sat a house worth coming home to. Its welcoming facade spoke of care, and family, and all the things he hadn't thought about for so long. He was homesick. Homesick for a place he had never been. He wanted a place of his own. He had lived in inns, and rooming houses and aboard ship, for so long, it seemed that was all he could remember.

They placed the carpet in the front hall, and carried the nursery crate to the master bedroom. It took all four of them to maneuver the heavy desk into the upstairs study. When they were ready to leave, Devin stopped on his way out to compliment the elderly owner on her lovely home and her good taste.

"Oh, thank you, but I didn't choose those things. I'm selling the house, you see, I'm only here to get it ready."

"Are you?" Devin took in the great hall once again, in admiration. "Is it final yet?" He asked, a mixture of hope and doubt warring inside.

"We're to sign papers tomorrow."

"Oh," he frowned. "You wouldn't change your mind, say, for a better offer?"

Helen gave him a look that would have shamed Satan. "I could never do that. I'm afraid it is out of the question. It would not be right."

"No, I suppose it wouldn't," he agreed. "My apologies." He bowed deeply before she walked with him to the door. "Good day, Madam."

"Perhaps, sir, you should return to meet the new owner. She's very attractive," she said, a mischievous gleam in her eye.

Devin laughed good naturedly, at the smiling woman. "Madam, if she were half as lovely as you, I should be lost instantly."

Helen smiled and watched him join the other men. She looked at the paper he had given her with his name, and an address where he could be reached, in case the sale of the house did not work out, and tucked it away, knowing she would not need it.

The following morning, Dorothea and Keith accompanied Katherine and her son into town, while Evelyn watched the Sawyer children at home. Keith had business to see to, and Thea had agreed to watch Gabriel and do some shopping while Katherine met with Helen Trendwell at the attorney's office to finalize the sale. Afterward, the three would meet for lunch, before they returned home.

"Thank you so much, Helen." Katherine said, as they stood outside the lawyer's office and she embraced the older woman. "Remember, you're welcome to visit anytime, and with your permission, I'm going to keep the name 'Trendwell' for the estate. Maybe it will bring me luck."

"Why, thank you dear, I think that's a splendid idea, and I *shall* visit you at Trendwell." She smiled, trying out the name for Katherine's benefit. "I hope you'll be as happy there as I was, but if ever…" Helen hesitated. "Now, don't take this the wrong way, child, but if for any reason you should decide not to stay, I have the name of someone else who was interested in the house after all. Just this week—imagine, all that time—and then two offers!"

Katherine left her, assuring her that she would not be moving anytime soon, and spent the half-hour left before lunch window shopping, and day-dreaming of the little things that would make Trendwell her own.

Captain Galloway left the dry goods store and stood in the warm September sun, surveying the busy street, when he saw her. He bolted down the steps and into the crowd, scattering pedestrians and animals alike, weaving his way through the shoppers, much as he had a long-ago day in the Boston marketplace. This time though, he did not take his eyes from the slim back and the pert bonnet perched upon the golden head. Feeling as though he moved in slow motion, he reached her, placing a hand on her shoulder when he came up behind her. "Katherine!" He gasped.

Grabbed from behind, she spun to face a tall handsome man with a crazed look in his riveting blue eyes. Dorothea stared. She noted the attractive, though haggard features, and the curling dark hair, and knew immediately who he was. Her mind churned with fear, and with pity, as the glimmer of hope died in his eyes. "I'm afraid, I'm not..."

Devin swallowed hard, his hands shook and his throat was dry. He felt like a fool. Of course she wasn't Katherine, he could see that now. She wasn't quite as tall, her hair was a few shades lighter, and her eyes were blue, and not the green he had so hoped to see. He had thought he was over this, seeing her on every corner, across every room. He closed his eyes. The last he knew, she had booked passage to England, and he had not been able to arrange a long enough leave to track her down—*Yet.*

"Are you all right, sir?" Dorothea asked, torn between what she felt was right, and loyalty to her sister.

Christ! She even sounded like Katherine, he thought, *or did she?* Perhaps what was left of his mind was playing tricks on him. "I beg your pardon. I thought you were someone else. I can't find her..." He finished disjointedly.

"We've all lost far too much in this horrid war," she sympathized.

"I'd sooner lose my life than my mind." He offered an apologetic smile, and as he looked upon the baby, a strange expression crossed his face.

Heaven, help me! Thought Dorothea, panic making her heart race.

Would he guess? Did he know this was his own child?

Devin smiled into the tiny visage, whose eyes studied him so seriously. He offered a long forefinger to be accepted and clutched in a miniature fist, and the small trust touched his heart. He never took much notice of children, nor gave them much thought, but somehow... He had a sudden revelation that he would like children of his own, a thought that surprised him. Perhaps it followed the general feeling of homesickness that had plagued him of late. *Perhaps you're getting old,* he chided himself. "A beautiful child," he said, as Thea stood in tense silence. "A boy?"

"Yes," she choked out, feeling trapped in a bad dream, glancing around, wishing Katherine would somehow appear.

"A son to be proud of," he complimented. "You're very fortunate."

"I'm afraid I must be going," she whispered, backing away from him. "I'm meeting someone." *Should she invite him?*

"Of course," Devin said, dragging his eyes from the baby to meet hers. "Again, I apologize, I had no right."

She nodded, and hurried off, thinking he had every right. Every right in the world.

Devin watched her go until she entered the hotel down the street, and did something he rarely did. He turned abruptly and headed for the nearest tavern.

Dorothea entered the hotel dining room and went straight to her sister. "I saw him! *Gabriels's father.* It was him. I know it was. And he looks terrible. I don't know how you can do this."

Katherine smiled benevolently. "You're guessing again. You think every man with dark coloring and blue eyes is De... Is him. And besides, he is very good looking," she said, looking down to the floor.

"*I know!* He is quite handsome, and the baby looks so like him, but he does not look well. He is quite distraught."

"Thea..."

"When he came up behind me, he called me, *Katherine!*" She put as much force into her whisper as she dared with the few other diners in the room.

Her eyes met her sister's in alarm, and Katherine rose to her feet. After all, he *could* be here in Portsmouth; it wasn't so very far away. She didn't even know where he lived before the Johnston's.

Finding that realization disturbing, she reached for her cross, in her old habit. She had never gotten used to not wearing it since that night in the cottage, when she had removed it, and placed it under her pillow. In the morning, she had forgotten it in her haste, and the time she had returned, she had not been able to find it. She lifted her sleeping son to her shoulder, and implored her sister to leave with her.

They met Keith on their way out, and explained that they had decided to go right home after all, and he went to have the carriage brought around. While the two women waited, Dorothea tried again, "Are you *sure,* you don't want to look for him? Now's your chance to tell him."

"I can't. There are things you don't know."

Dorothea played her ace, "He saw the baby."

"Oh…" Katherine faltered, unsure of herself. "Did he say anything?" She asked in a whisper.

"He said, 'he was beautiful. A son to be proud of.' Unless he harmed you in some way, it's not fair Kate!"

Katherine closed her eyes and hugged Gabriel closer. "I need time to think. *Please*, take me home."

Devin sat at a lonely table in the crowded barroom, and ordered his second drink. He went over and over the strange meeting, trying to put a finger on what it was that still bothered him, *aside from making a fool of himself.* Perhaps it was the knowledge of how easily he had jumped to the conclusion that it was Katherine, after all this time… *Or how happy he was to see her.* He laughed bitterly, and gulped the last of his drink. He was glad it hadn't been her. He had played the fool for her one time too many, and when he did see her again, *if he did…*

Mid-way through his third drink, he was feeling much better. Anyone could mistake an identity; it happened all the time. But, somehow, for those few moments, he had felt so close to her, and they looked so much alike, *they could be sisters…* The amber liquid sloshed from the glass, as he jumped to his feet, and fumbled to slap an overpayment on the table. Three blocks away, he burst into the hotel, nearly taking the door from its hinges. The dining room was empty.

Dorothea and her sister had left for home, and Devin could only wonder how close he had come to finding the one who plagued him. He had not seen Katherine with her son, that fateful afternoon, but someone else had.

Chapter 20

The cold night air matched the heart of the rider, on a horse as big and black as the night itself. Beneath a dark cloak, the black clad figure spurred the horse on, as they flew through the northern countryside in a desperate dash of hope.

Devin had not known earlier, that when J.T. was murdered, he was the fourth victim in a vengeful line that stretched from Gloucester, to Beverly, to Danvers. They were all good men, in the Federal Secret Service, all killed in the same manner after being tortured, and all, he was now certain, by the same man. J.T. may not have talked, but someone had.

Everett Price had never stooped to doing his own dirty work before, but now he was out of money, and in his world, if you were out of money, you were out of friends. He was desperate. Desperate and vicious, and looking for revenge. Devin had received word that Everett was on his way to Salem. *Salem and Maggie.* At the thought of his kind and jovial friend, he drove his heels down hard, spurring his mount faster, praying to the heavens he would reach her first.

The Golden Goose was dimly lit, as he threw himself from the heaving horse. Drawing his shotgun from the saddle, he cleared the steps in a single leap, to find the lock blown from the door. Inside, he stumbled upon the body of young Marcus, and his stomach turned over, as he knelt momentarily beside the boy.

A horrified scream split the night, and he bolted up the stairs to smash his shoulder into the door of Maggie's room, sending it to slam in splinters against the wall.

She lay across the bed, and kneeling over her—there at last—was the elusive Everett Price.

Devin's eyes met hers, and his heart was strangled by her look of anguish, while at the same time his soul flooded with a euphoric triumph. He savored the moment, feeling the power surge through his chest, turning his nerves to steel. A wicked smile formed, and a startled Price stared beyond the barrel of the gun, to meet the cold blue eyes of death.

Devin's quick gaze had taken in the scene, the torn dress, and the clothed man. He was in time. Price looked much the same, but his eyes were large in a too thin face, his dark hair graying at the temples. He was showing the strain of the past few years… *Aren't we all*, he thought, before finding his voice. "Is this how you get all your women, Everett?"

The other man glared at his adversary with eyes that spewed hatred, "*Galloway!*"

"Aye, finally, and you have no idea how glad I am to be the one to end your miserable existence. You're an infection on this earth, a vile contamination, *and look*, I hold the cure. For make no mistake, your life is over."

Price scrambled off the opposite side of the bed dragging Maggie with him as a shield. It was then Devin saw the ugly gash that ran the length of her jaw, and the oozing cuts that crisscrossed her chest; an intricate necklace displaying its beads of blood, and his rage soared.

Everett retreated into the far corner, seeking a means of escape, and the blade of the knife shone menacingly in the lamplight.

"Give it up, Price. There's no hole for you to slither into here; not this time."

"I'll kill her," he warned. "You know I will."

"She's a woman. Let her go, and I'll give you a chance to fight me, fair and square—but hurry—There's a patrol on their way here right now."

Price scoffed. "You don't expect me to believe that."

Devin shrugged, reminding himself to remain calm, even as his heart pounded, and Maggie stood with a terrified expression, her tangled hair matted with blood and tears, and her eyes locked on his. They waited.

Faintly above the night wind was heard the pounding of horse's hooves, and a few shouted orders. Everett cursed and glanced toward the window. Devin choked back the scream of anguish that rose in his throat as Maggie gasped and straightened, her eyes wide. She fell forward, to reveal the ivory handled knife, sheathed in her back.

The level of the shotgun never wavered. Fighting for breath, she pulled herself across the floor out of the way, while Everett reached for his holstered gun. Devin glanced at his friend and read the question in her dying eyes. "Marcus lives," he answered, and as she struggled to smile, he pulled the trigger.

Two weeks later, and a number of miles to the north, Katherine was in her room at the Sawyer home, putting the baby down for his afternoon nap. Evelyn would soon be moving with her to Trendwell, but until they could get everything prepared, and order linens and supplies, they were staying on with Thea and Keith. In fact, it was Dorothea's opinion that they should stay through the winter, and move in the spring.

Katherine sighed, watching her sleeping son. It was also Dorothea's often stated opinion that the child's father should be informed of his good fortune, and Katherine was beginning to think it was the only decent thing to do. Of course, Devin had one child already, she debated mentally, and it would surely cause him hardship if it were known that... From the front lawn came excited shouting, and Thea was yelling her name. She crossed the room and looked out over the sweeping front lawn to see a familiar carriage arrive, and a tall man in a federal uniform running for the house.

Her heart soared, and with tears of joy already streaming down her cheeks, Katherine whirled and ran for the stairs. Gaining the front porch, she threw herself into the jubilant celebration and the arms of her brother. She hadn't realized how fiercely she had missed him, until she held him in her arms and gazed into his eyes. *William! An element of her life, of her parents, a piece of her heart back where it belonged. Not only home, but home to marry Louise!*

Sometime later after the surprise had subsided, Katherine found William getting settled in his room, and took the quiet moment to introduce him to his youngest nephew. She paused in the doorway, holding the tiny bundle, and admiring her handsome brother. Broad shouldered, tall and blond, with his blue eyes and dark reddish beard, he looked more like Phillip than ever, but the smile he gave her was his own, a mixture of memories… A lifetime of brotherly teasing, love, and pride.

"Come on, I won't drop him."

Katherine smiled shyly, and placed the child in his arms.

"He's so little!" William exclaimed in awe, rocking the child carefully. "He's wonderful, Kate."

At a loss for words, Katherine couldn't help the tears that came again, this time in sadness.

"Hey," William reached one arm out, to pull her close against his comforting shoulder. "Did you think I wouldn't like him?" He teased, and she shook her head.

"It's that I don't know what to say… and you look so like father."

He led her to the sofa. "Come and sit down and tell me about this little guy. Thea told me some."

"That's all she knows," Katherine said smiling, now, before she grew serious, again. "I'm sorry I had to write you about father, and mother. It's an awful way to find out."

"I'm sorry I couldn't be here."

They sat in silence for a few minutes, until Katherine spoke again. "Everything's changed so much."

"I know he answered, I've seen more changes than I care to think about. But you know, even if the war hadn't come, things would have changed. It's part of growing up. At least we had what we had, while we had it. And now we have it to remember."

Katherine nodded, as they spent a moment together in the past. "I have father's journal, if you'd like it. Neither Thea, nor I, have had the heart to read it."

"I'd like that."

A light knock sounded on the door, and Dorothea poked her head into the room. "What do you think, Uncle, shall we keep him?"

He smiled broadly. "I think I've got the best-looking pair of nephews, and the most beautiful niece, in the world!"

"That's what I thought too," the younger sister replied, beaming, but she couldn't pass up the opportunity to press her point. "Don't you think his father would feel the same way?" She whispered.

Katherine put her hands over her face, and gave an exaggerated moan, Thea began to laugh, and William looked from one to the other. "I can only speak for myself, but if he were mine…"

"*All right, all right,*" Katherine said in good humor, rising to take Gabriel off to feed him, "if you're going to gang up on me, I'll consider it."

"Ha! I'll believe it when I see it," said Thea.

The middle sister did not surrender easily. "Speaking of '*Yours,*' William, you must tell us all about the wedding."

"Oh, yes!" Dorothea chimed in, and began to pelt him with questions, and Katherine gave her brother a sisterly smirk, as she headed for the door. "But wait," Thea, paused, "the coffee will be ready, and I'm sure Evelyn and Keith will want to hear too. Hurry, Kate," she called over her shoulder, and took William's arm, as they went down to the parlor, to catch up on all that had happened since they had parted.

William told them parts of his adventures, and how he had gone directly to Ezra upon his return home, and proposed to Louise, who had, of course, accepted. He didn't tell them of the point in battle, when his ship was damaged, and he feared he had waited too long, and the chance may never come.

Katherine joined them just in time to hear William say, "We will be married as soon as we can make the arrangements." "And Judith Caldwell *agreed?*" She asked incredulously, pouring herself a cup of tea, and going to stand by the fireplace.

"Of course," William spoke haughtily, sitting up straight in mock importance. "You don't think she would let such a good catch get away, do you? Besides, Ezra had already said yes."

"To your happiness," Keith toasted, lifting his glass of brandy high in salute, "*and* your mother-in-law."

"That's a contradiction, if I ever heard one," Evelyn mumbled to one side, and everyone joined in the toast and the laughter.

"How soon will it be?" Thea asked.

"Only a week or so I think, we're keeping it very small, we just need time to invite a few friends, and give you time to get there."

"That's pretty quick," Keith commented.

"I insisted," William smirked, "And if Mrs. Caldwell doesn't like it, she doesn't have to show up."

"I don't notice you saying the same about Miss Louise," Evelyn observed, and William grinned his agreement, as the others looked on affectionately.

"I guess the Johnston's won't be coming, being in mourning," he added.

Everyone spoke at once, "*Mourning?*"

"Oh, hadn't you heard? Ezra told me."

It was Evelyn who recovered first, "Mourning for whom?"

"Their son-in-law. I don't know his name. He was killed a few weeks ago. Very messy business." He turned to Keith, and lowered his voice, "Took a shotgun blast to the gut, poor bas…"

"*William!*" Thea and Evelyn scolded in unison, and Keith hid a grin.

For one, the brightly lit room grew dark, and four heads turned toward the fireplace, where a fine china tea cup shattered into fragments on the hearth. For the first time in her life, Katherine McKenna Lawrence had fainted.

A bold knock interrupted the sanctuary of her darkened room, and she lay silent, hoping whoever it was would go away.

They did not, and the knock came again.

"I'm not hungry, Alice, thank you," she called.

The door opened abruptly, and Evelyn trundled in, carrying a tray with hot tea, fresh cinnamon rolls, and a large glass of milk. Without a word, she placed it on the bed, went to open the drapes, and stood with arms akimbo. "It's *Thursday.*"

Brilliant sunlight flooded the room, and Katherine gave her a glaring look through swollen red eyes, before they closed again. "Is it?"

"You can't stay in here forever."

"Why?"

The older woman pursed her lips and silently tapped a foot on the thick carpet, thinking. At last, she went and sat on the bed, and began pouring out the tea.

Katherine's stomach rumbled and she opened her eyes. "I don't feel like eating."

"I know, but you might as well. Nobody ever died solely because they wanted to, and you won't be able to keep feeding that baby if you don't eat."

The young woman eyed her friend, pushed herself up on the pillows, and reached for the tea cup. She wrapped both hands around its warmth, took a sip and closed her eyes. "I can't believe it… I can't." Tears came again, and she used one hand to wipe at them with a crumpled gray and white handkerchief.

Evelyn's own eyes watered and she placed a soothing hand on Katherine's shoulder. "I hate to see you like this, Kate."

"Do *you* think I should have told him about Gabriel? I was going to ask your advice." Her anguished eyes looked beseechingly to her friend, and Evelyn prayed for the right words.

"I decided long ago, that you're too old for me to be telling you what to do."

Katherine shot her a skeptical look, but Evelyn only smiled. "You've had to make some very tough decisions, and I think you've chosen well."

They looked toward the cradle where the little one lay sleeping. "In spite of my little consequence?" Katherine asked.

"Life is full of consequences, but some aren't too hard to take, are they?"

Katherine began to eat. "I'm grateful to have him, especially now, but do you think I should have gone to see Devin?"

"More importantly, I think you would have. You know as well as I do, by the time you ever ask my advice, your mind is already made up."

This time Katherine smiled, but without humor, and Evelyn poured her some more tea.

"I think you're right. I never really believed I wouldn't see him again."

"William feels terrible, you know. He thinks it was his vulgar description that set you off."

"Oh. He knows me better than that—or he used to."

"*Don't you understand, Kate?* They don't know what's going on, and the longer you stay in here, the harder it is to explain. I mean, why should you care about him to this extent, unless...?" She glanced toward the baby.

"Oh." Katherine said, sitting up a little straighter.

"The wedding is set for next week. Do you think you could rally a little enthusiasm and try to act normal?"

"I suppose."

"That would be a first," Evelyn mumbled under her breath, and Katherine slapped half-heartedly at her arm.

Gabriel woke, mewling softly, and Evelyn went to collect him and pass him to his mother. "It could be worse, you know," she said, touching the downy dark curls and heading for the door.

"Yes." Katherine agreed, knowing she might never have had the baby, or the memories of that one night of happiness she had shared with his father. "Thank you, Evelyn."

"Kate?" Evelyn turned from the door. "Do you believe what they are saying?"

"What?"

"Oh, I guess you didn't hear the rest. William heard he was a murderer and a traitor, and he was shot by a federal agent."

Katherine's mouth opened in shock, and she recalled his pleading look when he had asked her to trust him. "No! Oh, it couldn't be! I know it couldn't," she cried, an anguished frown seizing her already ravaged countenance.

"I don't believe it either." Evelyn lifted a questioning brow. "I wonder what we could do about it." She closed the door behind her, and went down the hall, quite pleased with herself. There was nothing like righteous anger and a good cause, to bring one back to life, or at least out of bed.

Chapter 21

William and Louise were married on a crisp and beautiful day that crackled with promise, for everyone but Katherine. But this was their day, and she did her best. She hid her tattered soul, and laughed and smiled, and no one, with the exception of dear Evelyn, knew that her very heart was missing. She stood bravely by Louise's side, in her lavender satin, witnessing the exchange of vows and the giving of the rings, and if tears flowed then, who could say they were not tears of joy for her brother and her friend, and they were, in part. Only Evelyn, in her vigilant concern, noticed how often Katherine reached for her necklace, in habit, to find the smooth pearls she had chosen for the occasion, and not the solid piece of strength she sought.

After a small reception, at which Katherine deftly managed to avoid Judith Caldwell, the newlyweds departed, and the rest of the family returned to the Lawrence's Boston house that would now be William and Louise's home. There they would stay the night, and return to Portsmouth in a few days.

In her old bedroom, Evelyn helped Katherine remove her gown, so she could hurry in her chemise and petticoats to nurse Gabriel, nuzzling and kissing his velvet cheek. "I hate leaving him, even for a short time," she said, caressing his dark locks, and thinking he was more like his father every day.

"But you are…" Evelyn half questioned.

Katherine nodded, "Thea will watch him."

"I'm going with you."

Two ladies, in somber dress, alighted from a Lawrence carriage at one of Boston's main cemeteries. They proceeded unaided, to the Johnston family plot, but found no new grave at which to pay homage.

Katherine clutched the bouquet of white roses she had brought, and released a shaky breath. Her mind was a blank and she turned to Evelyn for guidance.

"Could be he's not in the family plot for some reason," her friend murmured, and took her elbow to steer her toward the caretaker.

"Help ya?" The disheveled old man offered, in his clipped New England speech, removing his soft cap in respect.

Evelyn spoke up. "Please, we're looking for a Captain Galloway." She lowered her voice when Katherine turned away to stare into the distance. "Devin Galloway."

The old man scratched his head, torturing Katherine with his contemplation. "Galloway… Galloway. When'd he die?"

"Recently, within the month, I think," Evelyn whispered.

"Nope. Got one Mista' Galloway and that's Robbie, and there's his missus, but they been heah a long while." He ran dirt-stained fingers through the white stubble on his chin. "Nope. I ain't got no more."

"Shouldn't you check the records?" Evelyn prompted.

"Don't need ta." He swung an arm out to indicate the long neat rows of gravestones that surrounded them in the late afternoon light. "I know 'em all lady, new and old, I been heah for yeahs. I'll check if ya like, but I know."

"Thank you, I guess it's not necessary," Evelyn said, taking Katherine's arm again.

"If ya don't mind my sayin' so, Missus, if he got it in the war, he could be anywhere, they don't all come home ta rest."

This time Evelyn didn't bother to thank him, and when the carriage stopped again, it was in front of the home of Cecil Johnston.

"You sure you want to do this?" Evelyn asked doubtfully.

"I'd like to know where he is," Katherine answered, her face white. She held her breath while Evelyn knocked, but there was no answer. She stepped forward and knocked longer and harder until she was pounding on the door, and the older woman took hold of her wrist to stop her, but still no one came.

"I'm sorry," Evelyn consoled, when they had again settled in the carriage.

Katherine turned to her with tears in her eyes. "There's nothing… Not even a wreath." He deserved so much better. From everyone, including me."

The days crept by with agonizing slowness, and Katherine tried to occupy her mind with the refurbishing of Trendwell, but her heart wasn't in it. Little by little it dawned on her that when she had bought it, she had secretly harbored the hope that somehow, someday, Devin would share it with her. Now that hope was gone, and she often found herself considering whether to ask Helen Trendwell for the name of the other buyer. After all, there was no reason not to go home to the cottage now.

Always, she changed her mind. The new house had been her hope for the future, and she was afraid if she gave up on it, she would give up on everything. There was her child to think of, and perhaps someday it would be his. She did long to visit the cottage though, and perhaps she would visit soon.

She spent comforting hours with the children, finding it a great help to view life through their eyes. In their sight, the world was a place of wonder, and the smallest joys were the most important. When she felt cornered by her thoughts, as she often did, she would seek escape by taking a long ride on her beloved Matilda. But no matter how far or how fast she rode, she could not leave her heartache behind.

A small flock of clouds huddled on the horizon, snow-white against the brilliant blue of the sky, while the October sun set the surrounding hills ablaze with color. Katherine, in her favorite riding clothes, had hastily braided her hair and donned her old overcoat, before riding out to survey the friendly miles of Trendwell. The crisp air painted roses on her cheeks, and numbed her gloved fingers, as she cantered the pathways and byways of her home, giving Matilda a thorough work out.

Both tiring, after the lengthy ride, she turned the large black homeward and let the animal choose the pace, traveling a quiet lane that would lead them to the main road. Katherine was drawn from her wandering thoughts when Matilda stopped and gave a soft neigh, her ears stiff in attention. Taking a firm hold on the reins with one hand, Katherine gave the horse a soothing pat, and spoke to her softly, while she searched the lane ahead for the source of trouble. Seeing nothing, she urged her onward, but Matilda only tossed her head in obvious distress, sending a tiny shiver of fear to slide down Katherine's spine. Struck by the deep silence of the surrounding woods, she grew more nervous. She urged the horse sideways so she could have a better view beyond the bend in the lane, and caught her breath. Hidden in the deep shadows of the trees, a lone rider sat waiting.

Her blood ran cold. Perhaps it was her already frayed nerves, or the rumors of a recent confederate raid in nearby Vermont, but she knew she was in danger. Wasting no time, she wheeled Matilda about, and sent her racing in the opposite direction, only to be brought up short when their path was blocked by a second rider, who seemed to appear out of nowhere. Katherine braced herself to keep from sailing over the horse's head when she reined to a sudden stop, and in the next moment she was snatched from the saddle by a strong arm, and forced face down over the back of the other horse, in front of the silent rider. "What do you want?" She demanded, trying to keep the panic from her voice, but he gave no answer and started down the lane toward his waiting accomplice.

She reached one arm underneath her to grasp the saddle horn and keep it from gouging into her side and would have untied the cinch holding the saddle in place, but she needed two hands. The blood was rushing to her head, and she began to feel ill, as she hung upside down from the plodding horse. Her mind raced. Even if she had a weapon, she couldn't reach it, but she could reach the nearest rein, and like lightning, her gloved hand shot up to snatch it, and yank the bit painfully, pulling the surprised horse in circles.

The rider was caught off guard, and sensing her advantage, Katherine forced her arm upward and the bullied mount reared, sending the cursing man to land on his back in the road. Clinging to her hold for dear life, she managed to pull herself into the saddle and gain control of the frightened beast. Much like before, she whirled the animal around and was about to dig in her heels, only to come face to face with three more mounted men, one of whom held a pistol aimed at her heart.

From time to time in her life, the headstrong young woman admitted defeat, if only temporarily, and wisely, she determined this to be one of those times. A time to wait, and watch, and see what could be learned. Bound and gagged against further resistance, Katherine was again hoisted to the back of a horse surrounded by the group of men. The one she had bested, and nearly escaped from, seemed to be their leader. But even so, he was the object of their heckling as he came to his knees in the dirt. She knew she had made a hateful enemy. As far as she was concerned, the relationship was established long ago, and the hatred was mutual. His name was Russo.

The little group paused upon reaching the main road, and pulled roughly from the horse, Katherine struggled to keep her footing when a blindfold was added to her bindings. The last view she had before the dark cloth closed off her sight, was the burning resentment that shone in Russo's black eyes, and beyond him, the last glimmer of the setting sun, gilding the road that led to North Hill, home, and her child.

Chapter 22

Once Katherine was blindfolded, she found herself dumped unceremoniously, onto the floor of a moldy old coach, and with plenty of time to think as her strange journey continued, she tried to put her rambling thoughts in order. Matilda would have returned to the barn, she knew, and even now, Keith and some of the hired men were probably out searching for her. Thea and Evelyn would be worried, and Amy… Gabriel would be awake, and hungry. At the thought of her son, a tightness invaded her throat and her milk surged to cause a painful fullness in her breasts. *But he was all right, he was safe, and they would take care of him.* The best thing she could do would be to keep her wits about her, and use whatever opportunity arose to return to him. *To all of them,* and this was the thought she clung to, while the carriage rumbled on in the twilight.

At one point, the quiet dirt road gave way to the washboard rhythm of cobblestone, and soon after she heard the hollow sound of wood. The rickety old coach pulled to a stop, and Katherine was hauled from the musty interior. She stood for a moment, besieged by the pungent odor of low tide carried on the evening breeze, before she was roughly grabbed by the arm and led through a doorway.

Inside, someone fumbled with a lamp, and it grew brighter. She was escorted across the room and sent sprawling into the dark, as a second door closed behind her. She had not been prepared for the sudden shove, and she hit the floor hard, unable to brace herself. She was not badly hurt, but lay still for a moment, pulling herself together, and wondering what in the world had brought her to this predicament.

Russo couldn't know she had been on the beach those nights, when she discovered the smuggled guns, unless someone told him, and the only ones who knew were Evelyn and Devin. At the thought of Devin, she closed her eyes against quick tears as a thousand memories flooded from her heart. It didn't make any sense. Russo had shot him, and she had saved him. He wouldn't have told on her, *but neither was he able to help her.*

How she wished he were with her now. The mere thought of that powerful body and confident attitude brought a smile in spite of her tears, and the thought that he was dead remained beyond her comprehension. She would never get used to it, never stop expecting him to appear at her elbow, the way he had so many times, to tease her, and look at her *that* way.

With a surge of anger, she sat up and raised her bound hands to wipe at her eyes and pull the blindfold off. The gag was loose already, from her work in the coach and she let it drop down around her neck, as she sat blinking in her nearly black world.

A tiny sliver of light shown under the door, and here and there in the rough plank wall, were spaces through which she could see the moonlit night without. She moved closer, and as she suspected, was in an old warehouse along the wharf on the harbor, but *why?* If her connection to Russo wasn't Devin, what was it? She needed to know, but at the moment, after all that time in the coach, she had more pressing needs, and began to search the small room, as her eyes grew accustomed to the darkness. On one wall was a dilapidated straw pallet with a questionable covering, and a stale smelling blanket that she normally would have burned. In the corner nearby, was a broken chair, a bucket of water, and an old chamber pot. She gave silent thanks, because she would rather have died, than have had to ask for one.

Hours later, she lay on the straw pallet, huddled in her heavy coat and covered by the old blanket, which seemed slightly less offensive in the middle of the cool night. Earlier, one of the men had untied her, and left her a supper of bread and beans, and although she disliked the strong black coffee that came with it, she savored its warmth, and drank a few sips to wash down the scant meal. Her full breasts were agonizing and she took the opportunity to expel as much milk as she could, spilling it into the straw, and ignoring the sadness that burned behind her eyes. Now, like any model prisoner, she lay quietly working at the rope that once again bound her hands. She had loosened the knot with her teeth, and was so deep in concentration, that she almost didn't notice the slight creak of the door.

It sounded again, and she froze, when a shadowed form entered her small prison, and silently crossed the room. She had wondered if they would come. From the coarse remarks, and leering looks she had received from all but one, a huge young blond called Hann, she had almost been sure of it, and had tried to prepare herself with what little was at hand. But, as the hours had come and gone in peace, she had relaxed. Now she got to her feet to face her intruder. Moonlight passed through the ill placed planking to cast the room in silver shadows, and she watched him move closer.

"So, Mrs. Macey, we are alone at last."

Russo. She had prayed it wouldn't be him. For a moment she was confused, until she remembered the name she had given him to keep him from finding her, long ago, and seeing no reason to correct him, she said nothing.

He spread his hands against the wall on either side of her and leaned closer, his foul breath hot against her face. "This time though, the circumstances are a little different, eh?"

Still, she said nothing, but turned her face away from him.

"Come now, you know what I want, and if you are nice to me, I'll be nice to you. Her plan is crazy."

Her? Katherine let him talk.

"And you being a widow, I would think…"

"A widow?" She asked dumbfounded.

"Oh, I checked," he told her snidely. "I had people looking for you, but you disappeared. I know your husband was killed at Chancellorsville. Walter, wasn't it?"

"*Yes*, Walter," she repeated, wondering just how stupid a man could be.

"You must miss him." His rude smile flashed in the silver light. "Enough talk," he said, pressing his weight against her and moving his mouth toward hers.

She struggled to pull away, so his wet kiss landed along her jaw, and thought she might be sick.

He sneered, as he reached inside her open coat and began to fumble with the buttons of her blouse.

She stood seemingly pliant, until he moved to kiss her again, and she brought her knee upward, as hard as she could, catching him squarely between the legs. *Exactly like William had taught her when she was twelve.* When he doubled over, she brought her knee up again, to smash into his face, and send him sprawling backwards onto the floor. Her instinct was to run, but she heard sounds in the outer room. Would they help *her*, or *him?* By the time he had risen to his knees, blood pouring from his nose, the tall blond filled the doorway, backed by the others.

"So, Bernie, she has brought you to your knees again," he crowed, in a heavy German accent. "Once was not enough for you?"

The other men guffawed, and Russo glared at them all. He was in agony. He had blamed the afternoon's incident on his skittish horse, not wanting to admit he had been outdone by a woman, but now... There she was, staring him down, and they were laughing again. He never expected such an attack. *Dio! No decent woman would know such things!*

He got painfully to his feet and came toward her, but the German stepped between them, towering above them both, and shook his head. "Nein."

The smaller man nearly boiled with anger and humiliation, and leaned around the giant to threaten her. "If you were a man, I'd kill you for this!"

"Perhaps," she answered, "if *you* were a man, you would have the courage to face me with my hands untied."

Russo was furious. He glared at the German, and the big man smirked at him, while the other men laughed in the background.

"If she were a man," Hann pointed out, "you would not be in here in the first place."

"Or would ya?!" Someone else hooted from the safety of the group, sending everyone but Russo and Katherine into near fits of hysterics.

"Just leave me alone with her for a minute," he begged. "One minute."

The big man rubbed his clean-cut jaw thoughtfully, and Katherine moved her bound hands to her belt, where she had hidden a stout jagged rung from the broken chair.

Finally, Hann spoke again, "Well, I would, Bernie, but I wouldn't want you to get hurt."

The fresh outbreak of laughter was too much, and cursing, Russo shoved his way from the room. Outside the doorway, he turned with a final threat, and Katherine met the chilling depth of his stare. "I *will* have you!" He swore through clenched teeth, before stumbling from the room. The other men filed into the outer room, except her protector.

He was quite a pleasant looking man she noticed, with his high cheekbones and short cropped light hair, as he untied her wrists. He smiled at her when he noticed the loosened knot, and for a moment he gazed into her eyes. He paused at the door, "Russo means what he says," he warned.

"So do I," she replied, "and I'll die first."

He studied her, deciding she did mean it, and he admired her spirit. "You won't have to worry as long as I am here, yah?" He glanced around the bare room. "If you need anything, you call me. My name is Günter Hann. We will get an early start in the morning."

Günter, too, meant what he said, for before dawn the next morning, she was awakened by a high-pitched wail of a voice that she would have recognized anywhere. *Cecilia!* What was she doing here? Crawling closer to the thin wall, she had no trouble hearing, and listened intently to the exchange between Cecilia and Russo.

"Did you get the brat too?" Cecilia demanded.

"No, the house was empty. It does not belong to him, I tell you. Her name is Macey, just like I said. I checked with her last night."

"That ain't all he checked last night," someone interjected, and there was muffled laughter and then silence.

"I can find out," Cecilia said.

"Dio! We do not have the time, and this damn plan of yours is piss poor if you ask me." It was Russo. "Are you sure your father doesn't know?"

"Oh, shut up! I got the money, didn't I! I got the ship. Daddy's been gone for months. By the time those notes are called in we'll be long gone, and she's, our insurance. Go see to the rest of the loading, and come back when they're done."

Russo left, and Katherine tore through what little information she had. They were smuggling again, that was clear enough—and Cecilia was involved! They had wanted Gabriel, but why? Thank God he wasn't at Trendwell. She could only think that Cecilia knew about herself and Devin, and was seeking revenge of some kind. But how would she know? And Cecilia must have stolen from her father to supply a ship, and wanted her for insurance of some kind… Footsteps sounded near her door, and Katherine scampered to her pallet, pretending sleep, when Cecilia entered and shook her.

"Cecilia!" She whispered in her best surprised voice, her eyes assailed by the woman's glaring red dress in the light of the lamp she carried. "What on earth are you doing here?"

Cecilia played the old friend, and Katherine let her go on about old times, and how circumstances change things, and how she needed Katherine's help to aid her dear father.

"You could have *asked* me." Katherine said, wryly, but Cecilia changed the subject.

"Dear Katherine, did you ever marry? I saw you in Portsmouth, with a baby."

That was how they had found her! Katherine thought quickly, this was a game she could not afford to lose. Perhaps if Cecilia were convinced Gabriel was someone else's child he would be out of danger.

"Yes, unfortunately Walter was killed…" She let her voice trail off sadly. "But I have a son," she added. "A wonderful son… Walter and I. He looks like his father." This, at least, was not a lie." She could almost see Cecilia's mind at work.

"Oh." Cecilia frowned, "It said in the paper, Walter Macey was single when he died."

Dammit! Katherine took a deep breath. She didn't know anything about Walter Macey, she had only listened to Russo, of all people, and now she was on uncertain ground. "Cecilia, can you keep a secret?"

The overdressed woman leaned forward in greedy anticipation, and Katherine tried to keep her voice normal, as she glanced away in mock shame. "You swear?" She waited for the blonde head to nod. "He promised to marry me as soon as he came back," she whispered dramatically.

Cecilia nearly cackled. "That's what they all say, but I'm surprised *you* fell for it!"

Katherine shrugged dejectedly, "We all make mistakes."

"Yes, everyone but the high and mighty Lawrences!"

"You promised!"

"Yes. Well, don't worry, there isn't anyone here for me to tell about your little bastard." She grinned, "I guess it can wait until I get home."

Katherine looked at her, rage burning in her chest. If it wasn't for the men in the other room, she would wring her neck. With deadly calm she changed the subject. "You had a child, too, didn't you?"

"Yes, and my husband is dead too. Kind of makes us the same," she tossed out.

Katherine lowered her eyes, "I heard he died terribly."

Cecilia's next words took Katherine's breath. "He deserved it, and I don't miss him."

Katherine drew a steadying breath and wished she could kill her twice.

Cecilia rose to leave, confidant her plan would still work—And perhaps Katherine was not so bad after all. *She had a bastard brat with Macey, and she had to have been seeing Devin at one time...* "You know, there was a time I thought you were after Devin."

In fact, she had been certain the reason she herself, had been unable to seduce him, was because he was in love with Katherine. She remembered her last attempt when he had returned home after having been missing for almost two weeks. She had stolen the key, and in the late evening, had slipped into his room. Unfortunately for her, her timing had been poor, and when he jumped, bellowing, from the tub, wrapping a towel about his waist, her father happened to be passing in the hallway. In a rage born of embarrassment, Cecil had ordered her from his house forever, and she had gone, leaving Everett's brat behind.

Afterward, she realized, that the gold cross she had seen against Devin's bare chest, was the same one she had seen so often on Katherine. She had been beside herself with hatred for her rival, but now, she could almost thank her for turning the tables on Devin, and taking off with Walter Macey. *So that's where she had disappeared to,* Cecilia thought. *She had gone off to hide while she had Macey's brat. And meanwhile, Devin had turned Boston upside down, looking for another man's whore! Oh, this was wonderful!* Cecilia chuckled aloud, deciding to let her in on the joke. "You know what, Katherine? The last time I saw Devin, he was still wearing your cross!"

She left, and Katherine stood staring at the closed door. Her hand lifted absently to her neck, where the piece once hung, warm and comforting, but her thoughts were far away, caught in the storm of one rainy August night of long ago.

Chapter 23

Plunged into the depths of despair, Katherine's newest prison suited her well. She sat in a small cubicle, below deck on the Christina, the small overloaded schooner that they had boarded in the early dawn. It was cramped and dark, but she didn't care. It seemed like weeks since she had seen the light of day anyway. Since the last remnant of the New England coast had receded in the distance, she had battled her doubt of seeing home and Gabriel ever again. Although she still didn't know why she was here, she knew Cecilia and Russo were on board. Two of the most ruthless people she had ever known, both of whom hated her overmuch.

The only friend she had now was Günter. When it was his turn to guard her, he would often sit on the inside of the little room and let her share the light of his lantern. She found that he was quiet and shy, and they passed many hours talking. In spite of her circumstances, Katherine found herself smiling at his gentle humor. He spoke often of home, and she wondered how he had come to be part of this terrible crew. This night he brought a book to her, and asked her to read to him.

To Katherine, it was a lifeline. A treasured reminder of another world, and a key to the passing of time. "Thank you, Günter, what a wonderful idea."

"Maybe not so good," he said.

"What do you mean?"

"I have stolen, but when you are done, I can put it back."

"*Borrowed,* then," Katherine corrected, with a smile.

"Borrowed, yah. You will read to me?" His cheeks turned pink as he confessed, "I have not learned reading."

When she offered to teach him, he was thrilled, and began relieving some of the other men who took turns on guard duty, so that they could have more time together. He was a fast learner and was making good progress, and she found his enthusiasm somewhat cheering. It wasn't until one night, when he began to talk about the future and the home he was going to build when the war was over, that Katherine realized there was more in his pleasant blue eyes than the love of learning. "…just a small farm, but my own." He went on in his heavily accented speech, "and… You won't laugh?" He stopped to plead.

She gave him a kind smile, and he continued, "I want to raise chickens. That is why I am here," he rushed on to explain, "I just need a little more money." He searched her face hopefully, seeming to need her approval, so she kindly gave it, and withheld comment on his method of attainment.

"There's nothing wrong with chickens, Günter, that's a fine dream," she encouraged.

"I have told no one, ever," he beamed at her and before he left, he kissed her on the cheek, and she let him hold her for a moment. It was nice to be held, to be wanted by someone kind, and big and strong, who could keep her safe, but it wasn't the same. It would never be the same.

"Will you think about it, Katherine?"

Drawn from thoughts of another man's arms, she became aware that he had proposed to her. It was out of the question, and it wouldn't be fair to him. She would always belong to Devin. Even now, his memory brought a quickness to her pulse and a renewed sadness to her heart. She couldn't love another, but she didn't want to hurt this kind soul, and she couldn't afford to lose him as a friend. "Günter," she said gently, "there's so much you don't know about me."

"I know you're the finest woman I have ever met," he hesitated, and blushed severely as she watched in amazement, "and I know I love you."

"But surely this is no time to make plans. Look at the mess we're in, and you can't get out now, it's too late."

The gentle giant took her hands in a pleading manner, "I will get us out of this, you will see. Besides, no one wants you hurt, you are only here for the ins…ins…"

"Insurance?"

"Yah, the insurance against that crazy captain, that hunts us like dogs. Cecilia says if he knows you're with us, he will leave us alone."

Katherine was puzzled. "Who?"

"Some say he is maybe Satan." He laughed. "The Dark Lord, they call him. Cecilia says she wants him because he killed her man, but all here know that is not the truth." He lowered his voice, "I was told, if her husband hadn't died when he did, Cecilia and Ambrose were going to kill him anyway, so they could take over everything for themselves."

Her breath caught, at Cecilia's cruelty, but she paid careful attention. "Who is Ambrose?" she asked.

Hann hesitated, "I have not met him. I know only that Cecilia and John Ambrose are partners, and at first, they made a lot of money bringing guns to the South. But they kept trying to make more, and now they have lost too many cargos. Unless we are successful this time, Ambrose will be ruined. No more money, and no more shares for men like me. Anyway, this will all be over soon, yah? So, you will think about what I said, Katrina?"

"Yes," Katherine answered absently, and when he walked away with the lantern, she was left more in the dark than ever.

The next evening, Katherine was doing her best to pace in the limited space allowed her. She guessed it was nearly time for Günter to return, and she was still wondering how best to tell him she couldn't marry him, when someone approached outside the door. There was muffled conversation and a slight argument, before the guard take his leave in a hurry. With growing apprehension, she waited for the door to open, and met the caustic glare of Russo.

Time stopped, and in that fraction, she registered that he had two faded black eyes, and his nose was crooked. Before she could move, he grabbed her by the shirt front and slammed her against the wall knocking the breath from her, while his heavy fist shot out to hammer the delicate bone of her cheek. She turned her face away avoiding the brunt of it, and when she hit the floor, she had the revelation that they had not been guarding her against escape.

She fought with all her might, but Russo sprawled on top of her, his hands grasping and beating. She kept turning her head, protecting her nose with her arms, claiming at least that small victory, and when he gave up, and tried to push her arms away to capture her mouth in an open kiss, she bit his lip.

He slapped her hard across the face, and caught her again with the back of his hand. Seeing she was dazed, he took the opportunity to rise up and unfasten his trousers with eager fingers.

Think, think! Katherine twisted and writhed, struggling to sit up, her hands were free, but she was pinned by his weight. He reached for her again and she pushed his face away and struck at his neck with the sharp wooden dowel she had hoarded. He ducked away, and she missed, driving it through his cheek.

He clutched his face and screamed.

She heard shouting above her own screaming denial, and watched through a fog when Günter came hurtling from the passageway, to sweep Russo off of her in one powerful leap. The rumble of thunder sounded in the distance, as both men rolled and crashed into the wall, and she watched in horror, as Russo pulled his pistol and fired, hitting her savior squarely in the chest.

More running feet sounded in the hallway, and wild shouting filled the hold, but Katherine paid no mind. Her sight was on the one who lay bleeding, while Russo rushed from the room, holding his face, and trying to button his trousers on the way. She crawled to where Günter lay in the corner, and lifted his head onto her lap. He was badly wounded, and she knew it was only a matter of time before the strong young man who had been her friend, *who loved her,* would die, and leave her once more alone.

His eyes fluttered open, "Katrina, you answer me now. Will you… when the war is over?"

She smoothed his hair, and whispered the words he wanted to hear, "Yes, Günter, when the war is over… I'll marry you." She kissed him then, tears falling freely, and she saw him smile, and when he closed his eyes, she knew he had gone home at last.

By slow degrees, her mind cleared. She was alone, and it was not thunder that sounded outside. She grabbed her coat and slipped it on as she ran for the stairs, only to be met by three men.

Her hands were bound behind her, and she was escorted aft of the schooner where Cecilia and the others stood waiting. They were watching a large frigate, magnificent in full sail, and sporting an ornate figurehead. The ship was gaining rapidly. Cecilia turned to look at Katherine's battered face and stared. She opened her mouth as if to speak but changed her mind.

Katherine thought they had all lost their minds when they began frantically waving their arms and caps at the pursuers, but, when

Cecilia gave the order, and Russo himself, lifted her over the rail and let her drop, she understood. When the frigate stopped to save her, they hoped to make their escape.

Surely, this was not the plan? Even Cecilia wasn't that stupid, Katherine thought, as she plunged downward into the foaming wake. She hit feet first, and the momentum carried her far below the surface before she could kick herself upward for another breath. The large ship was close now, and she waited, treading water with only her legs. Stray tendrils of hair clung across her face and the salt water stung her eyes, but she could see, and she watched in terror as the great ship sailed past, leaving her behind.

Her first thoughts were of her beloved son. *She had to live for his sake!* Her boots fit tightly enough so that they did not fill with water, but neither could she kick them off. She could normally tread water for a very long time, but the coat was heavy, and with her hands tied behind her, she struggled to stay afloat. The muscles in her legs were burning, and she tired and sank under the surface. *Only for a rest.* The cold water felt good against her face, even as it stung the cut on her lip, and she closed her eyes, listening to her inner voice… *You've been swimming since you were two, Katherine, I never thought you would drown… But does it really matter how it ends? Life is too hard, and full of heartbreak. Who would miss you? William and Thea… Amy… Thea would have to explain to Amy. Evelyn. Evelyn will be all right; she is stronger than you are.* She only hoped they would be safe from all the terrible things in the world. *There were bad people… people like Cecilia and Russo, with their dark hearts and cruel eyes…* She jolted to full awareness. *Sharks!* Her eyes flew open, and she fought the panic that rose in a scream she could not utter. She wouldn't think of the gaping mouths, and the sharp jagged teeth that could rip through flesh and bone, or how they were attracted by blood. She wouldn't think about how they could move silently through the water and strike out of nowhere, or their black lifeless eyes—*eyes like Russo's...* At least, she had escaped Russo, and maybe now, if he were caught, he would get what he deserved. *She wanted to know.* Even if she could only hear the battle from the distance, she needed to know if they were captured, and she struggled to the surface again determined to witness their downfall.

She could see both ships stopped some distance away. They were not coming for her. There must have been little or no fighting, for the schooner was being boarded. Her legs were leaden, and with the heavy coat pulling her down, she knew she would have to be satisfied with this last view of her captors turned captive. Still, fighting to the end with what strength she had left, she took another breath, and savored the warm sun on her face before she went down preparing herself to die.

This was odd, this drowning. She had never considered it much. It was almost as though it were up to her when to give up. She would live as long as she had the strength to go on. But she was weakening, and in the end, she knew it would be her physical strength that failed her and not her will. She didn't know if she were dreaming, floating in a semi-conscious state, wondering why she had tried so hard. *What difference did it make?* She had stopped trying to pull her wrists free. *Even if she were free to swim, there was nowhere to swim to. It was only a matter of time.*

Her last thoughts were of Devin. *She could be with him now. Cecilia said he had worn her cross.* She was glad. He must have discovered it that morning under her pillow. If she had thought of it, she might have given it to him, except for the fact that Cecilia would recognize it, and apparently, she had... She had never found him, but at least, wherever he had been laid to rest, he had something that was a part of her. *Yes, she was glad, and now she was glad Cecilia knew...* The ocean had always reminded her of his eyes. She searched the myriad images that she held of him, and found her favorite expression, the one when he held her after they had made love. The one full of tenderness and love, and... *Trust.* Her heart twisted. Another visage filled her mind again. Eyes of the same deep blue. The same trusting look. The eyes of their son. *Gabriel! She had to try for his sake*! But as strong as her will was, her body was exhausted, and this time she could not quite reach the surface. She said a silent prayer that he would somehow know she had not been a quitter. That she had died fighting. That she had tried... And that she loved him.

As close as she was, she could see the brightness of the sun overhead. Her lungs were burning, and with a final kick, she managed one more stolen gulp of air before she began to sink again, and the sea would claim her. *It's all right*, she told herself, giving herself permission to let go. She had done everything she could. *Her parents would be proud of her—And they would be waiting.*

As she drifted downward, she could see above her the tiny air bubbles that were the last of her life floating to the surface, *like seeking like. How strange...* Her tired mind struggled to register her last earthly vision, as a huge black bird swooped from the sky above

Chapter 24

Like a giant hawk diving on its prey, Devin kicked off his heavy boots and cleared the rail in a perfect arch. He had seen the man thrown overboard from the fleeing schooner but was determined not to lose his quarry. It was an old trick, and he had seen it before. It was his policy to first capture the ship, and return later for the unfortunate miscreant who was chosen to dissuade him. This time, though, he thought he had lost his man, as he stood on the deck searching the vacant blue main, until the waves parted for an instant, and in a last weak flurry, a final breath was drawn.

It was all he needed, and he sailed through the air to cleave the salty depths, hoping he was not too late. The force of his flight carried him downward, where a dark figure drifted helplessly. He grabbed the collar of the coat, and started upward with powerful strokes, to find the extra weight slowing his progress. He paused to push the weighted wool from the shoulders and discovered the bound hands. *Christ,* he fumed, their decoy hadn't stood a chance, and a picture of the heartless Cecilia flashed through his mind.

He turned the motionless victim back to, and flung an arm across the body. *Saints! A woman!* A woman bound and weighted, and he had left her to drown! *Katherine!* His soul cried out, but he pushed the thought away. *No, no, no!* Guilt and fear flooded his mind, and his lungs burned, as he propelled his burden to the surface, with a new burst of strength. The small dingy had been lowered and was waiting when he broke the surface to hand up his prize, and haul himself into the shallow boat.

As the men began to hoist them up to the ship, Devin knelt by the side of the hapless victim who lay face down in the bottom of the boat, his mind refusing to accept what his heart knew. A murmur passed among the men when he exposed the rope binding the slender wrists, and borrowed Tully's knife to cut the ties with shaking hands. He pulled the sodden coat from her shoulders revealing a long dark braid that reached a trim waist.

"*Captain,*" Tully offered helpfully, "He's a woman!"

Devin made no reply but bent to his task, placing his hands around and under the delicate rib cage, in an attempt to force any water up and out of her lungs. As he worked, a taunting vision of Katherine assailed him, and the pieces began to fall into place. *Of course… Cecelia… But no, she went to England… But she's here!*

The small boat was hoisted aboard, and set ably on deck, and the young woman coughed and parted with a good measure of the sea. Devin scooped her up in his arms, and lowered her to the smooth planking of the Athena. He glanced at the battered face for signs of consciousness, and for a single moment that he was always to recall, he froze and stared in disbelief, as this absurdity became his reality. *Was he losing his mind? Yes! No! Yes!* As if in answer to a thousand prayers, she had been dropped at his feet. *And he had left her to die!*

At this last thought, he cursed again, and placed his mouth over hers, gifting her with air from his own lungs. Time and again, he breathed for them both, anxiously watching her chest rise and praying it was working.

The long hair was dark in its wetness, and her lashes lay in moist spikes against her battered cheek. Her swollen face was almost unrecognizable, and he wondered still, if he were fooling himself, while his whole being cried out in confirmation. He studied the shadows under her eyes, the bruised mouth, the tortured wrists that told of a fierce struggle to escape her bonds, and his heart turned over. He had thought he wanted to hurt her in turn, for all the pain she had caused him, *but not this! Not this!* His voice sounded not his own as he called her name, *"Katherine! Katherine, can you hear me? I'm here, I'll help you!"*

She began to cough again, and then to breathe. She frantically uttered a name, and at this, Devin sat back on his heels and stared, while his heart shattered into even smaller pieces. But even then, that heart cried out at her terrible condition. He lifted her in his arms, and calling orders as he went, carried her into his cabin to place her on the bed. As her head hit the pillow, she moaned, and her hand fluttered in some dream inspired purpose.

Devin, sat on the bed and clasped the seeking hand in his own. He studied it, in its stillness, and swallowed hard, bowing to rest his forehead against it and bathe it with his tears. "Why, Katherine, *why?* Why did you leave me, and how did you come to this?" He wiped at his eyes, and stood to one side waiting as the surgeon entered and began his examination. His gaze swept once again over her bruises, and his heart filled with love, as much as he tried to deny it, and something deep inside him cried out for vengeance on her tormentors.

The surgeon, having salved and bandaged her wrists, finished and left, proclaiming bed rest and time the best healers. "Time will tell, sir."

Devin crept closer, and observed her shallow breathing, and tipped his head back in despair. Here she was, and already his torment had begun. There was the pain of her betrayal, the hurt. *Oh, God, how it hurt. Oh, God, how he wanted to hold her. To heal her.* He knelt by her side and touched his forehead to the pillow next to her shoulder, and closed his eyes, shutting out the gut-wrenching aguish that overwhelmed him. The Fates weren't through with him yet, and he could only wonder what lay ahead.

He rose, cursing himself, disgusted by his weakness. He had always thought fate was on his side, but now, he was not so sure. He ran both hands through his hair and laced his fingers around the back of his head in an effort to draw his thoughts together. Was this some kind of cruel joke, or Providence offering him another chance? And if it were, was he strong enough to take it? *Did he have a choice?*

Tully arrived with towels and hot water, and strangely quiet for once, bobbed his way out, after a sympathetic glance at both his captain and the sleeping woman.

Devin let out a long sigh of resignation. The least he could do would be to help her get well. After all, she had done that much for him. Still, he hesitated, almost afraid to touch her, and loath to admit it. In spite of his shaking hands, he began to remove her wet clothes.

Katherine stirred yet again in the comfortable bed. How many times had she awoken and looked around the room, only to fall asleep again? The last thing she remembered was being in the water. Her chest hurt, but her lip seemed a bit better, she thought, feeling it with her tongue. She had been here too long. *But where was she? A ship, yes, but the same ship? Was this the Christina? It had to be the captain's cabin, judging from the size of it, and the desk in the back alcove, but why was she here?*

Someone was seeing to her care, she knew, noting she wore an oversized nightshirt whose rolled sleeves revealed her wrists swathed in bandages. Her coat hung on one of the pegs beside the closet door and her clothes were clean and folded at the foot of the bed. A thick towel still lay over the pillow under her head, where her hair had been fanned out to dry. *Surely with such care, she was in no danger.* She struggled to dress and make her way to the door of the cabin, where she was met by a short man with a wreath of white hair surrounding his bald pate, and a kind look in his eyes.

"Oh, you're awake are ya, Miss? I was just comin' to check on ya."

Katherine held to the wall, her blurred vision and her aching head giving her pause.

The man appeared alarmed. "Here now, you'd best sit down, Miss," he directed, leading her to the table and chairs. "My name's Tully, Miss, and I'm to bring ya some broth, and some tea. Now you sit right there, and don't move, and I'll be back in a jiffy."

"What ship is this?" Katherine whispered, when she could get a word in.

"Beggin' your pardon, Miss, but I'm not allowed to say anything, until the captain questions ya."

The young woman's brow rose, and he went on to explain, "You were with *them*, Miss, which raises some questions, but I wouldn't worry, anyone could see… I'm not allowed to say, Miss."

"Is this the captain's cabin?" Katherine asked, knowing there was unlikely to be a cabin this size that did not belong to the captain of the ship, *but why was she here?*

"I'm not allowed to say, Miss."

When he had returned with the welcome liquids, Katherine downed the broth eagerly, discovering a hunger she hadn't realized, and savored the tea, while wondering if she were in some kind of trouble. She then asked to go on deck, to work the stiffness from her muscles and take some air. The man, Tully, escorted her and she was glad of it, for she was dismayed to find how weak she was, and there was no part of her that did not ache. This was clearly not the Christina. This ship was vast compared to the other, and she spotted the smaller ship sailing off to the starboard side. *The pursuer then. With the captain some called the dark lord? Were they pirates?* She closed her eyes. Reaching a quiet corner to rest in, supplied her with all the exercise she could stand at the moment. Still, she was enjoying the sun and fresh air, and Tully agreed that she could stay, but she noticed he was never too far away.

How long she sat dozing in the afternoon sun she did not know, but she stayed until she was approached by two jovial looking men. The older one, who wore a soft knit cap, removed it and bobbed his head in her direction. "Beggin' your pardon Miss, but the captain would like to see ya."

Katherine had no idea whether she was still a prisoner. Surely, the captain would inform her, but she could not deny the surge of apprehension at the summons. She got to her feet, and the older man put out a hand to assist her. "Thank you, Mister..."

"Hubbard, Miss, James Hubbard, and this here's Jimmy." He jerked a thumb in the direction of the younger man, who gave her a small nod and a lopsided grin that reminded her of a friendly hound dog. She followed the two men back to the cabin she had left earlier, and Tully followed behind.

Hubbard knocked and opened the door without waiting for a reply, and stepped aside so that Katherine could precede him. The bank of windows at the rear of the ship glowed with the descending sun, supplying the only light in the room, which left the tall bearded man who rose from his desk, in the shadows. *But still...*

Hope and disbelief rose together in her fogged mind, and her heart began to pound. *Devin?* It was a cruel trick of the light, that shone from behind, she knew, but her foolish heart was insistent. *Was she still dreaming? Had she drowned after all? The air had left her lungs,* her legs grew weak, and every nerve in her body came alive. She drew nearer, trying to make sense of what her eyes were now sure of, and still, she could not believe their witness. *Devin! Oh, Dear God, let it be true!* But surely her eyes were playing tricks on her. This could not be. *But it was. The hair was longer, the face bearded, but...* Their eyes locked, and she whispered the persistent thought aloud, "*Devin*."

"Miss Lawrence," he said coldly.

The truth righted her world, and resonated in her soul. *He was alive!* The joyous call ricocheted through her being, setting her alight with happiness. Her feet moved forward of their own accord, but at his warning look she faltered, and stopped where she was.

He stood with his arms crossed, staring with such a frigid intensity that she could not have sworn it wasn't hatred she saw on the beloved face. She could feel it, almost solid and tangible, reaching her from across the room, which only added to her doubt of this strange reality. *"Is it really you?"* She moved forward, and reached out a hand to touch the muscled forearm, at once a question, and an answer.

"War does not seem to agree with you, Miss Lawrence."

"Nor you, Captain," her voice was barely a whisper. This was not the Devin she had left behind on that long ago morning. *What had she done?* Tears started, and she moved her hand away. She wanted to run away again, and questioned what was holding her where she was. Perhaps it was the men blocking the doorway, or the look in his eyes that had changed at her touch, but she stayed, wavering on her feet.

Devin took her arm and turned to seat her in his chair, as the doctor and another man entered the cabin. "Why are you here?" He demanded, knowing he had to question her, and prove to himself and these men, that she was not involved. He could not have it said that he let her go because he knew her. *Loved her,* his heart and mind chorused, bullying his pride.

"I don't know," she said honestly, her voice sounding small and lost. "*I thought you were dead.*"

"You don't *know?*" He scoffed. "Are you aware that privateering and smuggling are punishable by hanging?"

She stared at him, caught between a dream and a nightmare, the embers of his touch on her arm still smoldering. "Am I on trial?"

"Call it an inquisition." He glanced at the waiting men who had started arguing amongst themselves when she mentioned his demise.

"Oh." *Was he serious?* "I know nothing of the cargo or its destination. I… I think I was brought as a decoy. I was kidnapped from my home."

Devin gave a short harsh laugh. "And why should I believe you?"

His taunting remark stabbed to her heart. *So that was how it would be.* He was full of resentment, and he would use this against her for his personal revenge. *Could he hate her that much?*

"Have you no answer?!"

Her heart thudded, whether from his tone, or his nearness, or the trouble she could be in, she could not have said. "No," she whispered. She stood up, meeting his eyes, feeling rather like a mouse before a hawk.

Devin's pulse quickened and he cursed his reaction to her. He had waited for this day, lived for it… And now he wasn't exactly sure what it was that he wanted. He wanted to hate her, or at least show her he could be as indifferent as she, but he couldn't, and the truth made him angry. "Have you any proof of what you claim?"

"No…" She tried to think. "How could I? I was out for a ride… And they were waiting."

He scowled. He wanted her to tell her story, and had bid the men stay as witnesses. There was no way she would be sent away with the other prisoners. As he watched her standing before him, he knew in his heart he could never let that happen. But part of him did want her punished. He wanted her punished because she had left him—*Or did he just want her? Dammit, he wanted answers!* He wanted to fight with her, and he wanted her to fight back. *Where was her spirit, her fire?* "Do you know what danger you could be in?"

This was more than she could bear. She was exhausted, and seeing him was such a shock she couldn't think straight. She spread her hands beseechingly, fighting back tears. "That's all I know. Am I not innocent until proven guilty?"

"You were caught red handed!" He barked, his temper rising.

Her chin raised a notch, *"At what? Drowning!?"*

Smothered laughter escaped from somewhere near the door, and Devin shot a black scowl in that direction, as he secretly reveled in her reaction. *There she was! His Katherine! His Athena, returning fire at last.* He ached inside. It was all he could do to keep from taking her in his arms, and in desperation, he grabbed her coat from where it hung on the wall behind him, and wrung it in his hands instead.

He could not make a fool of himself again. It burned at his pride to think how he had been reduced to a quaking mass of emotion, upon discovering it was she he had rescued. He had told himself he was over her, fooled himself into believing it, and now... He fought for control as that pride warred with his heart. He stalled for time, grasping at straws, and turned to face her. "What about Price?"

Price? It was too much for her confused mind. Her head throbbed, and her chest ached, and she needed to lie down. Her breast swelled with indignation, and her anguished eyes were all he could see as she leaned closer, filling his line of vision. *"What in God's name are you talking about?"* She searched his eyes for the Devin she knew.

They stood face to face, but neither had ever imagined a reunion would be like this.

He persisted, hiding from her soul-searching gaze behind more words... "Judith Caldwell told me all about Everett Price!"

Words that still made no sense to her. She closed her eyes and tried to make her voice stronger as she spoke, emphasizing each word for his benefit, "I have been beaten, and abused, and nearly drowned. I do *not* know Everett Price, I do *not* know what you are talking about, and I…have had…enough!" She paused, and her eyes fell on the strong brown hands as they worried the wool of her coat. Hands whose touch she longed for. She swallowed, forcing away the tears and the anguish, and a rush of desire to melt into his arms. Her pulse raced and her voice rose, "And that's my coat, dammit! And I'll thank you to keep your lecherous hands off it!" With that, she snatched the heavy garment from his sagging grasp, and swirling it over her shoulders she marched past the men and out the door into the waning sunshine.

The men, having witnessed the mutinous outburst directed at their captain, stood for a moment in awe of her courage, and no one lifted a finger to stop her. They looked at each other, and turned to Devin for direction.

He stood staring at the open portal, a strange expression that was half scowl, half smile etched on his face. When he noticed the men were watching him, he cleared his throat, and tried to think how he could best regain his previous status of unquestionable authority. "Well…" He said, and waited for words to fill the empty space between his brain and his mouth, but they were slow in coming. "Well," he tried again, "We don't know she's not telling the truth, and what we do know, seems to fit with what she said. Isn't that right, Hubbard?"

He spoke this last sternly, giving the sailor a keen look.

"Yes, Sir, you're right there, Captain!"

"Check the schooner top to bottom, and bring me anything you find that would support her story."

"Aye, Captain." The men spoke in unison and went out, struggling to keep straight faces.

Devin breathed a sigh of relief at their departure. It was important for a captain to be respected by his men. He laughed at himself, as he listened to their retreating comments, spoken, he knew, just loud enough for him to hear.

"By Jove, the captain's right lads, I believed her, didn't you?"

"I did," came Jimmy's voice. "Aye," said Tully, "The whole time she was moppin' the deck with 'im." Hurrying footsteps accompanied a fading gale of laughter as the men disappeared.

A pensive look replaced Devin's half-frown. He enjoyed the relationship he had with his crew. They were like family, and a bit of kindness had gotten him a lot more loyalty than harsh threats and severe punishments ever could. Of course, it depended on who you hired to begin with, and Devin considered himself a good judge of men.

But what of women? *What of this woman?* He thought, as he seated himself at his desk, who had… what had Tully said? '*Mopped the deck with him.*' He groaned inwardly. He had certainly butchered that reunion. *Was she guilty?* He knew in his heart the question was absurd, and the idea that she had been kidnapped made his blood boil.

He was glad she had come to life at last, although he knew she must be exhausted and hurting. At least now he could report that she had been questioned… He was afraid for a while she had changed, but the spirit was there, the strength he remembered so well. He couldn't remember everything she had said, he had been watching her eyes. At first, they had been wide with surprise, and dare he hope *welcome?* Then they had grown despondent and had shown her pain. When he said something else, they had practically crackled with fire, as she had set him down but good. He glanced about him at the cabin. He had spent countless hours alone here, and he wondered why the room now seemed so empty. He sat upright in his chair, an incredulous look replacing all traces of amusement on his bearded face, *"Saints,"* he swore to himself, she had called him lecherous, again… *And in front of his crew!* Leaving the cabin, to go in search of her, he was called aside by Tully, and it was to be some time before he would catch up with her.

Chapter 25

It was well after supper and the stars were high, scattered like so many diamonds across the black velvet night. Katherine stood with her hands on the rail, as she studied the dark expanse of ocean. The ship ran steadily under a soft playful breeze that stirred her hair and the full sleeves of her blouse. It was a beautiful night, quiet, calm, and… *Devin was alive!* She had escaped Russo, she hadn't drowned, and… *He's alive,* her heart sang again. She laughed aloud in pure joy, and then jumped at the voice behind her.

"What, may I ask, is so amusing?"

The deep voice that she could never forget, sent another surge of joy to her heart. She turned to find him there, as she had wished she would so many times, and gave a glad cry. The afternoon's fiasco forgotten, she impulsively threw her arms around him and hugged him to her, exalting in the vibrant rhythm of his heart beneath her ear.

"I thought you were dead," she whispered.

Devin stood seemingly immune to her embrace, his arms at his sides, and cocked an eyebrow at her. "Wishful thinking, no doubt."

His coldness cut to her heart, and she withdrew to stare again across the water, her tears now numbered among the sparkling reflections of the night. She tried to match his sarcasm, "Have you come to hang me from the yardarm, Captain? Is that to be your revenge?" She gave a short bitter laugh, thinking the world was a mad place indeed. "Is that to be my punishment for loving you?"

Devin stared at her back. He didn't know what was wrong with him. He only knew she made him crazy. He had been deliberately hurtful, and was instantly sorry. He wanted to throw his arms around her, and he wanted to throw her overboard, and... *What did she say?*

"You never said you loved me," he said, his throat growing tight.

She turned to look at him in disbelief. *Was it true? He didn't know she loved him?* She began to retrace in her mind the times they had been together, and that last night, when she had given him everything. *Surely, he knew.*

She stared up at him, and Devin was caught by the desperate plea in her eyes. *Did she love him? Saints, it was all he wanted in this world.* He stood for a moment in indecision, searching her eyes for his answer, and his heart ached at the sight of her tears. His hands reached to cradle her face, and his thumbs stroked the tears from her cheeks. This time it was Katherine who held her arms at her sides not knowing what he wanted of her. He stared, and she waited, wondering if he would kiss her or cast her aside. The world seemed to stop until he lowered his head, capturing her soul in a long questioning kiss, forgetting the hurt and anger, and all the confused passion she had caused his tired being to feel.

Her arms slid around him, as his came down over her shoulders enclosing her in his warmth, and Katherine's heart soared straight to the heavens. It was all she remembered it to be and more. How she had ever left him was a credit to her strength. But he was here, *and he loved her*, she knew he did. But he had always said he loved her, that wasn't the problem. The problem was Cecilia… *To hell with Cecilia.* She didn't know or care where she was. He was meant to be hers, and she owed her nothing now. The woman had tried to kill her. She didn't care anymore.

It was ever so slight, but he felt it. That small hesitation, and then again, her eager response… *But it was too late.* He lifted his head, and his eyes glittered like steel in the starlight. "Oh no, Katherine," he whispered. "Not again. Either you want me, or you don't, but we will settle this now. I do not understand this game you play!"

He took her by the hand and led her into the cabin, shutting the door behind them. Several lanterns burned within, and he seated her at the table in the center of the room, taking the opposite seat. "Now then…" he said, but each waited for the other to begin, and a long moment passed in silence before he spoke again.

She sat across from him, her hands folded on the table, her hair tousled from the breeze, and her eyes serious. She looked sad, and a little frightened, so he took a deep breath, and tried to keep his voice calm.

"Katherine. You know I love you." He hadn't meant to say the words, but as he spoke them, he knew they were truer than ever. He had thought he could forget, could hate her for what she had done, but as soon as he had seen her, and trembled at the thought that she had almost died before his eyes, he had known he still loved her. He had always loved her, and always would. He showed his palms in surrender, "I seem to be helpless in the matter, but if you can't love me, I would rather know the truth…"

"But I do," she interrupted, reaching for his hands across the table. "Of course I do."

He watched her intently. "Perhaps you and I have different definitions of the word."

Katherine shook her head, and her heart was in her eyes.

"Well?" He prompted, and when she was still silent, he slammed his palm on the table so loudly she jumped in her chair. "*What the hell is it then!?*" He cried out, but when she jumped so, he tried to calm himself. "All right, all right," he repeated, closing his eyes and showing his palms again. "Just tell me–for *God's sake*–for my sake–for *your* sake!" He buried his weary head in his hands and exhaled. "Tell me. Whatever it is, we can talk about it. Try me."

She studied him in wonder, but he was serious. She took a breath and spoke the hated words—The phrase that had haunted her night and day, and even now brought tears to blur her vision, "What about Cecilia?"

Devin frowned. "She'll be tried with the others I suppose, she may go to prison… or worse."

Katherine looked at him in surprise. *His own wife? Obviously, he had no feelings for her, but she was still the mother of his child.* "And me?" She asked evenly.

He shook his head impatiently. "I believe you. And if I didn't, do you think I would turn you in? I'd run away with you."

"I would like that."

"Yes, as I recall, you're fond of running away."

She lowered her eyes feeling the barb pierce her heart.

He took her hand again. "I'm sorry." He shrugged, running the other hand through his hair, "It hurt."

She nodded before she spoke. "Don't you think it hurt me? But you know I had to go," she said sadly. "I tried to stay away, but it wasn't working. I was going to look for you though."

Devin paid careful attention. His answer was here somewhere. "Now wait." He held up a hand to slow her explanation. "Why? What do you mean, you *had to go and why would you try to stay away*? If you loved me, and you knew I loved you, why did you leave me?"

Katherine was exasperated. "For Heaven's sake, Devin, you know *Cecilia is the problem.* You can't deny she stands between us. *Why do you pretend it doesn't matter?*"

Devin stared at her as if she had grown two heads. "Why are you so protective of her, after what she has done?" He scowled, "And what do you mean you were going to look for me?"

"I would have," she stammered, "but, when William came home… When he said that 'Cecilia's husband had died,' I…" She frowned at the bitter memory, and her voice lowered. "I wanted to die too."

Devin winced. *If she truly loved him, would she still care that Price was dead?* Now he would have to tell her. "He is."

"What?"

"Dead."

Now Katherine looked confused. "Who is?"

"Cecilia's husband, Everett. He's dead."

Katherine stared. She struggled to swallow, and forgot to breathe. Her heart slowed, and her eyes grew round. "What are you saying?"

Devin was uncomfortable, he wanted this over with. He repeated himself forcefully so neither of them could hide from the facts that stood between them. "Cecilia's husband, Everett Price, is dead." He watched the color drain from her face, and he had yet to tell her the worst of it.

"*Cecilia's husband, Everett?*" Her voice was very small. "But aren't you…"

"Yes, I'm the one who killed him."

Her mouth opened, but he hurried on before she could speak.

"I shot him, Katherine, I had to. Please understand," he begged, but she was not listening.

She was enveloped in the dawning horror of her simple error. *She had believed Cecilia.* Cecilia who had always been her enemy. Cecilia, who would do anything to hurt her. Cecilia who hated her. Cecilia must have been jealous that night, and she had been so caught up in her dreams she had lowered her guard, and in her shattered world had taken Cecilia at her word.

Tears filled her eyes, "*No…*" she moaned, rising unsteadily.

Devin was speaking, but nothing he said registered, "Please, I had to, he shot your father."

She was thinking of all the times she had turned away from him, hurt him, blamed him, and left him, when she needn't have. What if she had met him that first morning as they had planned? *How different it would have been. "No!" She needed air.*

As Devin had feared, she turned and ran from him. He caught her at the door before she could open it, and sobbing hysterically, she slid the length of the sturdy portal to land on the floor, a pathetic ball of misery.

He knelt and put a hand to her cheek. "Katherine, I don't know what to say. I'm sorry."

She began to cry harder at the gentleness of his touch, for all the time lost, for all that might have been hers. He could barely make out her words through her racking sobs.

"You don't understand." She took his hand in both of hers. "You don't understand. I thought *you* were Cecilia's husband. *All this time…* And when I heard her husband had been killed…"

"You thought I was Price?"

She looked at him helplessly, "No, I don't know who he is. I only thought you had married her."

Devin was incredulous. *"Married Cecilia?! But… Why?"*

"Because, Cecilia told me, that night at the ball, after I left you, after the garden, that you were her fiancé."

His brows arched upward. *"And you believed* her?"

Katherine shrugged dejectedly and didn't meet his eyes. "She showed me her ring. And she said if I didn't stay away, she would make your life a living hell, and I knew she could. I didn't want that. I loved you so much… from the first day, do you remember?" She blushed a little at her confession.

He smiled a little at her sincerity.

She continued, "It seemed too good to be true, so I guess it was easy to believe it wasn't. That's why I didn't meet you the next morning, and later on, when I went to see Cecil and he told me she had gotten married… of course I thought it was you, because—*I believed*—you were her fiancé. And well, people marry their fiancés, *don't they?*" She pleaded, gesturing with her hands, desperate for him to see it her way.

Devin stared at her, his eyes alight with compassion, as so many things began to make sense. He handed her his handkerchief, before he helped her to her feet.

She clutched at his shirt, her eyes closed in relief, and he held her close before lifting her and carrying her to the bunk. He settled her against the pillows and pulled a chair around so he could sit facing her, and took her hand. "Judith Caldwell told me you were in love with Cecilia's husband," he stated, wanting to make sure he understood.

"*You,*" she said, "but I don't know how she knew. Unless she was eavesdropping when I told Louise."

"And that day I saw you in town, you made it clear that you weren't alone."

"I was there with Ezra," she admitted, eyes downcast. "I was hurt and insulted, that you would marry her, and still try to be with me… I guess I wanted to hurt you back, because I wanted you to think more of me than that."

"But I did… I do. I think the world of you. Did I not make that clear?"

She squeezed his hand.

"What about that time on the beach, when you said there was someone else?"

"I meant Cecilia. I meant you had someone else."

"But you said you didn't love me."

"I lied," she confessed in abject misery, "so you would stay away. I was trying so hard to do the right thing. You have no idea of the agony of loving you, and believing I could never be with you."

She began to cry again, and he moved to sit beside her, putting his arm around her. "Shh, Love, I do, I do, but it's all right now."

"Not only that, but I failed miserably at doing the right thing. What would my parents say?"

"They would say it was love, Katherine. Those who know it, can understand it. It's over now, Love. Only..."

"What?"

"Well, you didn't give me much credit, did you? I mean, *Cecilia, for God's sake?*"

"I don't know. I guess I decided she must have trapped you, or it must have been an arrangement between you and Cecil or something. You *did* live in their house, and I used to see her with you all the time. I never saw her with anyone else, and she *was* with child..." Katherine placed a hand over her mouth, and her eyes widened again. "*That wasn't your child!*"

He sighed, full of compassion, "Of course not."

Her hand went to her heart, at the remembered pain.

Devin paused, studying the picture the way she had painted it, and noticed she was staring at him. "What are you thinking?"

"You were really never married to her?"

"Yes. I mean, no. I mean, *really not.* Of course not. What kind of question *is* that?" He teased, but Katherine was serious.

"Would you please kiss me?"

He smiled down at her, "That question is more foolish than the other one."

"No," she said, knowing he did not understand. "I would like one unmarried, guilt-free kiss, to remember what it was like."

"Katherine, they were all..."

She cut him off by placing a finger against his lips, a cry in her voice, "But I didn't know that."

He saw the regret in her eyes, and felt a surge of empathy for what she must have gone through even as she put him through hell. They had so much to make up for, and he wanted her to believe they would. "Does it hurt your lip?" He leaned closer.

"No, but if it does, you can kiss it better," she whispered against his mouth.

He tried his best, for in his kiss was all the compassion for the past, passion for the present, and hope for the future that he could give her.

She lost herself in the message. There was no guilt, no reason to hold back, nothing to think about but the bone-melting warmth filling her with love and contentment. When he lifted his head, she looked into his eyes. "Almost worth it," she whispered.

"Almost?"

"Mm, better try again."

He did, with great success, and she lay relaxed and warm in his arms, intoxicated with joy.

They talked about the past and the future. She told him about the kidnapping and Günter, including his proposal, soothing his concern with her kisses. She explained how he had died saving her from Russo, and Devin told her the big man would be buried at sea the next day when they reached deeper waters. "If they don't hang Russo, I'll kill him myself," he vowed, holding her closer. By the look on his face, she knew he was serious. A new thought came to her, "William said, that the man who killed Cecilia's husband, was a federal agent. Are you?"

Devin shrugged, "I work with them."

"Why did you kill him?"

He didn't know where to begin, there were so many reasons for Price to die. "He was a very dangerous man. He killed so many people. He shot your father, and he stabbed Maggie."

Devin kissed her temple, at her questioning look. He told her about Maggie and Marcus, and more of Price, and she told him about her new house, and William's marriage to Louise, and how she had gone to the cemetery afterward. "*I searched for your grave!*" She said, wondering if he could possibly know what that had been like.

He tried his best to imagine himself in her place.

They talked until Katherine fell asleep in his arms. For Devin, seeing a future rise from ashes, it was enough for the moment to hold her, and savor the thought that she loved him. His heart swelled. He watched her breathing gently against his darkly shirted chest, and thought this was one of the most important nights of his life. He knew there was more to be settled. He hadn't asked her about the name she was calling when he had first brought her on deck, because he hoped she would tell him everything of her own accord. She *had* said she loved him though, and this time they had tomorrow.

Chapter 26

That particular tomorrow dawned with an overcast, but bright sky, that pained the eyes. Katherine blinked awake to find Devin leaning on one elbow and gazing down at her. "Oh," she whispered, reaching a palm against his bearded cheek. "I was afraid it was a dream."

He smiled at her, his voice heavy with sleep, "It is a dream. It's mine. I've always dreamt of finding you, and now I have."

She smiled at him, winced, and put a hand to her face, I must look awful," she said, feeling the bruises that remained.

"You're beautiful," he said, his eyes telling her he meant it, as he leaned to meet one side of her mouth in a very gentle kiss that said much.

"I love you, Devin Galloway." She could say it now, so she did.

His kisses grew more urgent, and she longed to give herself up to his ardent persuasion, but as his mouth left hers to find the open collar of her blouse, she grappled for an excuse. "I need a bath."

Devin sighed. "As half-owner of the ship, I suppose you're entitled."

"This is our ship?"

He kissed her again. "Didn't you know?"

Katherine shook her head. "I've never seen her."

"I named her for you, you know, 'The Athena.'"

Her brow rose, *"The Warrior Goddess?"*

He nodded. "You reminded me of Athena the first time we met, when you came charging at me on that horse of yours. And then that night, when you attacked me in the Johnston's garden."

Katherine gasped. "I did not!" She slapped at him, as he sat up laughing.

She sat up too, swinging her legs beside his over the edge of the bunk, "You *do* know," she said, "that Athena was also the *virgin* goddess?"

He paused and looked at her sideways, "Damn, I'll have to rename the ship," he said, and relished her laughter. "I've got some things to take care of. Do you suppose I could have a kiss to see me through?" He gave her another sidelong glance, and she smiled, moving to straddle his lap, "For how long?" She asked, placing her arms around his neck in preparation.

"Too long," he grinned.

"Well," she said, "I'll try." She moved toward him still smiling, but when their lips met, the playful mood changed. It *was* too long. The moment he was gone, she would want him back. They had been apart so much already, and it was her fault. She wanted him to know how much she regretted it, how much she loved him, and how she would always be his. All this, she told him with her kiss.

Devin's arms tightened around her, and he fell back on the bunk, taking her with him.

Caressing, cajoling and very convincing, her tongue met his, transporting them both back through time, to a night of magic, shared and treasured. A dangerous moan sounded deep in his throat, and Katherine remembered herself, reining in her passions, and tapering her kiss to a last gentle touch, before she lifted her head to stare at him.

She watched him raise an astonished brow at her, and close his eyes again, breathing heavily. "Miss Lawrence!" He said at long last. "That was hardly a kiss to send a man on his way. It's more likely to put me in bed for a week!" His eyes flew open. "Perhaps that's what you had in mind?" He asked, hopefully.

Katherine smiled at him, a little shy, the blush of passion still coloring her cheeks. Her pulse was racing, and she could feel the hard length of him beneath her. She longed to say yes, but… "You have things to do," she reminded. "And I still need a bath." She sat up quickly, crossing her arms over her chest, as what was left of her milk pushed to the fore and dampened her shirt.

Devin drew a deep breath and let it out in disappointment. "All right," he said reluctantly, when she left the bed, to move across the room.

"And today I must thank whoever saved me," she added.

"You just did," he said, "But you can thank me again anytime."

"How did you know it was me?" She asked in surprise, loosening her hair and letting it fall to cover the front of her.

Devin, who had risen from the bunk turned to scoff at her, while he unbuttoned his shirt.

"I didn't. Do you think if I knew it was you, I would have left you there?"

She considered this. "Maybe," she teased. "I couldn't blame you if you had, could I?"

He was splashing at the washstand, and she watched the fascinating play of muscles across his broad back, as she waited for his answer.

"That's true," he grinned, toweling the water from his face. "But I wonder who would have suffered more."

For that he earned a heart-warming look.

"And you didn't know it was me, on the Athena, passing you by?" The thought of it haunted him.

"No, I only knew that…" she paused, remembering the moment when she knew she was going to die, *but she would spare him that,* "I had to try once more."

"Thank God you didn't give up. I can only imagine if you hadn't taken that last breath, and I had found out later that it was you I had left to die."

He kissed her wrist where the rope burns still remained to tell of her struggle, and Katherine tried not to stare too hard at the bare chest that filled her vision, and the gold cross that hung there. She raked her nails lightly through the crisp hair of his beard to change the mood.

"Do you think you'll ever shave again?"

"Do you want me to?" He asked, reminding her of days long past. He didn't tell her he had stopped shaving when she left him because nothing had seemed to matter anymore.

As he walked to the closet and pulled on a clean shirt, she studied him, her head tilted to one side, her brow crinkled in concentration. *Either way he was disgustingly handsome,* she decided.

"Well?" He prodded, posturing for her.

"I miss your dimples," she decided. "But you don't have to shave for me."

Devin gave no reply, but strode to the far wall to fold out a large brass tub from its storage cabinet. "It's early yet," he said, "I'll have the water sent in and I'll be back later with breakfast. There are a few more things we have to talk about."

She nodded, as he headed for the door. "Aren't you going to kiss me good-by?" She asked innocently.

"No, Miss Katherine, I don't believe I dare."

They did have to talk, Katherine thought, after Hubbard and some other men had made several trips, to fill the tub, and left her with an abundance of hot water. She had to tell him about their son. She should have told him last night, when they had gotten everything else out in the open, but she had held off, not quite sure how to go about it. But if things continued on their present course, and she very much hoped they did, she would be found out, and she wanted to tell him first. Each time she rid herself of the nourishing burden, as she did now, the thought of the small bundle she should have in her arms broke her heart anew.

She slipped into the steaming tub. *Yes, she had to tell him first, but how? There's something you should know*, she rehearsed mentally, while she luxuriated in the soothing heat. *I have a son. You have a son. We have a son. Why was it so difficult? He would be thrilled, wouldn't he? What if he didn't want children?* Katherine shrugged off the thought and began to lather her hair, trusting that when the time was right the words would come.

It was nearly an hour later, when she rose reluctantly, from the still warm water and looking with dismay at her shirt, tossed it along with her undergarments into the soapy water. From a peg on the wall, she borrowed his robe. It was a fine garment, of deep burgundy silk and intricate embroidery, but as she rolled up the sleeves, she raised a delicate brow in wonder. *It hardly seemed the type of thing a man would purchase for himself...* She rolled her eyes in self-disgust.

By now, the sun had broken through outside, and Katherine had hung her clothing up to dry by the windows. Her hair was drying too, and in search of a comb or brush she glanced around the room. They weren't by the washstand, and she could not bring herself to open the drawers built into the side of the bunk. Perhaps the closet, which somehow seemed less private since he had opened it earlier. Just when she opened the door, Devin entered across the cabin carrying a large covered tray.

"Katherine, I..." He stopped in his tracks, and barely remembered to close the door behind him. She was barefoot, wearing only his overlarge robe, and her hair, freshly washed, hung to her waist in damp amber waves. She looked wonderful. *She would look good in anything,* he thought, *or nothing,* and he stared.

Katherine, who had spun guiltily from the closet, grew warm under his persistent gaze. "Your mouth is open," she chided.

"I thought you would be done," he finished, setting the tray on the table.

"I washed my clothes, and I needed something… I hope you don't mind." She lifted her shoulders, indicating the robe. "I was looking for a hairbrush."

He crossed the floor and pulled open a small drawer in the end of the bunk, and placed his brush and comb in her hand. "With all my worldly goods, I thee endow," he whispered.

Katherine laughed nervously, and he smiled. But for a moment, there had been something in his eyes. Something she could not quite name.

"I brought breakfast," he said, turning away, "and someone is coming that I think you'll be glad to see."

"But I'm not dressed!" She looked around in dismay.

"You're perfect. Here," he took the quilt from the foot of the bed and placed it around her shoulders.

"What happened to your hand!?" She asked, capturing his wrist and examining the dark bruising across his knuckles.

"I… caught it on something."

"Both of them?" She asked doubtingly, glancing at his other hand.

He barely had her seated at the table, when to his relief a knock sounded, and she was on her feet again. "Cecil!" She greeted the old family friend, and he gave her a fatherly embrace, before they sat down.

"Katherine, I'm glad to see you up and about, and I'm so very sorry for all you've been through."

"Thank you. But why are you here? I don't understand." She looked from one to the other and the realization blossomed. They were all part of it somehow. Their acquaintance, Cecil's trips out of town, Phillip's letters… "Oh, but Cecilia."

Cecil shrugged, "I never thought she'd go this far."

"*You knew?*" Katherine asked.

"I didn't know they were going to involve you, and I am sorry for that, but yes, we have been keeping her under watch since the beginning. We let her get away with stealing the funds, leading us to the suppliers, and giving her enough rope to hang herself. Which is very much a possibility, I'm afraid." He stared across the room, "She was the only one careless enough to blow their cover."

"That's why I wanted to talk," Devin broke in. "We'll make port in a few days." He looked directly at Cecil. "You know, if Katherine had been involved, I don't know what I would do. I would never turn her in. I couldn't."

"You are overlooking the fact that she would never *be* involved." Cecil replied. "But neither would I."

Katherine listened to the exchange with a swell of gratitude filling her breast, and the older man continued, "She's like my own daughter."

A moment of awkward silence passed, while Devin raised a dubious brow, and Katherine kicked at him under the table with a bare foot.

Cecil turned slightly pink, "I meant..."

"I will take it as the lovely compliment it was intended to be," Katherine assured him, reaching to touch his hand, and he smiled appreciatively.

"What I'm trying to say," Devin continued, finding the words difficult, "is, I would not object if you want to keep Cecilia out of this. We've got what we need now. You could take her with you when we make port, get her out of the country."

Cecil studied the dregs of his coffee as if his answer were written there. "I thank you for your consideration. I know what it would take for you to go against your principles." He rose, and they stood with him, and he looked Devin in the eye, "The truth is, I wouldn't trust her for a minute. She has stolen a great deal of money from me. She stole her mother's jewelry. More importantly, she has threatened our lives, and the life of her own child. Her mother and the boy are in hiding even now. God knows how it happened… my own daughter, but she's worse than any of them. I'd be afraid to turn my back on her." He shook his head sadly, "No, thank you anyway, but it would be best if she were sent along with the others. It's out of my hands now, and yours too, my boy." Silently the men shook hands, while Katherine came around the table to offer a consoling hug, and Cecil strolled out of the cabin still deep in thought.

"That was kind of you," she said, when they had returned to their chairs and she had poured another cup of tea.

He shrugged, "I can't imagine turning in my own daughter."

"Devin," she started, jumping nervously into the tiny opening he unwittingly gave. "I have something very important to tell you."

He looked at her straight faced, "It's not that you're married, is it?"

"That's not funny." She smiled uncertainly, and watched him over the rim of her teacup, a gesture that at that moment he found unbearable. "Of course not," she added, searching his face for a hint of a smile, "I could never marry anyone but you." Katherine felt the warmth rise in her cheeks and glanced away. *They hadn't spoken of marriage.* "I mean, you're the only one I've ever loved," she said, meeting his eyes again, and lowering her cup to the table.

"These letters were found in the cabin of the schooner." Devin showed her the two letters that had been found aboard the Christina. One was neatly folded, and the other badly wrinkled, as though it had been crumpled and discarded. They were identical in content, explaining that Katherine was to be held on board the Christina, to guarantee the crew safe passage to Virginia.

"See, this one says Katherine Lawrence, and this one says Katherine Macey," he pointed out. "Is that supposed to be you?" He spoke casually, but all the way back from the Christina, the very thought of her sharing another man's name had twisted like a knife in his gut. *But she would have told him, wouldn't she?*

Katherine looked the letters over, and pushed them aside in disgust, "Part of Cecilia's brilliant plan… But why weren't they sent?" How were you supposed to know if they weren't delivered? Maybe there was another copy that was sent?"

Devin shook his head, "They left early. We had to scramble to be ready in time to follow."

"So, the plan changed. I was not '*held on board*,' I was thrown *overboard!*" She sighed and closed her eyes. "I used that name, because I saw it in the army office, after I discovered the smugglers. I went there for help, and Russo was there. I remembered his name from the beach landing. He was… *crude*, and I didn't want him to follow me or look for me, so I gave him that name instead. It was on a list posted on the wall… So, that's who he thought I was. When this all happened, and they thought I was Macey's widow, I just went along with it, because I thought it might protect…" She caught herself in time.

"I'm sorry," Devin whispered, rising and pulling her into his arms, realizing he'd had a small, but bitter taste, of what she must have gone through.

"It seems an easy mistake." She gave a short laugh and moved deeper into his embrace. She had seen the uncertainty in his eyes, in spite of his effort to hide it, and her heart twisted. She knew that feeling too well. She pulled his head down to capture his lips in a kiss meant to chase all doubt to Hell, where it belonged.

Devin thought he had found Heaven. "Now, what was that about you wanting to marry me?" He whispered against the side of her neck, tracing kisses along her jaw until he reached her mouth. Their lips met, and parted, and met again. *At last,* he thought, the mood was right. Not like the night before, when she had been exhausted, and overwrought, and there had been so much unsettled between them. Or this morning, when she had been vaguely evasive, and wanting her bath. Now she was willing, and there was that in her bewitching eyes that promised much, and stole his breath away, and had he a gun in his hand, he would have shot the poor man who chanced to knock on his door at that moment. Instead, he threw back his head in a frustrated moan that caused Katherine to smile as he went to answer the door.

Tully glimpsed Katherine through the opening and removed his hat from his bobbing head. "We're ready Cap'n, when you are."

"Thank you, Tully. We'll be out shortly. "Devin shut the door and turned to Katherine. "I'd forgotten." At her questioning look he answered, "The burial."

Katherine gave a small exclamation. She too had forgotten, and felt guilty for it. The revelations of the previous night had dominated her thoughts. "I want to go too," she said, "I'll get dressed." She hesitated, as Devin stood staring at her.

"I'll..." He cleared his throat, "I'd better wait out here," and obviously reluctant to leave her, he stepped outside.

Katherine hurried to dress in her trousers and battered boots. Her other clothes were still wet so she chose one of Devin's shirts, and covered it with a heavy cream-colored sweater that hung past her hips. Though overlarge, she decided it would have to do, and tying her hair with her old faded ribbon, she hurried to join him.

Devin waited outside the door with Cecil, and tossed her a smile when she made her appearance, asking his approval with her eyes.

"My clothes have never looked so good," he whispered near her ear, on their way to join the others.

Katherine noticed with a start, that Cecilia and some of the other prisoners had been brought on deck. Whether for fresh air, or the funeral, she did not know. She only noted with relief that Russo was not among them.

Devin noticed her reaction, and squeezed her hand in reassurance. He did not feel it necessary to mention, that the something he had caught his fists on, had been Russo.

Cecilia had no word of Katherine's fate. She had hoped she had drowned, and when she spotted her walking across the deck on Devin's arm, she shrieked in protest. *"You slut!"* Her gaze fell on her father, and she ran to him, "Daddy!"

Cecil stared right through her. "Don't call me that. You are no longer my daughter."

"But Daddy, you don't understand!"

"I understand perfectly well," his voice lowered, "you're a thief and a traitor, a would-be murderer, like a thing gone wild. Selfish and conniving, turning on your own family and friends. You make me ashamed."

With a scathing look Cecilia turned away. She would find no help here.

Devin, as captain, read the appropriate verses, and the shrouded body of Günter Hann was sent to rest, cradled within the tranquil bosom of the sea. In the silence that followed, broken only by the creaking of the rigging, Cecilia was the first to move away.

Katherine shed a last tear for her friend, and Devin put his arm around her to lead her to the cabin. Cecilia watched them, as Devin leaned close to whisper words of comfort, and Katherine looked at him adoringly. Once again, Katherine had survived and triumphed, and Cecilia was beside herself with rage. The silence shattered into fragments as her high-pitched voice raked the air.

"Katherine, you bitch!"

"Enough!" Devin turned and snarled at her, while Katherine froze. "Keep your mouth shut Cecilia, or "I'll have you chained below!"

But Cecilia was beyond caution, and unwisely she continued, "I bet she didn't tell you about Walter Macey! Did you Katherine? Did you tell him about your baby… Your little bastard?"

All who were left on deck stopped to stare, before Katherine came slowly to life. Once, when she had been powerless in the face of Cecilia's insults, she had let them pass, but no longer. Here was the reason she had been parted from Devin, and here was the reason she was now parted from her son, that innocent, whom she could not bear to hear slandered for circumstances that were no fault of his own. In quiet fury she marched across the deck toward Cecilia and no one moved to stop her.

For a space she was blinded, her one thought to protect her child from people like this. And Devin. Devin deserved better. The look of shock on his face burned in her brain, and the fire consumed her. She was going to tell him of course, but now she had hurt him one more time. Again and again, she had brought misery to the one she loved above all else, and all because of Cecilia. Her soul cried out for vengeance, but by the time she grabbed her enemy by the collar, and pulled her up close, she thought of Gabriel, and her vision cleared. She looked into the face of the seething woman, and realized there was no need to fight; she had already won. And there was a truer revenge. She would make Devin understand, *she would*, and she would go home with him to their son.

She stood in front of her nemesis, and spoke for her ears alone, "It's over, Cecilia. You've lost. You're going to prison. You may even hang. I can hardly fathom it. You were always so full of hate. Why? You had everything most people dream of. A home and loving parents. You never went without. Your jealousy has made your life miserable, and now your greed may be the death of you. But if not, and you live, wherever you are, whatever you're doing, never forget that I am free, and happy, with my son and his father." At Cecilia's shocked gasp, she continued, "Do you think you're the only one who can *lie*? You think you're so smart. I never even met Walter Macey, and if he died at Chancellorsville, he died too long ago to be the father of my child. You said you saw my son. Who do *you* think his father is? Strange, isn't it, that you, of all people, brought us back together. Live with that, for as long as you have left." Katherine released her with a shove, and turned her back and walked away.

In the next instant, she watched curiously when Devin hurled himself through the air in what seemed an oddly slowed motion, a strange cry tearing from his throat. He tackled her and carried her to the deck as a single shot rang out.

Silence settled once again, and Katherine pulled herself free and sat up. Cecilia's body lay sprawled on the weathered wood, blood forming a scarlet pool beneath her, a silver derringer in her outstretched palm. She turned and saw the smoking barrel of a pistol in the hand of Cecil, and she hurried to him. When she looked back, Devin was gone

Chapter 27

Katherine was still on deck, as far from the scene of Cecilia's death as possible. Devin had not reappeared since she had seen the cabin door close behind him, and she had not quite raised the courage to go after him. She paced the deck, thinking perhaps Cecilia had won after all, and the final straw had been cast. But she had come too far and was too close… She was still searching for the right words, but there was no point in waiting any longer, and she marched to the cabin.

She remembered another time, when she had gone to his door and hesitated, only to be found out. She paused, gathering strength from the sweet memory that engulfed her, and steeling herself, she rapped lightly upon the door. There was no answer, and she opened it and stepped inside, looking anxiously about the interior.

"Ah Katherine, I've been waiting for you!" He was seated at his desk, one leg slung over the arm of his chair, and when she entered, he poured himself a large brandy. By his slouching posture, and the look in his eyes, she knew it was not his first.

"False courage, Captain?" she asked quietly.

"'Tis not my courage that's lacking. Would *you* like some?"

"I don't need it," she replied patiently.

Devin put both feet on the floor and sat up a little straighter, studying her warily. Pushing the glass aside, he drummed his fingertips on the polished wood surface.

Katherine stood before the desk. "We have to talk."

"I should think."

She continued, "Haven't we been through enough to have learned to talk things through?" She asked pleadingly. "Shall we go through the rest of our lives the same way? Will you make the same mistake I did, and listen to Cecilia?"

"Is it true?"

"Well, yes, but…"

"Why didn't you tell me? I thought we talked things through, all of last night."

She let out a long breath, "I guess I was afraid."

"Of *me?* Do you not know you can tell me anything?"

"No, not of you." Katherine wasn't sure if he were angry. "Only that I had waited too long, and it got more difficult the longer I waited. I was going to look for you, at home… and I did try to tell you, this morning."

Through his protective fog, he studied the hopeful look in her eyes. *God,* he thought, *she was beautiful. And she was smart. And she was …honest.* And she did love him, he knew she did, it was in her touch and her every look—and the kisses she had given him that morning. She was going to look for him, *she had said that before.* Devin leaned back in his chair and crossed his arms over his chest, plopping his booted feet up on the desk. His fogged brain had fumbled through the months and math, long before she had joined him. "I know it wasn't Macey, and it couldn't have been Hann… Now, who else? *Who else?*" He frowned as if in thought.

Katherine picked up his brandy and took a drink, feeling the fire burn to her belly. "That's genuinely insulting, you know," she said with a slight grin, staring him down as though she were taking aim.

But he went on, "It must have been someone very handsome, I think, and *extremely* charming. Irresistible. Not lecherous at all. Someone you could trust… And you must have loved him very much."

She stared reflectively into the glass and then placed it down, before she began to speak, a small smile at the corners of her mouth, "Yes, he was handsome. The most handsome man I've ever known, and though I sent him from me, he assailed me at every turn, and it is true, I could not resist him. His kindness, his touch, indeed the mere sight of him, sent the blood to singing in my veins and made me weak with desire. Even when one night in his arms was to cost me my very soul, and cause me to live in shame the rest of my days, I could not help myself… So much did I love him."

His eyes locked with hers, and he stared so intently that she began to pace in front of the desk, gesturing with her hands.

"But then," she gave a short bitter laugh, "because I foolishly believed circumstances decreed it, I went away. I don't think he could ever know how difficult that was for me. To tear my own heart from my chest and leave it behind." She smiled sadly, as she remembered the needless pain of that morning. "Even then, when I was far away, that one whose path I know was meant to ever cross with mine, was with me, for God was kind, and by his grace would my love be with me always. Even now, when the obstacles are overcome, and the path is clear, should his father deny us, though my heart be broken, I shall not be alone, and will rejoice in his very image, and in the knowledge that in our son we are one forever. Yes, I loved the father of my child… And I still do."

His feet dropped to the floor, and she placed her hands on the arms of his chair, and leaned forward until her face was only inches from his, her heart pounding. *God, she wanted him*, the full impact of her love struck her like a blow to the stomach. She wanted to kiss him, and hold him, and to be held by him, not only in this moment, but for the rest of her life. "I tried to tell you this morning, and I would have, if we weren't interrupted. Please forgive me."

He stood, and Katherine straightened with him, watching him anxiously.

"Mine." He said, letting out a breath, "I knew," he gestured with his hand toward the desk, indicating the time he had waited. "I should have known right away."

"Of course," she whispered, as she stepped into his embrace, breathing a sigh of relief.

He stayed for a long while, stroking her hair, reveling in the words of love she had spoken, while her hands soothed the muscles of his back. "I'm sorry Katherine, for anything I said, and that I walked away. It wasn't the baby. It was the thought that you had found someone else. I should have known."

She looked into his eyes and found the love she needed. "It was my fault. I should have let you know, but I didn't want to make trouble for you, with Cecilia."

Devin nodded still in awe. "I had no idea. My own child and I've never seen him."

Katherine winced, at the weight of this last confession, "Well… You did. See him. Once." Nervously she plunged on, holding his eyes with her anxious gaze, and willing him to follow her. "Do you remember that day in Portsmouth, when you stopped a woman with a child?"

"I thought it was you."

"She was…"

"Your sister."

"Yes."

"I knew that!" He shook his head. "I mean, I thought of that later. There was something about her. *And that baby was mine?*"

"Ours," she corrected, her fingers finding and freeing the buttons down the front of his shirt.

"I was so close. If only I had found you."

"It doesn't matter now, but say you forgive me," she pleaded, as her hands pulled his shirttails free, and slid smoothly around his waist and up to his shoulders and her lips found that most wonderful place where his heart thudded ever louder in sweet harmony with hers.

He held her shoulders, and looked deep into her eyes. "Aye Love, I forgive you, but I swear to God, I'll never let you go again."

The words filled her heart and gave her courage. "In that case, would you do me a favor?"

"Try me," he rasped, her caresses warming him more than brandy ever had.

Her voice was barely a whisper. "*Love me now.*"

His answer flared from passion darkened eyes, "No more secrets?"

"None."

A warning voice taunted him still, but he shut it out. She loved him, it was clearly there in her face, a mixture of love and desire, and he loved her, and part of love was trust. "No doubts?"

"Never."

"You'll stay with me?"

"Always," she whispered against his lips.

She looked at you that way before, the voice insisted, as his mouth hovered over hers and his heart began to pound. *Oh damn*, he decided, *she was worth the risk!* Eagerly he claimed her, leaning her back upon the desktop and sending the brandy to the floor with a crash that left little doubt as to its fate.

"Your brandy!" She managed to gasp between his fierce kisses.

"Leave it, I don't even like brandy," he confessed against her mouth as his hands probed beneath her sweater to find the vital warmth of her skin.

Katherine considered this, although her mind was fast leaping to more interesting topics, as he persisted. "Is it me then, who drives you to drink?"

He slowed his caresses and raised his head to glance at her. "Aye, but no longer, for no drink can heat my blood, and fog my mind like the feel of your skin, and the taste of your lips. At your touch I am a drunkard, intoxicated beyond measure."

Katherine smiled in amusement at his words, flowery but touching, as he rolled his R's and slurred slightly. "Yes, perhaps it is best if you no longer drink," she laughed, and he looked at her questioningly. "I'll tell you in the morning," she said, pulling his mouth back to hers.

As he kissed her, Devin lifted her from the desk and carried her toward the door before setting her on her feet.

She questioned with her eyes, "You're throwing me out?"

He shot the heavy bolt and turned to capture her with his smile. "Not on your life, but I want you all to myself."

His smile faded, and she found herself lifted again, as they moved toward the bed, and he continued where he had left off, this time with no interruptions from the inquisitive and anxious Katherine.

He undressed her slowly and she stepped back in time, and into his arms, rejoicing in the feeling of his warmth against her.

She shivered.

"You're cold," he said, moving her to the bed and pulling the quilt around them.

"I'm nervous."

"Never be afraid of me, Katherine, I love you more than my own life." He kissed her and stroked her until she grew warm and relaxed. He explored her full breasts in wonder, sending her to the edge of ecstasy. He caressed her hip, and when she rolled onto her back, he pressed a kiss to the velvet softness of her stomach and thought of the child he had never known.

When he moved to capture her mouth again, she arched against him, wrapping her silken arms about his neck and burying her fingers in his soft curls as she always did in her dreams. He was hers now, *really* hers, and she reveled in the thought as well as the touch.

His tongue invaded her mouth and she met it hungrily, opening, welcoming, *remembering,* until the memory became one with the reality, healing her heart. Lost in his arms, she was hardly able to bear it, as he made her wait, made them both wait, long wonderous moments. He stroked between her thighs, and she knew only his touch, closing her eyes as he teased and tormented, and loved her to the very brink of her endurance, until she reached for him, looking deeply into his eyes. "No more waiting," she whispered, insuring her will with a silken caress.

When they came together at last, she met him with a willingness that captured him yet again, and enraptured him, and he gloried in the taking and the giving of this most wonderful love. Her hands gripped the muscles of his upper arms, and she gasped as she gave herself up to him body and soul, until her head fell back on the pillow.

He felt her surrender and her victory as one, and he too, found a release he'd thought never to know again, sharing with her in remembered wonder. Breathless, he collapsed beside her and embraced her, wanting to hold this moment forever. "You see, Love," he whispered against her temple, "It's the same, I've never forgotten."

"I never forgot you," she confessed, "Not for an hour, not for a moment… I've always loved you." She reached to straighten the cross that he wore, and he started to take it off.

Katherine caught his hand. "Please, keep it."

"But, it's yours."

She smiled, "I was glad when I heard you had taken it with you."

"I stole it." Devin said, looking as though he had never considered it quite that way before. "I didn't mean to, I only wanted to have something of yours until I found you."

At his confession, she smiled a soul reaching smile of satisfaction. "What is it?"

"Nothing."

Her cheeks were pink, her eyes sparkled, and he had to know.

"No, what?" he asked again.

"You love me."

"Yes," he said, "I do."

"I saw the Bluebells," she said, after a moment. "They were blooming, and they were beautiful—breathtaking, really. When did you do that?"

Devin looked a little embarrassed. "That October after you left. I had been to my parents' old house—they still own it—There are so many there. My mother planted them years ago—I brought some bulbs back. I was still looking for you, and I thought, if you came back and saw them... You would see them." He smiled, not sure if he wanted to finish the admission, "You would know, and you would remember me."

"As if I could ever forget," she said, her eyes full of love and unshed tears. "But there were so many. How did you..."

"I made my crew help," he grinned, "Tully, and Hubbard and Jimmy... all of them, and I never told them why. I am certain they thought I was crazy, but it was better than being in battle." He laughed at the memory.

They were quiet until something she had said, struck him as odd. "Who told you I took your cross?"

"Cecilia."

"Oh," he said, sorry he had brought it up.

Katherine rose up on her elbow to face him, a slight crease marring her forehead. "How did she know?"

Devin thought, the brandy still clouding his mind.

"She came into my room while I was in the tub."

At this Katherine raised a brow, and Devin hurried to finish. "But Cecil came, and he threw her out. If he hadn't, I would have. She was always after me," he said without guile.

"Yes," she said thoughtfully, "Well I can't condemn her for that. I'm just grateful she never caught you."

Devin groaned. "Please! Besides, I was hoping for better things."

She smiled and settled beside him. "Poor Cecilia."

"*Poor Cecilia?*"

"Yes, in a way I feel sorry for her. She just couldn't be happy. Can you imagine wanting anything that was worth trading family, friends, country… *everything.*"

He gave her a smoldering look, "Truthfully? I can."

Her heart melted and she snuggled closer. "Devin?"

"Hmm?"

"Did you ever stop to think, that in a war between the North and South, you're fighting Northerners?"

He nodded. "Yes, but both sides are fighting for what they believe in. And there's good and bad on both sides. These people aren't fighting for the North, they're robbing and cheating for personal gain. That's why I'd rather do this. My heart is with the Union, because I think the country will be stronger if the sides stay together, but I cannot say the South is totally wrong. I mean, slavery is abominable, but there are other issues."

Katherine smiled in admiration. "You make a pretty speech for a drunkard."

His thoughts were elsewhere. "Tell me about him." He brushed a hand across her abdomen. "Did you have a bad time?"

She hesitated, remembering, "I guess nothing out of the ordinary…" *If the ordinary was running the gauntlet through hell.* "Anyway, he was worth it, you'll see."

"I wish I had been there for you." He took her hand. "What's his name?" He looked at her, surprised he hadn't thought to ask sooner.

"*Gabriel,* after the messenger of God." She gave a short laugh. "I did wonder if God was trying to tell me something." And for strength. Do you mind it? You once said I had a strong name, so I thought you might like it."

Gabriel! His heart sang, and he flashed her a beautiful smile, his leap of faith rewarded. "It's a grand name. I'm glad to hear it." The name she had called so desperately that it had torn at his soul. *Their child.* It was fine. *Fine indeed!* He laughed aloud with relief.

"What is it?"

"Nothing."

"No more secrets, remember?"

"When I rescued you, when you came to, you were calling that name so frantically, I..."

"You were jealous," she whispered.

He laughed softly, "Yes, of my son, *Gabriel,*" he said again, liking the sound of it. "Gabriel... what?" He asked.

"Gabriel, 'T'."

"What's the 'T' stand for?"

She shrugged. "You never did tell me."

Devin smiled, remembering how he had teased her when she had asked. "As I recall, we were kind of busy," he said, running his hand upward to enclose a full breast and coax the nipple to a hardened peak.

"Tell me now," she whispered, closing her eyes.

"Thomas."

"*Gabriel Thomas.* That's nice."

"I like, *tonight* better," he teased, placing a warm kiss on her parted lips.

"Poor thing, though," she murmured, as his caresses continued to warm her.

Devin paused to gaze at her seriously. "What?"

She ran her palm across his ribs to tease him, as she rose up to cover his mouth in a lingering kiss that almost, but not quite, distracted him.

"Katherine, what is it?"

"Oh, one of those accidents of birth, I suppose," she said, pushing him onto his back while her hands sought out the warm hard strength of him that she wanted. She straddled his hips, and her breasts teased his chest as she kissed him hungrily, caressing him with her body.

Devin was in torment. Trying to concentrate on the conversation, and unable to ignore what she was doing to him. But even in his distracted state, he noticed there was something in her eyes, and the small smile at the corner of her mouth that told him it was a game.

"The doctors say there's no hope for it," she sighed, as she rose above him, teasing and withdrawing, challenging him with her eyes until the game caught up with her, and her breathing grew shallow.

"Tell me." He rasped.

"Poor thing," she whispered in his ear, "He looks just like his father."

Devin grinned appreciatively, but she had grown too serious to gloat.

His smile faded as she engulfed him, sinking over him with a deliberate slowness that took his breath away. Again and again, she caressed the length of him with her heated body, stopping to kiss him, and invite him to fondle her, until they were both at the brink of fulfillment.

Devin grew impatient, and with a soft moan he rolled her beneath him, bringing them both to an abrupt climax that left them speechless in their contentment.

They lay together in satisfied silence, until he raised his head to gaze at her.

"What?" She asked, self-conscious now that their passions were spent.

"Saints, Katherine, you amaze me," he whispered.

"I only wanted to please you."

"Oh, you do that. In fact, my love, I'd venture to say you barely need to try."

"So," she smiled, "you think there might be hope for us then?"

The look in his eyes told her all she needed to know.

The following morning Katherine again woke to find him watching her. "What are you thinking?" She asked sleepily, closing her eyes again.

"I was thinking that when we are married, we should have a small bed, so you will never be far away from me."

She opened her eyes, and closed them again, smiling, but saying nothing.

"Katherine?"

"I'm hungry," she said, remembering they hadn't had any supper.

"So am I," he said nuzzling her neck. Her stomach growled loudly in protest and he laughed.

"All right, all right, I'll get us something to eat," he chuckled, rising and pulling on his trousers, and sitting on the edge of the bed. "It must have been all that exertion from last night," he baited, giving her a sideward glance.

She brushed her palm across his bare shoulders. "Do you remember last night so well?"

"I do, Love. Am I not the happiest man in the world this very beautiful morning?"

Her heart grew warm and her eyes grew misty. "Oh," was all she said.

"And why shouldn't I remember?"

"Well…"

"I wasn't exactly drunk."

"You weren't exactly sober," she said, rising reluctantly from the bunk.

"I remember, *everything*." On his way to the wash stand, he gave her a wicked leer that made her laugh, "Will you wear this?" He held out his robe, inviting her to borrow it.

"Thank you. Did you buy this for yourself?" She hoped she sounded nonchalant, slipping into the caressing silk, and feeling the doubt in her heart.

Devin flipped his hair into place with the comb. "It was a gift," he gave her a knowing look, "from my sister."

"Likely story." Katherine looked at him skeptically, the corner of her mouth lifting.

"Honest! Who's jealous now?" He laughed, and snapped the towel at her, as she began to stalk him. "If I wanted anyone but you, I've had plenty of time, haven't I?" He said as he retreated around the room.

"Yes."

"And if I didn't want you, I could have left you in the ocean."

"You did," she reminded him, as they neared the bed again.

"But I came back," he defended, and paused as one of the pillows hit him full in the face, and he grinned. "So, you see, I want only you."

She cornered him by the bed, and threatened with the other pillow, but ready this time, he caught her about the waist with one arm to scoop her onto the bunk and crouch over her on all fours, holding her prisoner. "Marry me!"

It was barked like an order, and Katherine couldn't help but laugh. But seeing the uncertain look in his eyes her heart melted. *How could she not marry him. How could she ever be without him?*

Seconds seemed like hours to Devin as he watched her, trying to read her mind. He had never imagined himself in a situation such as this, as if his whole life depended on one answer.

Her gaze passed from his face, to caress her prison of broad shoulders and arms like rippling steel, and passed over his hard chest and the muscles of his stomach to the pillars of his darkly clad thighs. "What a *captivating* proposal," she mused, and was rewarded with a groan. She grinned as he shook his head in mock pain.

"Well?" He snapped.

On his face was a vicious scowl that had sent many a hearty sailor running about his business. From Katherine it elicited a raised brow and a mirthful *"What?"*

Damn, he thought, *it was his best scowl. What should he do now?* At a loss for words, he did what he most wanted to do. He lowered his head and kissed her, letting his heart speak for him.

Serious now, she moved her hand, and he held his breath as her palm grazed his stomach. Her fingertips teased inside his waistband before sliding upwards over his chest and caressing his neck as she pulled him down to kiss her again.

"Katherine…"

"Don't," she said.

"Don't what?" A puzzled look crossed his brow.

"Don't bark–at–me!" She exclaimed, as she tickled him under the arms in a sneak attack.

Wriggling in defense, he flattened himself against her, the full contact making them both pause. He wrapped his arms around her and rolled over pulling her, still laughing, on top of him.

Her laughter retreated before the look in his eyes, and her heart turned over, and this time it was she that lowered her lips to his.

Lost in her kiss, and all that followed, it was a long time before he realized she hadn't answered him.

Chapter 28

The Athena sailed like a queen through the gathering dusk, and into port in Delaware, her stately serenity at far odds with the apprehensive young woman who paced away in the heart of the grand vessel.

Katherine waited while the ship was secured, the prisoners were unloaded, and most of the crew had left the decks. She hadn't seen Devin for hours. As she studied the now familiar interior of the cabin, she tried to find the cause of her uneasiness. She wanted to reach port, *didn't she?* It was the first step in their journey homeward to their baby. But at least here, for the last few days, she had found some measure of happiness, secluded from the troublesome world as if on a private island.

Perhaps that was it, the return to reality, and the never-ending war that hung over the country like a black shroud, echoing uncertainty and despair. War or not, she tried to comfort herself, nothing in life was ever certain. What was to be, would be. But when Devin returned to collect her and escort her ashore, it did not help to see her uncertainty mirrored in his eyes.

Wordlessly, he took her in his arms and held her close before they left the ship and strolled through the newly fallen darkness. She could see little of the town, but she cared not, her natural curiosity crushed beneath the heavy load of doubt she carried. The streets were quiet at this hour, and as Devin knowingly led the way to a hotel she clung to his arm, wondering how much longer she could hold him, and fearing the answer.

They entered the dimly lit lobby and Katherine waited in the shadows, surprised to hear Devin register them as brother and sister, before he took her arm to escort her up the stairs. Halfway down the hallway he stopped at one room and opened the door to glance inside. When Katherine started to enter, he took her elbow and steered her to the room next door. Here he stood aside as she entered, and then followed her in, closing the door behind them.

Advancing into the center of the comfortable room, Katherine removed her coat and turned to him in question.

Devin smiled and shrugged. "I thought you might like a little privacy, and, *Miss* Lawrence, I don't want to do your reputation any more damage," he said, as he opened the door that joined the two rooms and set his bag down next door.

She smiled contritely, "I think it's a little late, to worry about my virtue."

He leaned one shoulder against the door jamb and crossed his arms, studying her, as she sauntered toward him, smiling as she spoke, "I am a lost cause, for I have been ravished by the best."

Devin's brow shot up, "*And did you enjoy it?*"

"I did." She laughed, "I'm wicked."

"Aye, wicked," he grinned, as he pulled her into his arms, and nuzzled her neck.

"I gladly proclaim myself a wanton woman if it means I may stay by your side," she stated, pulling his shirt from his trousers to run her hands up his bare back, her eyes smoldering with desire.

He paused only long enough to whisper against her lips, "Your room or mine?" and smothered her laughter with his kiss.

The sun had not yet risen when Devin sat up, throwing his long legs over the side of the bed and pulling on his trousers. At his movement, Katherine stirred, and moved behind him to hug him around the waist, as he pulled on his boots.

"Where are you going so early?" She asked, her voice heavy with sleep.

He arched against her, loving the feel of her against his bare skin, and turned to kiss her cheek. "I've got a lot to do, Love, go back to sleep. I've got to see that the prisoners are signed over, send word that you're safe, and make your arrangements."

He rose to put on his shirt and Katherine, pulled the sheet up to cover herself, as yesterday's bud of apprehension blossomed within her heart. "*What arrangements?*"

Devin was busy getting ready and barely glanced in her direction, "For your trip home.

"*My trip?*"

He stopped mid-step to turn his full attention on her, realizing there might be a hitch in his plans. With a worried look, he went and sat on the bed. "Come on now, Love…" tender fingers pushed a stray lock of hair from her face. "You know we're in the middle of a war. I've got to finish what I've started, and you've got to go home."

Her answer was neither loud, nor hysterical. It was a simple, but definite, "No."

Devin raised one eyebrow. As a captain, he was used to having his every order followed to the letter. The burly members of his crew jumped to do his bidding, but here was this… this… woman, who squared her shoulders, met him eye to eye and said, 'No'. *Very beautiful shoulders*, he added mentally, and took a deep breath. He reasoned, he pleaded, and still, she would be stubborn. "Katherine, be reasonable, for God's sake, I won't risk having you killed."

At this her eyes grew wide. "*What risk?* Where are you going?"

Devin sighed and caught her hand to kiss it, and moved to the adjoining door. "I'll be back for a late breakfast. We'll talk more then."

"Devin Galloway, if you're going to get yourself killed, I want to be there!"

He paused in the doorway to look at her.

"I mean it!" She sputtered in frustration.

He stayed only long enough to blow her a kiss before the portal closed behind him.

Katherine propped herself up in bed, and spent an overlong hour searching for a way he would let her stay. Though she longed to see their son, she couldn't bear to leave Devin, knowing he would be in danger. Deep in thought, she was startled when a timid knock sounded at her door, and embarrassed to realize she had no robe, or nightgown. She hastily wrapped the sheet about her, and went to open it. "Who is it?" She asked, cautiously.

"It's the maid, Ma'am we've brought your tea and the water for your bath. The gentleman ordered it for you before he left."

Warmed by his thoughtfulness, she lingered overlong in her bath, while, her mind raced far ahead. She didn't know yet how she would persuade Devin to let her stay, but she had more immediate things to take care of. She dressed in the same tired clothes, braided her wet hair, and pulling her coat around her shoulders to hide her questionable mode of dress, she started on her way. On impulse, she paused at the connecting door and opened it to look inside Devin's room. She smiled to see the bed mussed and his robe on a nearby chair. A few of his things were scattered across the bureau and wet towels draped the wash stand. He had seen to it that his room appeared more lived in than hers, and he had been with her the whole time.

She was immediately assailed by the heat of the day as she stepped into its brightness. The heavy coat was too much, but the streets were already full of people, and she would have felt naked without it. She was relieved to note, that, for the most part, people paid her no mind.

Her first stop was easy to find, as Devin had given her directions the night before. Down a narrow side street, she found the ladies clothiers called simply, "Ilene's," and she entered, trying not to wonder what business he ever had here. As she stepped through the plain doorway, she was surprised to find herself in a small entryway in the semi-darkness, and paused to let her eyes adjust. The tiny window above the door admitted a little light to show her the wooden stairway that led to the second floor. Seeing no other option, she began climbing carefully, wondering if she indeed had the right place.

Her doubts were banished when she entered a second door at the top of the stairs, and the merry tinkle of a bell announced her arrival into a clean and neat shop, flooded with sunlight. Therein she found the pretty dark-haired Ilene herself, eager to please, and Katherine was relieved to find some ready-made items. She purchased a white nightgown with a matching robe, exquisite in its simplicity, a new white blouse, and undergarments. Next, was a lovely green dress that Ilene produced from the back room insisting it was meant for Katherine. At further coaxing, the dress was tried on, and as Katherine admired the full sleeves of the soft flocked material, and the crocheted lace at the throat and cuffs, Ilene nipped and tucked for her, making the dress fit. As she labored, the proprietress chatted endlessly making her feel at home.

Katherine dressed, and while she waited for the slight alterations to be completed, she added a pair of low slippers of soft suede to her bounty. She paid with some of her own money, a few stray bills which had been in her pocket the whole of her adventure, and some new crisp bills Devin had given her that morning. Ilene, who had not flinched at the beautiful woman's current mode of dress, or her faded bruises, looked askance at some of the crumpled bills she was offered, trying to hide a grin. "It's a long story," was all Katherine offered in explanation.

After she made change, Ilene added a length of ribbon to the parcel waving away payment. Katherine thanked her, and being so reminded, added a box of hairpins, placing some coins on the counter, and waving away the change, which left both women laughing. With a promise not to forget her new friend, Katherine left in search of the general store. Her second destination, being a large establishment on the main street, was easier to find, and it did not take her nearly as long to purchase a comb and brush. She fleetingly considered new boots, her old favorites being pretty much ruined by their salt water bath, but she decided they would take too much of her limited funds. After all, she didn't know how long she would be away from home. Instead, she selected a tin of saddle soap to repair her boots, and reminded of soap, stopped to get some for herself.

She was on her way out, when a small stack of knitted shawls caught her eye, and she decided she'd better have one for the chilly nights. The workmanship was excellent, and the price most reasonable. She chose one of a soft cream color thinking of the lace on her new dress. As she paid once more, she thought she would like to buy something for Devin, but after wandering for some time, she could not decide on anything, and went on her way.

As she stepped outside, she was again assaulted by the heat of the day, but this time it was tempered by the delicious aroma of fresh bread, which practically dragged her to a nearby bakery. Inside, perspiring in the additional heat, she ordered the bread and two sweet rolls, and, juggling her packages, she headed to the hotel, thinking by the time she got there, she might be in need of another bath.

Plodding up the stairs and down the hall, she noted that the doors to both of their rooms were wide open, as was the door that joined the two rooms together. As the rooms were tidied, and the beds made, she dismissed the oddity as a careless oversight on the part of the young maids she had seen earlier that morning, and thought no more of it.

Dropping her bundles on her bed she slid out of her heavy coat, closed all the doors, and went immediately to open a window, seeking some relief. It was there she stood, awaiting a breeze that never came, when running footsteps sounded in the hall, and the door to her room burst open to slam the wall behind it with a force that rattled the windows. Her heart in her throat, Katherine spun in surprise to face a Devin she hardly recognized. Small rivulets of perspiration traveled down a face that was a vivid red, whether from heat or anger, she could not yet fathom. Damp curls clung to his forehead, as he stood gasping for breath and glaring in her direction. Regarding him warily, she questioned with a look.

"Where the devil have you been?!" He exclaimed, slamming the door and advancing into the room.

Taken aback by this unexpected abuse, Katherine fought the urge to answer in kind, while her mind fumbled to grasp the situation. At the moment, the best she could manage was, "What do you mean?"

He heaved an exasperated sigh, and wiped a hand across his brow. "I *mean*, where the hell have you been? That's what I mean!"

She glanced sideways at the bed. "Shopping," she stated, mentally debating how best to deal with this tirade.

Devin waived his arms furiously, and ripped at the buttons of his shirt, "*Shopping? Shopping!?*" He repeated, as he pulled the cloying garment off and rolled it into a ball. He too, took a sideways glance at the bed, and seeing its contents, went and pushed them aside, to sit back to her and wipe his face with his shirt.

Katherine approached with caution around the foot of the bed to find his face hidden. *"Devin?"*

His eyes appeared over the rumpled ball of cloth. At the quizzical look on her lovely face, he paused, and began to shake, and it was a moment before she realized he was laughing, and she wondered at his sanity. She stepped closer, and put a hand on his bare shoulder and he hugged her around the waist. "Do you want to tell me what that was all about?" She waited patiently, her hands finding the taut muscles in his neck and shoulders.

"I came to get you for breakfast."

"*Breakfast!* Oh, I forgot! I completely lost track of the time; it must be after noon! I'm so sorry."

He shook his head. "I thought you were gone. I thought you left… like before. The day after the ball, when I searched for you, and at the cottage… I thought you were upset about this morning and ran away."

She understood now, as her hands stilled on his shoulders and she hugged him to her center. "Oh," she whispered, "I thought you understood. There's no reason for that now. I only ever left you because, to my mind you were married. It was myself I couldn't trust… Nothing could ever make me leave you again." Haunted by visions of him slamming doors, and pounding the pavement, in search of her, she sought more words to reassure him, "Don't you realize how much I want to be with you? I always did. I'm sorry for those times, and I'll never forgive myself for hurting you, but you must believe it will never happen again, so we can go on from here. I love you." She rained soft kisses across his eyes and his cheeks until she found his mouth and sought to convince him with a kiss of gentle persuasion.

The thought that he believed her crossed her mind, as he answered her, and the kiss smoldered into a flame that engulfed her senses. Devin fell back across the bed taking her with him. "Ow."

Katherine opened her eyes at the sound and laughed at his puzzled expression, as he reached up to retrieve a small package from beneath his head, and hand it to her. Still smiling she rolled off his chest to open it, revealing her brush and comb and the offending tin of saddle soap.

As he rose on his elbows to look at her warped boots, his stomach growled loudly and she laughed again.

She looked around expectantly and grimaced, as she rescued another package that had been quite flattened beneath her. She shrugged, and began to feed him flattened bits of sweet roll. "You, see? You said we would have breakfast together, and so we are."

Devin playfully bit at her fingers, and turned on his side, to face her. "Don't you think you should just get new boots?"

"Well," she answered between bites, "I didn't want to spend too much."

"I've got enough money, Katherine."

She only shrugged, and got up to rinse her fingers at the wash stand, before moving back to her place at the window. "These will do."

He pretended to concentrate on the food he ate, but stole a look at her when he next spoke, "When we're married, you'll be free to spend whatever you will."

He had said it again, and she had seen him glance at her when he thought she wasn't looking, and that same look had been there. The look he had on the ship when he had playfully spoken part of the vows to her as he handed her his comb, and when he had barked it at her like an order. She struggled to put a label to that look… '*Love?*' Yes, there was that. She looked over her shoulder to catch him studying her, and she turned away again.

Devin rose, and went to the wash stand to rinse his hands, and splash fresh water over his bearded face and his chest. Toweling off, he went to stand behind her, at the window.

She was reminded of another night as he stood so close behind her, and she raised a silent prayer of gratitude that this was so different. There was no need to run, no need to hide, and she leaned back against him, "I was remembering…"

"The cottage?" He finished, as his arms came around her.

"Yes." She turned into his embrace.

"Katherine…"

"Hmm?"

"Every time I mention marriage, you turn away from me, and I would like to know why."

"You've never *asked* me." She gave a shy laugh, and it scraped across his dangling nerves.

He stepped back and held her gently by the shoulders, to better read her face, knowing there was more to it. "No more secrets?"

"I…"

"Just tell me."

"I want you to know…" She glanced down, before looking up at him. He waited.

"The truth is, I don't want it to be because of the baby. I wasn't trying to trap you."

"Katherine…"

"I know that women sometimes plan to do that, and I…"

"*Katherine.*"

"I would never do that. And I don't want you to feel…"

"*KATHERINE!*"

"What?"

"It is fairly obvious that you were not trying to trap me."

"Oh." She nodded, seeing the truth in his words. "Well, this is not the way I expected things to be, and I want you to know you don't have to marry me." She glanced away before looking up at him again, and was surprised to find his eyes closed and a smile breaking across his face.

Devin began to laugh. A rich sound that started deep within and rumbled upward through his chest. "Oh, but I do." He said at last, causing her to regard him wonderingly. He went on, pulling her close again. "It's not about the baby," he whispered. "It's the very reason I have survived these horrid years. I don't have to be here, you know. I had come to invest in the shipping, but I had planned to return to Nova Scotia, until I met you. My parents had recently moved there."

Katherine gasped and stared at him. Her mouth opened as though she would speak.

"I could have just gone back. But since that day, the first time I saw you, it has been my foremost thought, and my most cherished goal to call you my wife." He paused, and grinned down at her. "Maybe someday, I'll ask you."

She had been lost in his beautiful words and was caught off guard by his sudden change of mood, and she stood staring after him as he headed toward his room. True, he hadn't actually asked her, but she was happy. More so today than yesterday, for *hadn't he said his most cherished goal was to call her his wife? And wasn't that a lovely thing to say?* She nearly skipped over to the bed, and when he turned at his doorway, she balled up his soiled shirt and hurled it at him in mock anger, but she could not hide the smile that lit her face.

One hand on the door knob, Devin caught the shirt above his head and swept it to his waist in a deep bow. "My dear Miss Lawrence…" he began, and she laughed at the picture he made, so formally shirtless. He grinned, and flicked his brows at her as he continued, "would you do me the great honor of joining me for dinner this evening, before I starve to death?"

Katherine joined his mood and curtsied prettily, in spite of her faded clothes and worn boots. "Why, yes, Captain Galloway, I'd be delighted."

More seriously, he asked, nodding toward the packages on the bed, "Do you have something to wear?" She nodded, but he placed some bills on the bureau by the door, adding, "In case you want anything. I have business to take care of at the ship, and I'll need a bath. I'll be here around six. Oh, and there's a charity ball… Ladies Guild, or something, at the Governor's house, I thought we might go, if you like."

She nodded again, coming toward him with a look in her eye that made him wary. "I'm going to miss you," she whispered, twining her arms about his neck and giving him a long kiss that backed her words.

Devin took a deep breath and looked as though he would kiss her again, "I'm going to miss you too…"

"I know." She said, moving away from him, laughter trailing over her shoulder.

He threw her a grin and shut the door. When it immediately opened again, she turned, "I almost forgot," he dangled his gold pocket watch for her to see, before placing it on top of the bills. "Try to be here on time, hmm?"

Katherine crossed her arms and gave warning with her eyes, but was losing the battle with the grin that threatened to give her away.

"Oh," Devin added, "I don't believe any of the ladies will be wearing curly toed boots, lovely as they are." He shut the door and instantly opened it. "Are you sure you have something presentable to wear?"

The look she fired would have sent any blockade runner to the bottom of the ocean, and he ducked out quickly.

Chapter 29

After Devin had gone, Katherine unwrapped her bundles and laid out her new dress. It was pretty enough, but it was a day dress, and she had a sudden desire for something that would take his breath away. *Maybe Ilene would be able to help.* She washed and dressed in her new finery. Giving a last touch to her hair, she glanced in the mirror, and paused to look again. Her bruises had faded to a point where they were barely visible if she peered very closely, and the heat of the day had brought a bright flush of color to her cheeks. Excitement shone in the eyes that stared back at her, at the thought of the coming evening, and she hurried on her way.

This time, the tall blonde gathered more than a few admiring glances as she found her way without hesitation back to the dress shop.

"Oh, Miss Lawrence, you do look lovely!" Ilene stopped to admire her, as Katherine entered the shop.

"Thank you, Ilene. It's the dress, I'm sure. That's why I'm here. I need a gown…"

"Wonderful! I'd love to make you a gown."

"For tonight."

At the look on the young woman's face, Katherine's heart fell.

She knew it was highly unlikely she would find a suitable dress ready, and certainly there was not time to make one, but still… "Oh, Ilene, I know it's crazy, but is there nothing?" She asked, her eyes still hopefully searching the corners of the shop. "It's very important. Maybe we could add some different lace or ribbon to something?"

Slender dark brows arched and drew together in concentration, while Ilene did a mental inventory. "I'm sorry, Miss Lawrence, I don't …"

"Please, call me Katherine."

"All right, Katherine." The young woman paused, and seemed to study the one so called.

Katherine had a strange feeling the woman was weighing something far different than the question at hand, and stood patiently until she continued.

"I do have a few gowns that were never picked up, times being what they are, but I'm afraid…" Here she paused to look at Katherine again with a professional eye. "Wait," Ilene muttered, disappearing into the back room.

When she reappeared minutes later, she had a large box, which she placed on an already overburdened tabletop where she removed the lid, and lovingly withdrew a beautiful gown of cream-colored satin.

Katherine admired the long sleeves, the intricately embroidered neckline and tapered waist that flowed to a full skirt. Ilene turned the dress to show off a row of tiny satin covered buttons running down the back, and her smile broadened wider still, at Katherine's exclamation.

"Oh, Ilene, it's the prettiest gown I've ever seen. Is it someone's order?"

Ilene laughed brightly, "This is mine, but if you don't mind that, you're welcome to borrow it."

"Mind? Of course not, I can't believe I'm this fortunate, but are you sure? Did you really make it?" She asked, running her hand over the exquisite workmanship. "I've never had much patience for sewing," she admitted, thinking of the tiny stitches she had once fashioned in a head of dark hair.

"Yes, but I had help." Ilene looked around the little room as if amused by it. "I had a larger shop, and assistants, before the war," she broke off. "We'd better get this fitted, it will be a little short, but I'll think of something."

Katherine hesitated, "Oh, but if it's yours I don't want you to alter it," she protested.

A slim hand waived her words aside, "Now, don't be daft, if I needed to, I could make it fit a different person, every day of the week."

Katherine smiled, "But why should you? Your own dress?"

"Oh, I wouldn't do this for just anyone," she laughed.

Katherine persisted, "But why…" Her protests were stilled when the other's steady blue eyes held hers for a quiet moment, "Because I like you, Katherine." She said simply.

Once again in her room, Katherine paced before the window, her soft slippers making no sound on the polished wood floor. Instead of letting down the hem of the gown, Ilene had simply added a satin band at the bottom to create a double hem, and the rest was done in no time. The woman was a genius, and she could barely contain her excitement. She had returned for an early bath so her hair would have time to dry, and she would have plenty of time to get ready.

She had now finished her hair, pinning it up in an elegant style, and donned the beautiful dress, with the assistance of one of the maids. For the final touch, she added the pearl necklace and matching earrings that Ilene had insisted she borrow. She felt like a princess.

She heard voices in the next room, and surmised Devin had returned, and a bath was being readied next door. She could hear him moving about, and her excitement grew. *Is it his very nearness that affects me so?* Lighting the lamp to hold off the gathering darkness, she went again to stand at the window in contemplation. *Good Lord, I've been to bed with him… borne his child, and yet I am this affected because he asks me to dinner.* Of the many times they had been together, not once could she remember preparing herself for him… Except that fateful night at the cottage, and she hadn't had much time to think about it, and, she vividly recalled, she hadn't worn much. She blushed at the memory, and stopped to listen, realizing she had heard his door close.

Disappointment became a lead weight in her chest, slowing her movements. She went to the adjoining door and knocked lightly. There was no answer, and when she peeked inside, the room was empty. *Surely, he'd not forgotten?* But before she had time to think, a firm knock sounded at the other door, and she opened it to find a most precious memory.

Devin stood in full dress uniform, and when her eyes met his, he bowed low. The soft lamplight burnished the gold buttons and highlighted his dark hair, but it was his face that held fast her loving gaze. Katherine's heart turned over. Her eyes caressed the clean-shaven jaw that was so different, and yet so familiar, and when he smiled, she was lost.

If Katherine's thoughts were of the past, Devin's were very much riveted in the present and on the vision that greeted him. A warm smile stretching across his features, he studied her for an embarrassingly long time, before he spoke. "Good evening, Miss Lawrence," he said, his eyes never leaving hers. He produced a single white rose and presented it to her with a flourish.

"Thank you," she whispered, inhaling the delicate perfume of the fragile blossom. "The white are my favorite."

"I know."

Katherine paused in question, but he went on…

"The bud, does of course, pale in comparison to the full bloom of your beauty."

She smiled, completely captivated, "Does this mean you at least find me *presentable*, Captain?"

"Indeed, Miss Katherine, at the very least, presentable, and at the most…." he paused and shook his head with a smile, "Words fail me."

"That's a first," she teased, and laughing softly, she took his proffered arm and they started down the hall.

It wasn't long before Katherine noticed that this night was different. Devin's manner was very proper, and quite serious. He was courting her. Giving her what might have been, had their times and trails been different, and her heart melted.

They dined in a hotel, elegant by wartime standards, and although the food was fine, Katherine paid little attention to the meal. Devin carried the conversation. He charmed, he flattered, and he saw to her every need. If she were captivated by him before, she was doubly so now, when he had the opportunity to lavish her with his attention, and she was free to accept it.

The air was still warm, and the moon lit the way, as they strolled the main street to a private residence at the edge of town, where the fund-raising entertainment proved to be quite a fancy ball. Katherine was glad to find she was dressed appropriately, although the only approval she cared anything about was definitely won at the start of the evening.

Devin bought their tickets, and she found herself introduced to a Colonel and his wife, and a long blue line of names and faces that immediately blurred in her memory when Devin swept her into the crowd. They danced, they laughed, and when etiquette called for it, they changed partners, but she barely noticed, aware only of him, in her vision, her arms, and her heart. From across the room, he courted her with his eyes, caressing her, loving her with an intensity that made her blush, and she was ever conscious of his attention.

For each waltz he was there to claim her, his eyes smiling into hers. He swept her around the room in a dizzying whirl of sound and color, and Katherine was floating on air. She heard the music, and felt the strong arms holding her close. She looked up into his face and travelled back in time, to that magical night when she had first known she belonged to him.

She found herself wishing it were so… back before the years of pain and separation. Before the war, and her parents' deaths.

Devin sensed her mood and waltzed her off to the side of the room. "Are you all right?"

She brushed at one stray tear, dedicated to the past, and managed a smile, comforted by his warm concern. "Yes. I'm fine, honestly. I was only visiting the past for a moment." She glanced around, now feeling at odds with the determinedly gay scene that surrounded them. He whispered close to her ear, "I love it when you say my name," and she smiled, her happiness returning in part.

"Would you like to go now?" He asked.

She thought he sounded hopeful, so she nodded and took his arm while he said their good-byes, and he led her out into the night.

They were quiet as they strolled along, each lost in thought, and it was a little while before Katherine understood they were not going directly to the hotel. Devin, instead, had crossed the street and turned down a walkway into a park, where he approached one of the benches and gestured for her to sit down.

Katherine studied the moonlight reflected in the small pond a short distance downhill from where they were, but the beauty of the scenery was dimmed by the tenseness she sensed in him. The wind rustled a few stray leaves down the stone pathway, and she glanced at him warily. She knew he wanted to send her home, and she began to brace herself, hoping it wouldn't lead to an argument that would spoil their beautiful evening. Devin had paced several steps away, and stood facing away from her for a few seconds, his hands folded behind his back, and when he returned to her and knelt on one knee, she could only stare.

"Katherine," he began, and taking her hand, he stopped to smile and to breathe. "Countless times, I've been in battle… I have faced gunshot and cannon, and never have I been as frightened as I am now."

Her brow raised in question, and his smile broadened, the moonlit shadows painting his dimples deeper than usual.

"I said earlier, that since the first day I met you, it has been my most cherished goal to call you my wife."

At the confirmation of his intention, a great joy surged within, thrilling her heart, but she sat very still, wanting to catch every word.

"I'm asking you now, Love. Will you answer my prayers and say you'll marry me?"

Her heart swelled, when he sat beside her on the bench, and took her hand to slip a ring on her finger, but she was much more interested in the long sweet kiss that followed. He helped her to her feet and she shivered slightly without his warm embrace. Without a word, he removed his coat and held it out for her, breathing the sweet scent of her hair as she slid into it. Her hand came through the sleeve, and when her ring glittered in the moonlight, she paused to look at it. A large oval of some kind, surrounded by smaller stones, but it was dark and she held her hand up to try to see it more clearly.

"It's real," he teased, and she gasped and slapped at his shoulder laughing happily.

"I was only trying to see it."

"The stone is green, like your eyes and golden, like your hair," he supplied. "And if you hold it just right," he said, taking her in his arms, and whispering against her lips, "it lights with fire." He kissed her then, a long sweet kiss, both pure and passionate, that she was always to remember, and it did indeed light a fire in her heart.

He kept his arm around her, and they began to walk. It was nice to walk with him. Simply walk with him, and know he belonged to her—that he wanted to be with her always. "I love it," she said, truthfully, still breathless from his kiss, not caring what it looked like, only rejoicing in what it meant.

"I ordered it made in Boston…"

"Oh." She answered, wondering when, and how he came to have it with him. Certainly, he had not expected to find her *here*.

"The day after I met you."

Katherine stopped to face him.

"I also asked your father's permission the last time I saw him. I knew you were meant to be mine. I just had a little trouble catching up to you." He smiled and looked at her expectantly, "So…?"

She was distracted by the butterflies dancing in her chest, "What?"

He rolled his eyes and gave her a hopeful grin, "Is it a '*Yes*' then?"

"Oh!" Her smile spread across her face and into his heart. "What do you think?"

She kissed him, there in the middle of the street, in wordless consent, not caring if anyone were there to witness. A wonderful soul sharing kiss that filled his heart, and stole his breath, "Yes! Of course, yes! And thank you for this beautiful night, I shall never forget it."

"I love you," he whispered against her temple, "I love you so much." His hands slid down her arms, and captured hers. He looked down at the ground and off into the distance, and she knew what was coming.

"You know, Love, I can't take you with me… and if the worst should happen, one of us should be there for our son."

She nodded her head in acceptance, and felt his relief as he exhaled. *Maybe he was right.* And she was only as unhappy as someone who held the keys of heaven could be.

⁂

Back in the hotel, Katherine tossed and turned, and then surrendered the lonely bed that would yield her no rest. Devin had kissed her goodnight at her door, carrying his formal treatment of the evening a little too far for her liking. He had explained to her that he had to go out again. *But surely, he had returned by now. Maybe he hadn't wanted to wake her and was working in the other room.*

She pulled her wrapper on over her nightgown and paced the floor. She missed him, and they had been apart but a few hours. How would she stand it, when the day after tomorrow, she would sail for home on the Athena, and he would take the Christina, and continue on the intended route southward, in hopes of catching those who awaited the arrival of the cargo? She didn't like his plan, and she certainly didn't like spending one of their last nights apart.

Silently her steps carried her to the connecting door to his room, and she slipped inside, only to be disappointed, when she found that the room was still empty. Fighting the panic that threatened, she sat on the edge of his bed and tried to be calm. *He was doing what he had to do. After all, he was here because of his work… or maybe he had stepped out for some air. Of course he would come to her when he got back.* She fought the tiny voice in her mind that tormented her, *He's sailed! He's gone!* She trusted him. She did. *You did it to him,* the voice prodded, and she closed her eyes against the guilt that tormented her, along with the fear. *No. No, he wouldn't,* she chanted, over and over, *not after that beautiful proposal.* She looked down at the heavy golden ring on her hand, a shining reminder of his love even in the shadows, and she had almost won the argument, when Devin stepped into the room and her faith was rewarded.

"I thought you'd be asleep," he whispered, surprised to see her there, and coming to kiss her cheek.

"I was lonely."

"I'm sorry," he answered, taking off his coat and the dark shirt he had donned for his nighttime escapades.

"Where were you?"

"It is prudent to ready the Christina by night, the fewer people that see us, the better. He began to remove his boots, "Did you miss me terribly?"

She gave him an inviting look, easing into the pillows, "Come here and I'll show you."

Devin laughed, moving toward her on the bed, "*Miss Lawrence!* What would your fiancé say?"

Katherine thought for a moment, "He would probably shut up and kiss me."

Chapter 30

The next morning, Katherine forced open stubborn eyes to greet the new day. She hadn't slept much, and her head ached slightly, but when she passed a hand over her brow and noticed the unaccustomed weight of the ring on her finger, she smiled, remembering the night before.

Devin had risen with the dawn, preparing for their separate journeys, and now she hurried to her room to wash and dress. She too, had a few things to take care of, and there wouldn't be time tomorrow.

Wearing her day dress, her hair braided and wound into a neat coil, she entered the door to Ilene's shop and climbed the dark stairs, her progress somewhat slowed by the large box she was returning. The little bell rang when she entered, but it seemed no one was there to hear. She stood for a moment wondering whether to stay or go, when a voice sounded in the back room. *A very familiar voice.* Her feet carried her forward, her heart beginning to pound. *She must be mistaken.* She looked around the curtain and saw them as they embraced, and heard their whispered words.

Ilene was speaking, "I love you, and I'll never forgive you if you don't come back to me."

"I love you too," he answered. "Don't worry, and you be careful. Remember what I told you." He straightened, and shredded Katherine's false hope that she was mistaken. Her instinct was to run, but she refused to give in to it. She had run once, and what had that brought her? He might love Ilene, but there was no way he didn't love her—*Not after last night.*

The oversized box caused an over loud noise hitting the table, and when Devin and Ilene looked up, it was to see Katherine standing in the outer room, her arms crossed, inadvertently displaying the ring on the hand that rested at her elbow. Her color was high. "You've got two minutes to tell me that's your sister, and explain why you didn't tell me before." At the identical look of shock on their faces, she shook her head, "Never mind, I know she's your sister. Just tell me why…"

Ilene glanced at her brother with a mixture of trepidation and humor.

"I told you." He muttered, before turning to Katherine.

Devin's first thought was that she looked amazing in her new dress with her vivid coloring, and he felt a surge of pride. That was when he noticed her forced smile, and his second thought was that he might be in trouble. He didn't help his cause by stammering, "Katherine, you're early."

"Excuse us," he said to Ilene, before taking the hand of his fiancée to lead her out the doorway to the privacy of the landing, where he kissed her until she melted against him. He cupped her face in his hands, to better read her expression. "Tell me you were not thinking what I think you were thinking."

"Only at first," she whispered, letting go of the sick feeling that had assailed her, glad that the entryway was dark and private. "I…" She glanced down, avoiding his eyes, "I couldn't bear it if it happened again."

He gently lifted her chin, so that she focused on his words, *"Katherine, it never happened in the first place."*

She met his eyes in a mixture of confusion and comprehension. So real had his relationship with Cecilia been to her, she still had trouble remembering it had never existed outside of her mind. She considered this, as he led her into the shop where Ilene had discreetly made herself busy.

Devin held Katherine's hand reassuringly while he made the introduction, "Katherine, my sister Ilene. I call her Lee, among other things."

Ilene gave a confirming nod, and a warm smile.

Yes, Katherine had seen it of course, the dark hair, the blue eyes, and the dimples, though slighter on the young woman, were much the same. In fact, she had thought on first meeting Ilene, that there was a strong resemblance, but surely, they would have said something…

"A likely story," she jested, to cover her embarrassment and hurt at being left out. "But, why didn't you tell me she was your sister?"

Devin shrugged, brother and sister exchanged glances, and Katherine drew her own conclusion. "I see," she whispered, as she studied Ilene in awe.

The young brunette only smiled, but it was enough.

"How exciting!" Katherine exclaimed, and at the gleam in her eye, Devin thought it wise to change the subject. "Returning the dress, are you?" He went to retrieve the box.

"Oh, Katherine, I think you should keep it," Ilene spoke up. "Dev, told me he was going to propose, and I thought…" A hopeful look finished the question as she gave Katherine a sideways glance.

"Oh!" Katherine proudly presented the ring on her hand and the two women exchanged hugs.

"It would make a perfect wedding gown, don't you think?" Ilene said, with a happy laugh, and a teasing glance at her brother. "It was mine, and I would like you to have it."

"Oh, you're married…"

Ilene nodded, crossing the fingers of both hands.

Katherine asked only with her eyes.

"My husband is missing." She spoke quietly, glancing down at the floor before looking back to the woman she had felt an immediate bond with. I keep telling myself he'll be safe, and I pray day and night…" She shrugged helplessly.

"Oh, Ilene…" Katherine hugged her again, and Devin heaved a sigh, as the two women went arm and arm through the curtains to the back room. He followed, mentally adjusting his busy schedule. It was not to be the only time that day he would have a change of plans.

That evening in her room, Katherine relaxed in a warm bath. She was finished, but lingered lazily, resting her head back and reviewing the events of the day and what little she knew of the morrow. She had spent a delightful afternoon getting to know her future sister-in-law, until Ilene had to get ready for a previous engagement. Devin had met her at the hotel for an early supper, and would return again later to escort her to the Athena, where they would spend the night, and he would leave her early in the morning. It had been decided Ilene would return and accompany her, when the Athena sailed for home, in two days' time—*without Devin.*

This last part she pushed to the far reaches of her mind, and in her search for a happier subject, her eyes fell on her ring, that did indeed glow with fire in the lamp light, as her hand rested on the side of the tub. The sight of it, and the thought of its meaning, lifted her heart, and she concentrated on the future. Although she hated leaving Devin, she couldn't wait to see Gabriel again, *and Devin would return—Of course he would, and the war would end, and maybe soon they could be a normal happy family.* She paused to listen, when a loud noise sounded next door. She hadn't had time to move, when the adjoining door was smashed open, splintering the casing and her nerves as one.

Relief and anger, mingled with subsiding panic, when she recognized the door smasher as her very own. *"For Heaven's sake, Devin,* must you always…" She stopped at the sight of the gun in his hand.

Devin rapidly took in the scene, and allowed himself a deep breath. He holstered the colt, and just for a moment he studied the picture she made, locking it in his mind forever.

Her wet skin glowed in the lamplight, her slender arms resting on the sides of the tub, stretched forth as if in welcome. A few burnished tendrils had fallen loose to tease her bare shoulders and frame the lovely face whose eyes were full of surprise and questions.

His throat was dry, as he crossed to her side to give her a hand up from the tub, and a quick kiss. "Get dressed, Love," he whispered, handing her a towel, and going to look out the window.

Katherine surmised there wasn't time for questions at the moment, and did as he asked, dressing quickly in her faithful old clothes. The rest of her things had been sent ahead to the Athena, and when he turned to see if she were ready, she had only to grab her brush and comb. He swept her coat about her shoulders and they headed for the door.

"But where…" She wasn't going to ask, but she couldn't help it.

"You've got your wish, my love, though I dare say we'll both regret it," he said, when they had stepped into the hallway.

"What do you mean?"

"There's been a change of plans. You'll have to come with me. We're leaving now."

"But what…" Breathless from their hurried descent of the stairs she never finished.

Devin put his arm around her to hurry her through the darkened streets. The night was fairly warm, but a chill ran up her spine, when he reluctantly gave the explanation.

"Russo has escaped."

Chapter 31

The cabin in the Christina was below deck, small and cramped, with but a single narrow bunk. It mattered little. Katherine had practically been alone since they had come aboard. She paced the limited space, feeling once again a prisoner. Her mood was not improved as she recalled the few words she had exchanged with Devin that morning. Whenever she protested her near confinement to the small cabin, he would mumble something about her getting her wish, until that very morning when her frustration reached a boiling point, and she had snapped at him and he had stormed out.

Now, pacing the cabin, it came to her how easily she had given in, and agreed to journey home and wait for him. She had been reasonable and accepting. It was his idea to drag her off into the night, and now he was blaming her because she was here. "Ooh!" She spoke aloud. Her thoughts were interrupted when Devin strode in, and went straight to the desk to lean over his charts.

She stole a glance at him, and when she noticed he was back to her, the glance became a full-blown glare. Her target turned in time to catch the angry eyes lashing out at him, her arms folded defiantly across her chest, and although he could not have said why, the sight of her thus made him smile. "What's the matter with you?"

A furious groan was all she managed, and Devin gave a short laugh. He walked over to her, rolling the chart he had come for. "Miss me last night?"

Katherine was in no mood to be teased, and pulled away when he tried to slip his arm around her.

He paused momentarily, before he spoke with a bravado he did not feel. "Don't worry, Love, I'll make up for it later."

"Don't count on it!" She fired back, and because she had turned away, she did not see the uncertain look he gave her when he opened the door. "Have I told you lately that I love you?"

She turned to look over her shoulder. At his hopeful look, her heart softened, and she gave him a half smile before he went out. Katherine took a deep breath. *What was wrong with her?* She loved him so much. She had waited so long to be with him, and here they were at odds.

Her thoughts wandered, and she found herself picturing the recent scene as it might have been. She could have gone to him, put her arms around him… but she had missed her chance. She shivered inexplicably, and stared at the door, willing him back. It dawned on her that she was frightened, and it was not only the mission they were undertaking. She paced with her arms crossed, and searched within herself for the real reason. *Devin is afraid,* she realized, and that scared her more than anything.

Devin stood on deck in the sparse starlight, his eyes scanning the dark horizon, his thoughts on Katherine. *He was a fool to have brought her.* In the beginning he had been sure she would argue, and try to persuade him to bring her, and though he knew he shouldn't, he might have done so with a clearer conscience. He couldn't bear to send her away from him. What if she didn't get home safely? But in the end, she had been so reasonable about it, and when Russo had escaped… He was afraid to leave her aboard the Athena. He paused in his thoughts to curse himself. *Had he been too anxious to hustle her on board and take off?* He stood going over and over it in his mind. *Had he done the right thing?*

They were in a race now. Russo may have gone after Katherine, but more likely he would have headed south to try and warn his counterparts before Devin arrived to take them captive. Then there was the added threat of his own people patrolling the coast, who could not know that he had left early for his counterfeit run through the blockade. He now ran the same risk of anyone else trying to get through, and the odds were not in his favor. He swore under his breath. Yes, Katherine was in more danger now than ever, and it was his fault. If anything happened to her, he would never forgive himself.

He was never to know who it was that brought his fears to light, and it hardly mattered where the iron came from, that splintered the bow of the Christina. One blast after another, and the deck rumbled beneath his feet. For a second, he stood dazed, caught by the thought that now he was on the receiving end of what he had dealt out so many times. It was a most horrible feeling, and... *Katherine! Oh my God, Katherine was below deck!*

The Christina shuddered, and seemed to gasp a dying breath. She began to list, and loaded as she was, Devin knew it would be no time at all before she went down. The salvaged cargo had gone to auction, and they had loaded her with stone and bricks to ride low enough in the water to look like proper smugglers.

Earlier he had changed course and headed for the coast, but he couldn't be sure how close they were. His racing thoughts were interrupted when a manly bellow rose above the commotion of sliding cargo and running footsteps. Devin turned to look while he ran toward the cabin, shouting orders.

Katherine, affected by a strange calmness, moved about the cabin collecting things she might need. Yet, at the same time she knew she was acting oddly. It was as though she were watching the scene from far off, knowing the panic would come as surely as the water seeping under the door. When it did, she threw the portal open and had to hold to the casing when the sea swirled around her knees. Her stomach lurched when the panic gripped her fully, and the ladder in the gangway seemed just out of reach. In the dim light from the wildly swinging lantern in the cabin behind her, she could see a pair of booted feet above her on the ladder, and the strength of Devin's voice reached her through the madness. She grabbed for him when he slid down beside her in the now waist deep water, and together they climbed upward, his arms of steel anchoring her to the ladder from behind.

The ship began to roll, and Katherine lost all sense of direction when the sea poured in on them, blackening their world. She clung to her hold in the roaring hell, until Devin pulled at her hands coaxing her to let go. Gripping her around the waist, he pushed upward from the ladder. Her arm brushed the opening as they cleared the hatchway and shot through the dark water. Flailing instinctively, she could feel the tangled mass of canvas and rope that blocked their way upward.

Devin paused to release his hold on her and guide her hand to his belt, so he could use both arms to clear their path. Katherine held on for dear life, following his lead, their powerful strokes bringing them to the surface where they gasped for breath. Leaving the noise and confusion behind, they swam through the dark waters for what seemed like an eternity, until at last their feet touched bottom. Devin put a hand to her mouth and listened intently before signaling to her, and they crawled out onto the sand, and immediately hid in the nearby bushes.

"Have I told you lately that I love you?" She whispered in his ear, sitting in the circle of his arms.

His answer was a fierce tightening of his hold.

They watched hopefully, but learned little, and no others appeared to join them in their hiding place, where they spent the remainder of the night. At the merest hint of dawn, Devin roused the sleepy Katherine, who had dozed fitfully against his shoulder. "Come on, Love, we'd best be on our way."

She got up stiffly, a damp and sandy mess, and winced, rubbing her neck. The foggy shore was littered with debris, and some distance down the beach she may have seen the remains of a body. She had quickly glanced away, and refused to look again. The enormity of their situation struck her anew, and she looked nervously to Devin.

"We'll be all right," he spoke with assurance, but she was not fooled.

As he took her hand to lead her through the brush, Katherine took one longing look back at the splinters of their ride home.

They had walked in silence for some time and the day had grown warmer, when she decided to test his temperament. "Do you know where we are?"

He glanced sideways at her. "I know where we were. I'm not quite sure where we landed. I do know we're a long way from home." He let out a frustrated breath, and she stepped close to rest her head on his shoulder.

"I love you," she whispered, as his arms came around her.

"I'm sorry, Katherine. I'm so sorry." He kissed her by her ear.

"Don't. It's not your fault."

"It's my fault *you're* here. I should have taken you home."

"There you go, thinking you could have stopped me if I had decided to come with you." She paused to look at him, "I'm glad I'm here. I'd be crazy with worry, when you didn't return."

He smiled sadly, "I'm sure you're the only woman I've ever met, who would profess to be glad to be *here*," he stated, spreading his hands to indicate the surrounding swamp.

Her voice came low to thrill his heart, "I'd be glad to be anywhere with you, and we'll get through this together," and she gave him a kiss that was entirely inappropriate for the time or the place.

Devin sighed in appreciation, "How bad could it be, then?"

It was a brave thought they both clung to, while they journeyed through the unfamiliar countryside, spread before them in unwelcoming silence. Devin, ever thoughtful of her welfare, helped her through beach grass, and swamps, and briars and branches, until they came to a narrow dusty lane, overhung with tall oaks. In the refreshing shade, Katherine paused for breath.

"How far will we have to walk?" She asked, finding the thought of the distance between them and home overwhelming.

Devin looked across the distance contemplating the situation. "Probably between four to five hundred miles, unless we can find a Union ship close by, but that is not likely to be the safest option. I think we should keep away from the coast and out of sight. I'm hoping we can get back to the Athena before they leave, if we're quick enough. Tully was to wait for word if anything went wrong, but he won't wait forever. The problem is, my crew might not be the only ones who know we are down here."

"Russo?" She queried hesitantly.

He shrugged and gave a short laugh. "I'm not sure."

"The men you were after won't be caught now," she dared to point out.

"No," he urged her to start walking again, "but it's not a complete failure. They didn't get the guns, and Ambrose didn't get the profit."

That much had been accomplished before they left, she thought, but she remained silent.

The going was much easier on the roadway, but Katherine's relief was short-lived when Devin began to travel twice as fast as before. She was hungry and thirsty, but she was determined not to be a burden, lest he regret having her with him. And, she reasoned, if she were thirsty, he must be too.

They had gone quite a distance, when Devin grabbed her arm, and put a finger to his lips. He cocked his head to listen, and she stood motionless, hardly daring to breathe. The sound grew louder, and their eyes met, before they ran to hide off the side of the road, and peer through the bushes, to watch a small patrol of mounted Confederate soldiers clatter past. Katherine drew in her breath at the sight of the gray and butternut brown uniforms, and it struck her, that she was now the enemy in a foreign land. "What would they do to us?" She whispered after the riders had gone.

Devin shrugged.

"Surely, they wouldn't want you… us," she corrected, "You were only after people who would cheat them."

"Katherine, they would have wanted the guns at any price. They're hardly likely to thank me for cutting off their supplies."

"Of course," she murmured, feeling a little stupid and very weary. "It's… it's kind of a shock to be here, and to see…" She didn't finish, unable to put her thoughts of this strange reality into words.

"Come on," he said, rising and helping her to her feet. "We'll just make sure they don't find us."

Not far down the road, they came upon a neglected apple orchard, that was picked nearly clean by passing troops and fleeing civilians, but with what Devin gleaned from the highest branches, and Katherine scavenged off the ground, they gathered a small supply. After eating some, they stuffed their pockets and put what they could inside their shirts, laughing at each other's lumpy appearance. It was to be their last respite for a long while.

They ate on the go, stopping only now and then, to see to personal needs and get water when they could. The pace they traveled made talking difficult, and because they were listening constantly for any warning noise, there was little attempt. They walked in silence, but they worked as one, communicating with a look, a touch, a nod… and she loved him more than ever.

Mile after mile they trudged on, until it was too dark to see, and Devin called a halt. The night was chilly, and it was only then Katherine realized her old black coat had gone down with the Christina. She took a moment to mourn its loss, like an old friend, another part of her past, another casualty of this crazy war, but a minor detail in her present circumstance. Dirty and exhausted, without even a blanket, they lay down together and fell asleep immediately in each other's arms.

Chapter 32

Six Days, seven days, Katherine had lost count. Life had become one long blur of walking, blisters, and apples. At the moment she would have traded all the apples in the world for one hot cup of tea.

The area had become more inhabited, or so they had thought, when they began to see a house every so often, but they still hadn't seen any people. Together they watched the first house from the woods, a long hungry while, before approaching, and sneaking carefully into the barn. To their disappointment, there was nothing to be found.

The door to the small house, obviously deserted, stood ajar, and feeling like criminals, they entered to scavenge what they could. The former inhabitants had obviously not been rich to begin with, and what was left behind was poor indeed. They looked around carefully. It was an eerie feeling to stand uninvited in someone else's house, deserted or not, and Katherine stayed close to Devin. So close, in fact, that when he turned to speak to her, they both jumped.

Katherine gasped, placing a hand to her chest and he laughed, the tension broken for the moment. "Fine thieves we make," he whispered, grinning at her for the first time in days, and she felt a little better.

Devin found an old rusted knife, and a questionable iron pot in the kitchen, and a few small items, but that was about it.

Katherine stood with her hands on her hips, studying the empty dusty room until her eyes lit up, and she removed the grimy gingham curtains from the kitchen window, as her fiancé nodded in approval.

As they passed through the yard, he paused and returned to the well, filled the water bucket, and pulled out a good length of rope before he sawed it off with the old dull knife and carried the whole tangle, presenting it to Katherine like a grand trophy. They dropped into the bushes, breathing hard, and took stock of their treasures, until, nerves stretched to the limit, Katherine, started to laugh and couldn't stop.

"Very resourceful, Captain, I commend you."

Her laughter was infectious and the tension of the past days eased as he looked into her smiling eyes.

"Is that the best you can do?" He asked, gathering her into his arms on the forest floor.

"What do you mean?" She wriggled further into his embrace.

"I'd rather be kissed than commended," he challenged.

She tried, she really did, but it was difficult when she couldn't stop laughing, and it didn't help when he began to tickle her. It was then, they were startled by a raucous noise that filled the woods around them, and they froze, hearts thumping wildly, until they recognized the deafening caw of a huge black crow. Devin closed his eyes and swore, breathing a long sigh of relief, and Katherine sobered just enough to give him the kiss he had requested.

A lighter mood prevailed when they travelled on, and a quick scurry through the next empty house added to their bounty, most notably, three scrawny potatoes from a weed infested garden, and a worn and tattered blanket.

It was late afternoon when they came to a place that Katherine found most idyllic, under the circumstances. The path they followed, through a lightly wooded area, broadened, gradually turning sandy, and ending at the edge of a small creek. She turned hopeful eyes to Devin, praying they might pause long enough for a much-needed bath, but still, determined she would not slow his pace.

Devin put down the bundle he carried. "Oh, bless the Saints, I need a bath."

She clasped her hands together in delight. "Thank you, thank you." She threw her arms around his neck, and placed tiny kisses in rapid fire over his face.

"What's this?" He laughed trying to get his breath.

"I was afraid you'd keep going," she said, standing in the warm circle of his arms.

"We're making good time. I'm sorry I've pushed you so hard, not many people could keep up this pace. I think…" He studied her, his head tilted to one side, "as a reward, you shall have the first bath."

"Alone?" She asked, disappointed that he would not join her.

"I'd better look around a little," he explained, grinning at her, "You swim and I'll watch… I mean *take* watch." He flicked playful brows at her, "I'll get *my* reward later."

Her only answer was a grin, and a long slow perusal, over her shoulder, and she headed for the bushes at the water's edge.

Devin deliberately waited a few minutes before following in her footsteps. "*Oh, Katherine…*" He called, in a wheedling voice.

"Yes?" She answered warily, a smile lifting the corners of her mouth.

"I have something for you."

She had unbraided her hair and wore only her chemise and trousers, but stepped forth to meet him.

His gaze swept over her and he scowled. "Darn, too soon," he muttered, snapping his fingers in mock disappointment.

Wrestling a smile, she regarded him suspiciously, and crossed her arms over her chest, "What do you want?"

"Hmm…" He looked her up and down, leaving no doubt as to what it was he wanted, and she laughed as she put up her hands to hold him at arm's length. "I desperately need this bath, Captain Galloway, Sir."

"Umm…" Devin narrowed his eyes and considered her plea, but the more he studied her beautiful shoulders, her long slender arms that would twine about his neck, her thinly clad breasts that would tease softly against his chest…

He smiled to himself, "I just thought you might want… this!" With a dramatic flourish he produced the very thin and tired remains of a bar of soap.

Katherine gasped with joy, and cradled the gift lovingly in her cupped hands. "Oh!" She exclaimed, bringing the skeletal scrap to her nose to test its scent, not that it would have made any difference. "Honeysuckle!" She proclaimed the verdict, and at that moment it was the most wonderful fragrance in the world.

After taking her time with her bath and her hair, Katherine had rinsed her clothes, and spread them on the bushes to dry. She then went in search of Devin wrapped precariously in the freshly washed squares of gingham, tied together beneath each arm. She found him crouched before a small fire. There was a wonderful aroma coming from the old iron pot, and she inhaled the scent, her eyes closing for a moment in appreciation.

"Wild onion," he supplied.

She nodded, still taking in the scent, "Anything but apple."

Devin, busy adding a few more sticks to the flames, raised one dark eyebrow in a dubious salute to her costume, but she only shrugged, and grabbed hastily at her covering when it threatened to leave her.

He grinned broadly. "Never have I been so mindful of kitchen curtains. Do you suppose they'll flutter in the breeze?" He asked, stroking his bewhiskered chin and looking hopefully up at her.

She gave him a pointed look, "Why don't you wait a moment, I'm feeling a bit of hot air now."

He was still laughing, as he pushed himself languidly to his feet, and stretched, and she handed him the scrap of soap. "The water's quite chilly," she warned.

"Perhaps…" he nuzzled her neck, his breath hot against her skin, "you'll help me warm up later."

"You seem a bit over warm already."

He pulled her closer, "Mmm, you smell so sweet."

Katherine wrinkled her nose, "You don't," she whispered, laughing.

"Fear not, Miss Katherine, when I return, I shall smell like…" He held the sliver to his nose like she had, "*honeysuckle?*" He questioned skeptically, before heading down the path.

"Captain?" She called after him, and he turned to find her standing with hands on curtained hips. She gave him a mischievous smile, "I am *exceedingly* fond of honeysuckle."

He flashed a smile, and hurried on his way.

He was quicker than she, in part, because she had followed him a short time later, and done his laundering for him. Now, Devin, wrapped in the blanket that her curtain ingenuity had left for him, served up the sparse stew that was their first substantial meal in days.

Katherine ate from a battered tin cup that had two small holes where the handle used to be attached. She had to hold it at an angle so it didn't leak, but it didn't matter. After a diet of partially rotted apples, and a few shriveled berries, the potatoes tasted delicious. She savored the warmth of the broth, and there was some kind of meat. She noted the way it was cut in small round pieces, and glanced at Devin, who studied her while he speared a square of potato with the knife he had cleaned and sharpened. "It's very good, thank you," she said, and he nodded as he ate.

After supper, in the meager light that was left, they gathered their belongings and moved on a while, in case anyone should investigate the fire they'd had. Devin set up the new camp, and wondered where their next meal might come from, and what it would be.

They made love, as they had known they would, under a beautiful starlit sky, their intensity heightened by the playful words of the afternoon, and their long plight together. Afterward, Devin lay on his side facing her. With all the strength he had left, he lifted a silken tress across his face, to breathe in the sweet scent of her. "It would appear, my love," he whispered, "that we are *both* quite fond of honeysuckle." He stayed awake a long time, worried about her safety and regarding her strength with wonder.

Katherine, cuddled against his shoulder, slipped into sated slumber, trying not to think about the snake she had eaten for dinner.

Chapter 33

The sound of distant rumbling, seemed at odds, with the pale rays of dawn intruding into their mist enshrouded hollow. Devin shivered while he lay listening, and pulled the thin blanket more snuggly around Katherine's shoulder. He hated to wake her, and stole a few minutes longer, to study the delicate brows arched above a fan of long dark lashes, as she lay nestled against him, still fast asleep.

Each time he woke to find her near, he felt a surge of gratitude, and he knew it would always be so. Even here, in the middle of nowhere, on their fragrant bed of pine needles, the gladness touched his heart. They hadn't had a very good beginning, but God help him, he would get her out of here, get her home, and spend the rest of his life making up for it. This was his vow as he began the new day, and he sealed it with a light kiss.

She stirred and opened her eyes to find him staring down at her, and she moved to hide her face against his shoulder. "Am I still dreaming?"

"Would that you were, you could dream us out of this mess." He sighed, and kissed her forehead.

"Mmm… Where to?"

"Ladies choice," he whispered. "Wherever you say."

"Well… home, of course."

"The cottage?" He asked.

"I do miss the cottage terribly, but I've a wish to see you at Trendwell. Especially," she grimaced, trying to wriggle an achy hip into the unforgiving ground, "the big four poster in the master bedroom."

"That sounds perfect." He drew his other arm around her. "Tell me about it again."

This day brought change to the hell-bent, travel at any cost, that had become their habit. Several times, the road they now traveled had been attacked by pounding hooves, when small mounted patrols had thundered past, sending them scurrying for the bushes. For a while they had tried walking through the woods, but the brush was too dense, and they made too much noise, so now they traveled the edge of the roadway, nerves stretched taunt and hearts apprehensive. Holding hands, they moved cautiously through the day, and it was nearly dusk when the way broadened once again into open fields, and they stepped over a low stone wall into the shelter of the trees.

He touched her arm in warning, and she froze as still as a doe, when she heard voices carried on the twilight breeze. Over the thudding of her heart, a steady rhythmic sound etched itself in her mind, and they peered through the brush trying to discern its source.

Devin pointed, and there across the field was a small group of men. Shirtless, wearing gray and dirty trousers, talking while they worked.

The parting sun bathed them in shadows and Katherine squinted to see what they were doing. She scowled in disgust, realizing she was seeing a bloody carcass of some sort, there on the ground. *Some kind of hunting party,* she thought fleetingly, before her mind grasped the true picture through her dawning horror, and committed it forever to memory.

It was not an animal there on the ground, but what was left of a human being. And what she had at first thought a crumbled gray stone wall behind the shoveling men, now clearly became another, and another, as she focused on the line of butchered flesh, barely discernable in the sparse light.

Devin too, was caught off guard, and too late, turned her away from the grotesque sight. She closed her eyes in horror, and she knew the rumblings they had heard that morning, had been a different kind of thunder.

They moved as hollow shells, sleeping little and having no thought of food. They hadn't spoken, lost in their own thoughts, sickened and isolated, held captive by a common picture they knew would change them forever, and perhaps, each wondering what that change would bring to the other. They had been too close to death.

It was the third night, and she lay at his side, staring at an amazing night sky that brought tears to her eyes for those no longer able to witness such beauty. She was a prisoner of the thoughts that plagued her. *What if Gabriel were of an age? What if Devin had ended up a bloody mass in some farmer's field? And those men… What of their loved ones who waited at home? Some must have children waiting, tiny sons and daughters.*

She thought of the thousands of battles, named and unnamed, whose reality, to her current shame, had been little more than another headline in the newspapers. If this had been but a battle of stragglers in one small corner, what of the countless numbers who had died in so many other places. It was almost impossible to imagine. A gruesome picture of the infinite line of slain humanity, stretched out in her mind, their lifeblood seeping slowly into the dust from which they had come, and tears rolled silently down her cheeks. She closed her eyes in a wordless plea for it to stop. *How horrid, how wasteful, and how utterly, utterly, foolish.*

Katherine felt a great anger, and a powerful surging in her veins as life stirred within, filling her heart with longing. *She* was alive! And she needed to feel alive, and to stay alive, so she could get home with Devin and live out whatever time God would allow them. She listened to the heavy thud of his heart, and without hesitation she reached for him, roughly communicating her need. She began to kiss him urgently, beckoning him to share life and its gifts with her.

Devin was not displeased with her abrupt invitation. He had searched for some way to break the silent barrier which had held them for a time as one with the death they had witnessed. He had wanted to kiss her, to touch her, but thought he should give her time to deal with what they had seen. And, too, he was angry at himself—blamed himself—for not protecting her from the horrid truth of war. It was some of this anger he vented, taking his cue from her rough foreplay, and pushed her onto her back.

Katherine's hands left the front of his open trousers and came up to knead his shoulders and twine through his dark hair. She teasingly forced his head back as he undid her shirt and pulled her chemise down from her shoulders, his rough hands claiming, tormenting, and yet, soothing her. Greedily she reversed direction, pulling him down, and his hot mouth found her naked breast, his bristled chin causing both pain and pleasure when it swept across her tender skin. She arched toward him in silent appeal, their kisses passionately bruising, and he entered her in one quick movement, desperately filling her with the wonder of life and love, again and again in a glorious confirmation of being. When at last the unbearable tension shattered, carrying her to glowing heights, she floated, feeling she could join the starlit sky above—and very much alive. They clung breathlessly, holding each other. "Thank you," she whispered, looking at him with eyes full of love and tears, explaining all.

"My pleasure, Love."

The pair sat at the edge of the woods, growing bored, as they eyed what appeared to be another vacant house and dilapidated barn. Travel weary and famished, Katherine yawned behind her hand.

Devin glanced at her, and leaned over to graze at the lobe of her ear for a long moment.

"Mmm…" She closed her eyes, "Are you that hungry?"

He laughed; his breath warm in her ear.

"Aye, I'm hungry to have you as my wife, at home in that warm bed you keep threatening me with. The first thing I'm going to do, is bring you a hot cup of tea," he vowed, caressing the muscles on either side of her neck with strong fingers.

"Promise?"

"Promise," he answered.

She pondered a moment, "Devin?"

"Yes, Love?"

"What's the second thing?"

He chuckled wickedly, pulling her into his arms to hold her close.

"I do hope it's as good as it sounds."

"Try me," he whispered, before kissing her longingly.

"You'll get us home," she said, when their lips parted, and though it wasn't a question, it wasn't quite the powerful statement she had intended.

"I will, or die trying, I promise you."

Inside the small three-room house, they stood against the closed door, adjusting to the dim light. Devin held up a hand in warning and a blade of apprehension slid between her ribs.

Her fear did not fade when he crossed the room to pick up a knapsack from the corner. An examination of its contents yielded a small parcel of jerky, three dried apples at which Katherine wrinkled her nose, and a carefully wrapped portion of something that tasted like cornbread. It was old and dry and delicious—*but why was it here?* She was about to ask, when Devin graciously handed her the last of it, and hoof beats sounded in the yard.

Their eyes met in alarm. It was Katherine who yanked at his arm and pointed to the ladder that led to a trap door in the ceiling, and when the horses halted outside, the surprised pair had already scrambled up above. They closed the trap door just before a number of booted feet stomped into the downstairs.

Settled uncomfortably on the floor of the dusty attic they tried to count voices. Devin held up four fingers and Katherine nodded in agreement. It was difficult to hear anything but murmuring, until those voices were raised in laughter or anger, this latter when the one Katherine dubbed 'low voice,' discovered his missing rations.

"You ate my damn food!"

"I did not!" Screeched high voice.

"You must have eaten it, and forgotten." A third voice counseled.

"I did not!" The low voice bellowed.

An argument ensued, and then quieted, and just above their heads Devin winked at Katherine as she finished the last of the missing portion. It was to be a dubious victory, for the next day dawned bright and sunny, and they sat helplessly waiting, Devin chaffing at the delay. Throughout the morning, the heat increased until the attic air was stifling.

He removed his shirt and boots, and motioned for Katherine to do the same, but she shook her head and tried to explain with her hands that she didn't want to be caught without her clothes if they were discovered.

Later in the afternoon, the men were outside, but not far enough away for the trapped victims to make an escape. When Devin cautiously made his way from the makeshift commode he had fashioned from the junk in the corner of the attic, he was quite surprised to find that Katherine had removed everything but her underclothing, and was using her shirt to pillow her head above the dirty floor. He gazed admiringly at her, until it dawned on him that her complexion was oddly pale and her cheeks overly pink, and he crept closer to check on her. "Katherine?" He touched her hand, and in alarm, put a hand to her forehead to find her burning with fever.

At his touch, she opened her eyes and began to cry silently, giving him a pleading look.

"I want my baby, and I want my mother."

"I know, Love, I know," he whispered helplessly, cradling her head on his lap.

"And I need Evelyn."

"Yes, Love."

She didn't want to be weak, and reached a hand to touch the face she loved so well. "I'm sorry."

"Shh, it will be all right. Don't give up now."

Through the night he sat, quieting her murmurings and wondering what in the world he was going to do, until his answer came with the dawn.

Katherine had just gone to sleep, when the men began to stir below. Peering through the small vent he watched them saddle their horses and took stock of the situation. 'Low voice,' a portly fellow with a wreath of whiskers, was giving orders to 'high voice' and 'the peacekeeper' as they mounted up and rode off, leaving Devin deep in thought.

Three men… but he was sure they had counted four. If they were mistaken, and the men were all gone, he was wasting precious time getting her to safety, if not… *Was there one armed man waiting downstairs? Had some sound in the night given them away?* He had to make a decision, and the old loose boards that comprised the siding of the house had given him an idea.

He worked his way across the attic to the rear of the house and began pushing at the dry planks until he found one whose old rusted nails gave slightly. Carefully he forced the board outward and worked it back and forth until he could twist it loose, and turning it sideways, brought it inside, before working on the next one, making a space large enough to fit through. It was then a small matter to lower himself down, and with one glance at Katherine, jump to the ground.

Katherine didn't sleep for long and when she noticed Devin was gone, she sat up with a start. There was no time to contemplate the missing boards in the wall, before she heard the unmistakable sound of footsteps coming up the ladder. Grabbing her boot as the only weapon at hand, she sat poised to fire.

The trap door was lifted upward to reveal first, the tall crown of a wide brimmed grey hat, bearing a C.S.A. insignia, and sporting a rakish black ostrich feather, and as she let loose her best shot—the handsome face of her betrothed. Immediately she stopped reaching for the second boot, and put both hands to her face to cover a gasp, but it was too late. The leather missile caught him on the side of the head knocking his hat askew and pushing him backwards before he regained his grip on the ladder.

"*Saints, Katherine, it's me!*" He sputtered, above the ringing in his ear.

Her heart was still pounding, "But why are you wearing that hat?"

"It matches my jacket," he grinned, and as he came up the ladder, she could see the short gray coat trimmed with gold braid.

Katherine raised a hand to her forehead. "Are they gone?"

"Come with me, and I'll show you." He hurried to help her get dressed. "How do you feel?"

"Fine," she lied.

He eyed her with suspicion, and searched momentarily for her other boot, before he realized it was that very boot which had nearly knocked him from his perch on the ladder. Shaking his head at her gumption, he guided her down the spindly steps, noting how warm she was.

Katherine was a bit wobbly, by the time she reached the bottom, and she put out a hand to steady herself. She drew in a sharp breath, when she spotted a youth sprawled on the cot in the corner. "Is he dead?" She asked, her throat tight.

Devin put a finger to his lips, "No, I only hit him," he whispered, making a motion with fist against palm.

"*But, he's just a boy!*" She whispered in wonder, looking closer at the downy cheek.

Devin glanced at the owner of the second of two high voices. "Aye, a boy—with a man's gun," he corrected, showing her the holstered iron now strapped to his own hip.

She nodded, still staring at the youth.

"Come in here," he said, taking her arm and leading her into the other room.

She stopped and stared, for the bed was piled high with uniforms of all sorts and colors, and guns and military paraphernalia filled the corners of the room.

"Thieves and scavengers," Devin proclaimed, a look of disgust crossing his face, as he gathered a Union Major's uniform, he had chosen earlier. He helped her into a blue shirt and fitted her with an overcoat of blue wool, sans bullet holes, that fit her fairly well, topping it off with a union forage cap, in which he thought she looked adorable.

Katherine gave him a confused look. "Well, what *are* we?"

"We…" He informed her, ushering her to the doorway, and gathering a rifle, several canteens, and a knapsack he had packed, "are going home."

"Why the gray?" She asked, pointing a finger to indicate his new attire, and removing her overcoat to hold it over her arm.

Devin shrugged, and quickly gathered a few more items they might need. "It fits," he said, leading her out the door, and skirting the edge of the clearing with a watchful eye.

She raised slim brows in doubt, knowing he had certainly had his choice from the supplies in the room, but still, he looked very handsome with the rakish hat shading his bearded face. Though she still felt unwell, Katherine couldn't help teasing him, "You like the feather," she whispered.

Devin defended himself with a sidelong glance, and a killer grin, "*You* like the feather."

"Hmm." She considered this, as she studied him with fever-bright eyes. "Maybe." She smiled, but placed her hand on his arm to steady herself.

"Katherine…" Devin caught her wrist, and swinging the knapsack over one shoulder, bent to lift her in his arms. Still holding the rifle in one hand, he entered the circle of packed earth that was the yard, and crossed its dusty diameter.

"You don't have to carry me," she protested, but her eyes were closed, and her head lolled on his shoulder.

"Shh, It's all right." Devin's long strides had nearly closed the gap to the other side, when there came the whinny of a horse. Katherine lifted her head to meet his startled gaze, and for an airless moment they stayed frozen. She was puzzled when a smile claimed his face, and he turned and headed for the barn.

"*Saints, Katherine,*" he whispered, pushing the door shut with his foot, enclosing them in the deep cool shadows of the interior. He settled her in the corner, and stood for a moment admiring as fine an example of horseflesh as he had ever seen. "*Saints…*"

"You said that," she murmured, not unappreciative of the large and pretty mare with a white face, whose coat shone red-gold in the rays of sunlight that now began to reach between the rough boards of the barn.

"Katherine…" Devin whispered in awe, feeling like he had indeed found gold. "Do you realize, there's probably not a horse this fine left in the whole of the Confederate States?"

"Hurry then…" she urged, closing her eyes, knowing they would take the horse, "before those other thieves come back."

Devin shot her a protesting glance, but realizing he had no argument, he began to ready the mare.

Chapter 34

Mile after mile, the treasured animal carried them northward through the desecrated South. Devin rode the horse hard at first, keeping the rest stops short. He wanted to put as much distance as possible between them and the men they had stolen her from, but he was torn between their safe escape, and Katherine's welfare. Her fever had not improved, but each time he suggested they stop she encouraged him to go on, her head resting listlessly against his shoulder, while she rode in front of him in the saddle.

At dusk they forded a small creek, and shortly afterward, Devin turned off the trail to stop for the night. He climbed stiffly down and stretched, turning in alarm when Katherine slumped forward in the saddle. He caught her as she slid from the horse's neck and hurried to lay her down on a soft bed of moss.

"Katherine?"

She was far away, for in her mind a battle raged. She was caught on the front lines fighting to survive, her body waging war on the invader within. The attack was sudden and strong and Katherine was tired and weak. Her eyes fluttered open a moment, and she murmured something he didn't catch. He placed a palm to her forehead and when he felt her blazing temperature he cursed himself for listening to her and traveling through the long day.

Grabbing the canteen, he cradled her head on his lap while he tried to get her to drink. She was like a rag doll in his arms. He had to get her fever down, he knew, and in a near panic he knelt at her side. "Katherine? Can you hear me?" Hastily he removed her boots and clothing, and carried her to the creek. It was dark now, and he set her at the water's edge to remove his own clothes. As he pulled off his boots, she called for him and he leaned close to listen. "I'm here, Love, I'm here."

She struggled to speak. "If I don't make it home…"

"Shh, Love, you'll be all right," he whispered, his mind refusing to accept any other possibility.

"You'll take care of Gabriel. I know you will. You'll love him… love him for me."

Devin's heart twisted. He gathered her up and waded chest deep into the cold water. There was a tightness in his throat as he coaxed her, "Don't give up now." *I can't lose you. I won't go on without you.* "We'll go home together. We're very close." On and on, he talked, until his teeth chattered from the cold, and his arms ached. He had no idea how long it was before Katherine stirred.

"Cold… now. I'm cold." She shivered, and he carried her to their little camp and wrapped her in stolen blankets, and held her through the night.

In the morning, she was much improved. The glassy look was gone from her eyes, and her cheeks were no longer flushed with fever. It was a tired Confederate officer who waited while she dressed and took a few moments for herself.

"How do you feel?" He asked when she returned.

"Much better, thank you."

He smiled, and yawned behind his hand. He had held her close most of the night in case she needed his help in some way, and had only slept the last few hours before dawn.

"I didn't mean to be weak," she apologized, remembering her tears in the attic.

Devin hugged her tightly. "Katherine, you're the strongest, bravest, woman I've ever known."

She nodded her thanks and avoided his eyes so he wouldn't see the tears that threatened once again. She had lost her milk. She had tried to keep it flowing by relieving herself, but had felt the burden a little less each day, and now, with the time in the attic, and the fever, she feared it was gone for good. *She would ask Evelyn. Evelyn would know.* It saddened her to think she would never nurse her baby again, *or possibly, never see him again.* "Do you want to know the truth?" She asked, as she began helping to gather their belongings.

Devin scowled her into sitting, and took the items from her hands.

She managed a sad grin, and continued, while folding the blanket, "At the moment, I'd rather be as weak and spoiled as Cecilia, if it would mean I could be at home."

Her fiancé tilted his head to consider her, while his mind painted a picture of his future wife gowned in shocking pink ruffles, screeching at a half dozen servants, as they ran in six different directions to do her bidding. His face took on such a pained look, that Katherine paused in her labor, and watched his head shake from side to side, before he spoke. "Madam, this will never do. We must get you home at once."

It was perhaps a blessing that neither had much appetite, as they continued on their way, because once again, they were without food. It was for this reason they did not make the best time the next day, for hunger accompanied them on their ride. Devin made the stops to rest the mare longer, to forage in the woods for anything of sustenance. Each time, there was nothing to be found. Every mile seemed gleaned to the last berry by the many who had gone before. They could not have said later, whether it was the hunger, or the frustration born thereof, that caused them to grow a little careless. Katherine had leaned from the saddle to brush his lips with a kiss, to tempt his thoughts from food, and neither heard the approaching buggy until it was nearly upon them.

Thinking fast, Devin grabbed the reins, tugged the cap lower on Katherine's head, and pushed her forward so she leaned low over the horse's neck, hiding her face. He turned, and with great relief, faced a single woman driver, and raised a hand in greeting.

The young woman paused warily, sawing on the reins of the sorry looking horse attached to the worse looking buggy. "I need this buggy!" She spoke with a challenge in her dark eyes, holding her whip at the ready.

Katherine had fallen quickly into her role, keeping her face down, leaning over the saddle horn, and remembering to hide her ring. From where she sat, she peeked through the horse's mane at a pretty woman with long auburn hair, and once again felt the sting of jealousy… *The woman was clean!* Her hair was shining in the sunlight, tied with a pretty ribbon, and her beige dress, though worn, was spotless. Katherine considered her road dusted braid, hidden beneath her coat, and her dirty clothing. She frowned while Devin stood talking to *'the clean dress'* and wondered if they weren't both doing an awful lot of smiling. *Of course he was keeping them safe…*

When he returned to fetch her, with nothing but a whispered, "Keep your head down," and to tie her mount to the rear of the buggy, it was with a decided lack of appreciation that she conceded.

She heartily resented the ride that followed, in which she learned, as she bobbed along in the dust, feeling forgotten, that she was Devin's captive, being transported for imprisonment. She listened to him reel off his stories, and decided he was an excellent liar.

However, it was right between the delicate shoulder blades of *'the clean dress,'* that the full weight of her resentment settled. For *wasn't that tan shoulder much closer than warranted to the gray? And didn't the hands that fluttered like butterflies through the conversation, alight once too often on the gold braided sleeve above the hands that worked the reins?* It was only their current predicament that kept Katherine from leaping through the back of the buggy, when that hand brushed ever so slightly over the gray knee. That, and the comforting fact, that Devin moved discreetly away from the gentle assault.

He had no way of knowing that the small gesture became the thread that Katherine held to now, while she waited for him to reappear. The house they arrived at, was, like its owner, neat and trim, if a little shabby. The small barn where Katherine was 'imprisoned' housed a cow and calf, two pigs and some chickens, and Katherine was hard-pressed between petting them, and thinking of them as dinner.

She tried to nap in the fresh hay, but with time alone, thoughts of her sweet baby son tormented her to tears, and her empty arms ached to hold him. For what seemed the hundredth time, she sighed, and looked out the small window toward the house, and this time was rewarded with what she hoped to see. Devin strolled toward the barn with long confident strides, carrying a covered tray. He was clean shaven, and gave her a big smile when he spotted her peeking through the begrimed window. When he had kicked the door closed behind him, he set the tray on top of a nearby barrel and reached to take her in his arms. "Hello, Yank," he said, smiling down at her.

Katherine laughed, as he lowered his head and kissed her most thoroughly.

"Are you all right, Love?"

She nodded, "And you?"

"I missed you. I'm sorry it took so long. She was cooking." He kissed her again, and she caught her breath when his hand wandered to enclose her breast.

She closed her eyes, resting her cheek over his heart, until her eyes flew open. "I smell…"

"Perfume, I know…" He interrupted.

"…bacon!" She finished.

"Ah, bacon!" Devin changed course immediately, drawing her over to the tray and removing the covering with a flourish, to reveal a plate of bacon, ham, eggs, and toast. "Katherine, you make me forget what I'm doing."

"Perfume?" She turned questioning eyes in his direction, as she took a bite of the bacon, and closed her eyes in rapture.

Devin cleared his throat. "She's very… *friendly.*"

"So, I noticed," she agreed calmly, finishing the bacon, and picking up a piece of toast.

"But, look!" He offered excitedly, lifting another cover to reveal a still steaming pot of tea. "And there's milk," he added, so pleased with himself that she had to smile.

She cradled the cup in both hands, and took several sips, closing her eyes, and then frowned. "I wonder how she got everything."

Devin cleared his throat again. "I think I know." He grinned, and flicked his brows suggestively.

Katherine was occupied cleaning her plate. "How *friendly* did you have to be to get this?"

"Some… But not *too,*" he hastened to add. "She's more than willing for you to have a good meal. She seemed concerned you be treated well. You don't think I would…"

"No," she answered truthfully, "It's just that… *She's* so *clean,*" she tried to explain, not sure he would understand.

He smiled, and cut to the heart of the matter with simple male logic, setting her world aright, "But, she's not *you.*"

He caressed her hip and kissed her temple, and continued speaking, "I could hardly tell her I'm in love with my beautiful Yankee prisoner." He kissed her cheek.

She glanced around. Her hat and coat, her only disguise, were over by the stalls. "You don't think she'll come out here?"

"Mm, no." He kissed her neck, and whispered in her ear, "I told her you were dangerous."

Katherine grew warm. She set down the tea cup without looking and turned to meet his kiss, and it was a longtime before he raised his head to stare down at her.

"You see?" He said, catching his breath, "*Very dangerous.*"

"And don't you forget it!" She answered, releasing her hold for the moment.

He nuzzled her temple again, and kissed her throat, shooting sparks through her soul.

"Not the least bit likely, my lovely Major Katherine."

Afraid of getting carried away, she didn't move to close the precarious half inch of space between them. "Can we leave now?" She asked, hopefully.

Devin sighed and stepped away, holding both her hands in his. "Soon Love, I'll be back to get you."

Katherine had hidden her disappointment, and was rewarded sooner than she expected, when a short time later she heard voices and peered out to see *'Miss Clean Dress,'* take her friendly self off in the buggy. But not, she noted, before much too much giggling, and farewell patting of Devin's manly shoulder, as he helped her up to her seat, and kissed her hand.

Katherine wrestled with a slow burning resentment, when he opened the door.

His smile faded, and his brow rose in question, as he took warning from her petulant stance. "What's the matter?"

"She studied him for a long moment trying to remain rational. "Nothing."

Devin scoffed, "*Nothing?* Only a woman can say '*nothing*' and have it be meaning *everything!*"

She had to smile, and went to gather her things, but didn't escape his questioning gaze. "Well…" She began, trying to put words to her thoughts, "I don't know, I just don't like her. I mean, she doesn't know who I am, and I guess I can't blame her. *I mean, you are attractive.*"

"That's true," he chimed in, and caught a heavy blue overcoat with his face.

"*Somewhat,* attractive," she amended. "Let's not forget, she probably hasn't seen a man for months… maybe even years!"

Devin's threatening look was lost in a laugh, as he pinned her against the wall. "Is that so," he chuckled, leaning close. And how attractive would I be if I said there was a hot bath waiting for you in the house?"

Instantly she melted against him, turning so it was he, who had his back to the wall.

He wasn't exactly conscious of when her tongue slipped in to greet his, or how her hands slid beneath his clothing to caress and arouse him in new and exciting ways. He only knew she was full of wonder and surprises, that left him raging with desire, his heart thundering in his chest.

Katherine smiled, "Need I say more, my *extremely* attractive, Captain Galloway?"

He managed to croak a weak, "No," before she grabbed her things, and ran for the house.

"I mean, *yes!* Hey! "He called after her, but when he reached the house, she was already slipping into the tub.

"Oh, thank you, thank you, thank you!" She sighed, sinking beneath the surface and lathering her hair. "You look more attractive every minute," she grinned.

He groaned. "In that case, I can't wait until you're done," he countered, leaning in the doorway, and trying to catch his breath from more than the run across the yard. The sight of her in the tub wasn't helping.

Her heart beat rapidly under his close perusal. Kissing him that way had certainly been a two-edged sword. A delicious two-edged sword. She dunked under to rinse her hair and resurfaced.

"Thank you for the bath. I know you want to leave." She wasted not a second, thoroughly lathering herself.

Devin, who was possibly enjoying her bath more than she, gave her a small sheepish grin, followed the path of her clothes to the tub, and handed her a towel so she could wipe her eyes. "You're most welcome, Love, but it was her idea," he confessed, showering her with a bucket of rinse water, and leaning down to kiss her wet mouth.

When he lifted his head, she frowned slightly, "*That's odd.*"

"Hmm?" He answered, totally distracted by the trail of tiny bubbles sliding across her breast.

"But, *why*, do you think? She persisted.

"Why?" Devin sighed, and wandered around the room in search of something else to occupy his mind. "I told you. She was concerned for your welfare." He gave a short laugh and ran a finger over the pearl handle of the razor he had used earlier, and picked up the shaving brush. "She thought you might like a shave too, and insisted we stay for supper when she gets back…" His smile faded into a scowl, as he played the brush across the fresh bar of shaving soap, and stood staring at the foam. His eyes shifted to Katherine.

The skin prickled at the back of her neck, "What is it?"

"Something you said." His frown grew deeper, as the words she had spoken earlier came to him… "*She probably hasn't seen a man in months.*" His eyes sought hers, "When William left home, did he take his razor?"

"I don't know." A sick feeling began in her stomach.

"I did." He said, looking at her with dread.

Her blood ran cold, and she jumped from the tub grabbing the towel. "Where did she go?!"

He cursed. "She's gone for help! They're going to free you! Get dressed! I'll get the horse." She was already pulling on her clothes, and a minute later she ran from the house, slipping into her coat on the way, and swinging up behind him.

<hr>

They were well away from the house, and Devin had slowed the mare to a walk, before Katherine dared ask her question, "Devin," she whispered, "If they're Northerners, shouldn't we wait for them? If we told them who we are, wouldn't they help us?"

"I don't know… All the things I told her… I laid it on pretty thick, trying to convince her. What if they don't give me a chance to explain? What if they shoot me? Or hang me? *I want to see my son.*"

Tears sprang to her eyes at the anguish in his voice, and she hugged him tightly. "Well, when they see I'm a woman…"

He cut her off, "Maybe not the best idea either."

"Oh," was all she said, and he patted her knee, glad she understood his meaning.

"I can't believe I missed it, Katherine… *the horse, the buggy, the animals, even the hay!* We talked about it! Where there is *nothing*—she has everything. And the razor. I held it in my hand, I shaved with it, and it never dawned on me. The soap was new, but it had been recently used. How could I be so stupid!?"

"*We,*" she amended, and after a little more thought added, "The razor could have been left. There are extras at the cottage. We were tired. We were hungry… And it may not be what you think," she added, feeling the doubt in her heart.

"Hmm," he mumbled, clearly not ready to forgive himself.

They rode for a while, until Katherine, resting her head on the back of his shoulder, thought to ask, "How did you know she would be friendly to you, dressed the way you are?"

"I didn't have much time to think about it when she surprised us. I just took a chance because of where we are. That's why I chose one uniform from each side. Depending on who we run into, I thought you could be my prisoner, or I could be yours."

"That was very clever," she said. After further consideration, she added, "Next time you can be my prisoner."

He patted her knee again, appreciative of her effort to make him feel better. "Ha," he said, "I've been your prisoner since the day we met." And she hugged him a little tighter.

Later they came to a fork in the road and Devin cursed under his breath, circling the horse around several times in indecision.

"What's wrong?" She dared, feeling the tension in his body.

"She told me about the roads, but I don't know if she told me to go this way because it's the right way, or because it's the wrong way. What if she wants me to go *that* way, and she thinks I will, because she told me to go this way. *Saints*, Katherine, how could I have let this happen?!"

She tightened her arms around him, "Shh, you didn't," she comforted, while checking nervously over her shoulder. "Pick one," she urged, and added, "Follow your heart!"

"Right," Devin jammed his hat tighter on his head and charged down the left fork.

After a few miles, he turned and road through the woods until they came to the other road, which they travelled an equal length. Near evening, they left that road to, so it seemed to Katherine, ride straight up the side of a mountain. Up and up, they went, Devin guiding and encouraging, the mare straining and stumbling, and Katherine clinging tightly to her hold.

They camped near the top for the night, where the earth beneath their feet was nothing but smooth gray rock. No fire, no food. Devin was apologizing, when Katherine pulled a cloth holding what was left of the bacon, some thick slices of ham, and half a loaf of bread, from the large pockets of her overcoat.

He looked at her with surprise and gratitude, and she shrugged, "Once a thief...?"

They huddled together on the ground, Devin, awake and watching, urging her to sleep if she could. Shortly after dawn, they crouched together and watched the road far below, as five horsemen thundered past. Pursuers or not, they could not know, but at one point they slowed, and circled, before riding off again. It was with a great deal of relief and pride that she noted none left the road to follow their path up the hillside.

"You did it!" She praised, "I knew you would."

Devin sighed heavily. "I did it, all right. I still can't believe I didn't see it coming. How could I have missed it?"

Katherine gave him a sympathetic look. "Because she's a woman?"

"Nah!" He scoffed, but then gave some thought to her suggestion. "Do you think so?"

"You didn't think it was me on the cliff trail that night. I think a woman can get away with a lot. Maybe because we're considered less of a threat?"

"I guess you're right," he said, thinking of Maggie and his sister.

"Not, I hope, because you think we're less intelligent," she challenged.

His brows shot up, "Of course not! You know me better than that. I guess I just expect women to be less... *devious*, or something."

"*Oh*, ...like Cecilia."

He frowned.

"Weak?" She suggested.

"Well, no."

"Helpless?"

"No…" Devin squirmed a little, trying to measure old ideas about the weaker sex against Katherine's strengths, and the other woman's deception.

She smiled, and gave him a consoling pat on the shoulder. "All's fair in love and war, Captain."

He laughed harshly at himself. "She caught me completely off guard, but I see it now. She did overplay it a bit. I mean, she was *so* concerned about you. I said it myself… I wasn't paying attention." He shook his head; still disbelieving they had survived the close call. "Of course, I *was* rather preoccupied with my prisoner."

Katherine had not taken the time to braid her hair, and he pulled her into his arms and buried his face in the soft waves. "Which reminds me," he continued, "About that kiss…"

She gave a small laugh, her lips nearly brushing his. "What kiss was that?"

His arms tightened around her, "In truth, it was more of an attack than a kiss, and just as I was about to surrender *everything* you went into retreat. You fight most unfairly, Major."

"She who fights and runs away…" She tutored, her gaze lowering from adoring his eyes to caressing his mouth, "And I told you, all is fair in love and war."

"In that case, I shall have to mount a counter attack," he threatened, capturing her lips once more, before they went on their way.

Chapter 35

Long miles and longer hours, brought the close of yet another day, and it was in the deep purple shadows of a secluded glen, that they came upon a small stone church. Beautiful in its simplicity, the building inspired in Katherine a feeling that was a mixture of inner peace and heightened longing for their elusive homecoming.

It was not until they passed within the sturdy wooden portal, that they could see a large portion of the building had been blown away, leaving part of the side wall crumbled in ruins, and the roof partially open to the heavens. Nature, as she will, had begun to reclaim her purchase, sending creeping tendrils of vines over the tumbled stone, joining the peaceful sanctuary and the silvered woodlands in her inherent embrace.

Devin removed his hat, something scampered for cover, and Katherine grabbed for his arm, and then smiled. When the moonlight flooded within to bathe the altar and its wooden cross, it was quite the loveliest church she had ever seen. She spoke in a whisper, "Do you feel it?"

"Aye," he answered, "God is here."

They walked forward and knelt at the altar, where each was silent for a time, lost in their own thoughts and prayers. Devin had finished first and waited, watching her, and thinking her more beautiful than ever, kneeling there in the moonlight. By the time she raised her head and smiled at him, in spite of the tears in her eyes, he had decided to ask, "For what do you pray, Love?"

"Forgiveness."

Devin's brow furrowed in question, and she searched for the words to explain. "I can't believe the things I've done." She studied her folded hands where a tear had fallen and watched as he smoothed it away with his fingers.

He asked softly, "You mean with me? *Us?*"

She nodded but still didn't look at him when she spoke again, "I was raised, that it would be wrong to… to…"

"To love me?" He asked, devastated that her love for him should ever cause her pain.

Her eyes swung to meet his, as she nodded in agreement, and he had to strain to hear her, "Without marriage… But I love you so much, things just happened."

Devin sat beside her and enfolded her in his arms, "Katherine, it's not your fault, and it's not my fault. If it hadn't been for this stupid war, we could have been married a long time ago. I would have come to your parents' house and asked permission to court you. For a year, I would have sat in your front parlor for twenty-minute visits, trying to beguile you from across the room—Properly chaperoned of course."

The picture he created made her smile, "Would you wear a starched collar?"

"Oh, aye, very starched, and much too tight," he added, just to see her smile broaden, before he went on, "And then, I would have asked your father for your hand, and for another year we would have pondered and planned, and *maybe*, as your betrothed, I would have stolen a kiss—In a very proper Bostonian way, of course, and finally, on our wedding night, I would hold you in my arms and…"

He had leaned so close, she was sure he was going to kiss her, and the expectation crushed the air from her lungs. Instead, he lifted his head and looked into her eyes, liquid with tears and desire. "No, I don't think so," he whispered, "When you look at me that way, I would never have made it through the first afternoon. I should have ravished you there in your parents' front parlor."

"And I would have let you," she whispered, resting her head on his shoulder.

He smiled and brushed his knuckle across her cheek. "Only because you know it's right as much as I do. As far as I'm concerned, you were meant to be my wife, and I was meant to be your husband. I believe with all my heart that God brought us together. He knows what's in our hearts, Katherine. This love is a gift.

Tears were rolling down her cheeks now, making a dark spot on his jacket, and her voice came chokingly, "But, the first time I went to you, I believed you were married, and I cannot forgive myself for that."

He held her by the shoulders to look into her eyes, *"But, I wasn't!"*

"But don't you see, *I didn't know that*, so I would have done the same thing, even if you were, and it haunts me. What would my mother have thought?"

She buried her face in his shoulder again, and he held her while he prayed for the words that would make her feel better. "It's fate, Katherine… Why was it *your* cove the smugglers chose to use, and why did I have to be the one in charge of that investigation, and why were you on the beach that night, and why wasn't Evelyn at the cottage, and…"

"All right," she smiled weakly, loving him all the more, and vaguely remembering a most fervent prayer for guidance before she had decided to go to him that night.

"And…" Devin interrupted her musings with a recollection of his own, "…you were leaving."

"What?"

"You changed your mind, don't you remember?"

Her brows drew together and he went on, "You had turned around to go back to your room, and if I hadn't gone to close the window, I would never have known you were at my door."

She caught her breath as she did remember, and a blush claimed her cheeks as she recalled what had happened next.

"It was raining. But what made me remember to close the window? I mean, not before you came, or after you left, but at exactly the right moment?"

"Now you're pushing it," she smiled.

"Am, I? What made you leave it open?"

"So, you really think God brought us together?"

"Aye, 'tis fate. Say it."

"Fate."

"So, if it makes you feel better, I'm sure he forgives us."

She smiled, "*God* might forgive me, but you don't know my mother."

"I think your mother knew very well what it was to love someone that much. I saw your parents together. The way they looked at each other. Do you honestly think when they met, they didn't..."

Her eyes widened.

"We're only human," he continued, "and so were they. And I believe they are together now, and that they are watching out for us. Love is love, Katherine, and it is perfectly natural. Who was there to marry Adam and Eve?" He smiled at the look on her face. "No one. Yet they were brought together by God."

Her throat was tight, so she nodded her agreement.

"God takes care of me, Katherine. He's on my side. In spite of everything, I believe that."

"But why was it so difficult?" She challenged, "Why was it, that every time I saw you, you were with Cecilia, and why did I believe her, and why..."

He cut her off grinning, "That was our doing. Human evil, was Cecilia lying, human error, you being gullible and making assumptions, and I, being in the wrong place at the wrong time."

"And stubborn," she aided, desperately wanting him to be right.

"Aye, stubborn," he agreed. "I wasn't going to let you go."

"Well, we're together now."

"Aye, that's all that matters, we're together here." He smiled a heart-warming smile, "Will you marry me?"

"Yes, of course."

"I mean here. Now," he whispered.

"What?"

"Speak the vows with me here, 'tis a most special place."

Katherine stared, thinking how much she loved him. He helped her to her feet, and she removed her ring and handed it to him. Then he led her to the altar and began to speak, holding her hands in his. "I, Devin, take thee Katherine to be my wedded wife. To have and to hold from this day forward…"

She listened, enthralled, at the beautiful words, surprised he knew them all, and trying to remember them for her turn. She knew she would never forget the richness of his voice echoing across the cold stone, and the way each breath was revealed by the frosty air, making his promise a tangible thing. "…for better, for worse, for richer, for poorer, in sickness and in health, until the end of time.

She smiled at that, and then it was her turn to repeat the words back to him. She looked into his eyes, shining black in the moonlight and felt the vow with her heart and soul, changing the ending as he had.

When she finished, he whispered, "With this ring, I thee wed," placing the ring back on her finger, "What God hath joined together, let no man put asunder," and brushed her lips in a feather soft kiss.

Her heart was full, and he held her once again, whispering near her ear, "We'll do it over when we get home, but I swear, I will never feel more married to you than I do right now."

They stayed like that a long while, wanting the moment to last, Katherine, more than willing to be convinced he was right, and thanking God, and the Fates, and anyone else that might have persisted in bringing them together. When they broke apart, he took her hand in his, and that was when they heard the footsteps.

Unnecessarily, Devin put a finger to his lips and drew her into the shadows near the crumbled wall, where he picked up the rifle. They stood staring at each other, listening for breathless moments before he smiled, and stepped over the low broken boundary into the yard, with a curious Katherine close behind.

The moon shone through the overhead branches, and a slight breeze rolled the shadows of the embracing limbs across the earth, like so many entwined lovers. The dark and light patterns made it difficult to see at first, but by the time she reached his side, she could clearly see him raise the rifle and sight down its long barrel.

As she squinted to find his target, the wind stirred again, and the moonlight brightened to reveal a magnificent horned buck, standing proudly in the field beyond. Her breath caught at the beautiful portrait it made, bathed in the amethyst shadows, and she placed a staying hand on Devin's arm. Their eyes met, and he knew she could not bear to have the moment of magic shattered any more than he. He lowered the rifle to put one arm around her shoulders, and as they watched, a doe appeared, and together the majestic couple walked slowly away, pausing once to look back as though beckoning their human counterparts to follow. Katherine shivered, not wholly from the cold, and was hesitant, but Devin strode forth.

Standing alone, she tried to shake the strange feeling that the ghostlike pair had conjured, and was helped when Devin's soft laugh reached her through the darkness. "What is it?" She whispered to the shadows, not sure where he had gone. *"Please hurry."*

"I'm coming, Love," he answered, and appeared from the darkness, having sprouted some not so unfamiliar lumps in his absence.

"Oh, don't tell me…" she half pleaded.

"Look, apples! I told you God takes care of me."

"Yes," she replied, "But are you sure He *likes* you?"

Katherine woke, shivering in the cold church without Devin's warmth beside her. She groaned thinking of another weary day of travel, and endless apples. She recovered quickly, and bowed her head, giving thanks for the apples—*And thank you Lord, for letting us steal the horse*—she added. *Where would we be without the horse? Maybe Devin was right.*

Her faith was rewarded with a considerable warming of heart, when she found Devin heating and scraping a bottle of old dried ink, and painstakingly scratching their names into the marriage section of a much battered, torn, and water-stained book of records in the ancient bible beside the altar. She hugged his arm. With that simple act, he had wrapped her, yet again, in a blanket of love, a mantle of confidence, that would help her put the past behind them and embrace their future.

It was that new wave of love, that carried her happily through the final days of their journey, and when they at last rode within sight of the Athena, her heart was soaring—As full as the plump white sails that would soon be carrying them out to sea, and homeward at last. She refused to leave Devin's side amongst the cheers and celebration of their friends, or when he saw to the boarding and care of the horse. And she refused to let him discard the dashing cavalry hat, which she still held in her hands, when he scooped her up to carry her into the cabin.

Once inside, Devin set her on her feet and kissed her soundly in celebration. Again and again, he captured her mouth, rewarding himself, and letting go of the last of his fear that he would fail her somehow and not get her back to safety. So enthusiastic was he, that she gasped for breath, her cheeks flushed and her eyes dancing with happiness. She placed the hat on his head and stood on tip toe to kiss him again, winding her arms around his neck. What started as warm and playful, sparked by joy, changed in its midst, fanned by relief and gratitude, brought to flame by love, and she welcomed the spreading heat.

Devin lifted his head with a grin, "You like the feather," he teased.

She laughed aloud, "I confess, it is the feather. I *love* the feather."

He began to tickle her unmercifully, pulling loose her shirttails and torturing the bare skin beneath until she pleaded with him to stop, laughing so, she could scarcely speak the words. "Stop! Devin, please!"

"Devin?" A woman's voice.

They turned in surprise toward the bunk, where their play, no doubt, would have led them. Ilene stumbled from the bed, not convinced she wasn't dreaming. "Devin?! Katherine?!" One by one she grasped their arms and her hands slid down to enclose theirs, as though checking to see if they were real. "Oh, thank God!" She said, now hugging each in turn, crying tears of happiness. "When did you get here? *How* did you get here? Why didn't anyone wake me?" She embraced them both again, and Devin lifted her off her feet and twirled her around in joy. "I guess in all the confusion they forgot you were in here," he decided.

Katherine's cheeks pinkened to a deeper shade, and she struggled to tuck in her shirttails, shielded by Devin's broad back.

"Oh, 'tis glad I am to see you!" Ilene proclaimed again, "I thought we might have lost you." She took the arm of each and walked them to the table, "You must tell me everything over breakfast," she demanded, giving Devin's hat a quizzical expression that was so like her brother's Katherine laughed.

The day was passed recounting their adventures, eating and bathing. Katherine had bathed and washed her hair twice, but had not yet had her fill of tea, and to Ilene's delight, it was a very attentive Devin who refilled her cup. Strangely enough, at dinner that evening the conversation was awkward and the air hung heavy in the room. Katherine sat at the small table wearing the dress she had purchased at Ilene's shop. Her hair, brushed to a silken sheen, was left to hang in glorious golden freedom. Devin sat at the other end, freshly shaven, wearing a full sleeved white shirt and black trousers, his still damp hair curling at his collar. He could not keep his eyes off of her, even when poor Ilene, seated between them, posed another question about their ordeal.

"Dev?"

"Hmm?" He replied. He had been thinking how that golden hair would look fanned across the pillows of the soft bed which waited only a short distance away.

The dark-haired woman smiled knowingly. Her luck was no better a moment later when she tried the other end of the table where Katherine sat, thinking it oddly formal sitting like this across from Devin, after all they had been through together… and he really was quite the handsomest man she had ever seen.

Ilene hurriedly finished her meal and excused herself, gaining their attention only when she stood. With habit born of years, Devin jumped to his feet and helped her with her chair. "I'm sorry," he said, reluctantly drawing his eyes from Katherine, "Did you say something, Lee?"

"Yes, brother, I said I'm going to take a walk on deck." She grinned, giving him a pointed look. "It's a bit warm in here, don't you think?"

"Aye, a bit," he answered, walking her to the door, and helping her with her cloak.

"I think I shall be quite a while."

"You've always been my favorite sister."

"I'm your *only* sister, you big Ape, and as your only sister, may I offer a piece of advice?"

He gave a short nod, granting her permission.

She lowered her voice, "I suggest you marry the lady as soon as possible!"

Katherine felt her cheeks grow hot when his eyes locked with hers across the room, and in that moment, Ilene stepped out, and he closed the door behind her.

"You didn't eat much," he spoke, breaking the weighty silence.

Katherine's heart thudded heavily in her breast. "I guess I'm not used to it." Her chair scraped on the floor, and she was in his arms, being carried toward the bed. A prisoner of his thoughts, Devin fanned her hair across the pillow, and buried his face in the soft silken waves before claiming her mouth.

"You didn't tell her… about being married," she half questioned.

"I thought *you* might." At her look of sorrow, he smiled in understanding. "It's not quite the same, is it?"

She was relieved to hear him state her feelings, for she had been afraid he might be disappointed. She brushed the hair off his forehead, and caressed his freshly shaven cheek.

"It's all right, Love, can you see me explaining to my sister that I consider myself married even though it's not legal?" He shook his head and traced a finger across her soft mouth. "No, we'll do it again, because I want to be able to shout it to the world, and have no one be able to dispute it."

"Yes," she whispered, as his mouth closed over hers, and her whole being resonated with joy. For a few long minutes she gave herself up to his masterful kisses and soft words of endearment, until he regretfully withdrew from her embrace.

Katherine sighed feeling wonderfully content. After weeks of sleeping on the hard ground the soft feather tick felt like a cloud, and warmed by Devin's kisses she floated very close to Heaven.

"You know," Devin's sigh matched hers, but was born more of disappointment, "I guess I'll have to let Ilene share the cabin with you, and I'll bunk with the men."

Her eyes popped open, and he was heartened to see his own feelings mirrored there, until she continued, "Oh, *Ilene!*" Katherine sat up. "She probably thinks we're..." She scrambled off the bed smoothing her hair into place.

She had flushed so scarlet that Devin felt sorry for her. Having a sister on board surely did change things. "Not if we join her on deck," he offered, "But she knows about Gabriel, I don't see that..."

"That's different," she whispered, motioning with her hands for him to hurry, "It wasn't while... *Someone was waiting!*"

"I doubt that's what she's thinking," he lied comfortingly, and led her from the cabin, but not before pausing at the door to share one very long and intimate kiss, to last him through the night.

"It's going to be a long journey home," she whispered.

"I'll set a new record," he promised.

Chapter 36

"MR. TULANE! WE'LL MAKE FOURTEEN KNOTS OR DIE TRYING!" True to his word, Captain Galloway was making record time in his journey northward. The Athena's engines had never worked as hard or as long as they did now, with her bow slicing through the miles that separated her passengers from home. Tully teased that the boilers would burst, sending the giant screw propeller into the Southern States causing them to sink like a harpooned whale, and the captain would win the war singlehandedly. These outlandish theories earned the first mate a black scowl from his captain, and delighted applause from that one's sister.

Katherine, who had taken to wearing one of Devin's sweaters under her navy overcoat to fight the December cold, and keep him closer to her heart, waited anxiously, secretly counting down the hours that would bring her back to her child, and a time when she could be alone with Devin. The tantalizing kisses they shared in the dark passageways were wonderful, but only made their separation harder to bear, and she laughed inwardly when she found herself longing for the privacy and isolation of their previous weeks. *She was hopeless.*

She thought that fact was clearly evident, when Devin grew a bit overzealous in his nocturnal farewell, right outside the cabin. She leaned back, supported by his arm, completely intent on the pleasurable sensations of his tongue probing her mouth and the sweet yearning that blossomed within. His other arm, well hidden by her overcoat was busy caressing her naked back beneath her sweater, brushing the side of her breast in an unintentional teasing, that was proving too much for them both. The more she twisted toward his touch, the more he leaned forward in his effort to not drop her, and inadvertently backed her into the cabin door, which unbeknownst to them both, swung silently open.

Ilene, who sat within, reading, finally gained their attention by delicately clearing her throat, for the third time.

When Devin opened his eyes, the light in the cabin had the same effect as a dose of cold water, and Katherine, mortified, blushed to the roots of her hair.

Ilene, to her credit, kept a fairly straight face, but there was a merry twinkle in her eyes. "Good evening," she spoke as nonchalantly as she could, while wrestling the smile that threatened mightily, at the looks on the two surprised faces.

Devin recovered quite easily, "Good evening," he grinned at her, and then winked at Katherine, "Sweet dreams, Major," he whispered.

"It's almost time for my evening walk." Ilene offered innocently.

He smiled. His loving sister had become quite fond of walking the deck at all hours of the day and night. "No thanks, Lee. When you have permission, it's kind of like…" He searched for words.

"*Kissing your sister?*" That one supplied helpfully.

He turned to the blushing Katherine and gave her a very warm perusal, and flashed an appreciative smile at his teasing sibling. "Hardly." As he crossed the deck, they could hear his laughter carried on the night breeze.

Katherine latched the door a bit awkwardly and turned to join the other woman at the table accepting a welcome cup of tea.

"Don't be shy with me, Katherine. You two are hardly a secret after all." Ilene smiled, and closed her book. "You love my brother very much, don't you?"

Katherine nodded absently, tracing a pattern in the wood grain with her fingertip, "More than I can make sense of," she admitted, looking her future sister-in-law in the eye.

"You have a brother, don't you?" Ilene questioned, and when she received the agreeing nod, she went on, "Well then, you should be able to understand how pleased I am to see Devin so happy."

Katherine nodded and sipped her tea, thinking of William and Louise, and finding the new perspective helped her relax even more in Ilene's company.

"You know," the brunette continued, "he was such a different man before, when you were gone. I didn't know it was you, of course, but I knew something had happened. He was like an empty shell, brittle and unreachable. I only want you to know what a difference you've made, and understand that it means the world to me to see him happy again." She smiled, touching the other's hand to soften her words when tears threatened.

Katherine halted the march of a single tear, and struggled again with the heavy weight of guilt. Before she knew it, she had explained the whole story, including Devin's rescue, and why she had left him. Ilene knew most of their journey through the South, and this time Katherine had no trouble telling her about the strange little church, and how they had married each other, and felt somehow changed for their stay there. "Well," she said to the woman, now truly her friend, who had alternately laughed and cried with her throughout the telling, "now you know."

Ilene smiled through her tears. "That's either the most beautiful, or the most horrible story I've ever heard, and it seems to me, you were both terribly wronged by one selfish woman's lies. It wasn't your fault."

"Thank you for that," Katherine whispered, "It means more to me than you'll ever know. The way things happened… seemed to be out of my control. I'd never felt like that before." She lowered her eyes, "I don't know, Devin calls it fate. I can't explain it."

Ilene smiled knowingly, "That's love, Katherine. Has no one ever told you? Love changes you. Love changes everything." She stared over Katherine's shoulder and far beyond the small cabin. I'd do anything for my husband."

"Tell me about him," Katherine said, not meaning to pry.

Ilene paused and her eyes lit with pride. "Thank you for asking. It's been so long since anyone has asked. Devin knows him of course, but… He's a wonderful man. He's quiet, and strong, and one of the kindest people I have ever known. He loves books, and working with wood." The corners of her mouth lifted, "He often smells of sawdust… and leather and old ink, like his books…" She looked into Katherine's eyes, "And he's a Confederate officer."

"Oh, Ilene." Katherine hardly knew what to say, feeling the love in Ilene's words, and remembering the pain of being parted from Devin. She rose and went to put her arms around the despondent woman.

"You're not angry? I mean, you don't think that's terrible?" she asked, hugging Katherine's shoulder in relief at having shared her secret without losing a friend.

"About him fighting for the South?"

Ilene nodded.

"Of course not. I'm sure he did what he thought was right, and no one should do less than that."

Ilene lifted her head, "I'm so glad to hear you say that."

Numb fingers and toes, were never as welcome as they were than by the anxious passengers riding into Portsmouth. The skies wore heavy shrouds of gray, and the threat of snow accompanied the bone chilling northeast wind.

'Treasure,' as Devin had taken to calling the mare, was tied behind a hired coach heading post-haste for North Hill. Inside, the occupants spoke little, each for his or her own reasons. Ilene sat huddled in the corner of the forward seat feeling an imposition. Still, she was anxious to meet her nephew, and was glad to be part of this wonderful homecoming. She only hoped Katherine's family were as nice as she was.

Word of their arrival had been sent ahead, and Katherine, weighted with a ponderous burden of anticipation, sat forward in her seat, as if by so doing, she would reach her destination that much sooner. There was such a lump in her throat that she could barely breathe, and alternately, she squeezed Devin's hand and smiled nervously at Ilene, unable to find words for her feelings.

Devin, too, smiled at Ilene, in silent communication, touched by Katherine's demeanor. Like her, he was most anxious to greet his son, but unlike her, he did not already know what he had been missing. He was nervous, too, about to become an instant father, reality closing in with each passing minute. He craned his neck to see if their destination was in sight, and nagging suspicion and recognition grew at the same time, as they passed the turn to Trendwell and Katherine pointed out the house. He was heard to mumble something about fate under his breath, but he held his story for another time.

A half mile down the road, and around the corner, the coach turned in a wide welcoming drive. "Here we are!" Katherine sat even more forward in her excitement, "My sister's home, North Hill! Do come, Ilene!" She called over her shoulder, when the coach halted, and she hit the ground running, straight into the arms of her sister.

Devin laughed, helping his sister down, and she thanked him, but the words were lost among the shrieks of happiness as they were discovered. Grooms ran up from the stables, and everyone from the cook to the upstairs maid, poured from the house. Dogs barked, and horses whinnied to trumpet in the grand celebration.

Keith appeared with little Phillip, who had begun to cry because of all the shouting, and Amy, who was soon jumping up and down, singing an original version of 'Auntie Kate is Home.' The sisters, crying tears of joy, still stood locked in a grateful embrace. Amidst the euphoria and introductions, the party worked its way rather cumbersomely through the front door. There, a smiling maid was seen coming carefully down the stairs, carrying a mother's heart in her arms. That mother stumbled forward, for her knees had gone weak, and as the child was placed in her arms she cried out and sank to the floor, cradling and kissing him, and crying so, that she could barely see the sight she had so longed for.

Devin gave her some time, but he was eager too, and he put his arms around them both. When she turned her head into his shoulder, and placed the baby in his father's strong arms, no one could claim dry eyes—With the exception of Amy, who was still singing.

Katherine could hardly believe what she was seeing. Devin, home with her at last, and holding their child. It was a miracle. It was her triumph! And who better to share it with her, than *Evelyn?* Katherine looked around expectantly. "Where is Evelyn?"

She turned anxiously to her sister, who exchanged a nervous glance with Keith. "Thea, where is she?" Katherine asked, in growing alarm.

Dorothea stepped forward, her hands moving without purpose. "She's… Well, she's…"

Katherine waited a lifetime in those few moments, unable to breathe, while her sister searched for words. *It couldn't go wrong now.* She had made it home, she had Devin and Gabriel… *"She's all right, isn't she?"*

"Yes… yes!" Her sister reassured. "She's over at Trendwell." Again, she looked to her husband, who nodded encouragement. "She stays there now."

Katherine knew her sister too well, "What's wrong?"

Dorothea clasped her hands nervously and immediately opened them in supplication, willing her sister to understand, "She's…

different." She finished weakly.

"*Different?*" Katherine was alarmed now.

"She insists to be there day and night, except for coming a short time each day to check on the baby," Thea tried to explain. She has lived there since you disappeared. We hired a staff and they've been getting ready for you. We got your message that you were safe, weeks ago, but when you didn't return, she got more and more… She was adamant that you were fine, the whole time. She wouldn't accept anything else, and she wouldn't let us either. Not that we lost hope, but she… She's on a *mission* or something. She doesn't talk about anything but your homecoming, and she has a strange look in her eyes… Almost like her determination alone would make everything work out."

Keith stepped forward and placed an arm comfortingly around his wife's shoulders, "She's different, Kate. You'll see," he added.

Katherine's eyes narrowed, "Are you telling me she's lost her mind?"

"Yes," Keith said.

"No!" His wife said at the same time.

Footsteps were heard in the back hall, and the subject of their discussion came into view. For Katherine, the shock was sudden and complete, and she hoped it didn't show in her face. Evelyn looked *old*, and for the first time, Katherine contemplated her true age. The round pink face she remembered was thin and white, and there were dark circles beneath the once bright eyes, which were only now registering the shock she herself felt. Searching those eyes for the Evelyn of old, she watched tears form and fall, and the older woman came forward to silently embrace her.

Her tears fell as she gently rocked her friend, much like she had her child, and said a silent prayer of gratitude and hope. Moments passed, until, barely able to speak, Katherine chided, "Cat got your tongue, Evelyn?"

It was only a split second before she received her reply, "You're a sight for sore eyes, child… A sight for sore eyes." Then she whispered, her voice breaking, "I knew you would come."

When at last they held each other at arm's length, Katherine scolded her friend, "You've lost weight."

Evelyn grinned a ghost of her old grin, and brushed at a tear, surveying the young woman up and down, "Isn't that the pot calling the kettle black." She stopped abruptly, and frowned at Devin. "Well, Captain. You're the best-looking dead man I've ever seen."

Keith cleared his throat, and Dorothea gave her sister a knowing look.

Katherine only smiled and Devin laughed aloud, "It's a long story, Mrs. Wiley."

"You don't need to tell me," Evelyn replied, waving a hand. "She marched straight into Hell, spit on the devil, and brought you back with her."

Devin stood holding his son, and put an arm around Katherine, "You are precisely right, Madam."

The meal that was set before them that evening was aimed at rectifying some of the damage done. By the time Devin had finished his second helping of everything, and Katherine her third cup of tea, much of their story had been told, and the conversation had turned to a strange mixture of wedding plans and war.

Although the newcomers had missed President Lincoln's newly proclaimed day of Thanksgiving, it could safely be said none were more thankful than those gathered at North Hill, and few could be found in better spirits. The only disappointment of the entire day was to be had by the hostess, and perhaps the cook, when both guests of honor simultaneously, and most emphatically, turned down the dessert especially prepared for their enjoyment—freshly baked apple pie.

Chapter 37

The house at North Hill was in an uproar. Such had been the case since shortly after the homecoming, when Katherine decided she and Devin should be married before he had to return to his work—work and the war—which were one and the same, and which everyone tried not to think about.

He would leave after Christmas, taking Ilene with him to return to Wilmington. Katherine had seized upon the romantic notion of being married on Christmas Eve, leaving less than three weeks to make the announcements and arrangements for the guests.

It didn't seem like a difficult idea at first, since she planned to wear the gown Ilene had so graciously gifted her with, and the guest list, of wartime necessity, would be small. But, in the usual way of things, the details to be dealt with multiplied daily, and the challenges snowballed. Challenges Dorothea, Ilene, and Evelyn, were happy to help with, and Katherine happy to let them.

She couldn't get enough of her son, and her mind was constantly on Devin. Returning to the binding arms of propriety was not all that easy. They could hardly be living together when everyone arrived for the wedding, so she was staying at North Hill, while Devin had moved into Trendwell without her. To add to their frustration, Katherine had come up with the brilliant idea that they 'behave themselves,' for the weeks before they took their vows, so their wedding night would be all the more special. Her groom had reluctantly agreed.

It hardly mattered, because the very thing that would join them together, seemed most instrumental in keeping them apart. There were fittings and flowers, and food to be taken care of, and the men were back and forth to town for supplies. Their days were busy, and after being no more than arm's length from one another for so long, the nights apart seemed endless. So, it was easy to understand why, when one morning, she and Evelyn left for Trendwell, to confer with the staff about the reception, and greet some of Devin's friends who were arriving that afternoon, that Katherine was most anxious to visit her own home.

While Evelyn, more her old self now, headed for the kitchens to take charge, Katherine picked up her skirts and flew up the stairs. She paused at the door to the master bedroom, to take a deep breath and smooth her dress, before she knocked anxiously and peered around the door.

The drapes were open and the flooding sunlight revealed that the bed was empty. She blinked, and spotted him standing by the dresser in his bare feet, black trousers and a white shirt he had yet to button. His hair curled damply around his collar, and his newly shaven chin nearly shone. He glanced up in surprise, from the book he was reading.

At the sight of him, a familiar excitement blossomed deep inside, and surged upward like liquid fire to make her breasts tingle and her face flush pink. "Hi," she spoke with a breathlessness that had naught to do with her run up the stairs.

Devin's glance took in the whole of her, as she stepped into the room and closed the door, to stand with her hands behind her, still clutching the doorknob. She was stunning in a long-sleeved gown of burgundy taffeta, that complemented the sparkle in her eyes. Her hair was caught up in a gray snood, and the small pearls that adorned her earlobes made him want to kiss her there and feel her softness.

"Hi," he grinned, and belatedly thought to hide the book he had been reading behind his back, which of course, immediately caught her attention.

"What's that?" She asked, smiling and crossing the room toward him.

"What?" He stalled, his eyes shifting guiltily to the bedside table whose open drawer gave condemning testimony.

Katherine stalked him playfully, her eyes following his. "Ah, my voyeur has returned!" She teased, reaching her arms around him for the evidence.

Devin laughed and shifted the book high out of her reach, causing her to tilt back her pretty head, a position he immediately took advantage of by capturing her mouth with a kiss. Their play was forgotten when she slipped her arms inside his open shirt and he crushed her to him, kissing her most thoroughly.

He moaned deep in his throat, his kisses trailing along her jaw down to her neck where her pulse beat wildly, and up to her ear where his teeth clicked against a pearl, and his tongue played eagerly, sending exquisite shivers down her spine. Katherine ran her palms up his naked back, reveling in the feel of his powerful shoulders, and up the front of him over the rock-hard muscles of his chest. He moaned aloud, and it pleased her, so she did it again, pressing him against the dresser and darting her tongue over one flat hard nipple and then the other. When he threw back his head and took a deep breath, she kissed the corded muscles of his neck, before pulling his head down to capture his mouth, again.

He kissed her fiercely now, turning away from the dresser, and she found herself against the wall while he pressed into her, conveying his need. She pushed his head lower, into her modest neckline and the hot sparks of passion streaked across her very core. Devin fumbled with the buttons down the back of her dress until at last she could pull the garment forward and frantically work her arms from the sleeves, and slide from her chemise. Once free, she pushed his shirt off his shoulders. They came together, flesh against flesh, knowing this goal attained only fueled the fire for more. Katherine arched back in his arms, and this time it was she who moaned when his mouth came hot upon her breast and she held him there lost in the pleasure. She fumbled with his belt, and Devin took a stumbling step, as they moved in a passion blinded waltz toward the bed.

They never made it. At its edge, Devin knelt to help her remove the rest of her clothing, but she went down with him onto the carpet, and they joined quickly, furiously, spiraling to an ecstasy that left them breathless and exhausted.

When he was able to move, Devin drew a deep breath, and lay with one arm flung over his face. "I surrender," he breathed.

It was quite some time before Katherine rose up on her elbows, and surveyed their disarray. The pins that had held her hair were scattered across the carpet; her bodice was down around her waist, and her skirts up about her hips. Devin's trousers barely clung to one ankle, and there in the middle, lay the book he had tried to hide from her. She laughed and turned on her side to face him, smoothing her skirts down.

Devin lowered his arm and gave her a sideways glance, "What?" He looked around as she had, the difference being, his gaze kept returning to the vision she created, naked to the waist, lying beside him, and he nuzzled his face between her breasts unable to resist.

"I'm not sure you make a very good spy," she laughed.

"Oh?" He stretched to reach the small book of French that he had taken from the nightstand, "You mean this?" Turning to her, he once again held it high over her head and playfully raised his brow.

Katherine glanced up at the book, a grin playing about the corners of her mouth. "Yes, I mean that," she stated, her stomach echoing a familiar drumming when he began to kiss her breasts once again.

"Do you want it, Katherine?"

She laughed, and lay back on the floor, contemplating an answer to the double-edged question, while he did fantastic things to her with his mouth.

He moved up to kiss her neck, where a rapid pulse gave the lie to her coolness, and returned again to her breast, causing her to arch against him.

"Do you want it?" He whispered sweetly, lifting his head to look deeply into her eyes.

She smiled, and returned his gaze for a long moment, "Yes, I want it."

He returned her smile and her book, before lifting her in his arms, and placing her on the bed, where he undressed her, and made love to her so sweetly that she shed tears of joy when he was done.

"What is it, Love?" He asked, holding her close and gazing down into her eyes.

She pressed one palm against his cheek, "I love you so much," she whispered.

"And I love you…" he answered, and gave her a false frown, "and I *always have.*"

She answered with a sheepish look. "I always loved you too, but I didn't see how it could ever end well."

Devin leaned his forehead against hers. "But here we are."

Her gaze swept down the two of them, entangled in the sheets, and her eyes closed as she made a face of resignation, "So much for waiting until the wedding."

"Do you mind so much?"

She blushed prettily, remembering her behavior but a short time before, "Do I look like I mind?" The corner of her mouth lifted, "I only wanted something about our wedding night to be special…" She trailed off, embarrassed now for having spoken her thoughts out loud.

He touched her chin and waited until she looked at him, "Every moment I am with you is special. Maybe the one good thing about us being apart all that time, is that I will never, ever, take you for granted. Do you understand?"

She nodded smiling up at him, because she knew he was right, and brushed a hand through his curls as he kissed her forehead. When her arm fell to the bed, it landed on the forgotten book, and she picked it up to show him.

They grinned at each other.

"What were you reading?" She whispered.

"Why are you whispering?" He whispered back.

"Come on…" She coaxed a little louder.

"I wasn't reading," he confessed. "I told you before, I can't read French. I was only trying to remember the words you said to me at the cottage… do you remember?"

She nodded, "Oh yes, I remember very well."

"Well?" He prompted.

"Well what?" She asked, innocently.

Devin tilted his head to one side, "Would you tell me, *please*?"

"*Oh…*"

"*Katherine*," he cajoled.

"Well," she began, "do you remember any of it?"

"I tried to remember it, and write it down—afterward. I thought it might hold a clue to where you went. But I didn't have enough for anyone to make any sense out of it. *I don't know…* something about flowers and raisins.

At this charming admission Katherine gave him a big smile. "All right," she said, "are you ready?"

"I've been ready forever! Please tell me."

"I believe I said… *Devin, Je t'aimerai toujours. Tu etes la chanson d'mon couer. La fleur d'toute ma'jour"*

Devin was concentrating, trying to take it all in.

"Et ma'raison d'être. Sans toi, je ne'suis pas. " She finished and smiled up at him.

"Well?"

"What?" She asked, her eyes twinkling with merriment.

"What did you *say*?" He ground out between clenched teeth.

"That *is* what I said," she answered sweetly.

At the look on his face, she relented.

"All right, all right," she gasped, laughing.

The mid-morning sun showed the mischief in her eyes change, as she settled herself into the pillows, and regarded him with a soft glowing look that touched him deep inside. She began to speak softly, *"Devin, I will always love you. You are the song of my heart. The flower of all my days, and my reason for living. Without you, I am nothing."* She swallowed hard and blushed under his heavy scrutiny. "Well?" She whispered.

He studied her intently, "It *was* difficult for you to leave me, wasn't it?" He leaned back on the pillows and she moved into his arms.

She nodded, "I thought that was my only chance to tell you that I loved you."

"I wish I had understood it."

"That was the point." She smiled and then grew serious. "Because, I didn't think I had the right to tell you at the time, and I so wanted to."

"Well, it's fine now, Love." He gave her hand an encouraging squeeze, and decided to press his luck. "Tell me about this," he said, reaching into the drawer to bring out his handkerchief. He unrolled the cloth to reveal one dried white rose. "I don't remember this, last time."

"She lifted the delicate blossom by its stem, twirling it in her fingers. "It's the rose you gave me the night you proposed, I just put it in there when our things came from the Athena."

He kissed her on the forehead, and a thought struck him. "Wait," he ordered, disentangling himself and leaving the bed. After rifling through his dresser, he returned with a yellowed envelope, from which he handed her a flower much like the one she held.

Katherine frowned her question at him, trying to remember. *Had she given him a rose?*

"It was the night the Parker's had their Fourth of July party. You barely spoke to me."

"You were there with Cecilia," she defended.

The face he made, told her what he thought of that. "I was working with Cecil."

She digested that thought, even as he waved a hand to dismiss it, so he could continue.

"It was getting dark, and I was in the Johnston's backyard, and you appeared…

"Oh." She remembered, "I had picked it walking through the garden."

"You left it on the stone wall when you left."

"And you kept it?" She asked her voice catching.

He shrugged, pulling on his trousers and bent to give her a kiss, which stretched into two more. "The question *is*, Love, 'Do I get back into bed with you, or do you get up with *me* to greet our guests?'"

"Oh!" She jumped from the bed and grabbed her shift, "You make me forget myself!" she scolded, as she dressed.

He smiled, fastening the buttons of her gown, "I know exactly what you mean."

With a subtle hint from his fiancée, Devin had chosen a dark burgundy vest before adding his black coat, and now the handsome couple stood ready to descend the long stairway. One of them had cold feet. Devin had descended several steps before realizing Katherine was not with him, and he turned in question.

"Do you think your friends will like me?" She asked, suddenly unsure of herself.

He scoffed, and reached a hand up to her, lowering his voice, "Is this my hard-riding Athena? The take-charge shipping queen, who told me to use a grand frigate for *kindling?* The hell-cat adversary who bested me on the cliff trail?"

At this, she smiled a little, and tilted her head, "I did, didn't I?"

"I'll never forget it. Shall I go on? My fighting, clawing, half-drowned Major, who crossed enemy territory to get to her son? *Really?*" He stepped closer, "*…and did I mention, every man's dream in bed?*"

She shrugged, a little embarrassed at her momentary lapse, and straitening her shoulders and holding her head high, she took his arm ready to proceed. "I'm fine."

"You certainly are," he whispered in her ear, as they descended the stairs. She colored prettily, and swatted his shoulder.

They reached the drive and waited for the coach roll to a stop, and Devin stepped forward to lend assistance. Katherine waited as a buxom red headed woman stepped down, and he made the introductions. "Katherine, this is my friend, Maggie O'Leary."

The attractive woman was not so old that the exuberance of the hug she gave Devin, was not noted by his fiancée. "How do you do?" Katherine asked politely, careful not to stare at the scar that ran the length of the woman's jaw.

"Glad to meet ya, darlin'!" The bundle of energy greeted her with the same exuberant hug she had given Devin, and Katherine smiled.

A young and handsome boy stepped from the coach, and Devin continued, "And this is her son, Marcus."

Katherine shook hands with the dark-haired Marcus, whom she liked immediately, until he begged Devin for a tour of the stables, leaving her alone to play an awkward hostess to his mother.

"Won't you come in," she invited, throwing a last beseeching glance at Devin's receding shoulders, but she was on her own. "Lunch will be ready soon." She led the way to the parlor, but Maggie had stopped in the foyer to look around admiringly, before she spoke.

"You've done all right for yourself, catchin' my Devin, you have. He has a beautiful home here."

Katherine's brows arched slightly. She forced herself to take a deep calming breath. "May I get you some refreshment, Mrs. O'Leary?"

"A drop of wine would be lovely." She seated herself, while Katherine called for the wine, and tea for herself. She racked her brain for some topic of conversation, but shortly learned there was no need. Maggie O'Leary had the gift of gab, and needed only a competent listener to while away the time. She covered the weather, her trip, her feelings for Marcus and the home they had left… All her hostess need do, was nod and smile in the appropriate places.

Katherine was soon so relaxed in the flow of mundane chatter, that she was nearly daydreaming before the other woman's words brought her up short.

"…quite a night we had, Devin and me, in that hotel."

Katherine set cup to saucer. "I beg your pardon?" She asked quietly.

Maggie continued, completely oblivious to the woman's discomfit, "The night he rescued me. That's when I got this," she said, not shy about turning her head so Katherine could get a clear view of her scarred face, and pulling at her neckline to display a mesh of disfigurement covering her chest. "Stabbed in the back too," she said, making a motion behind her with her arm, "quick as ya please." I would have died that night, if it wasn't for Devin. Ended it with his shotgun, he did, and then stopped the bleedin' until they got me to the doctor, and waited with me to make sure I was going to stay on this side o' the dirt."

Katherine sat in shock as it all came together in her mind, *the stabbing, a shotgun blast…* "I'm so sorry. Was that…?"

"Everett Price, may he burn in hell. But my Devin saved me; I knew he would. Got there just in time, too. I love that man like my own son, I do, and he loves you, anyone can see it when he looks at ya. You're a lucky woman, you couldn't find better."

The bride-to-be had to smile, when the woman heaped praise on her beloved. She took another sip of tea, deciding she liked Maggie O'Leary after all. The woman was exactly as she appeared to be, no airs, no veiled meanings… Katherine's thoughts came stumbling to a halt once again, when she caught the tail end of the woman's last comment. "I beg your pardon?"

Maggie continued undaunted, "I'm just sayin' how glad I am that he found you, after that other one."

Katherine's heart squeezed. "*Other one?*"

"It's the truth I'm tellin', although he never did say who she was. But I know him. Broke his heart, she did. He thought she loved him, and then she disappeared. I didn't think he'd ever stop lookin' for her. Like ta drove him outta his mind. Why, if I could get my hands on that black hearted flirt, I'd wring her neck."

Two bright pink spots assaulted Katherine's cheeks, and an awkward silence flooded the room, until Devin, who had entered in time to hear the end of the conversation, went directly to Katherine's side and took her hand. "There was no other," he spoke for the benefit of both women, while giving Maggie a scold with his eyes, and indicating Katherine with a tilt of his head. "Shame on you, Maggie, letting out my secrets," he said, not unkindly.

Now, it was the older woman whose cheeks burned, at her blunder. "Oh my, I've stepped in it deep this time, haven't I?"

Devin turned to Katherine, a look of pleading in his eyes, and she, released from an awkward confession, rose graciously. "Would you excuse us?" She patted his arm. "I would like it if Mrs. O'Leary would walk with me in the garden."

In the barren winter gardens, there were no flowers, but there were evergreens, pretty dried seed heads, the vibrant stems of the red twig dogwood, and an icy December wind that cooled the embarrassment of both women as they walked in silence.

"Well now," the shorter woman spoke first, snuggling deeper into her cloak of thick Irish tweed, "I guess I couldn't have made a worse first impression."

"I believe that prize belongs to me," Katherine responded, more to herself than the other woman.

Maggie stopped abruptly, and screwed up her face, closing her eyes tightly, "Please-call-me-Maggie-and-I'll-know-you-forgive-me."

Katherine pressed her lips together to hold in a laugh, "All right, *Maggie*."

The red head bobbed up and down, "Bless your heart!"

"I can hardly blame you for being upset, if you care so for Devin."

"I do. He is very dear to my heart."

"It's a long story, what happened between Devin and me, I'll tell you some other time. They had reached the end of the walkway, and Katherine turned to look into the eyes of the woman she sensed would be her friend. "Suffice it to say, that whatever pain I brought to him, I felt ten-fold trying to avoid him, and I swear to you, I will spend the rest of my days trying to make up for it."

Maggie gave her a look of understanding, and they began to walk arm in arm, giving Katherine the courage to add, "I wasn't very good at it… *the avoiding part.* Would you like to meet our son?"

Devin delighted in the fast-forming friendship between two of his favorite women. Maggie was over the moon about the baby. And Katherine was blissfully unaware how this new friendship would affect her life in the very near future.

Chapter 38

The long-awaited wedding day dawned with but one small black cloud on the horizon. That cloud's name was Judith Caldwell. Katherine stood looking out the window of her room at North Hill, remembering the apologetic look on the face of her brother William, when he and Louise had arrived the night before with Judith in tow.

As soon as he found an opportunity, William had pulled his sister aside for a private word. "I'm sorry, Kate, Ezra is away, and once she heard we were coming there was no stopping her. She's as sure as she can be that you'll be glad to have her."

His sister's eyes widened in surprise, but there had been no time to answer, before Louise, spying the two of them together, seized the opportunity to join them, her big brown eyes pleading forgiveness. "Katherine, I'm so embarrassed. She wouldn't take no for an answer. You know how she is."

At the twin apologies, the bride had laughed and kissed them both. "Nothing can spoil my wedding." But, now, as she prepared for the most welcome event, she was not so sure. She couldn't shake the feeling that Judith was indeed a black spot on her plans, and her presence forbode anything but champagne and best wishes. She shrugged off the feeling. Judith was, after all, the nosiest busybody of them all, and it was, perhaps, only her deplorable curiosity that had brought her. And after all, a wedding was but a few hours and whatever happened, at the end of this day she would be married to Devin, and that was all that mattered.

She hurried to spend time with Gabriel and keep up the routine of trying to nurse him. With help from Evelyn's concoctions and advice, her milk was returning little by little, something Katherine considered another miracle, and for which she was extremely grateful. In the meantime, Thea continued to help as she had all along.

Thankfully, the journey from bed, to bath, to the old stone church was uneventful, and the wedding was beautiful. Devin, stepped straight from her dreams, in his dress uniform, and the bride was radiant in her ivory gown, with her hair elegantly pinned beneath a long veil. She wore her pearl earrings and carried, white roses and ivy.

What she could recall afterwards, was a blur of happy moments—Sweet Amy as her flower girl, Ilene, and Louise and Dorothea, preceding her down the aisle. Her joy as she followed them on the arm of her brother, passing Tully and the men from the Athena, Evelyn, bursting with pride, Cecil smiling at her, Uncle Roderick at Devin's side—and Devin, waiting for her. She recalled the rich timber of his voice, and the light in his eyes, when he spoke the words that would make her his wife.

She had spoken her vows in a clear steady voice, and her heart flooded with happiness as they were pronounced man and wife at last. She barely recalled drifting up the aisle and outside into the December sunlight. Devin paused to kiss her again, before whisking her away to their private coach for the ride to Trendwell. He settled next to her, and pulled a fur lined cape around her shoulders, "Hello, wife."

She laughed, and gave him a brilliant smile, "Hello, husband." Her eyes glowed with joy and they shared a tender kiss, after which she rested her forehead against his. "I can hardly believe this is happening," she whispered. "It seems like a dream."

"It does, and thank you, my love, for marrying me." Taking a flat velvet box from inside his coat, he opened it to reveal a beautiful necklace and earrings, that matched her engagement ring.

His new bride gasped at their beauty, "They're beautiful! Oh, but… You didn't have to do that. They must have cost a fortune."

"Why not? I've waited long enough to spoil you," he laughed.

She gave him a suspicious look. "But when I wanted to sell you my half of the Athena, you said you couldn't afford to buy her at any price."

"You are not married to a pauper, Mrs. Galloway."

Mrs. Galloway. She smiled at that, but was not dissuaded, "But the Athena…"

Devin could almost see her adding two and two, so he spoke quickly, "I said I couldn't *afford* to do it. I never said I didn't have the funds."

She tilted her head, suppressing a grin. "And how is that not the same?"

He took her hand, "It was my one link to you. I couldn't afford to give it up at any price. And you know you didn't want me to." His voice was teasing, but deep inside he hoped she wouldn't be angry.

"You're right," she admitted, after a pause, leaning to touch her lips to his, and linger there until all thoughts, save one, had flown from him.

His arms came around her, and she turned to lie across his lap and pull his head down, "Thank you, for being stubborn," she kissed him again, "and arrogant," and again, "and smarter than I was, and for not giving up, even when I hated you for it." She kissed him again, until he stopped to whisper against her mouth. "*Saints*, Katherine, did you really hate me?"

She grinned, "There was a moment, I think, born of frustration."

"And now?" He returned her grin.

She let him read the answer in her eyes, until his mouth lowered to hers, and she told him with her heart.

"So, you're not cross with me?" Devin secretly breathed a sigh of relief at this one last obstacle out of the way.

"*Let me think…* My brand new, wonderful, *somewhat* handsome husband, whom I love to death, has more money than I thought. Hmm…"

The coach turned into the drive at Trendwell, and Katherine sat up to smooth her hair into place. "I have something for you, too. It's home." She smiled, "I mean, it *is* home. Trendwell is *ours,* I had your name added to the deed."

Devin turned his head toward the window and watched the house come into view. "Thank you," he whispered in awe. "'Tis a grand gift. I know I told you of the first time I saw it. I had such a longing to be here. And to think it was *your* home, and I already had a family." I don't believe Helen Trendwell has forgiven me for trying to bribe her. She was still looking at me crossways in the church, and her daughter, too. I'll have to explain that I have not married you for your house. He laughed, and shook his head, and turned to her with a grin, "Fate is truly on my side, Madam."

Katherine thought of all the times she had cursed fate for throwing them together, and she smiled, thinking there just might be some truth to his claim, for he had won out, and she was so very glad he had.

It was well into the evening, and the small crowd had eaten and danced and toasted, and toasted some more. Katherine looked around the ballroom at the fire blazing in the fireplace, the twinkling chandeliers and the magnificent Christmas tree in one corner. Her eyes sought out Devin across the room, raising a glass with his men. He had exchanged his uniform for a black suit and a cream-colored satin vest, and her gaze lingered. She took a deep breath, and let it out in a long sigh of satisfaction. Everything had gone well.

Gabriel, had been put down for his nap when they returned home, and now, along with little Phillip and Amy, had been brought in to join his parents in the celebration. Katherine still wore her wedding gown, but had removed her veil, and exchanged her pearls for the necklace and earrings Devin had gifted her with earlier. She waltzed with their son in her arms, twirling around and around to the music, the glow of her happiness rivaling the jewels she wore. Devin could not resist joining them on the dance floor, and when he wrapped his arms around them, his eyes locking with hers over the head of their son, she was so filled with joy she could have floated above the floor.

It was then that Judith Caldwell loosed her sharp tongue to shred their happy bubble. She had seen the children at the wedding, but it wasn't until now that the obvious truth had dawned. The dark-haired baby, the proud man, the adulation in the woman's eyes… This was clearly an intimate family moment, and as usual, her mouth worked quicker than her mind.

Louise was standing next to her mother when reality hit like a bomb, and she recoiled from the impending explosion, even as she tried to stop it. "Mother, don't! *Mother!*" She hissed, in a warning whisper, but it was too late. Judith started across the room, and Louise began to search frantically for William.

The music stopped, and the happy couple swirled to a halt, when Judith reached them. Katherine, intoxicated with exuberance, and more than a little champagne, looked questioningly at the woman's face, and knew immediately something was wrong. "Mrs. Caldwell?" She scanned the room to see what was amiss. Everyone seemed to be standing stock still, and staring at the little group in the middle of the dance floor. She turned again to Judith.

The woman's eyes glowed with, righteous fury, and rage colored her cheeks. "I knew it!" She spat, with obvious disgust, "I knew no good would come of your behavior! Dressing the way you do… Living alone… No proper supervision!"

Her new husband stepped forward protectively, but Katherine handed the baby to him, to keep him occupied.

Judith's eyes never left Katherine as she carried on, "I tried! God knows, I tried…"

Devin burned inside, but took his cue from his wife, who stood calmly, her head held high, although a tell-tale blush had bloomed upon her cheek. He took a deep breath. And still the woman raged, "I felt I owed it to your mother, God rest her, a decent woman, and here you are with a… a… a…"

Katherine's head notched up, the look of warning in her eyes preventing her aggressor from taking one liberty too many, although the implication was perfectly clear, as she finished, "*…And flaunting him at your wedding! Oh, for shame, Katherine Lawrence! Shame on you, and shame on me for being part of it!*"

Katherine relaxed her fists, hidden in her skirts, and could barely contain the laugh that bubbled up inside. *She was Katherine Galloway!* And she found it hysterically funny that Judith hadn't been invited to be part of it in the first place —*It didn't matter*— Yes, she had a baby, but she was married to his father. *Where was the shame in that?* She searched her happy heart, but could find none, and decided to share this fine revelation with the poor distraught woman beside her. "I'm married," she said simply, a brilliant smile breaking forth.

Judith still simmered in the juices of a rich indignation, and Devin decided she had more than had her say, but Katherine's smile salved his temper.

Louise had recruited William and Keith's help in marshalling her mother, but too late, and now they stood behind the woman, embarrassed, and ready to drag her off if need be. Evelyn had come barreling across the room, with Dorothea and Ilene on her heels, and they too, stood mutely waiting to help. Roderick and Maggie stood behind Devin and the rest of the guests gathered close in support of the couple.

This was fortunate, for they could hear Devin's words plainly. "Madam, though it may be difficult for you, try to think before you speak," he rebuked, with such a charming smile, the insult was lost on Judith. "We are at war, and love, like everything else, has paid a dear price for it. Nothing has been as we have wished it these past years. You know this as well as anyone. Let there be no doubt, Katherine is my true and virtuous wife. I have spoken the vows with her on no less than three separate occasions." At this, Judith caught her breath, and Katherine looked sharply at her husband, as he went on…

"First, on board ship, as she stood in the presence of the captain, did I pledge to her all my worldly goods and vow my love." While he said this, his eyes met Katherine's and she gave him a soft smile, before he turned again to Judith. "Regrettably, we have no proof of this. Did you know we were on a ship that was attacked and sunk, and my wife almost drowned?"

Judith shook her head, hanging on every word.

"Yet again, in a most picturesque moonlit church, we spoke the vows together before God, and signed our names to the register." Here he paused for effect, sadly shaking his head. "That church was bombarded and left in ruins. By our *own* troops!"

Judith gasped, putting a hand to her heart.

"But," he continued, "the records remain, and God blessed my wife and I with a son. But because of the war, all of this was away from our home, our family, and our friends. So, though we were already bound to one another, we wanted to gather with our loved ones, to vow our love once again. To share it with *you*. And ask your blessings and best wishes." He directed a most sincere gaze at the offended one, not sparing her a flash of his dimples, while he reached for his wife's hand. "You can believe me, Mrs. Caldwell, when I tell you that I am more married to Katherine, than any man will ever be to any woman."

The room was very quiet, and not all eyes were dry, when Devin shifted his gaze to his wife, and back to Judith, his voice lowered, "We have paid our price to be together. So please, Mrs. Caldwell, celebrate with us, and give us the gift of peace."

Judith, nodded silently. "Hear! Hear!" Someone called out, and Devin signaled for the musicians to play. He passed Gabriel to Evelyn, whose eyes shone with a mixture of tears and approval, and waltzed Katherine away to the refreshment table.

He handed her a glass of punch, and watched, charmed, as she sipped, and her eyes locked with his over its rim. This time when he took it from her, and drank from the very spot her lips had touched, she only smiled—That soft secret smile that spoke volumes.

He turned her so that the breadth of his shoulders shielded her from view, and kissed her.

"Are you all right?"

"I am now, thanks to you," she said, picking up another glass of champagne. The bubbles tickled her nose, and she giggled.

"What is it?"

"I was thinking about the story you told, and how you twisted the truth."

He gave her a haughty look, and placed a hand sincerely over his heart. "I spoke no lie, Madam."

She smiled, *it was true,* "But, the first time…"

He rose to his own defense, "I did pledge you all my worldly goods."

"Yes, as you gave me your *hairbrush!*…And *you* were the captain!"

He only shrugged, grinning broadly.

"And…" she whispered, "that was *not* the ship that sank!"

"I never said it was."

Katherine glanced around to see if anyone could hear them, before she continued, "*And,* the church was destroyed *before* we went there!"

"I never said it wasn't." This time he was not able to suppress a laugh.

She smiled again, and sipped her drink, "True," she conceded. "But," she gave him a look of wonder, "You took a lot of little truths, and painted a picture the way you wanted everyone to see it, and word will spread that we were married before, and our son will be protected."

He grinned in satisfaction, "Merry Christmas, Love."

"Thank you," she whispered, and a mischievous smile played about her mouth.

Devin was caught by it. "What?"

"Hmm, I shall be leery of your explanations in the future."

"Speaking of the future," he smiled, and at the dark look in his eyes, her heart began a knowing beat. He slid his hand over his side where the inside pocket of his coat would be. "I have some papers here that say you are my wife."

"Oh?" She said, innocently, when he leaned close, his lips only inches away.

"And it's getting late."

"Is it?" She breathed against his mouth as it covered hers. The champagne lent fuel to the fireworks that flared with newfound intensity. Her pulse quickened, and she clung to him, opening to him, as he plunged her mouth with promise. "I take it you'd like to do something about that?"

Devin straightened and made a small noise in his throat. "Try me."

She stared, her lips dark and full from his kiss, and he hated to let her go.

Katherine, remembering herself, glanced around guiltily, and put a hand to her hair, taking a deep cooling breath. She handed him her empty glass, and taking his other hand, led him to one of the side doors.

Soon, Anderson, the new butler hired by Devin, was assisting Keith, in lighting the candles on the Christmas tree, while everyone watched appreciatively. The small band played several carols while they all sang, and amidst calls of 'Merry Christmas!' and 'best wishes!'

people began to take their leave, bearing gifts of champagne, whiskey, and cake.

Dorothea was taking care of Gabriel, long since asleep, and any overnight guests were staying at North Hill, leaving the newlywed couple alone in their home, except for the help, who discreetly retreated. Katherine stole a glance at Devin, who smiled and took her hand, bringing it to his lips for a kiss. "Well, Mrs. Galloway, how do you feel?"

She sighed and went into his arms. "Happy," she whispered, "so very happy."

Devin kissed her upturned mouth, and placed careful kisses along her delicate jaw to her ear. The large oval stone she wore there blocked his path, as he sought the petal softness of her lobe. He missed the pearls which were smaller and not in his way.

Katherine closed her eyes, savoring this moment she would always remember—Devin, *her husband*, kissing her in their home—it seemed too precious to be real. She sighed again, as his warm breath bathed her ear, and the familiar fires flickered to life. She turned her head inviting him to retrace his path to her mouth, but not before she heard the smallest sound of regret, forced to abandon his prey. They finished the lingering kiss and Katherine opened her eyes, to study him. "What?"

Devin took a long breath, "What?" He threw back at her, smiling.

She stepped away, and tilting her head in a most feminine gesture, removed first one earring, and then the other, all the while holding his eyes with hers. When she was done, she reached her arms around his neck to pull him to her, turning her face away at the last second, granting him access to the velvet spot he craved.

He took up the challenge with a zeal that turned the flicker to a steadily growing flame.

"Mmm…" she murmured, turning her head to gain the other ear an equal share of the exquisite torture. "*You like the pearls,*" she said, in a breathless whisper.

His soft rumble of laughter tickled straight to her toes. "Madam, you read my mind."

"I do," she smiled mysteriously, "although in truth, it is not difficult."

"Witch…" he rasped, "read this then," and his mouth covered hers in a kiss stoked white hot by their play.

When he lifted his head, Katherine gazed at him, catching her breath. "It says this…" Thinking of no better way to answer, she buried her hands in his hair and met his mouth again, returning every bit as much as she had received a moment ago. She moved against him, the satin of her gown sliding over the rougher wool of his clothing. Her tongue sought his in a daring dance, much like the flames that now leapt and danced within, burning upward and spreading downward until they became all encompassing.

She knew Devin felt the heat, when the deep breath he took swelled his chest, causing it to push harder against her aching breasts as he held her tightly to him. It was he who broke away from the kiss, and stepped back, his eyes glittering darkly.

She stared, her lips parted, paralyzed by desire and disappointment, when he held one hand up palm outward in a signal that called a halt to their activities.

The rapid rise and fall of her lovely breasts, displayed at the top of her gown, caught his eye, and he watched for a moment mesmerized by their beckoning softness. With a will of iron, he pulled his eyes away, glancing upward to the ceiling, and found his voice, "I do think it would be in our best interests, if we were to continue this conversation upstairs." Stoically he offered his arm, and she took it, but at the look she gave, his iron will began to melt.

Two stairs, three. Devin glanced over and met her scorching eyes again. Four stairs, five, he studied her pretty mouth, swollen from his kisses. Six. Seven steps, and his gaze passed along the line of her jaw, to the softness of her ear that screamed out for his attention, and the elegant line of her neck that beckoned him.

On the eighth stair, Katherine, warmed by his heated glances, hugged his arm more tightly to her, causing her breasts to push upward, nearly spilling out of her gown. Devin's step faltered, and at her questioning expression, he swept her into his arms and continued up the stairs and into their room, all the while planting fervent kisses on her eyes, her mouth, her ear, and on the tops of her breasts. He pushed the door shut with his back, and let her slide to her feet before him. *"Saints Katherine."*

Katherine, who had kept her arms about his neck when her feet touched the floor, mutely requested his kiss, and he complied, giving, taking, plundering, playing, until they were barely able to control the passion bursting between them. She was disappointed when he stepped away, and again held up a halting hand to give her pause. She stood breathing heavily, smiling at his effort to act cool and collected while his eyes blazed with a heat that seared her. She watched while he removed his jacket and cravat, boots and socks, before he returned to her.

When he did, he turned her back to, and wrapped his arms around her from behind. She gasped, and took a deep swelling breath, as his hands slid across her middle, and moved up to cup her breasts, causing them to overflow her bodice once again.

Devin, too, held his breath, his blood surging like molten steel. He ached to be inside her, feeling her softness draw him out and end this torment, but he vowed she would remember this night. He undid the buttons at the back of her gown, and it slid off her arms to puddle on the floor around her like a satin cloud. Layers peeled away like the petals of a rose, until she was his at last. Deftly, he removed the pins from her hair placing hot kisses in ever widening circles at the nape of her neck to send shivers of delight and desire radiating to every part of her body.

Her hair cascaded in a silken veil, caressing them both with its cool softness, while his hands found her breasts again, his calloused palms teasing her to ecstasy. Katherine's head lolled back on his shoulder and she abandoned herself to the pleasure, as his hands roamed over her, worshipping every inch of her skin. He captured her wrists and raised her arms out to her sides, sliding his palms over them, feeling the muscle, the strength and the softness that he marveled at, all the while whispering words of adoration. "Katherine, I love you so much."

"Then why are you torturing me?" She teased, her voice a husky breath against his neck.

His fingers ran the length of her spine, and encircled her to find each rib, each hollow, and smooth the planes of her stomach, before they moved to claim her very center. When he touched her there, the force of her desire shocked her, and she caught her breath. His hands slid away to caress her breasts again, their hardened peaks eagerly awaiting his return. She arched into his hold, her arms coming up over her head to clutch at the sides of his neck, as small murmurs of passion escaped her. She turned to unfasten his belt, and Devin stepped away to remove the rest of his clothing, an impatient Katherine helping with the last of the buttons on his shirt.

She went into his arms, melding her aching softness into the crisp dark hair of his chest, their scorching heat fusing them together. His kiss was fire and lightning, bolting through her to set every nerve aflame, and she felt she would die before she ever knew him as her husband.

Devin moved his mouth to her throat, finding the violent pulse that matched his own, and trailed downward to close over her breast.

She arched back, and let the sweet wet warmth of his love bathed her once again in bliss, his whispered name a plea for mercy, until at last he lifted her, and carried her to the bed… But still, he continued this prelude, this symphony he played upon her senses. He lowered his weight over her, pressing her into the softness of the bed and matched himself to her, palm to palm, arms, breasts, hips, and thighs so that no part of her was left unclaimed by him. For a long moment he looked into her eyes, as if he would search out her soul and claim that too, and then he began to kiss her. Her eyes, her chin, her jaw, the pulse at the base of her throat, every place he had touched earlier, he now branded with his lips and tongue. Her fingers wound into his hair. He returned to claim her breasts, each in turn, and blazed a scorching trail across her stomach to the flat plain of her hip.

Knowing now, what he intended, she gave herself up totally to him, in this marvelous baptism of love. He moved downward beyond her grasp, parting her thighs, and she followed his gentle urgings, forgetting to breathe, her fists holding fast to the sheets beside her, steeling herself against the raging thunder of his ultimate tribute.

It came as she knew it would, and yet, like nothing she had felt before. The iron grip of passion squeezing the life from her, and an all-encompassing tide of ecstasy, when life surged back anew, tumbling her senses until she was somehow separate from herself, lost in this torrential sea of passion.

Devin joined with her in the midst of her thundering climax, and whether it began again or never ended, she could not have said. He traveled with her in this strange breathless world, until the tower of passion he had so carefully constructed, came crashing down around them.

They slept. Man and woman. Husband and wife.

Chapter 39

Christmas Morning! Although the sun was far from rising, the thought came clearly, when Katherine opened her eyes to find Devin's sleeping face only inches from hers. She studied the long lashes, the straight nose, and his devilish dimples, innocent in repose. Her gaze passed over the dark shadows, shading the contours of his cheek, and came to rest on his mouth. Memories of the night before brought a thrill to her heart, and a blush to her cheek. At the soft sigh that escaped her, his eyes opened.

"Good morning, wife."

"Merry Christmas," she whispered, moving into his arms.

"Merry Christmas, to *you,* love. Did you sleep well?"

At her nod, Devin traced one finger across her cheek to brush at a stray strand of hair. "No more nightmares?"

She shook her head to indicate her negative answer, and touched a palm to his bristled cheek. "No," she spoke softly, "You've turned all my nightmares into dreams and all my dreams have come true."

"I pray they always will," he whispered, nuzzling her sleep-warmed neck with kisses.

The feel of his bewhiskered chin, struck sparks of pleasure that wove their way tantalizingly through her sleepy haze, and caused her to press closer to his warmth. "And what of your dreams?" She whispered, touching him where she would, and reveling in the freedom to do so.

For a moment he didn't answer, being totally absorbed in his labors, but he paused to lift his head and give her a wicked grin. "I've but one dream, love…" He lowered his voice to match hers, "and I think it's about to come true again."

It *had* been a night for dreams come true, and the banishing of nightmares. All but one, and it waited beyond the sturdy doors of Trendwell, cloaked in stark reality. It may be forced to wait a day or a week, but still, its turn would come, and the beast would raise its horrid head—The nightmare beast of war. Katherine returned his kisses and lost herself once more in his loving, determined to not think about how in the world she would survive his leaving.

In deference to the newlyweds, it was not until late afternoon when the family returned to share a Christmas supper and gather around the tree, supervised by Amy. Gabriel, to his mother's joy, was ensconced in her arms and was not about to be removed, and Judith, to everyone's relief, had pleaded a headache, and was not about to be missed. Ilene and Devin exchanged teasing banter, as brothers and sisters are wont to do, and Roderick was so solicitous of Evelyn, when they took their places around the gleaming table, that it caught Katherine's attention. Her eyes swung to Thea across the table, and interrogated her with a look.

Dorothea, in the way of sisters, confirmed with a look of her own, shrugged her shoulders, and pressed her lips together, all at the same time, struggling to suppress her laughter at her sister's expression.

Katherine wore a long-sleeved velvet gown of dark emerald, which showed to perfection the new string of pearls Devin had gifted her with that morning. With it, of course, she wore the pearl earrings to match, and the implication of his gift, tied with her recent memories, brought a merry twinkle to her eyes each time she glanced toward her husband. Her hair was simply tied back, and as she sat forward in her play with her son, the golden tresses slid forward to rest upon her velvet clad bosom. Devin could barely keep his eyes from her—A fact not lost on the small company, who each in his own mind, determined that the visit not be a lengthy one.

It was this thought that prompted William to act, as Evelyn was exclaiming over her new set of garden tools from Katherine… *and holding hands with Roderick?* With a look toward the company in general, he asked Katherine if he might speak to her alone.

Reluctant to give up the baby, she surrendered him to his father, followed her brother into the drawing room, and closed the door. She turned to him, her face a mixture of happiness and curiosity. William stood, handsome in his dark suit. *He had gained a little needed weight. If only he didn't have to go back…* She pushed her thoughts aside, and seated herself in one of the chairs in front of the fire, expecting him to do the same.

Instead, he turned to pace nervously, before he spoke. "I'm not sure about this, Kate. I don't want to spoil anything for you."

Her eyes lit with alarm.

"You're so happy right now."

"What is it?"

"Remember when you gave me father's journal?"

She nodded.

He cleared his throat, "I never read it. I couldn't."

She was already nodding in understanding.

"But, this morning, while we were waiting to come over, I had some time, and Christmas, you know, seemed like a good time."

Her stomach fluttered nervously. "*And?*"

He laughed a little, "There's nothing in it."

"*What?*"

"Well, very little since the war started, and nothing about Mother passing. That's why I didn't want to read it, I think. I was…" he laughed, a little embarrassed, "*afraid, I guess,* to read what he wrote about her. But he didn't."

"I did the same thing. That's why I didn't want to read it either."

William nodded in silence, "I did find these, though, tucked in the pages," he finished, handing her two envelopes.

Katherine examined the letters addressed to herself, her imagination running ahead to cross a thousand bridges.

"One is father's writing," her brother offered helpfully, "but the other is not."

"No," she answered, her voice quiet above the hammering of her heart, "It's Devin's." They stared at each other a moment, before she carefully broke the seals on the letters and began to read to herself.

"Kate?"

She looked up, her eyes full. "Father got this letter from Devin. It was delivered to him instead of to the house, before they sailed…The delivery boy was late getting to his own ship. He didn't send it on to me because… It's a long story, but father didn't think I would want to hear from him because… because of something I told him."

She stopped to skim the passage from her father again, written shortly before his death… *…I have seen Captain Galloway… He cares for you Kate, I am certain, so I am now forwarding this letter… I have a feeling things will work out for you. It is up to you, of course. …love to your mother and Thea… Hopefully I will be home…*

"So, it's good?" William asked doubtfully.

She only nodded, reading still, and he retreated to pace across the room, while she finished, and began to read the other letter.

Without knowing that he had done so, her brother had given her the greatest gift of all, and yet it broke her heart. For here were the words… The words she had prayed for so long ago, Devin had asked her to wait for him after all. Not only to wait for him, but to marry him.

William watched helplessly, as her tears came so steadily, he wondered that she could see. "Are you all right?"

She only nodded. Her heart soaring with the knowledge even now. She had been right about him. She had been so sure he would ask her. If only Cecilia hadn't interfered, if she hadn't been so shattered by her lies, if she had met Devin that morning, or if she had received this letter, everything would have been different. At the thought, the flood of sorrow and happiness began again. Of course, none of that mattered now, but to see the words, to hold the past in her hands… Blinking through the tears, she searched the missive once again for the lines dearest to her heart.

My Dearest Katherine … no right to ask … due to the circumstances… please understand, Katherine, I beg you… I have loved you from the first moment I saw you. If you cannot accept my proposal, at least wait for me to return, and give me a chance to win your heart. Until then, I shall keep you in mine, and live on this hope alone. Yours truly, Devin

She clutched the pages to her heart and glanced up to see that her brother had been replaced by her husband, who stood leaning against the doorframe watching her, and she smiled through her tears. "I got your letter."

He crossed the room to kneel in front of her chair, "William told me. I wondered what had become of it." He handed her one of his new handkerchiefs. "I wrote it that morning, when you didn't come to meet me." He paused, "I paid a boy for delivery. I wonder how your father ended up with it?"

"There's a letter from my father, as well. I guess the boy was late to ship out, and chose a short-cut. One Lawrence is as good as another, right?

"You'll forgive me if I disagree?" He grinned.

"He didn't send it to me, because I told him—both my parents—

that I didn't want to see you. I think they had hopes…" She hung her head, "He never got to mail it. Both letters were in his journal—I had them all this time—" She met his eyes and winced apologetically, but he only smiled kindly.

"Well, I'm glad it turned up. A man doesn't like to leave stray proposals lying around."

"Change your mind, Captain?"

"Never." His mood turned sadly serious, "But I'm afraid it's almost time to ask again."

At her inquiring glance, he finished, "Will you wait for me, this time?" He teased, knowing of course, she would be waiting for him, but trying to ease the pain of the fact that the time of his departure was fast approaching.

She smiled bravely, turning the white cloth over to examine the initials she herself had so recently embroidered, "Only if I can keep your handkerchief."

He kissed her then, and she clasped his hand and held the back of it to the beating of her heart, before they went to rejoin their guests.

When the letters had been explained, the small group toasted the couple, and the last of the gifts were handed out. A blushing Katherine had opened Devin's last gift to her, and though none were privy to its exact implication, the smoldering look the couple exchanged, told them all they needed to know. William put his arm around Louise, hiding a grin in her hair, while Dorothea glanced at Keith, and blushed herself, when she caught his knowing look. Roderick was seen to whisper something to Evelyn, while Ilene cleared her throat, and busied herself kissing her nephew's pudgy cheek.

Soon the family was ready to depart, with the exception of a protesting Amy, who was taken aside and whispered to by her mother.

What did Auntie Kate think was so great about a bar of soap, even if it was honeysunkle? And why anyone would want to go to bed early on Christmas was beyond her.

Ambiguous Time, giver and taker, was oppressively present, snatching the minutes away. In the dwindling days that followed, the desperate couple did their best to enjoy the hours and ignore their passing. They walked in the weak winter sunshine, rode the miles of Trendwell in the snow, and spent time sitting by the fire, and without realizing it, making the memories that would carry them through the lonely days to come. The baby had stayed in the room connected to their bedroom since Christmas night, and if anyone thought it odd that the couple felt the need to nap each afternoon when their son did, none spoke the thought aloud. All too soon, Katherine was alone.

She wasn't *completely* alone, of course, she told herself, she had Gabriel, there was a houseful of helpers, and she and Evelyn spent plenty of time together, now that Roderick had departed. Yet deep within, the loneliness, the terrible void she remembered so well, was there. She wandered the halls and rode the hills of Trendwell, her mind often occupied with the puzzle of who she was without Devin, and why she felt so much more herself when he was present. She visited with her sister, she answered Amy's questions, and contrary time, slowed to a crawl.

Dressed as her usual habit, in oversized shirt and trousers, and a heavy winter coat, she descended the stairway and crossed the foyer, ready for her early morning ride. Anderson, was instantly there to open the door, and she nodded to the kindly older gentleman, catching the smile that hovered at the side of his mouth, much like an annoying bumble bee he would like to brush away. She paused, blushing slightly, missing her beloved cottage where there was no one to witness her comings and goings or her taste in attire.

"Good morning, Anderson."

"Madam."

Nearly out the door, she stopped and turned toward the butler,

"Mister… Anderson, I… Sometimes, I may be a bit… *unconventional*."

"Yes, Madam," he answered, with a slight nod, the smile buzzing dangerously closer. It was not the first time he had been witness to her free-spirited nature. He especially liked it when she romped about with the children. And he had seen her ride like the wind across the fields, her hair spread like wings dancing on the air. But she was a lady still, in all things, caring, polite and friendly, and certainly life here would not be boring.

She waited, hoping he would say more, wondering if her words weren't woefully inadequate, but he didn't speak, and she turned to go.

"Madam?"

"Yes?" She turned, her eyes searching his, and finding the persistent smile had won out.

"I shall endeavor to adjust."

She flashed him a brilliant smile. "Thank you, Anderson."

Now she sat astride Matilda in the numbing January cold. With a gloved hand she turned up the collar of her coat, and blankly studied the toe of one shiny new boot. Her mind journeyed a familiar path, back to the morning Devin had left, after one last sweet night together. He had risen before dawn and dressed, asking her to stay in bed, rather than going downstairs to see him off. He would remember her there, he had said, soft and warm and sleepy, waiting for him to return.

Katherine had acquiesced, having shared a heart-breaking farewell with Ilene the evening before, not knowing if she would have been able to let them leave if she had followed them out to the coach. It hardly mattered, there was no good place, no good way, and no good time to say goodbye.

Matilda shifted beneath her, sensing the lack of attention from her rider, and Katherine came to, still staring at the toe of her boot. She chided herself, and patted the horse's neck, sighing inwardly, *Come back. Come back soon.*

She was not the only one praying for Devin's return.

Chapter 40

Devin! Devin, me boy, come to me! Maggie prayed, her eyes closed tightly for a moment, as though she could send the silent message by will alone. Her heart beating frantically, her large frame moved around her room at the Golden Goose, packing her trunk with a wild abandon born of fear. Ambrose was here! She was sure of it. Tall, blond, and handsome—John Ambrose—with his angelic face and devil's heart. She knew him on sight, and she knew the things he had done to people who had tried to stand in his way—*and she was one of those people.*

"*Oh, Mary, Mother of God,*" she prayed. Why had she gotten into this? *Damn her patriotic heart!* And why had she come back here? Everett Price had found her, and she had barely survived that encounter. *If it hadn't been for Devin*—At the thought of her savior, she closed her eyes, sending him another silent message. Oh, where would she go?! Where *should* she go? All she could think of was Devin, he would take care of her—*He said he would.*

"Marcus!" She called, jumping when he appeared, satchel in hand, looking at her with anxious brown eyes. Armored with the power of youth, he gave her a quick hug of reassurance before she took his satchel, and he took her trunk, and followed her down to the rickety old cart that stood ready.

John Ambrose watched that same cart pass down the street, with a smile of satisfaction and a gleam in his clear blue eyes. He leaned indolently against the wall, and took one last drag on the cheroot he held before crushing the stub beneath a highly polished boot.

Fort Fisher, the last of the Confederate ports, had fallen to the Union. The glory days of the blockade runners were over—his ships, his profits—all lost. He was ruined. All that was left to him was revenge on those who had worked to destroy his plans, and *that*, he would have… But he would need help. Pulling forth a fine gold pocket watch, he noted the hour, and with leisurely grace strolled toward his waiting horse.

Katherine was surprised, but not unhappily so, at the arrival of unexpected guests. She was in the drawing room, when the clattering of hooves came to a halt in the front yard. She went out to greet whomever it might be, heedless of the cold wind that gusted through her brown woolen dress.

She watched Maggie and Marcus climb from a small cart that had seen better days, but her welcoming smile faded at the look on the older woman's face. *"Maggie?"* She questioned, as the woman took hold of her arm.

"Oh, I hope I haven't done wrong, Dearie. I don't know where to go. Don't know what to do, so I came to Devin."

"Devin's not here, Maggie…"

"I know. I know."

Katherine put her arm around the shaken woman, and the story began to rattle out in bits and pieces while they walked toward the house. When they reached the front steps, she paused to survey the surrounding hills in the gathering twilight, and the chill in her core could not be blamed on the winter winds.

Katherine was still putting the pieces together. Maggie was sure John Ambrose was after her. Ambrose, who led the smuggling operation that had involved Cecilia and Everett Price. It was Ambrose, along with Cecilia who had put up the bulk of the money to get them started smuggling rifles to the south.

"They made a lot of money, they did. They could have walked away with millions, I'm sayin,' but no, the greedy guts. The more they made, the more they put back into the operations, ya see. but we was on to 'em, and they started to lose more and more. He's the last of the pack, he is, and it's hard to say who's the worst, himself or Everett."

Oh, my God! Katherine thought in disbelief. She sat in the drawing room, listening to the whole story… How Maggie had worked with Devin, listening and spying, and passing information from the tavern. How first, Everett Price, and then, John Ambrose, had found her… And now, the frightened woman had brought, *God only knew what danger*, to her very door. Her gaze touched briefly on the woman's scarred face. "Of course you should have come," she assured her, pouring out more tea and swallowing her fear.

The year matured with painstaking slowness, a solemn march through hollow days, set to the haunting dirge of war. She had invited Maggie and Marcus to stay, but she was determined not to live in fear. The tenseness in Maggie was palpable, and transferred to Marcus. Evelyn, as always, was a great help, befriending the nervous woman. There were gardens to be planned, knitting to be done, and babies to be held. The two women were becoming fast friends, and Maggie began to settle into a life she seemed to have forgotten existed.

Katherine felt sorry for Marcus. The poor boy seemed at a loss. She taught him to ride, if only in the paddock and around the yard, and to care for the horses, using her beloved Matilda and the newly acquired Treasure, as steps in the forming of this new bond. Together, they mucked the stalls and measured out feed, brushed down the horses, and checked their hooves. He was a good worker, and eager to learn. Pleased to discover he could read and write well, she introduced him to some of her favorite books, and had him help her with her paperwork. She had also begun to teach him how to keep the books for the estate, finding him to be capable and bright. On occasion, she asked his advice, and watched his chest swell with pride. But best of all, she took the time to continue teaching him to shoot the rifle Devin had given him at Christmas time, praising and encouraging, and watching his confidence grow. "There, you see! That was excellent!" She was truly excited for the boy, when his shot came close to center on the targets they had set up in the back field.

"Bravo, young man!" Anderson, whom Katherine had invited along for the outing, was equally encouraging as he readied for his turn. "You'll be an expert marksman in no time!" Marcus' eyes shone at the praise, and Katherine met the butler's look in mutual satisfaction. The three of them stood in the February cold, pink cheeked, their breath frosting the air around them, stomping cold feet in the snow, and happy for the moment.

She had confided her fears to Anderson, and if her eyes lifted now and then to scan the hills around them, he understood, because he did the same.

It was one of those surveillances that would return at least some measure of joy to her heart. Crossing from the main barn to the house, in the late dusk, she stopped to look around, and caught the rumble of a coach far down the road. She waited while it drew closer, and stepped into the shadows when it turned into the drive, and continued toward the house. When the door opened, she broke into a run, arms open in welcome.

"Ilene! What are you doing here? Are you all right? *Is Devin all right?*" In her relief, Katherine hugged her tightly and did not want to let her go. At last, she stepped back and wiped away tears, laughing self-consciously, "I didn't realize how worried I was about you, until now. I'm a mess of nerves."

Ilene took her hands in concern and tried to answer all of her questions, "Yes, all is well. And here?" At Katherine's quick nod, she went on, "There's been a change of plans. I'm done in Wilmington, but Devin has other things to do. He is transferring prisoners," she whispered, before Katherine could ask. "He sends his love. I came back as soon as I could. Are you sure you're all right? Have you been well? Has something happened?" She peppered her with questions, thinking Katherine didn't seem herself.

Katherine picked up her valise. "Let's go in and get you settled, and I'll explain. I'm so glad you're here."

"Well, that remains to be seen," Ilene laughed, and took her arm.

Life wove its way into yet another new normal, but the passing of time did nothing to dissuade her misgivings, Katherine kept close to the house, more now than ever, and made sure everyone else did too. She had never shaken the feeling, that Maggie and Marcus, were not the only ones who had found her the day they had arrived. The ghost of her kidnapping haunted her, and she missed Devin terribly. And now there was one more added to the household to worry about and keep safe, although she was certain Ilene could hold her own, and she was glad to have her back. It was these thoughts that kept her awake one night, while the rest of the house slept. These, and a savage April storm that would not quit. Lightning flashed, thunder roiled, and Katherine sighed aloud. The wind driven rain that lashed her windows mirrored her frenzied thoughts, and she threw off the covers. In spite of how tired she was, it was clear she would not get to sleep anytime soon. She needed a distraction… *Yes, she needed a book.* Pulling on a wrapper over her nightgown, and finding her slippers, she stopped to check on Gabriel, before heading downstairs. The candle she carried threw long shadows on the wall, on her way to the library, and once inside, she began her search for sanity.

She couldn't decide what to read, because she knew nothing would keep her attention well enough to distract her. She had gathered several weighty volumes when she froze on the spot, her arms full. She strained to hear past the driving rain, and the sound came again…*tapping?*

Someone was moving steadily along the porch. She blew out the candle and waited for her eyes to adjust to the darkness, the only light in the room the embers in the fireplace banked for the night. Her heart thudded in her ears, as someone clearly tried the front window.

The latch held. She followed with her eyes and forgot to breathe as the steps moved around to the side of the house. The window rattled, the latch was undone, and she waited, her heart in her throat. The sash rose and a booted foot stepped over the low sill. An arm appeared to clear the tangle of drapery, and she waited in horror while that someone climbed easily into the room.

Before the intruder could straighten, Katherine let fly with one of the heavy books, striking the shadowed form in the back, and he turned in surprise.

"Saints, Katherine!" Devin stood, rain dripping from his coat and the brim of his hat. "Leave it to you!"

"Oh!" The remaining books fell to the floor when he opened his coat, and she flew into his arms. "What are you doing here?!"

"I live here," he laughed between kisses, torn between holding her as close as possible, or holding her back so he could look at the face he had dreamt of. "The door is locked. I didn't want to wake everyone, and I saw a light… It's over, Katherine! It's over!"

"What?" She gasped, his words secondary to his presence, and his kisses.

He held her face in his hands, "Richmond has fallen, and Lee has surrendered, it's only a matter of time. The war is over, Love! The war is over!" He picked her up and swung her around in a circle, as she laughed and cried with relief and happiness.

The books lay forgotten, and the exuberant couple found their way up the stairs, Devin explaining to her how the end of the war was assuredly near. Katherine was so overwhelmed with joy she could not take everything in, and she could not take her eyes off of her husband. *He was home!* There would be time for her to tell him about Maggie and Marcus, and her concerns, and all that had happened in his absence. There would be time, because the war was ending. *And he was home! And whatever happened now had to be better!*

There would be time to tell her he was not home for good. Not yet. John Ambrose and his men, had been caught in the trap they had set for them. But there were many loose ends to be gathered and tied. It would take months before word would spread, and the war, that still rolled across the country like a runaway train, so hotly stoked, could be brought to a stop. He would tell her all of this, but not tonight.

They stopped to look in on the baby before passing into their room, where Devin removed his wet clothing. Katherine eyed the bed she had fled from in such anguish, and now returned to in exultation. Her nightgown too, was soaked through from holding him close, and was also removed. She never missed it.

Chapter 41

President Lincoln was dead. Six days after the Confederate surrender, he had been assassinated by the actor John Wilkes Booth. Katherine had admired his quiet eloquence, his wit, and his brave leadership. She grieved with the others, and found consolation in her thoughts. Throughout history, it seemed, when an extraordinary person was needed, there was someone to step in and fill the capacious shoes of leadership. She viewed this as the hand of heaven. It seemed to her, when an angel was needed, an angel was sent. This would explain Lincoln's aura, his silver-tongued phrases, and his thoughts that seemed above the common man. *Yes,* perhaps he was an angel, this Abraham, guardian of a young country that had lost its way, and having been sent by God, he was simply called home, his work on earth finished with the ending of the war. She would remember him that way.

The war-torn nation, had inflicted immeasurable damage upon itself. And although the end of the fighting became more of a reality every day, that reality was stark and somber. The wounds left in the wake of this disaster would take years to heal, and scar the decades to come. By the fourth of July, the country remained divided, even in their celebrations.

The family planned a quiet picnic at North Hill. William had been close to Boston when Lee surrendered, and he and Louise had arrived to stay with Dorothea and Keith. Devin was away once again, but not far from home, involved in the transport and paperwork of some of his captives. He had promised to return in time for the celebration.

Katherine returned from a long morning ride, feeling exhausted. She had, as always, not slept well in her husband's absence. She was relieved, though, to have her freedom restored knowing Ambrose and his men were no longer a threat, and she could travel where she would.

"Are you sure you're feeling all right?" Asked Evelyn, placing a caring hand on her forehead.

"Yes, I'm fine, Evelyn. I didn't get much sleep, that's all."

Evelyn and Ilene took Gabriel, and went ahead with Maggie and Marcus, and the staff. All of them, laden with food and supplies, traveled the path next door to prepare for the picnic. Katherine would try to nap while she waited for Devin, and they would join the others later… *Maybe much later.* She smiled to herself as she laid out the blue-green dress that he liked so well. She sank down on the chaise lounge in their room, and had barely closed her eyes, when she heard the front door open, and hurried to the balcony rail in greeting.

Her welcoming smile died in place as shock surged through her core and burned down her arms, causing her hands to tremble. There in the front hall—*In her home*—she looked down into the sneering face of Russo.

He smirked up at her, and she knew, that *he* knew, that she was alone. She stood, barely able to breathe. Her first thought, whether Devin was all right.

Russo unbuckled his gun belt and laid it mockingly on the hall table. Inch by inch he drew his sword from its scabbard, his eyes never leaving hers as he started up the stairs. His meaning was clear.

Katherine's mind raced, even as she whirled and ran along the hallway… *Why hadn't she kept a gun upstairs? What time was Devin coming home? Oh God, how could this be happening? Not now, when the war was over!* She scoffed mentally at this last thought… this had nothing to do with the war. This was a different level of hatred.

She ran to the spare bedroom where Devin's uniforms were kept and his sword stood in the corner. Diving across the bed, she turned and warily backed toward the weapon. Russo paused in the doorway as she unsheathed the sleek blade, and unconsciously took up the stance. Body sideways, feet apart, she hefted the sword to feel its weight and balance.

He was surprised to see her armed, but he laughed, pausing to roll up his sleeve. "Come now, you haven't the heart to kill a man, or the skill, I think."

"Try me." Devin's words came unbidden, giving her courage.

"Oh, I intend to," he said, his laugh hollow, a dark promise in his eyes.

The sword and the words she used belonged to her husband, but the surge of hatred was purely her own. How she longed to wipe the smirk from that hated face, scarred now, with a large jagged hollow in one cheek.

He moved to his left and she stepped to hers, watching his sword drawing little circles in the air, and his smile growing broader. She fought the sickening feeling that rose in her stomach. Her heart pounded, and the sword was heavy in her hand.

He feinted slightly to test her, and she parried with a ringing blow that surprised him. *Dio!* He had never seen such hatred as there in her eyes. Her face was calm, if a little flushed, and her arm did not waver. Only her bosom heaved with her effort, while her eyes shot sparks. *If looks could kill, he would be dead now,* he thought, as he stepped in and thrust low and upward.

Again, she parried, down and across with a strength that caused the handle of his sword to buzz in his hand. He had thought to find sport, a little amusement. To see the fear in her eyes, before he took her, *like all the others.* But this was no game. He did not want to kill her… *not yet.* Only to disarm her, and then to make her pay. He swung again, and again, and she met him blow for blow.

Katherine was already tiring. *His eyes…* It was her father's voice, back through the years, as she fenced with William… *Watch his eyes,* he counseled, *that is the secret. Where the eyes go the sword follows… Was it true?* She began to watch his eyes. He was no longer smiling. He glanced toward her sword arm, and like lightning the blade followed. She ducked to the left, and the tip of his blade caught her sleeve at the shoulder, *so close! Watch his eyes… an advantage. She had to find something!*

They were moving steadily now, testing, circling, booted feet sliding along the carpet. She kept her eyes on his. His hair clung to his forehead, and she noticed his labored breathing. Sweat dripped through his long sideburns, and she noticed for the first time how stifling the heat was in the room.

He attacked left, and then right. She met the first blow and the second with both hands on the sword. He was much heavier than she, and he wore a leather vest… *Could she outlast him in the heat?* He swung in an arc from over his head. She defended with her blade sideways holding on for dear life. The strength in her arms was going, and her palms were damp.

The back of her neck under her hair was wet with sweat. It made her shirt cling to her back, and trickled between her breasts. *No, the heat wouldn't do him in… at least not more than her.* He was heavier, but much stronger. *Think… think… Oh God, where was Devin? He should be here soon. Unless he was in trouble!* Her adrenaline surged again at the thought of him being attacked… *Attacking!* She had only been defending. *Russo wouldn't expect an attack.* Maybe she could surprise him. Summoning all her strength, she stepped in, thrusting straight on, aiming for his chest.

He parried, the strength of his swing knocking her sideways across the bed. The sword stung in her hand, but she hung on, dragging it with her, and coming to her feet on the other side. She was shaken, but it was a relief to put her arm down, if only for a few seconds. Once again, she engaged his eyes, watching him move around the end of the bed. *What was her advantage?* He didn't want to kill her right away. She knew that… *and she knew why.* His lewd comments had come back to taunt her, as she rolled across the bed. *No, he didn't want her dead. Some advantage. She'd rather die… No! Think! Think of something else… Devin!*

'Devin is fine.' She heard the words clearly in her mind, and they hummed with surety throughout her being, lifting her heart.

Russo had been watching her, trying to read her thoughts. *What would she do next?* He had never expected her to attack, and though he had thwarted her easily, it had unsettled him. But the thing that chilled him to the bone, was the smile that now came slowly to her face. *Madre di Dio, what was she thinking?*

He had been ready for her attack. *How?* As she studied his face, she knew. He was watching her eyes. *It may be the secret, Papa, but it is not a well-kept one!* But it gave her an idea. She would fake one way, and attack the other. Not with her sword, but with her eyes. She looked to his heart, and in a quick fluid movement, swung toward his right slashing downward.

Russo caught her look, and raised his blade crossways over his chest. Too late, he knew she had deceived him, and instead of thrusting straight at his heart, she had swung to the side. When he brought his arm up, her blade crossed his fingers at the hilt of his sword.

Dammit! The sword was too heavy. She had targeted his arm. She had felt the pull of the sword and was hopeful. Any contact would be a small victory. When she could see no wound, her heart fell, but seconds later, a thin white line appeared across his fingers and past his wrist. With a mixture of hope and horror, she watched tiny red droplets form along that line, to sit trembling, as though waiting for one another. Then, having gathered together, they began to travel in crooked rivulets down his raised forearm.

"You bitch!" he spat out. *She had cut him*! The blood was running to his elbow and soaking into his rolled sleeve. "But it is nothing," he shrugged, "You are too weak! You are a woman."

Katherine was beyond exhausted. *Was that supposed to be an insult? She had never thought of herself as weak, and she rather liked being a woman.* She studied the face, so ugly from the hatred within, and spoke without thinking, "But I'm not the one bleeding. And at least my nose isn't broken."

At this reminder, his shock was replaced by rage. She knew she had hurt him, and she had been as surprised as he with her success. But it wasn't enough. He came at her now like a mad bull—A bull with a wound that only made him more determined. She swung and blocked and did her best, but found herself retreating before his new-found fury. Around and around the room, backing, backing, both hands on the sword, blocking, and all the while tiring. Sweat stung her eyes, tendrils of hair clung to her face, and her arms burned as though on fire. She thought of Devin, and wondered where he was, as her hope diminished with her strength. She thought of her mother, and wondered strangely if she were watching her now. She pictured Gabriel, and the thought of him growing up without a mother broke her heart. She had no doubt Russo would take great pleasure in her torture. She would stop that at any cost, but *Dear God, she did not want to die!*

Damn, what was she made of, steel? Russo had never fought a woman before—*at least not one that had a weapon, and a chance to defend herself. Except for her.* He brushed at the scar on his cheek. *She did not have the strength of a man. But the endurance!* How he hated her. How he wanted to get to her, to make her suffer. *She would beg him…* He pulled his mind back to the present. First, he had to defeat her. Strain showed in her face, but still, there was the determination in her eyes. Her hair was wet now, and perspiration ran down her face, his eyes strayed to where her damp shirt clung to her heaving breasts. *She fights like a tiger! No, a lion, with her golden mane and challenging eyes.* She had the proud look of a lioness… *and she was not wounded.*

His hand did not hurt at first, but now it was excruciating. The slash was deep, with two of his fingers cut to the bone, and his wrist was now bleeding badly. Each time the swords clanged together, a wave of pain shot through his arm, and his grip grew weaker. *She would pay for that too*, he promised himself, while they circled…

"Auntie Kate! Auntie Kate!"

For a breathless moment they stared. So immersed had they been in their clash of wills, they had forgotten that someone else could enter the game. Now the rules would change. He had known as soon as he heard the child's voice that he had won, and he flashed a look of triumph, backing toward the door. This was almost worth the pain in his hand, and as he watched his opponent's expression, he realized with a surge of power, that this was not just any child. She must be very dear to her… *Had she not called out, 'Auntie'?* It must be the blonde child. The one he had seen often, as he watched the house. Earlier she was with the others, but now… This lioness would surrender for the life of the child. She would drop her sword at last, and he would have her. *Women were such weaklings.* This was his advantage. It was all he could have hoped for! He was tired, and he could no longer feel his fingers. Not only would she surrender when he grabbed the girl, but he would kill the child, and make her watch. *Yes, that would hurt her most of all!* Already grinning in victory, he stood near the doorway, and all the while the small steps came closer.

Katherine froze, while the dawning horror clawed into her chest, and ripped out her last ounce of hope. *Amy. Oh God, no! Sweet Amy, coming to get her for the picnic.* She could hear her humming as she came skipping up the stairs and that goddamned monster waiting for her! She stood rooted to the floor, and watched Russo's face flush with triumph, and his eyes cloud with evil.

"Auntie, Kate! Are you here?" The little voice echoed in the great hall.

"Amy, go home!" Katherine yelled, and saw his lip curl with contempt.

"But Auntie Kate, it's time for the picnic."

"Amy, go! Go now!" She screamed, hoping against hope, the child would mind her.

"But, Auntie Kate, you're going to miss it."

Amy had reached the top of the stairs. Katherine knew, because she had heard the tiny footsteps on the wooden edge, where the carpet ended. It was the only way the child could reach the railing. Now her steps were muffled by the carpet in the hallway. She prayed Amy would stop or go the other way, but in her heart, she knew she was coming.

And Russo was waiting. He leaned with his back against the open door, breathing heavily, the tip of his sword resting on the floor. Katherine's eyes lingered over the length of the blade. If she could capture it within her own body, Amy might go free. *Should that be her goal?* She wondered if it would hurt very much, or if she would feel little but shock when it invaded the fragile armor of her flesh. Her mind screamed in denial, even as she contemplated the trading of one life for another.

Her decision was made. This was a new battle now, and they both knew it. It showed in the look they exchanged, Russo's triumphant sneer, and the determined resignation in Katherine's gaze, her sole purpose to keep the evil from the innocent at any cost. Here then, was the advantage she had prayed for. It would give her the strength she needed. With new resolve, she turned her eyes back to his sword, six feet away, rising now like a silver cobra from the floor. While she watched, with his free hand, he fingered the handle of a long-bladed knife in his belt.

She slid one foot forward, and then the other. In calm detachment, she watched the blood drip from his fingers, while in the silence of the room, the ticking clock passed the precious seconds of life. The sound coincided with the dripping of Russo's blood. Tic, tic, tic, drip, drip, drip. *Did he notice?* She watched in hypnotic fascination as drop after drop seeped into the thick nap of the carpet.

"Auntie Kate!"

"*RUN AMY, RUN!*"

Russo grabbed for the child, but in his haste, he took his eyes off her aunt.

Katherine was at the door, breast to breast with Russo, her eyes wide with surprise, as they stared into his. The protruding half of her sword, was between them, her hands on the hilt, covered with blood. The other half disappeared under his rib cage and reappeared at the back of his shoulder. She saw the bloodied tip of the blade and heard it hit against the door when he fell back against it.

His hands were at her waist, one holding the handle of the knife caught between them, and the other splayed on her hip, as if to hold her there, in some macabre dance of death, while the blood flowed between them. He pulled at the knife, but Katherine pressed closer and it would not come free. With a crazed look, he raised both hands to her throat. She turned her head, attempting to avoid the grotesque fingers, when he gripped her neck and began to squeeze the life from her.

Not now! Not when she was this close to sharing a lifetime with Devin. Once again, she brought a knee up forcefully between his legs, and his hands fell away. With a strength born of pure will, she tightened her grip on the sword and pushed, sliding it upward to the hilt, and his eyes bulged in shocked surprise. He opened his mouth to speak, and blood gurgled from his throat and poured down his chin. *"Damn, you,"* he whispered, as he slid to the floor.

Her victory was brief. Katherine stared beyond comprehension. As she started to fall, she doubled over, holding her stomach, and a maniacal laugh echoed through the room.

Chapter 42

Amy had squealed and dashed for the stairs when the man tried to grab her, and Auntie Kate had yelled. Part of the way down, realizing no one was after her, she stopped. From her perch, she could see the door to the bedroom, but no one came out. *What was wrong?*

She sat on the stairs to think, her tiny brow wrinkled in concentration. *What had she seen? Auntie Kate jumping in the air with a sword. Did Auntie Kate have a sword?* And the man grabbed her hair. *He was scary!* Auntie Kate had yelled, and the last thing she heard was Auntie Kate laugh. *Maybe Uncle Devin was home, he always made Auntie Kate laugh. Auntie really sounded mad, though.*

Peering through the balusters, her eyes like saucers, feet ready to fly at the slightest movement, the little girl squirmed impatiently. The quiet continued unbroken, and she grew bolder, moving up the steps. After all, Auntie Kate wasn't yelling anymore. Maybe she would peek in, and if Auntie wasn't too busy, she might ask about the picnic. And if she didn't want to go now, maybe she would be nice again. *Auntie Kate was always nice, and she never yelled.*

When she reached the doorway, she peered carefully around the corner, and jumped in fright when her nose almost touched the side of the man's head. He was sitting sideways in the doorway, and there was a sword, and *blood. Blood everywhere…* She looked past him into the room, and what she saw made her squeal again and bolt for the stairs, and this time she didn't look back.

She could hardly see the path for her tears as she ran as fast as she could… *Auntie Kate!* Her Auntie Kate was lying on the floor, and she was all bloody! *She would get Mamma, that's what! Mamma could fix everything.* But with all the wisdom of her years, Amy knew in her heart that anyone with that much blood on them was dead… *Had to be. Oh, Auntie Kate, h*er heart cried over and over while her feet flew.

By the time she reached home, she was sobbing so hard she could barely speak. Dorothea, who heard her sobs and thought perhaps she had skinned her knees yet again, met her at the door. Her heart stopped at the sight of blood in her child's hair, and the moment she saw the poor little lips pressed to thin white lines, and the eyes too large for the pinched pale face, she screamed for Keith, and everyone came running.

They wrapped her in a blanket, and tried to comfort her, as the words came through her sobs—*unfathomable words*— "Auntie Kate is dead… and a man. They're all bloody and dead. The man tried to get me, and he pulled my hair, but Auntie Kate yelled and I ran, but then I peeked."

Dorothea's blood turned to ice. She met Keith's eyes, and then William's, and saw her fear reflected there. Keith spoke, hastily opening the gun cabinet, "Amy, was there only one man?"

Amy, comforted somewhat by the familiar faces, clung tightly to her mother's neck, and told what she knew. "One man, Papa, and Auntie Kate. They were upstairs in the bedroom, and Auntie Kate was mean. She yelled at me to go home. Then she laughed." At this, the group exchanged puzzled looks.

Keith knelt down to her level, "Amy, was Uncle Devin home?"

"No… I don't think so. Just the man who tried to get me, and she yelled real mean, and when I looked, the man was sitting up, and they were all bloody!"

"The rest of you stay here." William was armed and out the door with Keith right behind, racing up the path. They paused but a moment, in the shadows of the trees, and William noted the lone horse by the hitching post, and was relieved to think that Amy was probably right about there being only one man. With no movement or sound from the house, he knew they couldn't wait any longer. If his sister were hurt, they should get to her as soon as possible, and if she were… He couldn't finish the thought.

Thea and Ilene exchanged a glance at the order to stay, and joined Evelyn, already at the gun cabinet. So it was, that not far behind the two men, followed the younger women, skirts hiked high, rifles in hand, running for all they were worth, and Evelyn hustling along, armed with an enormous horse pistol. Louise, Marcus, and Maggie brought up the rear of the family group, with Marcus holding tightly to his new rifle. Not far behind, Anderson, lamenting abandoning his mistress in her time of need, brandished a shotgun, followed by a small army of the help from Trendwell, armed with everything from fire pokers to frying pans. At North Hill, the maids and the cook stayed to watch over the children, well-guarded by the footmen the grooms, and the gardeners.

They formed a plan; William, covered by Keith, dashed across the yard in a zigzag pattern and dove onto the porch rolling to his feet. When nothing happened, Keith followed as quickly as he was able, with his bad leg. Seeing the others rounding the bend in the path, he cursed to himself, and held up a hand of caution.

Devin, who had overseen the transportation of prisoners, and finished the hours of paperwork, was anxious to be on his way. Katherine was waiting. A family picnic seemed worlds away from this hell hole of a prison. On his way out, he passed down a row of cells, and paused when someone called his name.

John Ambrose stood close to the bars of his heavily guarded cell, "Going home, Galloway?"

The smirk on his face gave Devin pause, but he didn't show it. "*I am.* You're not."

"That pretty wife waiting for you?"

"That's right."

"Are you sure?"

Devin would have walked away, but something in the other man's manner raised the hair on the back of his neck. He stepped closer. "Why do you ask?"

Ambrose was enjoying his moment, and drew out his answer. He shrugged, "I guess I thought since Russo escaped, you might not be so sure of yourself."

Devin grabbed the man's shirtfront through the bars, and drew his revolver, "What do you mean!"

Ambrose looked him in the eye. "I *mean,* Russo's on his way to your place. In fact, he's probably been there a while now. I paid to get him out, and he's gone on a little errand. I would have gone too, but…" He eyed the shackles on his legs, and the extra guards at the door. "It would be a little more difficult."

Devin's blood ran cold. "I don't believe you."

"How do you think he escaped the last time? I paid for that too." He had the audacity to smirk even now. "Nice place you have. Big white house with green shutters, set back on that hill. Nice place for a man to live out his life, with a family and a good-looking woman by his side… *Or not.*" He shrugged.

The hammer on the gun made an ominous sound in the silence, "Who was it!?"

Ambrose laughed. "It is difficult to threaten a man who's going to hang. I mean, what do I care? You'd be doing me a favor, really." Long seconds passed. Devin was contemplating his next move, still not sure he believed him, when Ambrose spoke again. "I'll tell you. Because I owe him one. It was Lattimer." He gave an exaggerated sigh, "It's a shame, isn't it, when plans don't work out the way we…"

With a cry of rage, Devin shoved him back, and yanked him forward in one motion, smashing the handsome face of John Ambrose into the rough iron bars of the cell, and letting him drop to the floor. His mind reeled as he ran… *could it be true?* He tried to gather his thoughts and to remember what he knew of Lattimer, the newest member of his crew. *A plant? A traitor?*

In another part of the building, a door slammed inward, splintering at its hinges, and Devin, followed by several guards, stormed in. Lattimer jumped from his seat, but it was too late. The captain grabbed hold of him, and pulled him up close with a murderous look in his eyes, *"Did you let Russo go?"*

Lattimer hesitated a little too long, and Devin shook him, nearly lifting him from the floor. "Yeah! Yeah!" He said. "What difference does it make? The war's over, and I needed the money."

Devin's blood boiled, *"When? Damn you! When!?"*

"Last night!"

"You're a dead man! Do you hear me!? A dead man!" He gave one punch, square to the other man's jaw, and shoved him toward the guards to keep himself from doing murder—and he was gone.

Keith signaled to the others, and they crossed the yard. They readied to enter the house, when pounding hooves sounded on the drive, and Devin thundered into view. At the men's urgent signaling he pulled up short and leapt from his horse, fear hitting his stomach with the force of a cannon shot. Keith filled him in as quickly as he could, but watched him turn white under his tan. Devin looked at Dorothea and his heart lurched at the fear in her eyes.

On the hall table they found the lone pistol, but Devin was already up the stairs heading for the room he shared with Katherine. It was empty.

On his order, Anderson and the servants had spread out to search the first floor. The others went cautiously up the stairs, except for Marcus, who had boldly followed his hero up, and had already started down the hall, checking rooms as he went, his rifle at the ready. *She had to be all right, she had been so kind to him and his mother, she was… she was…*

He could not find words, and so it was but a keening moan that alerted the others to his discovery— *"She's dead!"* Marcus sobbed, and he ran from the doorway, looking now like the young boy that he was. *"They're both dead!"* He cried, passing the others at the top of the stairs.

Devin tore down the hall when Marcus cried out, the words the boy had spoken, so incomprehensible they might have been a foreign language. He jumped and aimed his colt, when he got to the doorway, before realizing that Russo would never move again. His mind took in the sword snuggled in the man's belly, and the one in his hand, and he swallowed hard, steeling himself to look across the room. When his eyes fell on Katherine, a strangled cry escaped him, his brain spurring his heart, driving him to accept the inconceivable horror, as time stood still.

She lay where she had fallen, half on her side, one leg buckled under her body, her hands holding her stomach, and from her fingertips to her elbows, and her neck to her knees, she was covered in blood. He forced himself to move into the room, listening to the echo of a voice from another day. A day so unlike this one—*a day of sanity*—Katherine, laughing at his teasing, and promising to wear a dress for his homecoming. It came to him now, that he had seen it in their bedroom—his favorite. It was there on the bed waiting for her. *Like he would wait for her for the rest of his life. How could this happen?* He had been so close to being home with her. *A few hours. After all this time. All they had been through—Hours—Minutes!* He went to her in a fog of disbelief.

As the others rushed into the room, Thea gasped and threw herself down at her sister's side, sobbing her name. Ilene stepped around one of the men in the hallway, and followed to place a consoling hand on the distraught woman's shoulder. Maggie began to pray.

William had tried to warn the women away, and now stood shielding Louise, awaiting word, and glancing periodically at the body in the doorway, trying to understand the scene before him.

Keith, too, studied the dead man. *Could Katherine have done this?* He turned to consider his sister-in-law; her hands covered in blood. *Yes, she could have done it on stubbornness alone, and to protect Amy, she would have.* He swallowed belated rage, as he thought of Amy, and eyed the sword lying on the floor. A blade of death, shining in the afternoon light. And then his eyes lit upon the knife…

Evelyn, like the others before her, ignored William's warnings, and went straight to Katherine's side, as Devin reached for his wife. He straightened her leg, and rolled her onto her back, leaning close… And everyone spoke at once.

"She's got a pulse," said Evelyn, who did not hesitate to place her fingers at the young woman's throat in spite of the blood.

"*Katherine,* can you hear me?" Thea, brushed the hair from her sister's face.

"…The sword is *clean,*" Keith spoke his thoughts aloud, "and so is the knife." The room went silent, and all heads turned from Katherine, to Russo, and back again.

"*That's his blood!*" William said quietly, able, now, to take a closer look at his sister, daring to hope it were true. A bubble of pride rose in his chest, to force out the tears he had so valiantly battled.

"*Please, Katherine!*" Devin blurted, leaning over her, praying to feel her breath against his cheek, *"She's breathing!"*

"Check for wounds," Evelyn ordered, running practiced hands over her neck and throat, and gently opening Katherine's mouth to peer inside.

Carefully the women opened the blood-soaked shirt, and lifted her camisole, steeling themselves, but finding no wound. Devin didn't realize he was holding his breath until he let it out in a rush. They turned her to look at her back, and again Devin held his breath. Again, nothing… and they lay her gently down. Evelyn continued her examination, patting and prodding. "I don't see anything," she concluded, deep in thought. She shared a glance with Devin, "Shock? Or could be she's passed out, or hit her head," she said, running practiced hands over the back and sides of Katherine's skull.

Devin desperately looked to his sister-in-law.

Dorothea stared at her sister through tears of heartbreak turned to hope, and with a fierce will in her heart. Now that Katherine was lying on her back, Thea thought she could see her breathing, but looking at her, it was hard to believe she was all right, and it was difficult to see through her tears. Not trusting her eyes, she placed her palm on Katherine's chest to feel the faint rhythm there and leaned close. "Kate, can you hear me!?"

Katherine struggled just beneath the surface of consciousness. *Was she drowning?* It was much like drowning. But this time she could not break through to the surface. She couldn't move. *Her throat hurt—and her hands, and her arms—and there was the smell of blood… Something was wrong… She should get up; Thea was calling…*

Katherine felt the touch, and opened her eyes to see the faces of everyone hovering above her. Her sister was crying and stroking her hair, and her brother was smiling down at her. *Devin… Devin was here, holding her hand, and Evelyn, looking worried. Ilene and Louise, and…* "Amy?" She struggled to ask, but she didn't think it came out right.

"She's safe," Thea assured her on a sob, as Keith knelt to place an arm around his wife, hiding tears of gratitude in her hair.

The army of workers had crowded into the hallway and word had spread. Marcus returned to see for himself, hoping his reddened eyes didn't betray him. The women banded together using their wide skirts to shield her while some of the men wrapped Russo's body in a blanket and took it away. They didn't want Katherine to see, but it didn't matter. *Nothing else mattered… Amy was safe and Devin was here.* She tried to squeeze his hand and surrendered to exhaustion once again.

Katherine did very nearly sleep the sleep of the dead. She hadn't said much, or seemed much aware, when the women had bathed her, and washed her hair, and tucked her into bed, except for half-conscious whispers about Amy, and Gabriel, and of course, Devin.

No one mentioned Russo. Following Evelyn's lead, they held their questions, and gave only reassurance in her struggle with shock and exhaustion. The doctor, who had been summoned, could only agree, "She should be fine, with plenty of rest," he told Devin, "There is some bruising on her throat, but I don't think it will be a problem."

Devin watched and waited an eternity, deeply touched that the name she uttered from time to time was his own. *What she went through,* he thought, shaking his head. She had faced that man, *that animal,* and fought him to the death, but she appeared so helpless now… And although he had been waiting for it, he was surprised, nonetheless, when she stirred and opened her eyes to look around the room.

"Oh," was all she said.

"Hello Love." He kissed her on the forehead, and sat on the edge of the bed facing her.

She blinked and frowned, as though she might have been dreaming. "Russo?" She rasped, and he helped her with a drink of water.

"Gone, Love, it's all over. Everything is fine, now."

He watched while she brought her thoughts to order. "Did I kill him?"

He hesitated. "Aye, Love," he spoke softly, placing a strand of hair behind her ear.

"Good," but her eyes sought his for affirmation.

"You had no choice." He took her hand. "You did what you had to do, and I'm so proud of you. But I'm so sorry that you went through that. I can't believe what happened. I wish I had been here when you needed me." His voice broke.

"It wasn't your fault," she whispered. "You're here now, and I will *always* need you." She motioned for him to move beside her, and he stretched out, grateful to hold her at last. She placed a kiss over his heart, and rested her head on his chest.

"I can scarcely believe you defeated him." He gave a short harsh laugh, "And yet, at the same time, I'm not completely surprised. But, *how did you?* How could you?"

Her eyes closed, "I couldn't let him hurt the child."

"Amy was unharmed, you saved her life." He changed course when she shook her head, and he knew that was not what she meant. "Gabriel is safe. He was in no danger. He was at your sister's, remember?"

"No…" She pulled his hand under the covers to place it low on her abdomen, where she reveled in its warming touch through her gown, "This child."

Epilogue

The end of the War Between the States was formerly declared on August 20, 1866.

On a beautiful July afternoon the following summer, the Lawrence families were gathered together at the cottage built by their father. Not a single wisp of a cloud dared blemish the beautiful evening sky, and the departing sun sparkled across gently breaking waves.

William and Louise, Dorothea and Keith, Evelyn and Roderick, and several more friends, in-laws, and outlaws, had joined Katherine and Devin and their family. Children played, tents were pitched, and food cooked over open fires. There was love and laughter, but most of all, there was peace.

Katherine stood on the bluff and waved to Devin, who was down on the beach supervising the children. She watched as he directed them, holding their daughter in his arms. The last rays of the sun and the playful breeze caressed her face, and her heart swelled with joy. But there was something more. An indefinable bond with those who had come before, and the generations yet to be, in this special place. In a sense, this would always be home, and they would always return here to gather strength from the past and hope for the future—And no matter what happened, the love would live on. She turned to look behind her at the cottage, glowing with light, and realized that life had come full circle. Here again, was the magical light of love that touched all who came near—And she would be its keeper.

In Acknowledgment

With heartfelt appreciation and love for my circle of family and friends who have encouraged, helped and supported me on this crazy path. You know who you are, and I could not be more grateful. My circle is a dream catcher.

I feel it's only fair to warn you… there's more.

Coming soon: '*A DREAM ALLOWED.*' A Regency romance. Of course there is love,

"Denial of something does not make it non-existent."

But there are rules.

And stay tuned for book two in the Keeper Series

'STEP FROM THE SHADOWS'

About the Author

Lesley M. Avery grew up in New England, where her appreciation of history began. She loves autumn, candles, carpentry, Christmas, and of course, romance. When not reading, writing, fixing things, or drinking too much tea, she may be found letting the dog in or out… or out and in… or out.

If you enjoyed this book, kindly leave a review or drop a comment to the author.

Lesleymavery.author@gmail.com

Facebook.com/LMAveryauthor/

Lesleymavery.com